NICOLA CORNICK

One WICKED Sin

HQN™

Recycling programs
for this product may
not exist in your area.

ISBN-13: 978-0-373-77487-6

ONE WICKED SIN

Author's Note

A few years ago I was reading a book about the Battle of Trafalgar when a small note at the bottom of the page caught my eye. It referred to the Napoleonic prisoners of war on parole in the small town of Tiverton in Devon. The idea of foreign prisoners being permitted the freedom of various small towns across Britain intrigued me. It was very difficult to find sources for this neglected aspect of British history, but as I gradually discovered more about the parole prisoners, as they were called, so I became caught up in a story idea involving a heroine who falls in love with the enemy....

One Wicked Sin is Lottie's story. A sophisticated woman of the world, the veteran of many love affairs, Lottie finds that her life falls apart when her husband divorces her. A future as the mistress of a renegade Irish prisoner of war seems her only hope. And of course two such experienced and world-weary characters as Lottie and Ethan will never fall in love.... Will they?

In November 1813 an uprising of all the 60,000 prisoners of war in Britain was thwarted by the authorities. Lottie and Ethan's love story is intertwined with this true event.

For Andrew, with all my love, now and always.

One WICKED Sin

"When lovely woman stoops to folly
And finds too late that men betray
What charm can soothe her melancholy
What art can take her guilt away?"

—*Oliver Goldsmith*

PROLOGUE

July 1786

IT WAS THE SOUND of the stones against the window-pane that woke her with a rattle like heavy rain on a winter's day. She lay still for a moment, engulfed in sleep, and then the sound came again sharp as gunfire. She opened her eyes and stared at the high shadows on the ceiling. Dawn was breaking, creeping into her bedroom and dimming the candlelight. The connecting door was open and she could hear her governess, Miss Snook, snoring in the room beyond.

A third rattle of stones sent her scurrying to the window, pulling back the heavy drapes and pushing up the sash. It was a beautiful morning outside. The sky was a soft, new blue and the sun was rising over the meadow in ribbons of gold.

"Papa!"

He was standing on the gravel sweep outside her window. As she watched he let the remaining stones trickle from between his fingers and then he raised his hand in a salute.

"Lottie! Come down!" It was a whisper, carried to her on the light breeze. She cast one dubious, furtive glance toward the connecting door but Miss Snook's snores were louder than ever. On bare feet she scampered along the corridor, down the stairs, its faded pattern gray in the pale light, and across the stone floor to the front door. The house was still with that special early-morning stillness that preceded the first stirrings of the day. Everyone slept.

He met her on the steps, kneeling down to enfold her in his arms, and she knew at once he had not been back that night, for he smelled of smoke and ale. The odor of it was in his hair and on his clothes, and his cheek, as he pressed it against hers, was rough with stubble. Beneath those smells, faint but still exotic, was the familiar scent of his sandalwood cologne. She had always loved it.

He held her very tightly and spoke very softly into her ear. "Lottie, I am going away. I wanted to say goodbye."

His words and the urgency she could feel in his touch sent a chill through her, the cold creeping up from her bare feet to wrap her entire body and set her shivering. She drew back and looked at him. "Away? Does Mama know?"

She saw a frown come into his eyes, those brown eyes so like her own, and then he smiled at her and it felt for a moment as though the sun had come out, though for some reason she was still afraid.

"No," he said. "It is our secret, sweetheart. Don't tell anyone that you saw me." He straightened up. "I'll come back for you soon, Lottie. I promise I will." He touched her cheek. "Be good."

The church clock struck a half after four as he walked away down the drive. Lottie stood listening to the mingled chimes and the crunch of her father's footsteps on the gravel until his tall figure turned into the lane at the end of the drive and vanished into the early-morning mist. She wanted to run after him, to catch his coat and beg him to come back. She was terrified. Her heart was thumping as it did when she ran and she could feel the tears pricking her eyelids. The sun was rising above the hills now, big and bright, shimmering golden on the mist, but Lottie felt very cold.

She was six years old and that was the way in which her life ended the first time.

CHAPTER ONE

London, July 1813

"THAT IS THE FIFTH gentleman this week to demand his money back." Mrs. Tong, resident procuress of The Temple of Venus, strode into the opulent boudoir with a hissing swish of angry silk skirts. "One hundred guineas that cost me!" She put her hands on her hips and viewed with utter exasperation the woman sitting at the dressing table. "You are supposed to be an investment, madam!" Her genteel accent was slipping under duress. "I hired you as a novelty, an attraction, the most notorious woman in London. I did not expect a shrinking virgin." She threw her hands up. "He said that you were so cold you unmanned him. You are supposed to be scandalous, so behave scandalously! If Lord Borrodale wanted a block of ice in his bed he would be at home with his wife!"

Lottie Cummings sat silently under the tirade pressing her hands together to prevent them from shaking. In the week that she had been under Mrs. Tong's roof she had learned that the mistress of the bawdy house was prone to these bouts of anger when her girls upset her, and what could be more upsetting than an unsatisfied customer demanding a refund? Money was Mrs. Tong's lifeblood; no wonder the bawd was furious.

Lottie hated this place, hated this work with a deep loathing that stalked her from the moment she woke to the moment she tried to escape the nightmare through sleep. She had never imagined that being a courtesan would be like this. She had thought herself so sophisticated, so experienced. She had even—God help her—imagined that she might take to the world of the demimonde like a professional. After all, how difficult could it be? She was a woman with a certain degree of confidence and worldly knowledge. She had once believed herself quite talented in the amatory arts. Before she had seen the reality of a courtesan's existence she had even thought that she could take the customers' money and enjoy their attentions.

Her bravado was in tatters now. Her confidence had failed her. *She had known nothing.*

Nothing of the degradation of being spoken of as though she were not there, discussed, dismissed, like a piece of meat. Nothing of the contempt customers would show her, exercised over her because they were paying and so they could behave as they wished. Nothing—if she was being brutally honest—of the downright repulsiveness of some of the men. She had only ever slept with good-looking men before and that had been no hardship. She had chosen her lovers. Now they chose her.

She could not bear this. She thought that if she remained one minute longer in that house she would run mad.

But where could she go?

There was nowhere. Her family had cast her out and her friends disowned her. She was not qualified to perform any job and she was too notorious to be offered one. Plus she owed Mrs. Tong a considerable amount of money: There was the bond taken as security against her health and the tire money to trick her out to look like a whore. She had been caught in a net of debt designed to ensure she never escaped.

She looked around the boudoir with its golden chairs shaped like seashells and the bed draped in swathes of purple. All the colors were loud and shockingly taste-less. She would have hated the room for its tawdry pre-tense at glamour had she not already hated it far more deeply for representing everything she had become.

"I don't understand you." When Lottie did not speak, Mrs. Tong sat down heavily on the purple bed. The mat-tress gave a sigh. "Gossip has it that you were giving it away for free to all and sundry during your marriage," she continued sharply, "yet now you are to be paid for it you act the outraged innocent."

Lottie set her lips in a tight line to prevent the words of repudiation from spilling out. She could not afford to antagonize Mrs. Tong further if she did not wish to be thrown on the streets. That was her reality now. Sell herself—or starve. And she could not be too particular about the purchaser.

She fidgeted with the pots on her table, with the rose- and lavender-scented creams for the skin, which were so strongly perfumed that they made her want to sneeze violently, and with the bright, harsh paints and cosmetics that were supposed to enhance her beauty but which in reality marked her out so brashly as a courtesan that she might as well have worn a placard.

She wanted to smash her hand down and scatter them to the floor.

"I find it difficult," she said, "that is all."

Mrs. Tong's face tightened into disapproval. "God knows why. How many men have you had?"

"Not so many."

Not as many as the scandalmongers said.

Mrs. Tong sighed. For a brief second there was a glint of something softer in her eyes, the memory, perhaps, of what she had once been before she had bought and sold other women to make her fortune.

"You should pull yourself together," she said, with rough sympathy, "or you'll be selling yourself for a shilling outside the theaters, and that won't suit your ladyship, either. At least here you have a roof over your head." Her cynical gray gaze flicked over Lottie. "You're not getting any younger, are you? And what else can you do now you're divorced and disgraced?"

"Nothing," Lottie said. "Nothing," she repeated quietly. Goodness knows, she had thought about it. She had searched desperately for an alternative. All doors were closed to her, all respectable trades impossible. Working for a living had once seemed laughable, something that other, less fortunate people did. Now it seemed her only choice was to make a living on her back.

"I'll try harder," she promised, attempting to keep the desperation from her voice. She did not want Mrs. Tong sensing her near despair, did not want to give the other woman an even greater hold over her.

"See that you do." The bawd rose to her feet. "There's a party tomorrow night—a few of the girls and a few of my most select gentlemen." Her eyes bored into Lottie. "I shall expect you to play your part."

Lottie felt a wave of horror and sickness rise in her throat. She swallowed hard and nodded dumbly.

I will not be sick. I will not.

There was a knock at the door, and Betsy, one of the other girls, small, dark and plump, stuck her head around.

"Begging your pardon, Mrs. Tong, but Lottie's next customer is here."

"Ah." Mrs. Tong sounded gratified. "Well—" she cast Lottie a sharp glance "—see you send this one away satisfied."

The door swung wider. Out on the red-and-gold carpeted landing, Lottie could see a man waiting. He was wearing a green coat and an excited, lascivious expression. John Hagan. He was an acquaintance of hers from her previous life, a man who had always wanted to have her and was now prepared to pay to fulfill his fantasy. She could not refuse him. Panic clawed at her chest. It made her catch her breath.

"I can't—"

Mrs. Tong turned on her as swift as a striking snake. "Then you can leave now."

It came then, the despair, crushing her, sapping her will. So many times in the past few months she had been close to it and had not quite given in. At first, when Gregory had said he was to divorce her, she had thought there had been some terrible mistake. Then he had sent her away, refused to see her, returned all her letters unopened with chilling ruthlessness, and she had realized that there *had* been a mistake and it had been hers. She had broken the unwritten agreement between them, become too indiscreet. The press had reported on her exploits and made her husband a laughingstock. She had damaged Gregory's reputation too openly, too flagrantly, to be forgiven. She was to be punished.

She had written to her family but they had chosen not to help her. Her friends, it seemed, were not friends at all, for they did not want to know her anymore. The only two people who might have helped her were abroad and out of reach. Gregory had paid handsomely for the case to be hurried through the courts, and on the day that the divorce had been granted he had served notice on her to leave her house. She was destitute. And through all of the long, painful process of the divorce she had not quite believed it was happening.

She believed it now, now that she was ruined.

Hagan was approaching, chest puffed out, his tread confident. Mrs. Tong was wreathed in smiles now, bowing him into the room. Lottie clutched the folds of her negligee to her throat.

"My dear Lottie, what a delight to see you once more…" Hagan was fulsome in his triumph, bowing over her hand with pretense of gentlemanly conduct, this hypocrite who had watched her fall into the gutter and now came to exploit her. His eyes roved over her transparent wrap, dwelling on the swell of her breasts and dropping lower. Lottie's mouth felt dry, her heart beating so hard she shook. She bent her head and fixed her eyes on the riotous pattern on the carpet.

"One hundred guineas," she heard Mrs. Tong say and saw the madam hold out her hand for the money.

"My dear Mrs. Tong…" Hagan sounded pained. "I

have heard stories that our little harlot here—" spite colored his voice "—can be somewhat disappointing. I'll pay *afterward,* not before, and only if I am satisfied."

Mrs. Tong was hesitating. Lottie could feel the heat of Hagan's palm on her shoulder through the thin material of her wrap. She shuddered deep inside. When it had come to a choice between starving to death or selling the one remaining commodity she still had, she had not hesitated. It had been her choice, if one could dignify a decision to which there was no alternative with the word *choice.* She had sold her body in order to survive and she would have to do it again, over and over until she was old and raddled and nobody wanted her. And that would not be long, for as Mrs. Tong had pointed out she was scarcely in the first flush of youth.... The cold shudders rippled down inside her again as she thought of the future.

Hagan's hand slid to her breast, fumbling. She could hear his breathing change and grow heavier with excitement.

The future starts here.

"A moment."

They all jumped.

A man was standing in the doorway, one shoulder resting against the jamb. He was in black-and-white evening dress, and against the raucous color of the brothel with its damask walls and peacock drapes he looked stark and almost too plainly attired. He was tall with black hair cut short and eyes of a startling, striking blue in a lean, watchful face. Lottie felt Hagan stiffen, as though sensing a rival.

"Sir—" Hagan withdrew his hand. His face had reddened. "You intrude. You must wait your turn."

The stranger's eyes met Lottie's. His gaze was so bright and piercing that she felt her breath catch. Odd, she thought, that in that moment there was something in his eyes that looked almost like reassurance. Odd and impossible, an illusion, for then he smiled and any impression of gentleness was banished. He strode forward, self-assured, dangerous.

"Oh, I do not think so," he murmured. "I don't wait in line."

Hagan opened his mouth to speak but it was Mrs. Tong who intervened now, a sweep of her hand silencing him.

"My lord…" Lottie could not quite place the tone in the bawd's voice. There was deference there, certainly, but something else too. Wariness? Lottie had known all manner of men, from overrefined dandies to brutish bucks, but she had never met a man whose presence felt quite so elemental. There was danger in the room. She felt it in the air and with a prickle down her spine. Suddenly the atmosphere was alive.

"I am sure Mr. Hagan would not mind waiting," Mrs. Tong said smoothly. "If you would be so good, sir… Can I offer you a glass of wine perhaps? On the house?" She was already shepherding Hagan toward the door. The newcomer stood aside with studied amusement to allow him to pass. Lottie let out her breath on a sigh she had thought was silent until the man cast her a quick, appraising glance.

The door closed.

"You are Charlotte Cummings?" the stranger asked.

"No," Lottie said. "Not anymore." The only thing she had wanted from Gregory was money. He could keep his name. It was no use to her. "I am Charlotte Palliser now," she said.

The man inclined his head. "I had heard that the Pallisers had disowned you."

"They cannot take my name," Lottie said. "I was born with it."

He did not reply at once. He was watching her with that same acute interest that he had shown from the moment he had set eyes on her. His gaze held no sexual appraisal, only a cool calculation that made Lottie shiver for there was no softness in it at all.

"May I?" He gestured to the armchair. She was surprised he troubled to ask permission. Such courtesy sat oddly with the sense that this was a man who would take what he wanted whether anyone opposed him or not.

He sat down and crossed one ankle over the other knee, lounging back with a casual grace. His whole body, so long and lean, looked elegantly relaxed and yet Lottie thought it would be a mistake to dismiss him as yet another fashionable Corinthian. There was too much forcefulness beneath the surface, too much power and intensity banked down.

"Who are you," Lottie said, "that Mrs. Tong allows you to dictate to her and does not even make you pay in advance?" It appeared that he was not intent on hurrying her into bed, whoever he was.

He laughed. "Ethan Ryder, at your service." There

was a wicked spark in his blue eyes. "And I pay afterward." He raised an eyebrow. "I do believe you're blushing. How singular—in a courtesan."

Lottie turned her face away. He was right. She felt vulnerable, almost shy. This was a man who seemed to be able to strip her feelings bare with no more than a look, and she, no matter what people said, was no brass-faced strumpet.

"Mrs. Tong called you 'my lord,'" she said. She knew that she sounded doubtful. He looked more like a horse master than an earl, for all his fashionable attire. At one time she had known the entire peerage and she had never met him before. She knew that she would have remembered him.

"How quick of you to notice." He still sounded amused. "It's no lie. I am the Baron St. Severin. Oh, and the Chevalier D'Estrange for good measure."

"You're *French?*" Lottie looked up, startled. He did not sound French and it was beyond unlikely. She had no grasp of politics and no interest in gaining one, but even she knew that there was a war on.

"I'm Irish." He smiled at her, full of charm. "It's a long story."

"An Irishman with a French title?" Lottie said. Something clicked in her mind then, a memory of her drawing room in Grosvenor Square and her bosom bows gossiping over the latest *on dit*, picking at it like crows.

What had they said of Ethan Ryder, the Irish soldier of fortune? She remembered that he was a famed swordsman, a crack shot and the best cavalryman in his regiment. It was rumored that he never lost at games of chance, that he took risks other men would run from, that he was cold and calculating where others were rash and foolish and so he never made a mistake, but waited and waited and wore his enemies down until they took the false step, made the blunder that gave him the game…. And beneath the stories there were the whispers; that he had killed a man in a duel; that he had escaped from the deepest dungeons; that he could pass unnoticed through an opposing army like a ghost….

Napoleon had weighed Ethan Ryder down with titles and money for his devotion to the French cause. He was a soldier of fortune indeed.

She saw the smile deepen on Ethan's lips and a certain hard light spring in his eyes, as though he knew exactly what she was thinking and what she was about to say.

"Oh," she said. "Yes. You are the one who is the bastard son of the Duke of Farne and the circus trapeze artist. You betrayed your father and ran away to France as a boy and joined Bonaparte's *Grande Armée*. I heard," she said slowly, "that you had been captured by the British and were a prisoner of war."

"I am all of those things." He sounded imperturbable as though mere words, even harsh ones, had long ago lost the power to hurt him. "And you," he said, "are the divorced former wife of a fabulously wealthy banker, the disgraced *Ton* favorite, now ruined and forced to sell herself to survive."

The words fell quietly into the hot little room, but Lottie still flinched. It seemed, she thought, that Ethan Ryder was a deal more comfortable with his situation than she was with hers.

"You express my circumstances most graphically," she said tightly.

He put his head on one side, his blue eyes narrowed on her face. "You don't like to be described like that, do you, Lottie Palliser?" His tone was soft but it was not gentle. There was no compassion. Lottie wondered if he could look into her soul and see the tarnish there.

"You don't want to face the fact that you chose to become a courtesan because you preferred survival to starvation," he went on, "but it is the truth, just as all the things that you said about me are the truth." His lips twisted in a parody of a smile. "I think that you and I are very alike, Lottie." His voice was quiet. "We're both survivors, both adventurers. We don't believe in martyrdom."

"We're both *prisoners*," Lottie said, unable to erase the bitterness from her voice. She made a slight gesture. "Should you not be locked up, my lord?"

He shrugged, supremely elegant and supremely unconcerned. "Plenty of people think so, my father included."

"And yet," Lottie said, "you are free."

This time he shifted in the chair, tension in the line of his shoulders now. "If you call it freedom. I gave my word not to try to escape—my parole—and in return I am penned in a country town in the middle of no-where, with nothing to do all day, waiting for the war to end."

"Then what are you doing here in London?" Lottie asked. "Have you broken your parole?"

Ethan shook his head. The candlelight caught the sheen of blue in the deep black of his hair and made his eyes look deep and fathomless. "All officers are permitted to come up to Town once in a while if they plead urgent personal business." He gestured around the boudoir. "And what could be more urgent and personal than visiting a Covent Garden brothel?" He smiled at her. "I require a mistress," he said. "That is why I am here. I have come to ask you if you will accept the role."

CHAPTER TWO

LOTTIE DID NOT ANSWER him immediately. Ethan watched her as she got to her feet and walked away from him. The room was small; there was not far for her to go. He sensed her need to escape. She was like a trapped bird in an exotic cage, like the golden canary that sat mutely in the cage by the window.

"You hate this life, don't you," he said. It was a statement of fact, spoken without sentiment or gentleness. It was a long time since he had felt sympathy for anyone.

"Yes." She did not turn back to look at him. Her shoulders were slumped. The saucy transparent negligee she was wearing with its swansdown trimmings was like a mocking reminder of her status. After a moment he saw her reach for a shawl from the bed and wrap it tightly about herself as though she were cold.

"I should not hate it." She sounded defiant. "God knows why I feel so demeaned. You are right that I chose this life rather than starve." She turned and looked at him. "And anyway, I used to like sex." She sounded vaguely surprised. "I used to be rather good at it, too."

Ethan laughed. Such plain speaking in a woman was refreshing and unusual. He had heard that Lottie Palliser was an unusual woman but he had not expected her to be quite like this. "That doesn't mean you would be a good courtesan," he pointed out. "Nor that you would like the work. When money changes hands it alters matters. It is like being a mercenary soldier. You put yourself up for hire and cannot always be scrupulous about who pays or what you have to do for the money."

She laughed, a rich throaty sound. "A nice analogy." The humor fled her voice. "It was naive of me to imagine I could step easily into a role like this."

There was far more to it than that, Ethan thought. He had heard what had happened to her and knew that the scandal of the divorce and her ruin must have shattered her world and stolen her certainties. No one could remain unchanged by so cataclysmic an experience. Gossip had painted her as a promiscuous harlot, but the woman he saw now was very far from bold. Experienced, certainly, but no shameless whore.

He stood up and walked over to her, taking her chin in his hand and turning her face toward the light. Her skin felt very soft beneath his fingers, but it was difficult to see the real woman beneath the layers of paint.

"Wash your face," he said abruptly.

Her chin jerked in his hand—evidently she disliked taking orders—but after a moment she freed herself and walked over to the basin, where she poured some water from a big china jug and splashed it on her face. The result, when she came back to his side, was astonishing. Her skin was now bare of cosmetics, a pale creamy color sprinkled with freckles. He let his gaze wander over her. Her face was heart-shaped, tapering to

a neat little chin, and her eyes were wide set and dark
brown beneath flyaway brows. Her mouth was pale pink
and looked sulky by nature; it also looked shockingly
erotic, which sent a spike of lust through him. Desire
gripped him, strong and sharp, taking him by surprise.
All his tastes were jaded, including his lust for women.
He had not expected to want her much. He needed
her—he needed Lottie Palliser specifically because of
her scandalous history—but he had not calculated on
desiring her, as well. He continued with his appraisal,
blue eyes narrowed now, aware that his blood was beating a little faster and harder and that he wanted to taste
that tempting mouth.

There were fine lines about her eyes. They gave
character and a certain world-weary cynicism to her
face. The color of her eyes, too, was fascinating, as deep
and smoky as strong coffee, rich, shadowed, promising
endless pleasures.

He put out a lazy hand and unpinned her hair. It un-
coiled in thick dark strands over her shoulders, autumn
hair with shades of bronze and chestnut and very dark
gold. He ran his fingers through the strands and found
it to be soft as sateen. She stood absolutely still beneath
his gaze, stiller than a hunted mouse. He pulled the
shawl from her shoulders and it fell in a puddle about
her feet.

She was naked beneath the sheer lacy robe. At such
close quarters Ethan could feel her warmth and smell
the faint sweet scent of jasmine on her skin. Her breasts
pressed against the lace, rounded and voluptuous, the
nipples dark through the transparent white. Ethan's
body stirred again. Their eyes met. That lush mouth

had a tiny smile lifting the corners now. She knew he wanted her and it pleased her. He felt another kick of lust. He leaned forward, kissed her.

She made no move to twine about him or press her body against his as a more accomplished courtesan might, skillful and eager to please. She stood quite still, her lips warm and soft, slightly parted, beneath his.

He stepped back wanting her all the more.

"How old are you?" he asked abruptly.

Her smile vanished and he saw a flash of expression in her eyes—calculation?—but she answered readily enough. "I am eight and twenty."

"I had heard," he said, "that you are three and thirty."

She did not trouble to hide her annoyance. She stepped back from him and scooped up her shawl, once again wrapping it close about her, hiding her nakedness from him.

"If you knew, why did you ask?" she snapped.

"Why bother to lie?" he countered.

"Because, as Mrs. Tong has not scrupled to point out to me," she said bitterly, "I do not have many more years left before I will end on the street. If I can steal a few back then why not?"

Ethan felt a curious stirring of sympathy. So it was more than hurt pride. She was fearful for her future. He suspected that it would make her more inclined to accept his terms. She was desperate to escape the tyranny of the whorehouse and the threat of a life as an old doxy, eking out an existence in the gutters. How low she had sunk.

He resumed his seat, settling back, watching her.

"So what do you think of my proposition?" He asked. "Do you accept—or not?"

She sat down on the edge of the bed, her feet in their swansdown-trimmed slippers, swinging.

"How blunt you are," she said, watching him with those brown eyes.

Ethan smiled. "It is a simple proposal," he said easily. "I am aware that you dislike this new life upon which you have embarked. I'll not force any woman to my bed. So—" he shrugged "—if the offer is not to your liking then I shall go elsewhere."

She took her time thinking about it. He respected that. He had not expected her to be clever. Surely no intelligent woman would have got herself into the situation Lottie Palliser was in, cast out by family and friends, destitute because the sum of money her former husband had been obliged to pay her on their divorce had apparently been spent on settling dressmakers' and other merchants' bills. He wondered idly if there could have been more to her downfall than was commonly known and then acknowledged that it hardly mattered. He needed a woman with an outrageous reputation, someone who was scandal personified. Lottie fitted the bill to perfection. He wanted her to accept because she was ideal for his purpose.

"Are prisoners of war allowed to keep mistresses?" she asked mildly. "I would not expect you to be accorded so much freedom."

"I could keep a pet lion if I wished," Ethan said, "as long as I could afford to feed and house it. I have every freedom except my actual liberty." He spoke with more bitterness than he had intended, looked up and saw that she was watching him with interest but with as little compassion as he had accorded her, as though he were a specimen on a doctor's slab. It was odd to be watched with the same detachment with which he customarily viewed the world. It made him feel a curious flash of kindred spirit for her.

"And can you?" she asked. "Afford to feed, house and clothe me?" She stretched, her body rippling beneath the negligee. It was consciously erotic and his body reacted instantly even as he knew his response was being manipulated. "I should warn you," she continued, "that I am more expensive than any pet. My former husband—" dislike colored her tone "—claimed that I cost more to keep than his most valuable racehorse."

"I can believe that." Ethan gave her an appreciative smile. "Yes, I am rich," he added. "I've done well for the bastard son of a circus performer." He took several bags of coins from his pockets and placed them on the table. The money clinked softly and he saw her eyes widen. Some of the gossip had evidently been true then—Lottie Palliser did have a mercenary and acquisitive nature. That was good. It meant that she could be bought if the price was right.

"Those sound like guineas," she said.

"They are." He pulled on the neck of one of the bags, allowing the golden coins to spill out across the table and watched the expressions flit across her face. Greed, calculation… "There is sufficient to pay Mrs. Tong for the cost of losing your services," he said, "and to buy you a new wardrobe and pay your fare to Wantage on the mail coach on Friday."

"Friday would not give me enough time to purchase

a new wardrobe," Lottie said. "Such matters are not to be rushed."

Ethan smiled. "You will have to buy ready-made gowns," he said.

Lottie frowned. "How cheap and vulgar."

"But necessary. I have to return to Berkshire in two days' time. You will have one day to go shopping before you join me." He glanced around the gaudy room. "I'll give you enough money to pay for lodgings until then. I doubt Mrs. Tong would wish you to stay here and I imagine you wish it even less."

Lottie chewed her lip thoughtfully between straight white teeth.

"Wantage, you say?" She raised her finely arched brows. "I have family living near there. From what I remember, it is the back of beyond."

"It's not such a bad little town, though you will find it parochial," Ethan said. "It is up to you," he added gently. "You can be a whore in a London brothel, prey to all those men who used to bow respectfully over your hand in your own drawing room, or you can be my mistress in the back of beyond—with enough money at the end of our association to set you up wherever you please."

Again he watched her as she weighed the benefits and drawbacks of his offer. It was an emotionless negotiation, he thought, which was exactly how one should appoint a mistress.

Lottie slipped off the bed and came over to the table. She cast him a suspicious look and then opened the other two pouches to check the contents. She even bit one of the guineas.

"It is not counterfeit," Ethan said. "I do not cheat." He smiled. "Do you not trust me?"

"I do not know." Lottie gave him a searching look. "There is something about this whole business that does not feel quite right."

She waited. Ethan kept his expression blank. He was a consummate card player and this was one hand he was not going to reveal. She was right—there was much more to the business than he had told her—but the less she knew the better.

After a moment she laughed. "Don't tell me—you will be paying me to keep quiet and ask no questions as well as to occupy your bed. Well—" she gave a slight sigh "—I am accounted most frightfully indiscreet but I can try to hold my tongue, I suppose, if there is money in it for me."

"That," Ethan said, "would be ideal."

She nodded. "Why do you want a mistress?" she asked, as blunt as he had been.

Ethan gave her a look that made her blush again. "Why does any man?" he said.

He saw a cynical expression touch her eyes. "There are many reasons why a man likes to boast his sexual prowess," she said dryly. "Sometimes it is because he is impotent, or he prefers men to women but wishes to disguise the fact…." Her voice faded. She gave a little shrug, inviting his response.

"My motives are not so complicated," Ethan said. "I am bored. I'm likely to be a prisoner of war for the duration of this conflict and I need to pass the time somehow. What better way than in bed?"

It should have been a convincing enough reason,

but still she hesitated, her dark gaze narrowed on him, as though she knew he was being less than open with her.

"Why me?" she said. "You asked for me specifically."

"I did," Ethan agreed. Again she had surprised him in remembering that detail and realizing that it had significance. "I have a certain reputation for scandal," he said. "If I am to take a mistress then it is only appropriate that she should be the most notorious woman in London." He took her wrist in a light grip and drew her close. "I want a woman who will be outrageous, ostentatious and—"

"Obliging?" Again she gave that little half smile that quickened his pulse. Something dark and hot shimmered in her eyes. "I used to be all of those things." She sounded almost wistful.

Ethan laughed. "So I heard." He traced a finger along her full lower lip and felt her body hum with the echo of his touch. His body was already tight and primed and hard, wanting her.

"So, Lottie Palliser," he said. "You have had enough time to decide now. What do you say?"

"YES," LOTTIE SAID. She did not hesitate. She knew that perhaps she should, for there was something about Ethan Ryder's story that did not ring true, some element that struck a note of warning within her. But then there were the bags of gold, so many guineas, the like of which she had not seen for months, years even. And she liked the element of danger and recklessness that burned in Ethan Ryder. It kindled excitement in her blood for the first time in months.

"I would be an abject fool," she added, "to refuse the offer of so rich a man in order to stay here and be subject to the whims of a multitude of poorer ones."

She saw his teeth gleam in a smile. "An admirably pragmatic approach."

Lottie gestured doubtfully to the gaudy bed. "Do you…would you like…"

She could hear the uncertainty in her own voice. The brief flash of confidence was already failing her. She knew she must seem gauche as a virgin debutante. There had been a time when seduction had seemed so easy. She thought bitterly of James Devlin, her final *affaire*. That was where it had all started to go wrong. She had fallen hopelessly in love with Dev, and it had been the single most stupid thing she could have done. When he had ended their association she had been utterly distraught, searching for comfort and solace with other men, whilst at the same time desperately trying to hide her hurt. It was difficult; she lived her life in the goldfish bowl of *Ton* society, forever under scrutiny. She could see now, with the benefit of time and hindsight, that in her grief she had become careless and too indiscreet. What she had thought had been secret had become common knowledge. And Gregory's patience had snapped.

She had heard that Gregory was to remarry, to one of the Season's most eligible heiresses. Evidently the scandal that had ruined her name had left him spotless. But then, he had the money and the power to wash his reputation clean. In fact his influence was so great that even had she told the truth of his sexual proclivities, no one would have listened to her. She hoped that his little virgin heiress would not be too shocked. She was afraid that she would be.

She turned back to look at Ethan Ryder. He was good-looking, attractive in that dangerous, devil-may-care way that had once been so appealing to her. Two years ago it would have taken one look for her to resolve that she wanted to take him to bed. Now she felt racked with nervousness. Her whole body was trembling. What on earth had happened to her? She was not sure, only that the court case had left her with not only her reputation in tatters. She had changed. Somewhere along the way all her certainties and all her confidence had been hammered into the ground.

She fumbled with the ribbon on her robe but Ethan's hand closed over hers, warm and firm, stilling her shaking fingers.

"No," he said. "I wouldn't. Not here."

Lottie closed her eyes briefly. She felt a curious mixture of relief and chagrin. It was so foolish to be irritated that he did not appear to want her when she was also relieved that she did not have to play the whore for him here and now. Perhaps he was another, like Gregory, who preferred men. Perhaps it was only the pretense of a mistress he wanted, the appearance of being as other men. Gregory had wanted a wife to act as hostess, but more importantly he had wanted the camouflage that she gave him. Yet she doubted that of Ethan. When he had kissed her she had felt the need in him as hot and sharp as a whetted knife. She had known that he wanted her.

His fingers released hers. He stepped closer to her so that his breath stirred her hair. His lips brushed the line of her jaw, sending little shivers of awareness along her skin. She looked into his eyes and saw again the hard glitter of desire.

"They are watching and listening," he said softly, "to make sure that you do your job properly this time."

Lottie spun around, her gaze searching the paneled walls of the boudoir. Of course they would be watching her through spy-holes, keyholes, peepholes, the whole prurient range of the brothel's trade. Perhaps Mrs. Tong had even taken John Hagan's money on the promise that he could watch her with Ethan before Hagan had her himself. She felt sick, hot and naive not to have thought of it before.

"I don't perform for crowds," she said defiantly.

Ethan smiled. It deepened the lines at the corners of his eyes and made a crease appear down one lean cheek. He had a crease in his chin, too. It did not soften his looks. In fact it gave even more resolution to a face that already had no gentleness in it.

"If it comes to that," he said, "neither do I." He moved away. "Put some clothes on. We're leaving."

Lottie let out her breath on a sigh. "Thank you."

Ethan held her eyes for a long moment. A smile still tilted his lips. Heat shimmered between them, robbing Lottie of breath. She felt flustered, taken by surprise. Then he turned away and scooped up the bags of guineas. "Don't thank me," he said. "I'm simply protecting my investment." He sounded impatient now. "That old procuress would only rob you blind if I left you alone to deal with her. I don't want you costing me more than is necessary."

Lottie scrambled in the wardrobe for a gown and shoes. Most of the clothes Mrs. Tong had provided her with were unpleasantly cheap quality as well as cut to enhance every asset she possessed and to fall off at the slightest touch. There was not a single tasteful garment among them other than the one gown and spencer that she had brought with her from home, from her lost life. She bundled them up under her arm. The cupboard smelled of stale scent. With a pang of loss she remembered the bottles of perfume she had once bought at Piver's and at Rimmel's in the Strand. Flower-scented gloves had been one of her favorite indulgences in the old days…

"Are you ready?" Ethan still sounded impatient. How long did he think it took a woman to dress? She did not even have a maid to help her. She opened the cupboard again and dragged a cloak about her shoulders then grabbed the canary's cage from its hook.

"Is that your bird or are you stealing it?" Ethan raised one black brow.

"It's mine." It was the only thing she had taken with her from Grosvenor Square. She looked around and raised her chin. "I don't want anything else from this godforsaken place."

"An understandable sentiment," Ethan said, "but not very practical. I am not prepared to pay to dress you from scratch."

Grumbling, Lottie gathered up some underclothes, stockings, gloves, a shawl, two fans, a feathered headdress, a couple of gowns and a parasol, and threw them into a small bandbox she had found at the back of the cupboard.

Ethan took her hand. His touch made her tremble. She felt disturbed. Misgivings stirred for the first time; more stark choices; stay in this hellhole or go with a virtual stranger. He slanted a look down at her, his gaze sardonic.

"Scared?"

She wished he could not read her so easily. It seemed extraordinary—and deeply inconvenient—that he could. She looked up and met his eyes boldly.

"No, of course not."

"Liar." A smile curled his lips. There was a hard light in his blue eyes. "It is your choice, Miss Palliser."

"You are the lesser of two evils," Lottie said.

His smile deepened, sending a quiver of awareness like a lightning bolt through her. "Or perhaps the devil you know?" He murmured.

"I don't know you," Lottie said.

"But you will," Ethan said. "You will."

It sounded like a dangerous promise.

CHAPTER THREE

THE GREEDY BAWD had taken him for almost every guinea he had on him. Ethan was not surprised but he was wondering if it was worth it.

He sat opposite Lottie Palliser in the hackney carriage and watched her as the shadows skipped across her face in bars of light and dark. She was not at all what he had expected. How many times had he thought that this evening? How many times had he had the opportunity to change his mind, discard her and choose another, more biddable and accomplished woman for the role of mistress? How had he, the most cold and calculating man in the kingdom, ended up with a courtesan who seemed almost as nervous as a virgin, accompanied by a canary that could not sing? He shifted with irritation, with himself, with her, with the damned canary. This was too important a mission he was engaged on; he could not afford to ruin it all on a whim because for some inexplicable reason he preferred Lottie Palliser to another more compliant mistress.

And yet Lottie Palliser was no shrinking innocent. Despite the ordeal of her divorce and disgrace there was spirit in her still, a little crushed, perhaps, but he could see the ghost of the woman she had once been. That was the woman he needed, the scandalous, hedonistic pleasure-seeker who would outrage the populace of a small market town and keep their attention firmly on her, leaving him to pursue his business away from their prying eyes. He needed a decoy, a distraction. Lottie Palliser was going to be that woman.

The first part of the jigsaw was now in place. Mrs. Tong had been suitably shocked and furious to lose the services of the most notorious jade in London—even if she had been hopeless as a whore—but had been unable to resist the lure of the money. The madam would undoubtedly tell the world and his wife how the scandalous Ethan Ryder had walked into her brothel and paid a king's ransom to walk out with Lottie Palliser as his mistress. Everyone would be talking about it from London to Land's End, which was exactly what Ethan desired. Before she even arrived in Wantage, Lottie would be the most infamous mistress in the country. She would set the town by the ears.

"London by night." Lottie was sitting forward, holding the curtain back so that she could look out of the carriage window. "I have missed its amusements."

There was something wistful in her tone, a regret for all she had lost, perhaps. For it did not matter how much he paid her at the end of their association, Ethan thought. She would never regain the life she had once had. *Ton* society was closed to her forever.

"How did you come to this?" he asked. He was not sure why he was even interested. Lottie's misfortunes were none of his affair. And yet he wanted to know how a seemingly intelligent woman had got herself into so desperate a situation. He was curious about her.

He could feel her eyes on him in the darkness of the carriage as though she was thinking about how much to tell him, whether to lie, perhaps, and paint her case as more sympathetic than it was. He was as indifferent to her scrutiny as he would be to her falsehoods. She would read nothing in his face. He just wanted to know her story. It would pass the time since the traffic was slow at this time of night.

"You know what happened to me," she said, after a pause. "You told me yourself."

"I know what happened, not why."

She turned away, hunched a shoulder. "My husband divorced me because I became too careless and indiscreet in my love affairs." For a split second, in a shaft of light, he saw her face, remote and hard. "I always was imprudent," she said. "I liked the danger. But I let it go too far. I was too reckless."

Ethan smiled.

I liked the danger....

He understood that because he liked danger, too. He liked the risk and the thunder in the blood and the race of the pulse, for what else was there to live for when everything you cared about had been taken away? He had been right. That instinct that had told him that Lottie Palliser was wild as he, a kindred spirit, had been correct. It should make her perfect for his purpose.

There was quiet but for the roll of the carriage wheels over the cobbles and the clop of the horse's hooves. Outside the nighttime world spun about them with its glitter and gaiety, the noise of the crowd, the taste of excitement in the air.

"I can understand why your family might disown you," Ethan said. The Pallisers were very high in the instep and divorce, scandal, would be anathema to them. "But surely you had friends who would help you—"

A quick shake of her head silenced him. "I tried to seduce the husband of my best friend," she said. "That was her second husband. He refused me. I had already slept with her first one."

It took a very great deal to surprise Ethan. This did not even come close. Besides, he had heard some tone in her voice that betrayed her, that was at odds with the brashness of her words.

"Are you trying to shock me?" he asked.

Her eyes gleamed. "Am I succeeding?"

"Not remotely."

"Oh well…" She sounded cross, like a thwarted child. "I could try harder but to tell the truth I cannot be bothered to do so."

"You wanted your friend's husband," Ethan said. "Why?"

He sensed her surprise. "Do you know," she said slowly, "no one has ever asked me that before?"

"Well?"

"You sound like a stern governess." She sounded petulant. "I don't know! I was bored, he was handsome…."

Ethan knew she was lying. He could hear it. He also knew she would not tell him the truth. Not now, not yet, if ever. Lottie Palliser had been badly hurt and that damage had made her draw her defenses so tight no one would ever come close to hurting her again. He understood that. He had been doing something similar since he was fifteen years old.

"You have an interesting concept of loyalty to your friends," he said now.

"I have no concept of loyalty." She sounded tired. "And it was not even worth it. He had a tiny penis and was only concerned for his own pleasure in bed."

Ethan laughed. "How disappointing to lose a friend and gain so little in return."

A small smile lifted the corner of her mouth. "That was the least of my betrayals. I deceived Joanna several times over." She sighed. "Even so, I think she would have helped me, but she has been out of the country for over a year, in Scandinavia and Russia, or somewhere equally far-flung. I forget. I wrote to her but the letter probably went astray. Geography is not my strong suit." She gave an irritable little shrug. "Must we speak of this?" He could feel her gaze resting on him. "There is no need for us to *talk,* is there, least of all about me?"

"Not if you do not wish." Ethan was amused. For as long as he could remember he had had women desperate to tell him their life stories. He had been the one trying to escape the intimacy.

Lottie shifted on the seat and he caught a faint scent of her jasmine perfume, fresh and sweet. The hunger gripped him again, as razor-sharp as it had been in the brothel. It was a very long time since he had had a woman. As a prisoner of war he had had little opportunity to satisfy his lusts and had grown accustomed to ignoring them. Instead he had focused all his energies on the long, dangerous, treasonable game he was playing. Yet now it seemed that Lottie Palliser's intriguing combination of reticence and experience was proving a great deal more seductive than he had ever imagined.

At first he had thought she was acting the prude to titillate the jaded palates of Mrs. Tong's clientele. An experienced woman playing the virgin was not unusual, but in Lottie's case it would have been pointless since everyone knew her history. And at no point had she attempted to deny her promiscuity or the infidelity that had led to her downfall. That honesty interested Ethan. Not a single woman of his acquaintance would have been as open as Lottie had been with him, and he admired her for that unflinching truthfulness.

She moved slightly on the hackney carriage seat and he heard the rustle of her silk skirts.

"How did *you* come to this?" she asked, turning his question back on him. "Since you seem so anxious to speak to me, you can tell me how you came to be a prisoner of war."

"I was captured at the battle of Fuentes de Onoro in Portugal," Ethan said. "When Wellington discovered who I was, he sent me back to England as a prisoner."

"How careless of you to be caught." Her voice was cool. "The British must have been delighted to lay hands on you when you have been a very public affront to your noble father for so many years. In fact—" her voice changed, became thoughtful "—I am surprised that they let you loose."

"They kept me locked in a prison hulk at Chatham for a year." Ethan spoke lightly, dismissively, even as he clenched his muscles with repudiation of every memory the words conjured, memories of the Black

Hole, a prison a mere six-foot square at the bottom of the hold, with no light and barely any air. Men had been driven mad in there and begged to die. Men had been clapped in irons, half starved, flogged until they could not stand. He felt as though he could still smell the stench of the hulks, feel the filth on his skin beneath the fine lawn of his shirt and hear the cries of those who had run mad. He would never forget it.

"That must have been vile." Lottie's voice was soft, as though for all his apparent unconcern she could feel his hatred seeping through.

"It was." He shut his mouth tightly.

"Why did you fight for the French?" He could feel her watching him in the darkness of the carriage. "Do you hate the British so much that their enemy is your friend?"

Ethan laughed. "I don't hate the British. Why should I?"

There were about a hundred answers to that one but he was not going to supply them. Like her, he would always hold back to protect himself.

"Then are you a mercenary, no more than a soldier of fortune, taking the Emperor's money?"

Lottie Palliser certainly knew how to provoke a man, Ethan thought ruefully. Perhaps silence would have been preferable after all.

"I am no mercenary soldier," he said stiffly. "I fought for Napoleon because I have principles. I believe in what he is doing."

"Principles." Lottie said the word as though it were foreign to her. "How extraordinary." He saw her smile.

"Most men I know are unprincipled bastards. So you believe in—" she hesitated, "—liberty, fraternity and… the other one?"

"Equality," Ethan said. "Yes, those are the beliefs of the revolution."

"An odd sort of equality that sets one man up as an Emperor over the others," Lottie said. "But then, I have never had much interest in politics so perhaps I am missing some crucial point. I fear that affairs of state bore me." She yawned.

"Fortunately I have no desire to talk politics with you," Ethan said. "I did not buy you for that."

The air in the carriage cooled as though a breath of frost had blown through. Ethan saw that he had angered her with the blunt reminder of her situation. She still had plenty of pride. She turned her face away from him, her expression haughty. The carriage had slowed down at the meeting of two streets; it jerked forward and Lottie lost her balance, putting a hand out to steady herself against the door frame. As she moved, Ethan heard the unmistakable chink of coin, and expensive coin at that. Guineas. There could be only one place she had got those from. Their eyes met and in that moment he realized what she was about to do.

She was going to cheat him and run away.

Lottie had a hand on the door, already had it half-open with the noise and lamplight spilling in from the street outside the carriage. Ethan made a grab for her arm, felt the velvet of her cloak slip and slither between his fingers and caught her about the waist a second before she jumped.

"Not so fast."

DAMN HIM. HE STILL sounded unperturbed. Was there nothing that could ruffle this man's calm?

Lottie half sat, half lay across Ethan's lap, breathing quickly and feeling as trapped and furious as a cornered cat. Ethan's arm was as unyielding as a steel band about her waist. She shifted a little, trying to ease his grip, and immediately the bag of guineas she had stolen from him bumped heavily against his thigh. He slanted a look down at her. His lips turned up in a grim smile as he extracted the purse from the pocket of her cloak.

"I thought so. When did you lift that from me?" He sounded mildly interested, as though the pickpocketing habit of a society lady-turned-whore was a matter for careful consideration. Lottie felt her temper tighten further.

"I took it whilst you were negotiating with Mrs. Tong," she snapped. "You weren't paying attention to me."

He nodded. "I underestimated you."

He ran his hands over her in an impersonal search that felt oddly like a caress. Lottie trembled a little beneath his touch. She felt tense as a bow, frustrated, furious, to have been caught out, yet alive, aroused, and dangerously close to the edge.

"There aren't any more," she said. "I only had time to take the one."

"And then you were going to run away from me."

Lottie did not reply. She saw the cynical smile deepen on his lips.

"Where did you plan to go?" Ethan's face was so close to hers that she could see the planes and hollows illuminated by the skipping lamplight. His expression was dark and unrevealing. Some men were easy to read, Lottie thought, easy to understand and even easier to manipulate. Ethan Ryder was not one of them.

"I have no notion," she said. "I had not thought that far ahead."

"So only the theft of my money was planned?"

Ethan's voice was smooth but there was contempt beneath the surface. Well, she was not going to apologize. Perhaps it was wrong by conventional standards but she had moved so far beyond convention that she no longer cared.

"Yes," she said. She met his eyes very directly. "I planned to rob you from the moment I saw all those lovely guineas." To have a little money would have given her back a tiny measure of control and the chance of freedom, she thought. Fate had presented her with an opportunity to wrest back some power so she had tried to take it. The fact that she had almost succeeded was infuriating. She had come so close—and then she had failed.

"You were going to cheat me," Ethan said. He grabbed her upper arms and held her still.

"Of course I was," Lottie flashed. "You would be a fool to think I would do otherwise." The anger bubbled up in her again. How many times had *she* been cheated, used and discarded? It had been her turn for a change.

"I thought we had an agreement," Ethan said. She could feel tension in him, wound tight. The hands that held her were merciless. "Where is your loyalty?"

"I have already told you that I do not possess such a quality."

"And now you have demonstrated it." His tone was still level. "I do not think that you understand. As my mistress I expect you to be faithful to me, to show me a modicum of honesty and certainly not to try and rob me and run off."

"Surely you did not trust me anyway?" Lottie said disdainfully.

"Naturally not." He sounded dismissive. "But that does not mean I wished to be proved right."

"And yet you are not even angry with me." For some reason this enraged Lottie all the more, as though his refusal to be provoked meant that she had failed twice over.

"You mistake me," Ethan said. "I *am* angry." He raised a hand, eased back the hood of her cloak and tangled his fingers in her hair, bringing her face forward so that they were very close. She could feel the fury in him now, as elemental as fire. It was a shocking contrast when he kept his voice so steady.

"I don't show my feelings very often," he whispered. "You should bear that in mind if you wish to please me in the future."

Lottie made an enraged sound. "Please you? I have no wish to please you! Surely you have realized that by now?"

"You are ungrateful." He sounded amused. "I could have left you in that brothel servicing half of London."

"Instead you bought me to service *you!*"

"I gave you a choice," Ethan said. His words were

cool but the undertone was fierce. "I told you I did not want an unwilling mistress. You did not have to come with me."

"Then I would not have had any money, would I?" Lottie said, furiously.

There was a pause and then Ethan laughed. "I do believe," he said pleasantly, "that you are even more mercenary than I suspected."

He cupped her face between his hands and kissed her hard. Lottie could sense the heated anger but beneath that was an equally turbulent desire. It fed both her fury and her need. In the brothel she had known that he wanted her and yet he had chosen not to take her. His control had baffled her where another man would simply have indulged his lust. Now though, Ethan's control was slipping, ignited by an anger she sensed went far deeper than mere annoyance at her deceit. She could feel a fury in him that was dark and ungovernable and went as deep as his soul. It was no wonder that normally he kept so tight a grip on it.

Ethan slid his tongue along her lower lip, delving into her mouth, plunging inside to taste and plunder. It made her head spin. Only an hour before she had felt desolation at what had become of her. Now that misery and frustration fused into an anger so great it met and matched his. He ravaged her mouth and she kissed him back as fiercely and as furiously as he took her.

She moved to straddle him on the seat of the carriage. She could feel the long hard ridge of his erection against her thigh and she pressed down on him and heard him groan.

"This is what you *bought*," she said against his

mouth. "See if you like it." She bit him, not gently. He jerked back, swearing, then rolled her over on the seat so that she was beneath him now, her legs tangled in a waterfall of silk and lace petticoats, his weight holding her down. She lay panting, looking up at him. He was breathing as hard as she, and there was a dark, feral light in his eyes.

Ethan pushed the cloak off her shoulders and pulled down the bodice of her gown with a violent movement that almost ripped the flimsy material. He cupped one breast, taking her quickly into his mouth. Lottie squirmed. Desire flamed through her, shocking her with its heat and ferocity after so many months of cold, empty misery. She opened her body and her mind to its dark, demanding tide, her entire being burning up with anger and wild need.

Ethan bit down on her breast, more gently than she had bitten him, and she gasped as her body jolted with the mingled pain and pleasure of it. In response she tangled her fingers in his thick dark hair and pulled hard.

He swore again before returning his mouth to her breasts, covering them with tiny kisses that made her skin tighten and shiver, rosy pink from the torment of his lips, tongue and teeth. He slid one hand up her thigh and she reached for the band of his pantaloons, feverish to feel him inside her and put an end to this driving need for possession. It was fury and it was escape, but it was pleasure, too, as she felt the palm of his hand rough against the soft skin of her inner thigh and she arched, desperate to draw his touch to the very core of her.

The carriage jerked to a halt, almost throwing them

off the seat. Ethan caught Lottie close in his arms to prevent her from falling, and for a second she stared up at him, seeing in his face the same welter of emotion there that she felt inside, the fury, the confusion and the need. Then his expression turned blank and she wondered if she had imagined that flash of feeling.

"Where are we?" Lottie said. She felt confused and adrift. The anger and desire were ebbing swiftly now and the cold desolation rushing back to fill all the empty corners of her soul.

"We are at Limmer's Hotel," Ethan said. "I stay here when I am in town." He shifted, straightening, and Lottie sat up, smoothing down her gown with hands that shook slightly. Another minute, she thought, another second, and he would have been inside her. She had wanted it, wanted him, with so fierce a hunger it had stolen her breath. So why did she now feel so cheap and sad and worthless?

She drew the cloak about her tightly as though trying to drive out the cold.

"Limmer's?" she said. "How very disreputable."

She saw Ethan smile. "How very appropriate."

He swung open the door of the hackney carriage and jumped down, threw some coins and a word of thanks to the coachman and turned to help Lottie down the steps. As she moved toward the doorway of the hotel he stopped her with a hand on her arm.

"A moment," he said softly. He looked her over, straightening the cloak with a gesture she found oddly touching, pulling the hood up over her disordered hair. His hand touched her cheek in a brief caress. She could not be sure whether it was accident or design but it sent a quiver of sensation right through her body. She searched his face for another glimpse of that elusive emotion she was sure she had seen before but there was no sign of it.

"That was not bad," Ethan said. He spoke lightly, mockingly. "Perhaps I shall get my money's worth after all."

And in that moment Lottie knew never to expect tenderness from Ethan Ryder. She berated herself for seeking it, hoping for it. This was about sex and money, nothing more. That was the cornerstone of her new life. And she had best not forget it.

CHAPTER FOUR

ETHAN WONDERED if he was destined to spend the rest
of the evening and very possibly the foreseeable future
feeling angry; angry with Lottie, angry with himself
and angry with the two of them in combination. It
seemed more than likely.

He had been absolutely furious to discover that Lottie
had attempted to steal and run away from him. Such
treachery should have amused him, bearing out as it did
his assessment that she had no integrity. But instead of
amusement he had been possessed by a red-hot rage that
had been as inexplicable as it had been out of character.
It had been sufficient to make him lose control, to want
to possess Lottie with an angry desire that had been
fueled by her equally uninhibited response. He was a
man who never lost control, least of all with a woman,
and this had been unprecedented. Choosing a mistress,
sleeping with her, should have been the simple part of
his plan. Instead it was mysteriously turning into the
most complicated aspect.

And now he was furious for an entirely different
reason. The fierce lovemaking with Lottie, which had
almost reached its culmination in a hackney carriage
of all places, had left him feeling shaken and disturbed.
Neither were reactions that he associated with making
love to a woman. He was not accustomed to being at

the mercy of his own passion and he did not care for the feeling. The unwelcome emotion had been enough to make him want to put some distance between them.

Lottie had not replied to him but had swept ahead of him through the doorway and into the dingy interior of Limmer's Hotel. She carried herself with dignity and Ethan was forcibly reminded of the fact that no matter her current ruin and disgrace, Lottie Palliser was descended from a very old and aristocratic family indeed.

He followed her inside. Lottie's arrival was causing considerable interest in the dark and dirty entrance hall. Several sporting gentlemen—for Limmer's was known as a haunt of the hunting squirearchy—were ogling her and even the pale desk clerk had a gleam of excitement in his eyes. Lottie was looking about her with haughty disdain. Ethan was startled to realize that in her velvet cloak with her hair peeping from beneath the hood and her face bare of cosmetics she looked more like a young ingenue than the veteran of many scandalous love affairs.

As he watched, a slim gentleman in the buff breeches and navy coat that was the uniform of the 1st regiment of Napoleon's Carabiniers stepped forward to bow to Lottie with languid elegance.

"*Enchanté, madame,*" he said. "Colonel Jacques Le Prevost at your service." Turning to Ethan he raised his fair brows expressively and continued in French: "My God, St. Severin, I thought you were visiting Madame Tong's Temple of Venus to find your mistress, not Almack's Assembly Rooms!"

Before Ethan could respond, Lottie had smiled

prettily at Le Prevost and replied, in perfect French. "You mistake, monsieur, I am fresh from the whorehouse not the schoolroom."

Le Prevost choked. "Madame!" He recovered himself and his hazel eyes lit with appreciative laughter. "All that, a sense of humor and perfect French, too? You are a fortunate man, St. Severin." His gaze narrowed speculatively on Lottie. "Perhaps Wantage will not prove so tedious a posting after all."

"You will have to make your own entertainment," Ethan said, taking Lottie's arm. "Jacques was previously on parole in Reading," he murmured to her. "It is where all the richest and most influential French officers are sent and the society there is good. He is less than impressed to be sent to Wantage's rural backwater."

"I am becoming more resigned to my fate by the moment," Le Prevost said, slapping Ethan on the back. "You had best take your English rose away, my friend, before her jealous countrymen snatch her back." He made another elegant bow to Lottie. "Your servant, *madame*. I shall look forward to knowing you better."

"I did not realize that you spoke such good French," Ethan said, as he and Lottie turned the stair. "Were you a studious child?"

"That seems unlikely, doesn't it," Lottie said. "No, I was no bluestocking. In fact my governess, Miss Snook, despaired of me. But my grandmother was French and my mother spoke to us a great deal in that language so I learned almost despite myself."

"Us?"

"My brother, Theo, and I." Lottie hesitated and Ethan saw a shadow touch her eyes. "He is…away."

Ethan took a guess. "Fighting the French?"

He saw her mouth turn down at the corners. "Yes. I have not heard from him in months. I am not sure…" Her voice trailed away and he knew what she meant.

I am not sure if he is even still alive….

"I'm sorry," he said.

She shrugged. Her expression was bright and hard and she looked uncaring, but Ethan was starting to know her a little now. He knew this was one of the things that hurt her. Matters might have been very different had her brother been present to help her when she needed him.

"It is of no consequence," she said lightly. They walked slowly along the upstairs corridor. It was dark and quiet here, but from the floor below wafted the scents of food and the roar of the racing crowd.

Lottie cast him a sideways glance. "How did you learn *your* French?" she asked.

Ethan smiled. "I had to learn quickly when I joined Napoleon's cavalry otherwise I would have been cantering left when everyone else was galloping right." He shook his head ruefully. "I did not have your facility with languages, though. I found it ridiculously hard. If I had not had such a talent with horses I think they would have thrown me out on my ear."

"How old were you?" Lottie said.

"Seventeen," Ethan said. "I was fifteen when I ran away from home, seventeen when I joined the *Grande Armée*." He squared his shoulders. He could still see the youth he had been, brash and tough—or so he had thought—already hardened by experience and yet still a boy underneath, and a scared one at that.

"Very young," Lottie said, echoing his thoughts. "I was wed at seventeen," she added quietly.

Their eyes met and once again Ethan felt that disturbing tug of affinity between them. There was a hollow feeling in the pit of his stomach and behind it an overwhelming urge to take Lottie and hold her tightly and lose himself in her so that the world and its intolerable conflicts might be held at bay a little longer. He hesitated a moment, a part of him rebelling against his need for her, rejecting the intimacy. But his instincts could not be denied. He took a step toward her, pulled her into his arms and kissed her.

She made a soft sound as his mouth touched hers, though whether it was from pleasure, surrender or something else he could not be sure. Her lips were as plush and smooth as the richest satin and he wanted to plunder them, but he held back, exerting control, wooing where he wanted simply to take. He felt hesitation behind her response. She seemed shy, almost innocent. It was such a contrast with the almost-feral passion she had shown in the carriage. Yet there was nothing feigned about her uncertainty. Once more she was the vulnerable woman he had glimpsed amidst the brazen setting of Mrs. Tong's Temple of Venus.

He drew her into his room, closed the door quietly and stood with his back to it, looking at her. The hood had fallen back on her tousled brown curls. She looked young and pale and ravishing. How was it possible for such a hardened wanton to look so very appealing?

Why did he even care? The desire in him kindled to a deeper, hotter wanting. He had to have her now.

"Now, where were we?" he said.

FOR THE LIFE OF HER, Lottie could not repress a little shiver. Ethan saw it and paused, his eyes narrowing on her.

"What is it?" he said. "In the carriage—"

"I know!" Lottie burst out. She could not help herself. She was too anxious to keep quiet and pretend to a sexual sophistication she no longer possessed. She knew he wanted an accomplished mistress. He had said as much when they had descended from the carriage. A pity, then, that he had bought a fake.

"I was furious with you in the carriage," she said. She glanced at him from under her lashes. He was watching her closely, and she could see from the heated intent in his eyes that he wanted her—but he was very still, very controlled, concentrating on her words rather than her body. She felt a tiny breath of relief that he was not a man to pounce on her, force himself on her, as some had tried to do.

"It was good to be angry," she said. "It meant that I was not thinking. But now I am no longer angry and I cannot…" She made a little, hopeless gesture. "The truth is that I have lost my confidence, my lord. Every time I see a bed now it makes me feel nervous rather than amorous. And I don't think it's funny!" she added, seeing that Ethan was laughing at her. Suddenly she wanted to cry. Torn between laughter and tears, furious with herself, she scrubbed viciously at her eyes with the back of her hand.

Ethan shook his head, the wicked smile still curving his lips. "Of course not," he soothed. "Of course it is not amusing." His lips twitched. "I had no idea you were so conventional, though. I had thought your amorous adventures must have taken place in vastly more exciting places than a mere bed."

He came toward her and eased the cloak from her shoulders. His hands were warm on her bare skin. He stroked her upper arms gently, as though she were a skittish animal. It was comforting. Lottie started to relax, allowing herself to be quieted.

"As I see it, we have two alternatives," Ethan continued softly. "Either we can make each other angry again—which should be all too easy to do given our somewhat volatile relationship—or..." He paused. "I can help you try to overcome your aversion to beds as furniture and to regain your confidence. What do you say?"

Lottie's heart was suddenly racing again. Her breath hitched in her throat. There was no escape. She knew there was not. She had taken his money and now she would have to pay his price. Even so, her lack of confidence flaying her, she sought excuses.

"I am not certain," she said, "that you are the right person to help me."

Ethan looked quizzical. "You think my technique will be inadequate?"

"No," Lottie said, smiling despite herself. "How like a man! I think your technique is *too* good. I need someone who is not too skillful or experienced so that they don't expect too much or become impatient with me—"

"No you don't." Ethan was caressing her again in

gentle strokes, up her bare arms, down again. It was extremely pleasant and distracted Lottie from all her worries. "You need me," he continued. "You need to be seduced."

Seduced. The word hung in the air between them. It sounded tempting. Lottie shivered a little with nerves and anticipation.

"You see this as a challenge," she said.

Ethan smiled. "Perhaps there is an element of that in it," he said. His smile faded. His gaze keen and hard rested on her. "Make no mistake, Lottie," he said. "I bought a mistress and now I want what I have paid for." Heat kindled in his eyes. He ran one finger down the curve of her arm, making her shiver. "To have to work for the pleasure is quite exciting," he added. "If you had planned this as a harlot's trick you could not have read me better. I hate a conquest to be too easy."

Another shiver rippled down Lottie's spine, awareness mingled with apprehension. "How ridiculous," she said, a little unsteadily, "to need to seduce your mistress. It isn't too late," she added quickly, as Ethan bent his head to feather a kiss across her collarbone. "You could find another mistress. One you do not need to coax like a virgin."

"It is far too late for that," Ethan said. He pressed a kiss in the hollow at the base of her throat. She could feel him smiling. Lottie's pulse raced. She knew Ethan would feel it beating like a trapped bird against his lips. She felt a little faint.

Ethan released her and stepped back, holding her lightly by the wrists, looking at her. Suddenly Lottie hated the fact that she was standing there in the garish, tasteless gown that had been the first thing she had grabbed to escape Mrs. Tong's whorehouse. The dress screamed harlotry like a street seller. She stiffened and Ethan released her and gave her a questioning look. There was a smile still in his blue eyes but behind it a flame burned, and she recognized it for desire and felt her wayward heart flutter.

"It is all right." He spoke gently. Somehow—how was it possible?—he had read her mind and sensed her distress at the tawdry gown. "We can get rid of it."

Lottie's lips curved into a shaky smile. "How practical you are."

He smiled back. "It is a pleasure to be of help."

He brushed his hands down her arms, from her shoulders to her elbows, and the dress, running true to form, fell off her like an empty shell. She wore no stays for she had dressed in haste. She heard Ethan's breath hitch as his gaze fell to her shift. It was her own, a sheer and delicate scrap of silk defiance in the face of Mrs. Tong's vulgarity and so fine that her nipples showed like a shadow through the material. It also molded the voluptuous roundness of her breasts. Though she was not a tall woman she was built with generous curves and as she had aged she had despaired of the way that all of those curves had sagged slightly as though they were getting tired. She supposed that she could hardly blame her breasts for drooping a little; she was fairly weary of life herself at times.

Yet Ethan did not seem to dislike the fullness of her figure for he was smiling and the sharp light of desire in his eyes ignited further.

"Delicious," he said softly, and Lottie felt a ripple

of awareness course through her. She waited for him
to remove her shift, but instead he cupped her face in
his hands and kissed her again, slow and sure, his lips
moving against hers with the gentlest of persuasion
until she parted for him and answered him hesitantly,
their breath mingling, the touch of his tongue soft
against hers. She felt the surge of response in him, the
triumph and the need to possess, and for a moment she
felt afraid again before he reined in his reaction and
drew back. He was breathing a little harder and she
could sense the impatience in him and yet he mastered
it with iron control.

She raised her hands so that he could draw her shift
off and cast it aside. Then she stood naked before him
but for her stockings and shoes. She found she had
to turn her face away from his scrutiny. She did not
know why this was different from her bravado in the
brothel where she had paraded herself barely dressed
in the transparent negligee. It felt different, though. It
felt honest, as though more than her clothes had been
stripped away.

When she risked a look at his face the unashamed
appreciation in his eyes stole her breath.

"You're beautiful," he said. His gaze pinned hers as
she looked away. "Surely you know that?"

Actually she did not. She could not remember anyone
ever telling her. She knew that Gregory had chosen her
for her prettiness as well as her family connections
because he had wanted a wife who was an adornment
to his position. But Gregory had never admired her as
a woman. He had appreciated her only in the cold way
that he valued a piece of china or glass. Her lovers had

thrown her pretty compliments, it was true, but she had often thought that was just part of the game, insincere, giving her the words she wanted to hear. Ethan sounded as though he really meant it, and although the cynical side of her berated her for her credulity, she desperately wanted it to be true.

"I…" Her heart was beating so hard and fast that the words seemed trapped in her chest. She felt self-conscious and had to smother a sudden insane urge to grab the cover from the bed and cloak herself in it. Yet at the same time she felt hot and dizzy and excited, a spiral of lust curling low in her belly.

Arousal.

She remembered the sensation but her memories seemed a pale and empty thing beside this burning reality.

Ethan took her hand and she almost jumped. Of all the places to touch her when she was naked… He was gently coaxing her to sit on the edge of the bed, then to lie back, spread and exposed to his gaze. Her stomach squirmed again in helpless desire as he allowed his gaze to travel over her from the crown of her head to her feet. He eased off her shoes and let them fall, then rolled her stockings down and cast them aside.

He came down beside her, still fully dressed, resting on one elbow. "You still look terrified." His fingers touched her cheek in a reassuring caress then moved to brush the tangle of hair back from her brow. "I had hoped to banish your fear a little by now."

Lottie turned her lips against his fingers. "You have," she whispered. "If you stop now I will probably kill you."

He laughed then swooped down to take her lips again in another deep kiss. He was less careful now, less controlled. She could feel his restraint slipping. Yet still he held something back even as the kiss took her to a place that was heated and sweet and intense, a place that she never wanted to leave.

They were both gasping when they finally drew apart.

"Take off your clothes," Lottie whispered. "This feels very unfair."

Ethan rolled over to shed his coat, casting it carelessly across the room. He pulled off his neck cloth and threw aside his shirt, barely repressed impatience in each gesture. Lottie watched. She had seen more than her fair share of naked men and had mostly found the male form a disappointment, oddly shaped, flabby, or even downright ugly. Men generally looked so much better with their clothes on. Her grandmother had told her so before she wed at seventeen and Lottie had never had cause to doubt her.

Not Ethan Ryder, though. His body was firm and lithe, whipcord strong, his shoulders wide and his chest hard and muscled. Lottie thought his thighs would probably be equally heavily muscled from so many hours in the saddle and she felt a little light-headed to think about it. Her mouth was dry and her blood felt drugged, heavy with lust.

"And the rest," she prompted, as he paused. The glitter in his eyes as he looked down at her was bright and hard, desire distilled. Her heart thumped.

It took him only a moment to discard the rest of his clothes, and then he stood before her entirely naked and magnificent with it, strong, powerful and, as Lottie could not help but note, with an enormous erection as impressive as the rest of him. Her throat felt as dry as sand now. She waited for him to return to her, to straddle her, to take her.

He did not. He stood looking down at her, his gaze as powerful as a physical touch. Lottie shifted restlessly beneath it. Then he was beside her again, touching her with gentle, reverent strokes; the line of her shoulder, the curve of her hip, the hollow of her elbow and the softness of her stomach. He kissed the underside of her breast. Lottie shivered. She reached for him, thinking that she really must show some of the initiative that would be expected of an experienced mistress, but he returned her hands firmly to her sides.

"No," he whispered. "Lie still. We do this my way."

He returned to his ministrations, firm and yet tender, his touch leaving a trail of fire in its wake. He nibbled the soft skin of her neck and her shivers intensified as his breath caressed her skin. His mouth moved lower, discovering the soft hollow of her collarbone again, licking and tasting her skin. She found herself arching up to meet him, wanting him to take her breasts in his mouth, aching for his touch. Frustratingly, infuriatingly, he left them alone. Instead she felt his tongue explore the curve of her belly and flick teasingly into her navel. The cool air breathed across her damp skin and she shuddered, need coiling within her like a tight knot.

"Please…"

She had not meant to beg, had not realized that she

would want to do so. She felt the sweep of his smile against her stomach.

"Ah…" There was a wealth of satisfaction in his voice.

He raised himself up to take one of her tight nipples into his mouth. She almost screamed; her mind spun away with pleasure. He was pulling it, tugging it with his teeth, the tiny bite mingling with the ecstasy that threatened to melt her very bones. She could not stop the trembling. The muscles jumped and quivered in her belly, and she reached again for him, blindly, but again he pressed her back down into the bed, his lips and hands tracing caresses across her skin from her stomach to her breasts until she moaned. She had never felt so vital, her body alive, all thought banished, a creature of sensation alone.

"You are driving me to madness…." The words were torn from her and she heard him laugh before his lips returned to her breast to torment her anew.

Lottie writhed, desperate to feel him inside her now, but again he evaded her grasp and resumed the slow, tantalizing mastery of her body, pressing his open mouth to her skin, his touch as hot as a brand. This time when his trail of tiny kisses reached her throat again he raised himself above her and his lips returned to her mouth, demanding, insatiable, all control lost. He plundered, but whatever he asked she gave more. There were no memories to haunt her here, no experience to draw on because she had never felt this way before, never felt this pitch of pleasure that was mingled somehow with exquisite tenderness.

"Please," she cried again, and this time she did not recognize her own voice. "Now…"

This time he slid a hand down to part her legs and she felt the cool air against the damp heat of her cleft. Her body plunged into another spasm of helpless hunger. He was poised above her, the touch of his fingers soft against the softer skin of her inner thighs and sliding toward the burning core of her. When he stroked her there she cried out, thinking she would come at once, all restraint lost. His fingers paused in the slow circles they were tracing.

"Wait," he whispered. His breath skittered across her skin racking her with shivers. She heard his voice laced with humor and wickedness. "Not yet."

"I cannot help it!" Another shudder shook her body. Desire, irresistible, unendurable, raked her. She could feel herself poised on the edge, suspended in restless, intolerable need, before one smooth stroke of his hand sent her flying into the abyss, the pleasure exploding through her body, her mind light and free. Gone was the shame and the confusion of the past weeks and months, the misery that had stolen her certainties and wrecked her confidence. She felt vivid and alive and for one terrible moment so grateful to him that she thought she loved him.

The blinding light faded a little from her mind, the brilliance dying. Gasping, she lay back on the bed, her body slick with sweat. She became aware of Ethan still kneeling between her parted thighs, still hard and erect and not one whit sexually satisfied. Truly, she thought faintly, she was a terrible mistress, grasping after her own pleasure so greedily with no thought for his.

"I'm sorry—" she croaked, and saw a frown crease between his brows.

"For what?"

"You told me to wait...." Her body still thrummed with pleasure like the last echo of music.

His expression lightened. "I am flattered you could not."

He tilted her hips up slightly and slid inside her, forcing a gasp from her because she was so tight around him. A new assault of sensation cascaded through her.

"Oh!"

He held himself quite still as her body instinctively adapted to his, cradling him, enclosing him in its heat. Then he rocked inside her, a tiny movement, a deeper penetration, creating a tumult of feeling. Her body tensed about his, clenching him tightly, and she heard the breath hiss between his teeth. Looking up into his eyes she saw the strength there and the power and knew he would not be provoked into hurrying this. Her body melted further into blissful sensation.

He took her slowly, so slowly, easing out, sliding back so deeply that she felt not only ravished but that she had abandoned everything to him, her heart and her soul, with each stroke. It was so exquisitely tender that it stole her breath. Lottie closed her eyes and gave herself up to the sensation of his loving, drawing him to her, eagerly seeking all that he could give and demanding more.

The rhythm changed, became more urgent. Lottie drew him in deeper still as each thrust drove them both toward an inexorable climax. At last he abandoned all control and plunged into her, crying out, entangling his fingers with hers and gripping tightly as the final thrust toppled him over the edge, sweeping her with him. This time it was darker and more intense than before. She was taken beyond the boundaries of all experience. In some profound way she could not understand, she knew he had claimed her.

Lottie allowed her body to lie quiescent and her mind to float as light as a feather in the darkness. She did not want to test her feelings. It seemed too dangerous, for fear that she, Lottie Palliser, once the most sophisticated of society matrons, might have offered up her heart as easily as her admittedly nonexistent virtue.

Yet eventually thought and feeling did return and she could not keep it out. She felt superbly replete, ravished in the best and most satisfying of ways. The other less physical, more emotional outcomes of their lovemaking she tried unsuccessfully to ignore. She felt vulnerable in a different way now. There was a hollow beneath her heart when she looked at Ethan lying in abandoned pleasure beside her. She wanted to hold him and rediscover the tender closeness they had achieved. She wanted to see love in his eyes.

She tried to make light of the thought, telling herself that she was confusing love with gratitude. Ethan had reminded her of how spectacular physical love could be and for that she was immensely indebted to him. That was all there was too it; she felt no deeper feelings for him, could not allow herself to do so. Nevertheless she felt cold, her stomach dropping in despair, for no matter how she had pretended to view love as a sport and recreation in the past, she had never quite been able to disassociate it from emotion. God knew she had tried. She had taken a score of lovers and claimed it was simply for amusement yet each time she knew she had been searching for something deeper and more elusive, and each time she had emerged with her heart scarred a little more.

Ethan rolled over, opened his eyes and smiled at her and her heart did another little dizzy skip and her despair deepened. *No, please no.* She could not be such a fool as to fall in love with him when she barely knew him, and what she *did* know with clear hard certainty was that he cared nothing for her and would only use her and then discard her.

"Thank you," she said very politely, hiding behind barriers, protecting herself. "That was very nice."

Ethan laughed. "I am glad to have been of service." He raised a brow. "No more running away?"

Lottie shook her head. She knew it was far too late for that. "No more running away," she whispered.

Ethan pressed a kiss on the damp skin of her belly, and Lottie shivered, reaching for the covers to shield her as though they could help protect her heart as well as cover her nakedness.

"I'm hungry," she said as her stomach rumbled. She was glad to be distracted by another very basic physical demand.

Ethan sat up and reached for his clothes. "They do an excellent dinner here," he said, "if you like plain roast beef."

"That sounds delicious," Lottie said. Her stomach rumbled again loudly. She appeared to be going downhill rapidly in the mistress stakes. A professional courtesan would surely waft fragrantly away at the end of a sexual encounter, her mystique and sophistication still intact even if nothing else was, rather than demand to be fed, having worked up an immense appetite. It was then that she realized she had not eaten for days. She had been too nervous and unhappy in Mrs. Tong's brothel to be able to face food, the sight or even the smell of it. Now she felt ravenous.

"They mix a fair rum punch here, as well," Ethan said, shrugging himself into his jacket but abandoning his cravat in a crumpled heap on the chair.

"I should have had one of those before we started," Lottie said.

"We didn't need it," Ethan said. He dropped another kiss lightly on her lips and went out, and Lottie lay in sated abandonment, the sheet draped across her stomach, watching the dance of light and shadow out in the street.

Ethan had been right, she thought. He had been the one she needed and he had been skillful and gentle and considerate, and she was enormously grateful to him for restoring her confidence and reminding her how glorious making love could be. She was so grateful to him, in fact, that she wanted to do it again at once—or as soon as she had eaten and given her food a little time to settle since she did not wish for indigestion.

Yet there was more to this than the simply physical. If—*when*—she made love with Ethan again, she knew she would tumble all the more deeply into those disturbing and inappropriate feelings she was starting to have for him. It was her nature. In the past she had pretended not to care about her *affaires* when in reality she had been consistently hopeless at treating them with the superficiality they warranted. It was why she always got hurt and always ended up rushing to the next lover. She was not sure what she was looking for, only that she never found it.

She certainly would not find it here with Ethan.

This was a man who had bought her for his pleasure and she knew she should not forget that. He had been bored, wanting a mistress to pass the time. She was the woman chosen. And though he had shown her patience and gentleness, there was no more to it than that, and she would be mistaken to read something into their relationship that was not, and never would be there.

She rolled over, drawing the sheet about her to ward off the sudden chill of the room. She felt acutely vulnerable, needing to rediscover the old Lottie with her sharp edges and sheen of protective sophistication. She *would* become the perfect courtesan now, cool and detached. She could do that. It was her future.

When Ethan came back it was with a tray loaded with food to satisfy even the lustiest appetite, and after they had eaten he read the newspaper and Lottie wrapped herself in a sheet and sat in the window seat watching the passersby on George Street on their way to the balls and the theaters. She felt oddly distant and detached from that world of the *Ton*, the world she had lost. In an effort to ward off her piercing loneliness she turned to Ethan again, this time setting out quite blatantly to seduce him, and they made love with a fierce intensity. But although it was deliciously pleasurable, in the aftermath Lottie felt even more lost than before.

CHAPTER FIVE

ETHAN WOKE FIRST. He lay listening to the sounds of London stirring, the street vendors setting up, the rumble of the milkmaids' carts, voices, the clop of hooves, the sweep of the brushes of the crossing boys. He had always liked London. He liked its anonymity and its bustle, its entertainments and its pleasures. Paris was a beautiful city, grand and self-important, but London had always held a special place in his heart, which was odd since he did not much care for England and the English.

He shifted slightly, careful not to wake Lottie, who was curled up beside him in a soft, trusting bundle. He watched her for a little while and found it surprisingly pleasant. She slept easily, lightly, with a little smile on her lips as though in sleep she could set aside the unhappy memories that shadowed her waking moments.

Ethan had never spent an entire night with a woman before. He had been very careful not to do so, for such behavior implied some sort of commitment he was not inclined to give. With Lottie he had no choice, although he supposed he could have taken another room. The hotel was not full. But such an idea had not occurred to him and now he wondered why not.

He had slept fitfully. Lottie had fallen asleep after they had made love a second time, snuggling confidingly into his arms, her hair spread across his bare chest like a swathe of silk. Ethan had lain awake and listened to her breathing and felt her warmth, and he had been disoriented and confused, as though he had come home to a place of peace and fulfillment that he had not even realized he had been seeking.

Nothing, he thought, had gone according to plan the previous night. He had wanted the notorious Lottie Palliser, the most scandalous divorcée in London, not a surprisingly vulnerable and appealing woman whom he had had to woo into bed. And yet making love to Lottie had been as profound as it was sweet. It had felt intimate and seductive in a different and far more dangerous sense than the simply sexual. For a few brief hours it had drawn them so close he had almost thought he cared for her.

He had made love to plenty of women in his time and had almost always enjoyed the experience with an uncomplicated and unquestioning pleasure. He had never particularly wanted to prolong the time he spent in their company out of bed. He had never experienced an ounce of genuine feeling for any of them beyond admiration of their amatory skill or appreciation for their sophistication. So it made absolutely no sense that having made love to Lottie Palliser he had felt a peculiar, unfamiliar and completely unwelcome mixture of emotions. The experience had seemed to be weighted with far too much significance. He had felt disturbingly as though he had bedded a bride rather than a new mistress. What had started on his part as no more than a lesson in skilled seduction had ended as something far more profound.

It had been an illusion.

He shifted again and Lottie made a soft sound of protest and reached for him, cuddling closer to his side, instinctively seeking his warmth and the comfort of his body. Ethan felt a powerful urge to pull away from her—he felt almost *afraid,* for pity's sake, as though she was asking for something he could not give—but he mastered the feeling, as he had conquered so many emotions in the past, and propped himself on one elbow, stroking her hair gently, enjoying the silken run of it through his fingers. Her skin was very soft, too. He liked the voluptuousness of it when so many women were as brittle as twigs. Lottie was plump and yielding, curved in all the right places. Ethan allowed his hand to drift over her bare shoulder and down to the rounded turn of her elbow. She rolled over, reaching for him, her nipples brushing his bare chest, her breasts pressed against him in their delicious fullness. Ethan felt again the wickedly strong urge to lose himself in her. She was like a drug to him, he thought, as he started to kiss the opulent whiteness of her breast, so sweet, so tempting. At the corner of his mind fluttered a warning; he had never felt so strong an attraction to a woman and he had certainly not expected it with this one. It went against both sense and expectation.

Involvement was dangerous. Emotion was dangerous.

For a moment he hesitated but the fierce clamor of his body could not be resisted. It was only sex, he thought, and it only blazed so strongly because he had denied himself for so long. He had bought her. She was his, and his alone, to take. His blood burned hotter at the thought.

Lottie opened dazed, sleep-filled eyes and smiled at him and his heart gave an odd, errant thump. She shifted accommodatingly, and he rolled lazily on top of her, making love to her in slow, dreamy strokes that heightened his pleasure beyond anything he had ever imagined. He felt as though he was giving up something of himself to her and he tried to resist, tried to hold back, but the gentle demand of her body and the greedy need of his own senses drove him on to abandon all barriers and claim her over and over as his. He was shaking when they fell apart, shocked and drained by the intensity of the experience, their bodies slick and wet with sweat, the room hot and the sun high in the sky.

"How lovely," Lottie murmured, eyes closed, as she pressed her lips to the point of his shoulder. Her eyelashes were spiky dark against the curve of her cheek and there was a little smile on her lips that was self-satisfied and very knowing.

"I am so pleased you have rediscovered your enthusiasm for it," Ethan pushed down the rumpled sheet and ran his hand over the bare swell of her hip, wondering how he could still want her when he had satiated his need over and over. He felt as though he was grasping after something he only half understood, finding it but losing it again, a never-ending quest. For so long he had been entirely self-sufficient through choice and necessity. With Lottie he felt as though he was surrendering something of himself and he fought against it even as wanted her; he wanted to know her, explore her, learn her over and over, deeper and deeper.

It had to stop. He was bewitched.

Ethan sat up, running an impatient hand over his hair. Physical love, he thought, should be simple. Strangely, it was proving to be damnably dangerous. He was behaving like a lovesick boy when in fact he was no more than a man enchanted by the novelty of a new mistress. He was about to pull the sheet up and turn his back on Lottie's nakedness, demonstrating the lack of power she had over him, when he realized that she was trying to cover herself and turn away from *him*. Contrarily that annoyed him. He yanked down the sheet and pushed her back onto the mattress so that she was lying there completely naked and exposed to his gaze.

"Don't cover yourself," he snapped. "I like you to be naked for me."

She toyed with the edge of the sheet, evading his eyes, trying stealthily to draw it toward her.

"I need to dress…."

"No you don't. You're a mistress and a mistress should be naked for her lover if he demands it."

She looked up and her eyes were defiant. "You are discourteous and I am too fat. So let me get up, damn it!"

Ethan could not deny the first part of the sentence— the damnable need he had for her was making him churlish—but it was the second part that interested him.

"You're *what?*" he said.

"Fat." Beneath her defiance he glimpsed a flash of despair. "I used to be rounded and dimpled. It was fashionable. But then when I…when Gregory started the divorce proceedings I was unhappy so I ate." A slight smile quivered on her lips. "Then I had even less money because in effect I ate it all away."

"You ate because you were unhappy?" Ethan frowned. He had not given much thought to what she had done in the months after her husband had thrown her from the Grosvenor Square house and the divorce had ground its way scandalously through the courts. He had assumed that her life would have gone on much as before, which was naive, now he thought about it. With little money, abandoned by friends and family, denounced as a wanton and vilified if she stepped outside the door, what could she have done?

"I ate cake and pastries, biscuits and ice cream," Lottie said, "until I was sick. I read copies of the *Ladies' Magazine* and ate and slept all day." She reached again for the sheet and this time Ethan did not stop her. "I suppose," she added, "that should I fall into even greater penury I could live off my fat, like a camel."

"Camels store water in their humps," Ethan said, "not fat."

"It is the same principle," Lottie said. She sighed. "Please let me dress."

"A moment." Ethan put out a hand and touched her wrist lightly. "You did not seem self-conscious before," he said.

"I forget," Lottie said simply. "I feel the same inside. Then I see myself in the mirror—" she nodded toward the pier glass on the wall "—and it shocks me."

Ethan raised a hand and smoothed her hair away

from her face. "I like it," he said. "You are not thin but I like that. You look very pretty to me."

Her eyes opened wide. *"Pretty?"*

"Delightfully curved. Voluptuous." He leaned forward and kissed her. She returned the kiss hesitantly, almost innocently. "We must make love in front of that mirror," he said, against her lips, "and then you can see how beautiful you look."

She blushed. *"Beautiful* now," she said dryly. "How you flatter me, my lord."

"Your body is divine," Ethan said. "Something else of which I must convince you?"

"Later," a delicious smile lit her eyes. "I really must wash and dress."

Ethan rang for hot water and fresh towels whilst Lottie wrapped the sheet about her and started to rummage through the bandbox she had brought with her.

"What do you do today?" She was kneeling on the floor, looking up at him as he dressed. She was barefoot and tousled and once again Ethan felt that strange pang of emotion as he looked at her, the tug at his heart. He could imagine her, alone in her exile, sending a maid out for pastry and cake and cream, whilst in the outside world her husband destroyed her reputation and dragged her name through the gutter. A harsh anger gripped him. Whatever Lottie had done, he thought, Gregory Cummings's behavior had been disproportionate and unforgivable, taking a hammer to crush a butterfly.

"I have business to attend to," he said, a little abruptly. He wanted to escape the warm intimacy of the room. He needed to break the spell, to refocus his mind upon the urgent plans that had brought him to London.

"Of course," Lottie said. She got to her feet and shook out the one respectable gown she had brought with her. "This gown needs pressing," she added, "if I am not to parade about Town tricked out like one of Mrs. Tong's harlots."

"Go and buy some new clothes," Ethan said. "I want you to have something suitable to drive with me later in the park and an evening gown for the theater tonight."

Her gaze flickered to meet his and he sensed her unease. "We are to go out in public later?"

"Of course," Ethan said. "If I wished to sit quietly at home reading then I would have stayed in Wantage." There was a tap at the door and a manservant brought in a steaming jug of water. The man shot Lottie a look, glanced at the tangled bedclothes, and went out smirking.

"Yes, I see." Lottie sounded subdued, her head bent, but Ethan could see her frown. "I thought—" She started, stopped. "I did not realize that you would wish to—"

"To flaunt you in public?"

She looked up, troubled. "Yes, I suppose so. The fashionable crowd were my acquaintances when I was married. It is awkward—"

Ethan shrugged, once again repressing that wayward sympathy. There was no room for sentiment and he knew it; he had a very particular purpose for her. She had satisfied his physical needs, for the time being at least, and now she would play another role, that of the ostentatious mistress about town. He was intent on creating as much gossip as he possibly could, diverting the attention of the authorities from his true interests and activities. Lottie's part in his plan was to act as an eye-catching diversion.

"I understand that," he said. "But you have a different role now. Besides, you will not be obliged to speak to any of your previous acquaintances, merely to be seen by them."

"Of course," Lottie said. Her voice was bland but her mouth turned down at the implication of his words, that she must display herself before her previous acquaintances marked out as his mistress. Ethan knew she was struggling to repress her protests. Lottie Palliser did not take easily to the role of accommodating Cyprian, he thought.

"You will be with me," he said. "That will protect you from any discourtesy."

"I am sure it will." She could not quite erase the sharpness from her tone. "No man of sense would wish to find your sword at his throat."

"Then that is settled," Ethan said. He put out a hand and drew her toward him. He felt a moment's hesitation in her but she came to him easily enough. He kissed her, long, hard and deep, a claim, an imprint, a statement of possession.

"You're with me now," he repeated softly when he let her go, and he felt a powerful flare of possessiveness. He kissed her again until he felt her relax and respond to him and then his desire caught like a flame again. He was breathing hard when he let her go and he felt shaken.

What the hell was wrong with him?

She sat looking at him, a luminous light in her brown eyes, soft hair falling gently about her bare shoulders, her body pure temptation beneath the twisted sheet.

Ethan stood up, wanting to be gone yet wanting to stay with her, too. The conflict in him puzzled and disturbed him.

"I have left you some money to buy the gowns," he said brusquely, gesturing to the bag of guineas on the table. "Buy something suitable. I don't want you looking like a debutante."

Her gaze was very clear as she held his. "I know what you want from me."

Swearing under his breath, Ethan went out, down the stairs two at a time, out into the street. He lengthened his stride, putting physical distance between himself and Lottie as though trying to outrun the emotions of the previous night. He felt a sense of relief to have escaped something he could not put a name to but which felt infinitely dangerous.

LOTTIE HAD SEEN Ethan's relief when he left. It had been in the haste with which he had gone out of the bedchamber; it had been in the tense line of his shoulders and the briskness of his departure and the fact that he had not looked back. She sighed a little as she gathered together the clothes she needed for the day. The intimacy of the night that she and Ethan had spent together had been illusory. She knew that. Physical closeness meant nothing. They were still essentially two strangers who were bound together for as long as Ethan paid for their association to continue. That was their relationship, no more. The previous night she had determined not to become emotionally involved with him and make the same mistakes that she had in the past. He could give her nothing of himself. He did not wish to, nor should she wish it. Her future was as a professional courtesan for as long as she had the looks to sustain the role. She would be particularly bad at her new job if she tumbled into love with every protector who crossed her path.

In truth, there was little to look forward to in Ethan's plans for the day, Lottie thought. They would bring the horrible social embarrassment of displaying herself in public for the first time since her divorce. She shuddered. Everyone would point and gossip as though she was an exhibit in a freak show. The *Ton* could be very cruel. She knew she had to be strong but she felt as vulnerable as a kitten. So she needed clothes. She needed clothes to wear as armor, to protect her and give her an outward shield against the harsh talk and accusatory stares. Plus a big hat, perhaps, for her to hide behind.

There was a knock at the door—the maid to take away her gown for pressing. Lottie handed it over, then glanced across to the table, where Ethan had left a small bag of coins for her expenses that day. She smiled wryly. If Ethan Ryder thought that would be sufficient to buy her an evening gown and all the accessories she required, then perhaps he did not know women quite as well as he claimed. Then she remembered that she had tried to steal his guineas and run away the day before. She let the coins slip through her fingers. Under the circumstances, she thought, it was perhaps surprising that he had entrusted her with any of his money at all.

She touched the money and let it run through her fingers. Once again the desire to take it, to use it to escape, stirred in her. She could run away from this life and from the ignominy and shame of having to appear in *Ton* society as Ethan's paid mistress.

Except that she had no one to help her and nowhere to run…

She straightened up. She would dress like a courtesan and smile until her face ached and pretend that she simply did not care, whilst she hid the molten shame of it deep inside.

CHAPTER SIX

ONCE, WHEN SHE HAD been a leader of society and a *Ton* hostess, Lottie had enjoyed driving in the park at the fashionable hour of five in the afternoon. She had done it to see and to be seen, to set new fashions and to hear the latest *on dit*. Now it seemed that she and Ethan *were* the *on dit*, which was, Lottie supposed, exactly what Ethan had wanted. She tried to keep her gaze fixed straight ahead in order to avoid meeting the eyes of her former friends and acquaintances, but it was difficult. Jumbled impressions slid past her as the phaeton rolled along. People were stopping to stare; they were even pointing, which was frightfully ill-bred, and they did not trouble to lower their voices:

"There is that damned traitorous bastard Ethan Ryder with his shameless mistress…."

The sun was bright and it made Lottie's eyes water even though she had bought a bonnet especially designed to shield her face. She could feel herself growing hotter and hotter under the scrutiny of so many censorious eyes. She drew herself up straight and tense in her seat.

I will not cry. She repeated the mantra fiercely to herself, over and over in her head, as she had when she was a little girl and the other children had teased her because she was a fatherless poor relation. She had scrambled up from that lowly place and had become an influential member of the *Ton* herself. She shuddered when she remembered the pride she had taken in wielding that social power. She had never imagined that one day she would topple off her lofty pedestal. Well, she had learned that lesson now. Perhaps if she were ever in a position of influence again she might be a bit kinder. She sighed. Not that *that* was likely to happen. She was beyond disgrace, ruined well and truly.

The carriage slowed because of the press of people and other vehicles and she heard one debutante, all pretty blond curls and demure blue eyes say to her friend:

"She used to be Mrs. Cummings, you know. She was married to a most frightfully rich and proper banker, but she simply could not prevent herself from running around Town with any man who asked. They say she takes after her father in being so loose with her affections…."

The girls' titters of laughter lingered as the carriage swept past and Lottie felt hot with mortification and anger.

She glanced at Ethan. He had hired a superb high perch phaeton for this outing, all sparkling green-and-blue livery and pulled by two showy gray horses. It was a neat way to show his haughty relatives that he cared nothing for their disapproval, Lottie supposed. She wished she had his self-assurance.

As though sensing her thoughts Ethan took one hand off the reins and dropped it over her tightly clasped ones in a comforting grip. He shot her a blazing smile.

"Are you enjoying this?"

"Of course not!" Lottie said tartly, forgetting that she had promised herself she would uphold the role of obliging mistress even if it killed her. "I hate it! All those people staring and tattling! I do not know how you can do it, my lord. I don't know *why* you do it."

Ethan slowed the horses and turned slightly toward her. His smile faded a little and he looked rueful. "I do it because they are bullies, Lottie," he said softly, "and they should not be allowed to win. When I was a small boy I had to accept the judgment of others that I was inferior because of my birth." His jaw tightened. "Now I accept no man's judgment but my own." He squeezed her hands. "Remember that you are worth a dozen of that foolish matron over there, or that posing dandy."

"I *was* that foolish matron not so long ago," Lottie said, with feeling. "Now I suspect my function is to be a Terrible Example. Chaperones will scare their charges into conformity with the threat that if they misbehave they will end up like me."

"They would have to behave pretty badly for that to happen," Ethan said. "You are more of an example of how one can get away with reckless behavior for years."

Despite herself, Lottie felt her lips twitch. "I fear you may be right." she said. She smiled ruefully. "Whichever way you look at it, I am the worst of bad examples to the young."

There was a devilish light in Ethan's eyes. "How true," he murmured. "And you are about to become an even worse example, I fear."

He allowed the horses to slow to a walk and then

drew her toward him. She read his purpose in his eyes and placed a hand against his chest.

"I cannot kiss you here in the Park," she whispered. "We shall probably be arrested for violating public decency!"

"I had no notion you were such a prude," Ethan said. "We may kiss one another wherever we please."

He kissed her, whilst all about them the crowd dipped and whispered. The sun was hot and the noise roared in Lottie's ears but she was aware of nothing but Ethan's lips on hers and the strength in his arms as he held her.

"There," he murmured as he released her. "That was not so bad, was it?"

Not bad at all, Lottie thought. She felt hot and confused and dizzy. Somewhere along the way she had definitely misplaced her town bronze. She smoothed her gown, intent on covering quite how much that brief kiss had affected her.

"Ethan!"

Up until that moment, no one had addressed or even acknowledged them. It had been uncomfortable but hardly unexpected. Now Lottie looked around to see that a tall man on a bay stallion had drawn alongside the phaeton. His presence was causing almost as much excitement as the fact that he had stopped to speak with them.

"I apologize for interrupting you," the man said, smiling broadly, "but I felt I had to make my presence known before you vanished beneath a tide of disapproval. How are you, Ethan?"

"Northesk." Ethan drew rein and leaned over to

shake hands with the newcomer. "I didn't know you were back in London," he added in a slightly mocking tone. "I thought you had settled abroad for good."

The other man smiled. "I heard that you were in England so I made a particular effort to return." He laughed and Ethan laughed, too, and embraced him. The crowd of onlookers murmured with surprise.

Ethan turned to Lottie, who was almost expiring with curiosity now. She knew that the Marquess of Northesk was the heir to the Duke of Farne and therefore Ethan's half brother. She had never met the Marquess in society because he had been in exile for the best part of ten years, banished abroad after a shocking duel with his wife's lover. It was interesting, she thought, that there was at least one member of his family with whom Ethan was evidently on good terms and looking at them now she could see a faint family resemblance. Ethan was very dark, where Northesk had auburn hair as rich and red as a fox's pelt. Ethan's eyes were vivid blue, where Northesk's were deep brown. The real resemblance, she thought, lay deeper than in coloring. It was in their bone structure, their gestures, in the slant of a head or the movement of a hand that was almost a mirror image. It was odd seeing together the Duke of Farne's offspring down the right and the wrong side of the blanket.

"May I introduce my half brother Garrick Farne, Marquess of Northesk," Ethan said formally to Lottie. "Garrick, this is Lottie Palliser."

Lottie saw the flash of surprise in Northesk's eyes to hear her introduced thus. Evidently he already knew who she was. But he smiled and bowed very gracefully, gesturing to the gawping crowds.

"A pleasure to meet you, Miss Palliser. I do believe that you and my reprobate brother are causing a sensation."

"That tends to be your brother's style, so I believe," Lottie said. She looked from one to another. "Forgive me," she added, "but I was not aware that Ethan was on speaking terms with any member of his family."

Northesk laughed. "It's true that I am the only one who acknowledges him." He shook his head. "I fear Ethan's politics are deeply misguided, but for all that I admire the tenacity with which he holds to them."

"Northesk and I grew up together," Ethan said. "He was the only one who tried to protect me from those who sought to ram home the hard facts of my base parentage." He spoke lightly but there was a shade of expression in his voice that Lottie caught; these were old wounds.

"I was forever dragging him out of fights at Eton when he felt he had to take on all comers," Northesk said. "Ethan and I are almost of an age, Miss Palliser— our esteemed father grew very bored very quickly when my mother was carrying me. He looked around for diversion—"

"And I was the result," Ethan finished.

Lottie felt a pang of surprise. She had not realized that Ethan and Farne's legitimate heir were almost the same age. The Duke was renowned for his philandering and it seemed he had paused only long enough to get his wife pregnant before he had resumed it.

"I wish you had told me you were in Town," Northesk was saying to Ethan. "Are you free to dine tonight?"

There was a pause. Once again Lottie sensed the

conflict in Ethan and felt all the words unspoken. "I don't want to embarrass you, Garrick," Ethan said in a low voice, and Lottie heard the sincerity and true emotion in his voice. "You have been more than generous to me in the past, but it is impossible. Our father—"

"Can go hang," Garrick Northesk said, shrugging. "What can he do? He cannot disinherit me. Besides, I am at least as scandalous as you."

"You have more than done penance," Ethan said, "and society welcomes you back. Whereas I am an enemy of the state."

Northesk shook his head. "I agree that it is unfortunate that you are a French prisoner of war," he said dryly, "but you know full well that half the French officers are related to the British aristocracy anyway, and we all dine together and it is frightfully civil."

"Some aspects of the situation are far from civilized," Ethan said, and now there was so much bitterness in his tone that Lottie jumped. She glanced at Northesk and saw swift sympathy in his face.

"I understand," he said. "I am sorry." He hesitated. "How is Arland?"

"I do not know," Ethan said. "Naturally I am not permitted to see him."

There was a silence. A summer breeze teased the ribbons of Lottie's bonnet.

She could hear the stir and murmur of the crowd about them. Northesk's bay stallion shifted with a clatter of hooves as though something of his master's tension had communicated itself to him.

Lottie put one hand on Ethan's arm. He was looking at his brother and Northesk was looking back and some sort of wordless communication seemed to be taking place between them. Ethan's face was as hard as stone.

"Who is Arland?" Lottie asked. She could feel the patter of butterfly wings in her stomach, though she had no notion why this seemed so important. But she could feel it, the tension in the air.

Ethan glanced down at her. His eyes were blank. For a moment she thought he was not going to reply. Then he said, "Arland is my son. He is a prisoner of war in Whitemoor Gaol."

ETHAN KNEW LOTTIE would ask questions. In his experience, women always did. They wanted to soothe, to help and to heal. But nothing could heal him and he was certainly beyond help. He had made the same mistakes as the father he despised and now he could not even protect the son that he had so carelessly brought into the world. The despair and self-loathing seethed in him, poisonous and dark.

Somehow, with automatic skill and intuition, he appeared to have steered the phaeton onto a quieter stretch of the park, out through the gates and toward the livery stables. He slowed the horses now that they were out on the street. He had no idea how they had got there. For all he knew he might just have rampaged through the fashionable crowds leaving mayhem in their wake. Well, if he had flattened half of the *Ton* in his urge to escape it was probably no loss. And they could only hang him once.

Lottie put her hand over his on the rein, and he

waited for the questions, the probing, unendurable
sympathy.

"I'm very sorry," she said.

He could not respond. He thought of Arland, incarcerated for six months in the prison hulks and now
confined in Whitemoor, the gaol built on the Lambourn Downs three miles from Wantage. His son. A
prisoner.

"I am surprised that they let you loose," Lottie had
said the previous night, and he remembered that he
had made some mention of the fact that he had been
locked up in his time in a Chatham prison hulk. What
he had not said was, "The reason the authorities give me
my freedom is to taunt me. They hold my son captive
against my good behavior and so I dance to their tune,
knowing that were I to try to escape, Arland would be
flogged, or tortured or locked in some hellhole until
he runs mad…."

He shuddered as the unendurable images flooded
his mind.

He had begged the British authorities to give Arland
parole. He had offered himself as hostage, to lock up
in the prison hulks as they willed, if only his son was
allowed his freedom. He had offered his very *life* for
Arland's and they had laughed in his face.

Truly he was the most abject failure as a father.
Arland would be better off without him.

"Arland must be very young," Lottie said softly.

He is seventeen. No more than a boy.

Ethan cleared his throat. "I do not wish to talk about
it."

Lottie did not reply. He waited for her to say something else, to try to comfort him when he was beyond comfort, or to reproach him for throwing her sympathy back in her face, but she did not. She sat calmly beside him whilst the world moved on around them and he was locked in his private hell. When he glanced at her he saw that her eyes were troubled but she did not speak. After a moment she touched his arm very gently with her gloved hand and he felt it through to his soul. The wordless gesture of comfort surprised him.

I want her.

Once again desire took him, the feverish need to claim her so that he could lose himself in her for a while. He would never be able to wash out the indelible stain of failing his son. He could only try to ease the hurt for a little.

He felt enormous relief as he turned into the livery stables and threw the reins to a groom. He jumped down and lifted Lottie from the seat, handing a great deal more money in tips to the grooms than he needed in his hurry to be away, to be alone with her, to forget for a little while. The hackney carriage back to Limmer's seemed to take forever. He sent the chambermaid scurrying from their room, her cleaning abandoned, and turned to Lottie.

"Come here," he said, a little roughly. This time he was not even going to question why she was the one he needed. He simply knew it to be so.

LOTTIE SAT IN THE BOX at the theater and tried to concentrate on the play. It was *He's Much To Blame* by Thomas Holcroft, and one of her favorites. In the days when she had been a *Ton* hostess, attending the theater had annoyed and frustrated her because all her friends and acquaintances had insisted on visiting her box to gossip and chat, frequently talking all the way through the performance. They had assumed that she, like them, had been there, not to see the play—that was almost irrelevant—but to flaunt her latest diamond necklace or indeed her latest admirer.

Tonight, though, since no one was talking to her but were all talking *about* her, it did mean that she could try to concentrate on the play. Except that she could not, of course, for she was thinking about Ethan.

They had not spoken about Arland, or indeed about anything, since the drive in the park that afternoon. At Limmer's Ethan had made love to her wildly, desperately, as though he were trying to drive out demons from his mind. It had been all consuming but afterward Ethan had got out of bed and gone straight out without a word, down to the taproom, and Lottie had lain there and tried not to feel like a cheap harlot. She knew that Ethan had used her to escape from an intolerable reality, the reality of his son's imprisonment. She had heard the pain in his voice when he had spoken of Arland. And she had also wondered if, without Northesk's intervention, Ethan would ever have mentioned his son to her at all. She thought he probably would not have done.

A chill had set in about her heart at the thought. She knew she could not reach Ethan. He would not talk to her. Yes, he would take physical comfort from her but he wanted no other intimacy.

Ethan had a son. The boy must be very young, barely more than a child. And Ethan himself must have been almost as young when the child was conceived. Who had his mother been? Where was she now? And how had Arland fallen into the hands of the British? Lottie's mind tumbled over all the thoughts and questions but she knew there was no point in asking. Ethan was not a man to confide.

He sat beside her now, his attention focused, like hers, on the stage even if his thoughts were, like hers, far from it. He looked handsome in evening dress of plain black-and-white. The only adornment to his clothes was a fine diamond pin in the folds of his cravat and a signet ring with the arms of St. Severin engraved upon it. There were at least two of Ethan's younger half siblings in the audience—Farne had had a large legitimate brood as well as several by-blows. One of Ethan's half sisters had walked out ostentatiously when she had realized that Ethan and Lottie were present. The others had remained, glaring at them at first and then pointedly ignoring them. Lottie had found it rather amusing.

She knew that Ethan had deliberately chosen to appear austere in his personal dress that night. *She* was the one designed for his adornment. Her gown was scarlet, cut very low to reveal almost all it could of her breasts without allowing them to actually fall out of the neckline. Her magnificent necklace of diamonds had been hired for the night from Hatton Garden and only served to draw more attention to her bare skin. There were matching diamonds twinkling in her hair and clasped about her bare arms. They were outstandingly fine jewels and they marked her out as Ethan's exclusive property. He was, she thought, showing the whole of London that not only was he so scandalous that he could flaunt an infamous mistress and not give a damn for anyone's opinion, but also that he was so rich that he could trick her out with a king's ransom in jewels.

Beneath the gown she wore a shift of the finest silk, which rubbed provocatively against her skin, making her achingly aware of her body and even more conscious of her role as Cyprian. It was as though every inch of her was stroked to an almost unbearable pitch of sensual tension, encouraged by the knowledge that once they returned to Limmer's Hotel, Ethan would strip her of everything but the jewels and make love to her again and again, with shattering intensity.

It was on this thought that she turned her gaze from the stage to the audience opposite, where a young woman with very glossy brown ringlets and a tall, fair handsome young man were making a very late and very showy entrance.

Lottie caught her breath. The girl was unknown to her. She was very young, perhaps only just out, and there was a quality of sweet, fresh excitement in her face that gave Lottie a pang to see. It made her feel old and worn, every inch the cynic she was. The girl was pulling the young man into his seat by the hand and he was protesting in a good-natured fashion, but he was laughing, as well, indulgent and well pleased with himself.

It was James Devlin.

Lottie felt her heart catch and then start to race. Her fingers tightened about her fan until the struts creaked.

She had not seen Dev for over a year. They had

parted on civil terms—of course they had; there was no other way to leave a lover if one had style—but inside she had been breaking into pieces, trying desperately to hide the grief she had felt on losing him. Dev had gone traveling—he was something of an adventurer— and she had gone on to try and ease her pain with one of the footmen. Well, two of them if she were honest, though not both together since that was not her taste. So foolish of her, she thought now, when both servants had been in Gregory's pay and so would say anything in court that he desired of them.

Dev looked directly across the theater and their eyes met. Lottie felt as though her heart would jump out of her chest. He looked just the same: handsome, debonair, careless, *heartless,* pleased to have caught himself a rich fiancée….

"One of your former lovers?" Ethan had leaned forward and was watching her with a sardonic gleam in his eye. He spoke softly. Lottie hastily tried to rearrange her face—she was not at all sure what expression had been showing. She did not want Ethan to see how she felt, not when he was infinitely capable of hiding his own emotions. But it was probably too late for her to dissemble now. He was quick, and perceptive, and would have seen her instinctive hurt.

"One of the many." She kept her tone light. "I will furnish you with a list if you wish to know whom to avoid."

"That won't be necessary." There was a shade of amusement in Ethan's tone. "However…" He hesitated. "Perhaps a general idea of the number of pages it might run to…"

Lottie met his gaze. "A great deal fewer than a list of your conquests would, my lord."

"Touché." A smile touched his lips. "I ask no questions. Only—" he paused, as though weighing his words "—you seem a little distraite. Did he hurt you?"

Oh, she had been hurt, so desperately lost and grieved. Yet for the first time she could see that it was not Devlin's fault. He had simply been himself. She was the one who had invested her feelings too heavily in what had only been a light *affaire*. She could not blame Devlin for her behavior. She felt strange to admit it. It had always been easier to lay her ruin at his door than to take the responsibility for it herself.

But Ethan was waiting for his answer and his gaze was acute. She smoothed the wrinkles in her gloves and avoided his eyes.

"Not in the slightest," she said. "He was a diversion. I told you last night—I get bored so easily and handsome young men are equally easily found."

Ethan did not reply and she was not sure if she had convinced him. When the play finished they did not take the private exit from the box—of course not, Ethan would not wish to slip away unseen—but went down into the foyer where the crush of people was hot and oppressive. Once again, as in the Park, Lottie felt the looks and the censure, heard the whispers, and even saw some ladies draw their skirts away from her as though to touch her would be to risk contamination. Her head spun with the heat and the lights and the smell of bodies pressed close, and she tried to smile and appear as arrogant and unconcerned as Ethan did, but it felt so hard. The smile did not reach her eyes; it was slipping away from her even as she tried to force it to stay.

And then there he was, James Devlin, right in front of her, and the crowd fell back and Dev turned to look at her and she saw the dismay in his eyes and the dread he was too slow to mask. She could see that he did not even know how to address her. Something of his unease had communicated itself to the young girl at his side, for her bright, happy expression had started to fade to uncertainty. Behind her an older lady, her mother perhaps, shifted uncomfortably, backing away from Lottie as though from a leper. The debutante shot Devlin a look of combined entreaty and fear.

This is how it will be for you, Lottie thought, watching the girl's face. You will have heard the gossip that Devlin has always been a ladies' man and you will always be wondering which were his conquests....

"Mr. Devlin..." Lottie found her poise. She smiled impartially at the group. They should cut her dead, of course, but it was too late for that. They were all trapped by this accident of fate.

"How do you do?" she said. "I hope you are well."

Dev's face relaxed a little. "Madam..."

Lottie turned to Ethan. "May I introduce Lord St. Severin?"

Now Dev was smiling, relieved, flushed with pride like a boy confronted with his childhood hero.

"My lord," Dev said, "it is such a great pleasure.... When I was growing up in Ireland I heard stories about you, and I have studied your exploits with great admiration—"

"Surely you mean with interest rather than

admiration, Mr. Devlin," Ethan corrected gently, "since I understand that you have served as a member of His Majesty's British Navy?"

There was a ripple of relieved laughter in the group that Ethan had saved Dev from a treasonable *faux pas*. Lottie put her hand lightly on Ethan's arm. She felt strong, hard muscle beneath her fingers. Odd that she had never seen James Devlin as a gauche youth until tonight, when beside Ethan's power and authority he seemed diminished somehow, still handsome but almost untried.

"You must excuse us," she said, drawing away from the group. "I wish you all a good evening."

They went out into the street and the night air was fresh on Lottie's skin and eased the ache in her head.

"That was gracious of you," Ethan said. "You could have caused a scene."

"That would have been bad *ton*," Lottie said lightly.

"And you are cousin to a Duke. I do not forget it, even if others do."

She could not place Ethan's tone and when she looked at him his face was expressionless. He was watching her closely, his blue eyes dark and watchful.

"You are quite well, I hope," he added.

"Quite well," Lottie said. "I have the headache…that is all."

But her words rang hollow, and Lottie had seen Ethan's gaze fall to where her hands were still clenched and one of the delicate wooded struts of the fan had snapped clean in two.

IN THE MORNING Ethan woke her with a hand on her bare shoulder, and Lottie stirred, feeling warm and content for a moment before she saw that he was fully dressed and about to leave. The light in the hotel bedchamber was dingy and pale, showing the dirty windows and the dust on the floor. Ethan sat down on the edge of the bed.

"I have to go now," he said. "My coach leaves for Wantage in an hour. You may stay here at Limmer's if you wish or find lodgings wherever you choose for the next few days. All I require is that you will be on the coach from Oxford on Friday." He nodded to the table. "I have left you sufficient funds to cover your shot and to buy you a few gowns, as we discussed." He laughed. "Try not to be too extravagant. Oh, and make sure that you dress to make an impression when you arrive."

Lottie gaped. If she had thought him parsimonious the day before, the fortune he was now leaving with her took her breath away. "You have left me *all* those guineas when I tried to steal them from you two days ago?"

She could hear the smile in his voice. "I am confident that you won't run off with my money this time."

Lottie frowned, trying to read his expression in the half-light of the room. "I don't know how you can be so certain," she said.

"Nothing is certain," Ethan said, "but I trust you to be in Wantage next Friday."

"You *trust* me?" Lottie said. She was beginning to wonder if she was still asleep and dreaming. "Are you mad?" she burst out.

"Not at all." Ethan stood up. "We have an agreement,

do we not? The terms of my parole mean that I must return to Wantage today, but you need more time to make some necessary purchases, so… " He shrugged his shoulders.

"Yes," Lottie said, "but to leave me here alone with the money!" She struggled upright. "I could fleece you, run away, cheat you like I tried to do before."

"So you could." Ethan sounded unconcerned. "But you won't. Not this time."

Lottie shook her head. "I wish I had your confidence," she said. "I thought you would at least ask someone to be my banker and keep an eye on my spending."

"There is no need," Ethan said. "Is there? You will not play me false."

He bent and kissed her. His lips were cool and firm, the kiss no more than a brief caress, and yet she shivered down to her soul. "You're a strange man," she murmured.

"It's only business, Lottie," Ethan said. "It makes better sense for you to throw in your lot with me just now. That is all."

He raised a hand in farewell, picked up his bag and went out, closing the door softly behind him. Lottie heard his steps retreat down the stair and fade away. A door closed in the distance. Some impulse prompted her to run to the window and she curled there on the seat as he walked away, his stride long and confident. He did not look back. She felt piqued.

She sat puzzling over what he had said. In the growing light she could see the fat bags of guineas sitting on the table. Greed and excitement possessed her. How much money was there? What could she do with it? Where could she go? She glanced out of the window again. Perhaps it was a trick. Perhaps Ethan was waiting for her to play him false.

"I could fleece you, run away, cheat you like I tried to do before."

"But you won't. Not this time."

Damn him! How could he know? How could he be so sure of her? What had happened to her in the past two days that meant that Ethan was right? Trust and loyalty had scarcely been her watchwords up until now. In fact they had barely been in her vocabulary, and then only so that she could behave in an opposite manner.

Her feet were cold. She slipped back into the warm folds of the bed. It felt empty. She knew that she had to get up, get dressed and go shopping in order to distract herself. She could not dwell on Ethan's absence and the peculiar space it appeared to leave in the vicinity of her heart. It could not be love; she had told herself from the start that she must root that out before it started to grow. So it was boredom. She had to be entertained. She hated her own company. That was why she was missing Ethan already—because she had no resources for solitude.

"It's only business, Lottie," he had said. Well, absolutely. If he could be so detached then so could she. It was only what she had resolved the previous night. Ethan was right. It made sound sense for her to throw in her lot with him until a more advantageous offer came along.

No one knew that better than she, opportunistic Lottie Palliser, without a trustworthy bone in her body.

IT WAS ALREADY HOT out in the street. The bright disc of the sun was rising with a hazy coppery light that promised an airless summer day in the city of London. Ethan shouldered his kit bag and strode away, resisting an almost overpowering urge to glance back to see if Lottie was watching. He concentrated instead on the road ahead: the street vendors already setting up their stalls, a closed carriage rattling across the cobbles, a drunken lord propping himself up against a wall as he tried to make his unsteady way home.

Strange that it seemed so hard to leave Lottie behind. His mind was full of images of her: Lottie wrapped in his arms sleeping after they had made love, of her reaching out to him to try and comfort him over Arland's incarceration, of her face tight with misery when she had seen James Devlin at the theater. She had rebuffed his attempts to reach her then, just as he had rejected her comfort earlier and perhaps she had been wise. Theirs was a commercial transaction, physically pleasing but not requiring emotion.

Ethan squared his shoulders. Cold, ruthless calculation had brought him this far in his plan and he reminded himself that Lottie was a pawn, a piece in the jigsaw, no more than a bit player in the grand scheme. Once his strategy was complete he would leave without a backward glance. He would pay Lottie off as agreed—he was a man of his word no matter how twisted and treacherous had become the world he lived in—but then he would never see her again. There was nothing profound in their relationship. Nor would Lottie herself wish there to be. Her sole concern was for money, and when they met again it would be on the cold, mercenary terms of a man and his paid mistress.

He turned into the courtyard of The Swan with Two Necks Inn. They were harnessing the horses. The clock on the stable chimed the quarter hour. There were fifteen minutes before the coach departed and his fellow passengers were assembling. A pretty young wife on the arm of a self-important husband cast him a look from the corner of her eye and gave him a covert smile. He bowed to her politely but with no acknowledgment of the implied invitation. There were two clerks in sober black; an older woman in shabby gray and a frumpy bonnet, who was probably a housekeeper or companion; and a man he guessed was a merchant or shopkeeper, sleek and prosperous-looking in a new jacket and embroidered waistcoat. Of the man who had been shadowing him from the moment he had set off to London a week before, spying on him, there was no sign. Perhaps he, too, had been enjoying the decadent pleasures of the city the night before and had overslept. One thing was for certain—the spy would have nothing to report other than that Ethan had spent his time in profligate debauchery. He would know nothing of the letters that had been exchanged, the messages passed. He would have seen nothing, for Ethan was a past master at covering his tracks.

Ethan smiled to himself. The British authorities did not trust him. Of course they did not. They were wise not to do so. But they would never uncover his plans.

His skill lay in hiding everything he did in plain sight right under the noses of his gaolers.

Not only *his* own future and freedom depended upon his talent for deception, but that of his son did, too. Every move, every plan he made, had the ultimate aim of freeing Arland from the hell of prison and his fellow captives along with him. Once it would have been enough to win Arland's freedom and for the two of them to escape, but Ethan had seen enough of the prison hulks and the harsh gaol regime to know that he could not allow any of his comrades to suffer and perish under such vile conditions. Men were starving, frozen half to death, living in filthy cells, beaten until they gave up the unequal struggle for life. He, with his passion for justice, could not let that pass unchallenged. There were nigh on sixty thousand prisoners of war in Britain. When they all rose up in revolt at one and the same time and seized their captors' weapons, they would make one hell of an invading army. The time was not yet ripe but it would come. He was working to make sure of it.

Ethan's grim smile faded as he thought again of Arland, incarcerated at Whitemoor prison, high on the Lambourn Downs above Wantage. He knew that was why the authorities had sent him on parole to that town. They wanted to remind him of Arland's suffering each and every day. They wanted to punish him; to make him suffer, too. And they had succeeded. He thought of Arland in the dark of the night when he could not sleep, tormented by the vision of his son in captivity. He thought of Arland whenever he saw the outline of Whitemoor's towers against the horizon.

Ethan had offered himself in return for Arland's freedom, offered his very life in return for that of his son, and the authorities had laughed in his face because they held all the cards. They held him and they held Arland and they allowed him his liberty as a form of torture whilst his son was locked up. It was their revenge for the way in which he had embarrassed his noble father and the British establishment.

Ethan knew that Northesk had gone to the Duke of Farne and had tried to persuade him to use his influence for Arland's release. His half brother was a good man, the only good man in a family of self-serving hypocrites, but he had failed. Nothing could obtain Arland's liberty. So now Ethan plotted and planned, slowly, carefully, as the months of his captivity passed, and inside he chafed against the fear of what was happening to his son. He should have known he would never be able to protect the boy, he thought bitterly, as he threw his kit bag up onto the roof and took his seat inside the coach. He should have known that in the end he would prove to be just like his father.

Ethan swore softly, under his breath. Soon, he promised silently. Soon we will both be free. Nothing and no one could come between him and his plan.

CHAPTER SEVEN

SHOPPING FOR HER ROLE as Ethan's mistress was a delicate affair, Lottie thought. She had no illusions as to how she would be received in Wantage society. Her position as a member of the demimonde and her style, her taste and her extravagance would be equally and roundly deplored. She would not be able to patronize a provincial dressmaker even if she wished, for doubtless they would refuse to serve her in case her lack of morals was contagious. So she needed to do all her shopping now, in advance. On the other hand, she simply could not visit the shops and emporia that had welcomed her when she was Mrs. Cummings, one of the leaders of society. They, too, would shut their doors in her face now that she was disgraced, which would be utterly mortifying. But that was the beauty of London. Whereas once she had shopped at the most fashionable addresses in order to see and be seen, now she could slip unnoticed into the warehouses and wholesalers at the less modish end of town, in Shoreditch and Cheapside and Newgate Street.

So it proved. She haggled over the price of silk stockings, found a very fetching straw bonnet at half the cost she would have paid in Oxford Street and tried not to exceed her budget. Eventually she had worn through her purse and realized that she would have to carry all her purchases back to Limmer's because she had failed to leave sufficient cash to pay for a hackney carriage. Such a plight had not befallen her before. Even when Gregory was in the process of divorcing her, he had been meticulous in paying her an allowance, employing a maid for her and permitting her the use of a small mews house in Mount Street. It was only when the papers were signed and sealed that he had withdrawn all support, making it clear that he had done his duty by her to the letter and that she was on her own.

Her purchases were heavy and the day was hot, and she paused on the corner of Arundel Street and the Strand to rest and draw breath. As she waited, a carriage turned down toward the river, driven at a spanking pace. Lottie stood and watched. Once, she thought, that would have been her in the carriage, cutting a dash through the streets of London, setting the fashion, spreading the *on dit,* at the center of the dizzy, glittering whirl of *Ton* society. With a wrench of memory that felt almost like a physical pain, she recalled the deep luxury of the green velvet seats in her landau, how soft and smooth the material had been beneath her palms, how the carriage was designed to be open and show the occupants to advantage, how people had flocked to greet her when she rode in Hyde Park. Crowds had stared, in much the same way that she was staring now. They had not gaped as though at a freak show, which was what had happened when she had driven out with Ethan yesterday. They had watched in envy.

"Make way there!" The coachman was shouting, and the horses, maddened by his use of the whip and skittish in the crowded, narrow street, were starting to prance and shy between the shafts. The noise was deafening; the rancid smells of the street engulfed Lottie: stale food, manure from the dray horses, rotting fruit, mingled with the scent of unwashed bodies with an edge of fear now as the coach forced its way through the crowd.

The whip caught someone in the throng and there was a roar of anger as the crowd surged forward. Someone jostled Lottie and she dropped one of the hatboxes. It rolled into the street like a hoop, straight under one of the coach's wheels. The carriage drove over it, squashing it flat. Lottie gave a little cry of despair and darted forward to try and retrieve it, but it was too late.

She was so close to the carriage now that she could reach out and touch its shining side. She felt like a little street urchin faced with unimaginable riches, opulence that was forever beyond her grasp. She looked up and for one impossible moment her eyes met those of Lady O'Hara, a woman she had once counted as her friend. Then that matron raised her nose to the perfect angle to look down and cut her dead, turning away to speak to the gentleman at her side. The footmen riding on the back raised their sticks threateningly to disperse the crowd, the carriage surged forward, and then it was gone.

The street was empty and quiet, the crowd melting away. Someone made a disparaging remark about the Quality and their careless, dangerous ways. Lottie scrabbled for the flattened hatbox. Even as she did so, she knew that her purchase was damaged beyond saving and this time she did not have Gregory's bottomless wealth to draw on for a replacement. She blinked back the tears of anger and frustration at the sheer unfairness of it all.

"Lottie!" She heard the cry from behind her. For a moment her heart lurched to think that one of her old acquaintances might have recognized her there on her knees in the gutter. But the tall gentleman in scarlet regimentals who was striding toward her was no mere acquaintance. He caught her and pulled her to her feet, scooping her up in his arms.

"Theo!"

She felt quite giddy with shock, relief and joy as her brother spun her around. It was what she had been praying for daily since word of Gregory's plan to divorce her had shattered her world. There were only two people she believed in enough to think they might save her. Joanna Grant was one, despite the shabby way in which Lottie had treated her. The other was her brother, and here he was, at last, come to help her and take her away. He would aid her in putting her life back together the way it was meant to be. Once again, she felt a huge surge of relief. She raised one hand to Theo's lean, bronzed cheek, trying to hug him and hold on to all her parcels at the same time.

"You could have written!" she scolded. "I thought you were dead. Oh, Theo, I am so happy to see you!"

Even as she held her brother close, Ethan Ryder's image appeared in her mind. She felt a little odd, weak with gratitude that her life would change now that Theo had returned, yet touched by a strange disappointment that she would not see Ethan again. She would not join him in Wantage now and continue to carve out her role as the most notorious mistress in the kingdom.

She hugged Theo harder, closing her eyes to blot out the guilty picture of all her purchases. She wondered if Theo could afford to repay all the guineas she had spent. The alternative was simply to disappear. Yesterday she would not have thought twice. Today she felt a stubborn need to prove to Ethan that she was a little bit trustworthy by returning his money. How odd. How inexplicable.

"Same old Lottie!" Theo was holding her at arm's length now and eyeing the bandboxes and brown paper parcels with fond exasperation, which for some reason irritated her. Perhaps it had been the sight of Lady O'Hara that had disturbed her, for clearly she was not the same Lottie *at all*. There was no town house in Grosvenor Square anymore, no landau, no bottomless bank account, no bosom bows in the *Ton* deferring to her fashion sense.

But Theo was still speaking and her irritation melted away under the warmth of her pleasure in seeing him again.

"I went to the house in Mount Street that you said you had moved into…" he was saying.

"So you *did* get my letters!" Lottie exclaimed.

"Not for a long time." Theo's expression sobered. "The postal service is poor and I have been on the move regularly." He glanced at her, a slight frown now between his brows. "I heard about your divorce, though, Lottie. Even in Spain it was the *on dit* from home."

Lottie pulled a face. "One would hope that there were more important things to talk about during a war."

"It's the gossip from home that keeps one going,"

Theo muttered. "Unless it's about your own sister, and then it is mortifying." He ran a hand over his hair. "Look, Lottie, do you want me to call Gregory out?"

Lottie thought about it. It was extraordinarily tempting. "No," she said reluctantly, after a moment. "I don't think that there is much point in that."

Theo visibly relaxed. "Well, thank goodness for that," he said. "Because I would do it, of course, but really—" he shook his head "—I expect he was justified, if your previous indiscretions were anything to go by."

"Let us not discuss that in the street," Lottie said hurriedly. She felt stung by Theo's criticism but she did not want to quarrel with him within seconds of seeing him again. "Is there somewhere we can go to talk?"

"How about Gunter's?" Theo said. "We could sit inside, away from the crowds."

Once again, Lottie prickled at the implication that he wished to hide her away. Theo had always been conventional, of course, far more conventional than she, and, if she were honest, a tiny bit of a stick-in-the-mud and more than a little bit of a social snob. So perhaps it was no wonder that he disapproved of her now. Still, he had taken her arm—and some of her parcels—and was setting off at a military stride, and she had to hurry to keep up. Soon they had turned into Berkeley Square and Theo had ushered her through the doorway and to a small table right at the back where he placed her in a dark corner and sat between her and the room. Lottie imagined that if he could have made her invisible he would have done so, the notorious sister, the embarrassment on the family escutcheon.

He ordered a pot of tea, most conventionally. She, rather defiantly, ordered a frozen fruit punch.

"Are you back in England for good?" she asked as the waiter sped away to fulfill their orders. "If so, perhaps we could set up house together—" She stopped, seeing his face fall. It was foolish of her, she thought, to imagine that Theo would want her to live with him. The truth was that if he were home he would wish to wed an heiress and for that he would need to be untainted by her scandal. He had little in the way of fortune and although he had had a successful army career—very successful judging by the colonel's crowns and stars on his uniform—she understood that he needed to consolidate that, which meant that he could hardly consort with the divorced sister who had brought disgrace on the family. She told herself it was only practical, but the realization hurt. Still, if he could not acknowledge her openly he could at least help her find somewhere to live—and pay her bills. Her heart eased again and she leaned over to touch the back of his hand.

"Thank you," she said softly. "I am so happy you have come back to help me."

"Like a knight in shining armor," Theo agreed, his discomfort of a moment ago slipping away. He squeezed her hand. "You know I love you, Lottie, and I will always do my best to help you."

Lottie felt the happiness blossom inside her. "Of course I do," she said. "And perhaps it would not serve for us to take a house together, but at the least you could help me to find a small place away from London where I might live quietly—" Once again she fell silent, this time warned by the stiffness in his body and the shame in his eyes.

Theo fidgeted with his teacup, swirling the spoon around in the dish. He evaded her eyes. "I would like that above all things," he said, "and I swear I will help you just as soon as I can, Lottie, but first…" He stopped and swallowed hard. "The thing is, we need you to do something for us. King and country and all that." He looked up, his brown eyes pleading for her understanding. "It's monstrous important."

"What is it?" Lottie said. She knew it was bad. She could feel it.

"It's to do with Ryder," Theo said.

Lottie's heart jumped. She felt a little sick. "You know about Ethan?" Her eyes widened. "You know everything, don't you? You know about Mrs. Tong and the Temple of Venus—"

Theo made a slight, dismissive gesture. "It doesn't matter," he said.

"Yes it does!" Lottie was furious. She felt shamed and dismayed. "Why did you not say?"

"Because I thought it would embarrass you," Theo said, "to talk to your brother about your time in a brothel." He looked up and Lottie's heart did another unpleasantly giddy skip to see the anger in his eyes.

"You always were the architect of your own downfall, Lottie," Theo said. "If you had not played Gregory false—"

"You know *nothing* about that," Lottie snapped. "Nothing!"

"All right." Theo raised his hands in a pacifying gesture. "But you let it get out of hand, Lottie. You took it too far. What else could he do when you had cuckolded him and made him look such a complaisant fool? And then to be so deep in debt that you had none of your settlement left, and had to earn a living on your back—"

"That's enough," Lottie said. There were tears of anger and betrayal in her throat. She gulped them back. "I don't need you to rehearse all my faults to me," she said. "And if you require some sort of favor from me it might do your cause more good to *try* to be nice."

"Of course," Theo said. He ran an agitated hand through his hair. "I'm sorry. You know it is only because I care for you, Lottie, and do not like to see you in these straits."

"You do not like to see me in them, but you are prepared to take advantage of them," Lottie said. "Try not to be such a hypocrite, Theo, and tell me what it is that you want."

Theo nodded. It gave Lottie some small satisfaction to see that he now looked more uncomfortable than she felt. She was too bruised and bitter to be embarrassed anymore. She had thought that Theo's return meant that there was someone to whom she could turn for help. Instead he wanted to use her.

"Well?" she said sharply, when it seemed that her brother was at a loss for words.

"Ryder is of interest to the government," Theo said, glancing over his shoulder in what seemed to Lottie to be a ridiculously conspiratorial manner. "I assume that you know his history?"

"He is a French prisoner of war," Lottie said.

"He's a renegade," Theo said viciously, "a traitor to the British."

"He's Irish," Lottie corrected, surprised by the surge of anger she felt to hear her brother's words. "His father may be a member of the establishment but Farne is still an Irish peer. And Ethan's mother was an Irish girl, so I understand." She glared at Theo. "Perhaps he did not think that he owed loyalty to the British. Perhaps he thought that loyalty and respect have to be earned."

"Farne did his best for him," Theo said. "He had him educated with his legitimate sons, would have bought him a commission in the British Army had he wished it. Did he not tell you?"

"No," Lottie said. "I know little of his family or his history. I only met him two days ago," she added, "and we did not spend much of our time in conversation."

Theo blushed. "No, well…" He cleared his throat. "Ryder was wild. All that gypsy blood."

"Because the Dukes of Farne have always been up-right, respectable citizens," Lottie said dryly, "with their gambling and their mistresses and various other ancestral vices… Or is that different because it is sanctioned by society?"

"You are sharp today," Theo complained.

"I have every right to be," Lottie said. "My own brother wishes me to be a government-approved whore, unless I miss my guess. And to think that before I was only doing it for the money," she added bitterly. "Now I suppose you would say it is my patriotic duty to sleep with Ethan."

Theo shifted in his chair. "We only want information, Lottie," he said. "Where he goes, whom he associates with, any letters, contacts, that sort of thing. He's a dangerous man and we need to keep a close watch on him."

"Then lock him up!" Lottie said. "He would be easier to watch under lock and key, would he not?" She frowned. "From the moment I met Ethan I wondered why on earth he had been given his liberty if he is such a dangerous prisoner."

There was a pause. "I'll allow that there is an element of revenge in it," Theo said carefully. "Ryder has embarrassed the British authorities by his outspoken rejection of his father's politics."

"So they leave him free—" Lottie broke off, suddenly seeing the truth. "Whilst his son is imprisoned," she finished. "He is tormented by the knowledge that he walks around at liberty whilst Arland is in some hellhole prison and he can do nothing about it. That is true cruelty, Theo."

Theo shrugged uncomfortably. "War is a dirty business."

"How did Arland Ryder come to be captured and imprisoned?" Lottie asked. "He cannot be much more than a boy!"

"He's seventeen." Theo fidgeted uncomfortably. "I do not know the details of it but I understand that the boy lied about his age in order to join the French army and be with his father. They were both captured at the Battle of Fuentes de Onoro in 1811."

"He can only have been fifteen then!" Lottie stared in horror. "This is not war! This is a personal vendetta!"

Theo looked away, embarrassed. "Let us not quarrel,"

he soothed. "The truth is that Ryder is also useful to us at liberty. He may lead us to other conspirators."

Lottie stared at him. "Ethan is involved in a conspiracy? To do what?"

"If we knew that for sure we wouldn't be requiring your help," her brother said. "We suspect that Ryder has been involved in planning the escape of some of his fellow officers from various parole towns, and with the breakout of prisoners from some of the hulks and gaols for that matter." Theo looked up and met her eyes. "There were mass escapes in '11 and last year, and Ryder is known to be an expert in planning and strategy. We think he is active in a countrywide network of agents who facilitate prisoner escapes."

Lottie thought of Ethan. He was not the sort of man to sit quietly by, waiting for the war to end. He would chafe at the inaction. Theo might well be right.

"We are giving him enough rope," Theo was saying, "so that he will hang himself and anyone else involved in his treason."

Lottie shivered at the image. "And you want me to find out what it is that he is involved with," she said bleakly. "You want me to betray him."

"You would be well rewarded for your help," Theo said eagerly. "I know how important it is to you to regain your place in society, Lottie."

"Not even the government can help me there," Lottie said dryly.

"Well, maybe matters cannot be as they were," Theo agreed, "but there would be a generous sum of money and a house somewhere where you could start over, marry again perhaps, with wealth and respectability behind you. I think that I could even persuade the family to accept you back if I explained, discreetly of course, that you have been…"

"Whoring myself out for the sake of King and country?" Lottie said sweetly. "You set yourself too high a task, Theo. The Pallisers will never take me back. And I am not sure that I would want them to do so," she added. "If they cannot help me when I need them then I want nothing of them."

"I thought that you were a pragmatist, Lottie," her brother said. "Take their charity if it is offered and be thankful." He paused. "I think I would be able to persuade them and—" there was a wealth of sincerity in his voice "—I swear I want to help you. I want it above all things."

Lottie looked around at the couples chatting, laughing and drinking in Gunter's. A young buck had drawn his phaeton up outside and had come in to fetch an ice cream for his fair companion. The sun was shining, the day bright with promise, and yet Lottie felt again that odd sense of detachment she had experienced when she had seen Lady O'Hara's carriage. This was no longer her world. She had forfeited her right to it. And what had she gained in return? Nothing but a temporary role as Ethan Ryder's mistress and a handsome payoff at the end of their association. She knew there was no other future for them. The shockingly tender lovemaking of their first night together had counted for nothing and she should not allow it to influence her. She would be a sentimental fool to do so. She had promised Ethan nothing other than her sexual fidelity for the length of their *affaire*. She owed him nothing. She had only herself to rely on.

And here was Theo offering her the tempting chance to regain, if not her original place in society, then a home and sufficient wealth to make her almost respectable again, offering, too, his influence within the family to take her back into the fold, smooth over her indiscretions and make all well again.

She was not sure that she believed he could do it, but she *wanted* to believe it. She wanted to believe it very much, almost as much as she wanted Theo to save her and restore her to her rightful place in society. And he *was* saving her in his own way. Her sore heart eased a little at the thought. Theo did want to help her. He was her brother and he loved her. It was simply that there was a price to be paid for his help. And if she paid that price, if she pleased him, she would regain his approval as well as feel secure in his love.

She drained the fruit punch. Its alcoholic sweetness made her head spin on such a hot day. A lady in the most adorably roguish and fashionable bonnet crossed her line of vision and Lottie was shot through with sadness. She wanted to regain all that she had lost, to be rich, never to have to sell herself again simply to survive, to be *safe*. Oh, she wanted to walk on soft carpets, to smell the scent of cut flowers as they reposed in a priceless china vase, to ride in her own smart landau again and become once more a part of the world she had lost. She wanted it so much that she felt breathless at the thought, her heart constricted in her chest as though it were in a vise.

She would do anything to go back.

"So you want me to work for you." Lottie tried to sound businesslike but beneath her cool tone she found she felt a little sick. The memory of her short time with Ethan tugged at her again. It was so little to build on when it was fleeting and illusory and when Theo was offering her heart's desire: money, comfort and a return to the life she once knew. Yet for some reason the urge to remain loyal to Ethan gripped her fiercely. She felt torn. She found that her hands were shaking at the thought of betraying him, and she pressed them together to still the trembling, hiding them in her lap.

"It is not really spying, Lottie," Theo was saying persuasively. "It is simply…passing information on to us if there is anything that you think might be useful…"

"Spying," Lottie said. "You should be honest and call it what it is."

Theo shrugged uncomfortably. He looked up and his dark eyes met hers. "So," he said. "Will you do it?"

There was a long, long silence. Lottie could hear the chink of china and the murmur of voices and the sounds of the carriages outside in Berkeley Square. She felt hot and shaken, and the sweet echoes of the time she had spent with Ethan—such a short time and yet so intense and so compelling—kept running through her mind.

Ethan would leave her. Men always did. There was no forever and they had never for a moment promised it to each other.

She wanted to be rich again. She wanted Theo to

smile at her with a brother's love and approval. She wanted him to save her.

She took a deep breath.

"Very well," she said. "I'll spy for you."

CHAPTER EIGHT

THERE WAS A LARGER than usual crowd in Wantage Market Place on Saturday afternoon waiting for the mail coach from Oxford. Ethan was gratified; he had spread the word of Lottie's arrival assiduously and would have been disappointed if the natural curiosity of the townspeople had not resulted in a crowd. The appearance of so disreputable a woman as Lottie Palliser, her role as his mistress, a bird of paradise amidst the dull sparrows of this little market town, was bound to cause a furor and that was precisely what Ethan wanted.

The Wantage Parole Agent had summoned him for a meeting as soon as he had heard the rumors of Lottie's impending arrival. Mr. Duster was a fussy little man, neat and precise in his person and his dealings, very anxious to do everything by the book. The book in question this time was the Transport Department's rules and regulations governing the conduct and terms of parole for prisoners, and Mr. Duster was flicking through it irritably when Ethan was shown into his office.

"This is a bad business, St. Severin," Mr. Duster had said, waving Ethan to a chair and summoning a servant to fetch him a glass of wine. "I can see no reference in any of the regulations to whether or not a prisoner of war is permitted to keep a mistress. Really, it is most remiss of the department not to have covered this eventuality."

"Surely," Ethan said, "the absence of any rules against the keeping of mistresses suggests that it must be permissible?"

Duster looked at him sharply as though suspecting Ethan of making fun of him. "I cannot be sure," he said. "And I certainly cannot make such a decision on my own initiative. I have written to the Transport Department for a ruling."

"Of course," Ethan said, inclining his head. "Thank you."

"Why on earth you need to bring such a woman to Wantage completely confounds me," Duster continued.

Ethan shrugged elegantly, a French habit he had picked up over the years.

"What can I say, Mr. Duster? I am bored kicking my heels here on parole. Your town, whilst charming, lacks amenities, and I have been used to a far more exciting existence."

"I cannot see why you do not use your time as the other officers do," Duster said, running an exasperated hand over his sweating forehead. "Can you not learn a musical instrument or practice your fencing? Those are the occupations of a gentleman."

"Keeping a mistress is also the occupation of a gentleman," Ethan said dryly. "You must forgive me. I have no taste for either the theatricals or the games of billiards in which my fellow officers indulge, and my swordplay is already of a high standard. I confess that I far prefer amorous games."

Duster had reddened and puffed up like a turkey cock but he had not forbidden Lottie's arrival. And now, as the Oxford coach turned into the square, Ethan reflected that he was going to look the most abject idiot if Lottie had played him false and absconded with the money. A wry smile tilted his lips. Had he been a fool to trust her with several hundred guineas?

Jacques Le Prevost had insisted on accompanying him to meet the carriage. "I am here as your friend, St. Severin," he said, clapping Ethan on the shoulder. "If *Madame* fails to arrive I will take you to the inn to drown your sorrows, and if her arrival outrages the populace—" he gave a very Gallic shrug "—I will stand as your second when someone calls you out for offending public decency."

"Very good of you, Jacques," Ethan said. "I appreciate it." The outside passengers were descending from the coach now. Naturally Lottie would have taken an inside seat. He imagined that it would be indignity enough for her to travel post rather than in a private carriage. Rattling along on the outside would have been out of the question.

One by one the passengers descended the steps: a clergyman clutching a Bible and with a face as tightly pinched as if he had a stinking Stilton cheese under his nose; a couple with a small child; a shabby-genteel female with a small portmanteau, who could have been a governess companion. And then a bonnet appeared, followed by a gloved hand clutching a gilded cage that contained a small, silent canary. Ethan let out the breath that, until that moment, he had not been aware he was holding.

"*Enfin*," Jacques murmured.

Lottie, Ethan realized, was making an entrance, just as he had requested.

She paused on the top step of the mail coach, looking around her with acute interest. She was wearing an enormous and extremely fetching straw bonnet tied under her chin with pink ribbons. Her dress of white muslin was what was known in London as in the naked style, for it was cut with a high waist to emphasize the bosom and then cut low over that same bosom to reveal as much naked flesh as possible. It was also light and airy to the point of transparency. She was wearing a spencer over the gown but it was also cut to show off her figure. What the good burghers of Wantage would make of such indecent fashion, Ethan thought, was anyone's guess. He liked it well enough. Suddenly the three days' abstinence since he had last made love to Lottie felt like a total desert.

"If you could hurry it up a little, madam," the harassed guard was saying as he checked his watch, "we do have a schedule to keep."

"Ethan, darling!" Lottie cast herself into his arms, canary and all, and gave him the sort of kiss that was best enjoyed in private. It was long and deep, an outrageous embrace to display in front of a fascinated audience of the assembled citizens of Wantage. Lottie tasted of sweet, wicked temptation that almost swept Ethan away, plunging him into a maelstrom of heated memory and back into that hot, intimate night at Limmer's Hotel. His body tightened with undeniable desire.

Then she released him and stepped back and Ethan saw in her eyes that she was laughing—the kiss had meant absolutely nothing to her other than that she was playing her part to the hilt—and Ethan felt an odd sensation, as though he had stepped off a cliff into thin air. For a moment he felt a naive fool for wanting to recreate what had been between them on those nights in London, the honest feelings, the sweetness of true intimacy. Had he not been the one who had walked away swearing that such closeness had been no more than an illusion? Had he not wanted a sophisticated mistress who would make no emotional demands on him? Yet still he felt discomfited for some obscure reason. He felt angry with Lottie for dissimulating and with himself for wanting it to be any other way.

Everyone was staring at them and whispering. Lottie's fellow passengers were gathering their baggage and whisking away as though the sight of such immorality on the streets might be infectious. Respectable housewives with their marketing baskets could not quite disguise the gleam of prurient curiosity in their eyes. Many of them had gathered specifically in order to be shocked and outraged and they were determined to have their money's worth.

"I am so sorry, darling," Lottie said, peeling herself off him, a wicked glint still in her brown eyes, "but my bonnet was so vast that I took up two seats in the carriage so I am afraid that you will have to pay the cost of another passenger."

"Jacques," Ethan said, recovering himself, "if you would be so good? I fear I do not have my pocketbook with me."

"*Enchanté*," Le Prevost murmured ironically. He bowed to Lottie. "*Madame*, such a very great pleasure to see you again."

"*Merci, monsieur.*" Lottie's smile was delicious, flirtatious, and Ethan was almost knocked flat by a wave of possessiveness that was unexpected, unwelcome and, he thought, completely inappropriate when the object of it was a woman who had been bought for a few hundred guineas and would no doubt sell herself again for a few guineas more. Nevertheless, desire gripped him like a vise. He needed to remind her of who was paying her bills. The odd tension that possessed him tightened a notch.

Lottie slipped her hand through his arm. "I have portmanteaux," she said, fluttering her eyelashes at him. "Several of them."

"I am sure that you have," Ethan said, a little grimly, wondering how much of the money he had given her was left.

"I am afraid," Lottie continued, as though she had read his mind, "that I rather exceeded my allowance, Ethan darling. They will be sending you the bills from London." She smiled limpidly. "I did warn you."

"You will have ample opportunity to earn the money back," Ethan said, even more grimly. He gestured to a porter from The Bear Inn who was loitering in the hope of business. "Pray get a cart and take these portmanteaux to Priory Cottage," he said. "Hopefully you will be able to fit them all in one barrow."

Lottie was looking around the market square with a certain amount of disfavor. "A duck pond!" she said. "How quaintly pretty!" She sighed theatrically. "I know that you said that Wantage was a parochial little place, Ethan darling—" her voice was carrying to everyone in the vicinity "—but I did not expect it to be quite *so* provincial. I am sure that I shall simply expire with boredom here!"

"I shall endeavor to keep you occupied," Ethan said smoothly. "Try not to be too disparaging," he added, lowering his voice. "After all, we do have to live here."

"Which is a great pity," Lottie said. "Could you not persuade the authorities to send you somewhere more congenial? Are there any shops?" she continued, without waiting for his reply. "I cannot live without shops!"

Well, he had wanted London Lottie, Ethan thought wryly, the frivolous social butterfly, the woman who lived for entertainment and required to be perpetually amused. And that was what he had got. He could scarcely complain now, now that she had regained all her town bronze and had become the creature he had wanted.

"Perhaps you could develop an interest in history," he suggested. "Wantage is an ancient town, the birthplace of King Alfred the Great."

Lottie gave an exaggerated yawn. "You know I am not bookish, darling. History? A remedy for sleeplessness, no more." She squeezed his arm. "Do we have to *walk* to my new home?"

"Yes, of course," Ethan said. "There are no hackney carriages here."

"I should have bought another pair of shoes when I

had the chance," Lottie mourned. "I will ruin my lovely new slippers on these dirty streets."

"I should think you have sufficient shoes in those portmanteaux to open your own shop," Ethan said.

"Seven pairs only, darling," Lottie said with a vague wave of her hands. "Just enough for one pair for each day of the week."

They cut through a narrow little cobbled alleyway from the marketplace into a square where the parish church loomed tall over the houses.

"How quelling," Lottie said, shuddering. "I feel it is disapproving of me."

"You will need to get used to it," Ethan said. He gestured toward a pretty brick-built villa standing back from the road on the north side of the church. "This is Priory Cottage. I have rented it for you."

Ethan paid off the porter, who was out of breath pushing a handcart laden with five portmanteaux and had almost got stuck in the narrow alleyway, and pushed open the door of the cottage. By now there was an indiscreet tide of people who had followed them from the marketplace and were gawping on the pavement outside.

"I do believe," Ethan said, as he ushered Lottie inside, "that Wantage has never seen anything quite like you before."

"Well, that was what you wanted, was it not?" Lottie said, a slight edge to her voice. "I have barely begun to be scandalous." She walked past him into the neat parlor, untied the ribbons of the enormous bonnet and cast it onto a chair. "The house is charming," she added, looking around, "but Priory Lane, next to the church? Could you be any more inappropriate, darling?"

Ethan laughed. "I can be much, much more inappropriate, I assure you."

He unfastened the buttons on her spencer and slid it from her shoulders. The dress was extraordinary, he thought, the pristine white of debutante garb and yet cut so low that her lush breasts were practically spilling out of it. She looked like a despoiled angel. It was impossible to look at her and not be consumed with lust and he was not even going to try to repress his feelings.

"Turn round," he said abruptly.

He saw her eyes widen at his tone. "Ethan, darling, I have just arrived and require a pot of tea rather than a—"

"Turn around," Ethan repeated. He could see a crowd on the pavement outside the house, peering in through the window, whispering and fluttering as though this were a royal visit and they were expecting something spectacular to happen. Well, he would give them something spectacular to talk about, though it would hardly be as respectable as a visit from the king and queen.

Lottie's gaze narrowed on his face and for a moment he thought she was going to argue with him but then she turned slowly so that she was facing the window. Ethan stepped behind her and lifted her hair away from the nape of her neck, pushing it forward so that it spilled over her shoulder and across her breasts. He put his hands on her upper arms and started to kiss the side of her throat and the soft curve where her neck met her shoulder. Her skin felt warm and soft against his lips and she smelled of sunshine and roses. Lust speared him again.

He could feel how tensely she held herself beneath his hands. "Relax," he murmured.

"I told you in London that I was not accustomed to an audience." Lottie's tone was tart. "I find it distracts me. Your crowd of busybodies is all of three feet away on the pavement outside with no more than a pane of glass between us. I have been here five minutes only and already you make a harlot's display of me."

"You made one of yourself in the marketplace," Ethan said. "And that is why you are here. You are my mistress. I want there to be no doubt in anyone's mind that you enjoy that role." He nipped the skin of her neck softly. "You said," he added, sliding his tongue down her nape, "that you had barely started to be scandalous. It is time to live down to your reputation."

He felt her tense again and wondered if she was going to refuse, but then she closed her eyes and dropped her head forward in the most perfect submissive pose. Ethan slid the white gown off one shoulder and allowed his lips to trace a path across the skin he had exposed. The low-cut neckline of the dress fell farther still, almost uncovering her breasts now. She did not adjust it, despite the milling crowd staring in through the glass.

Ethan had not been sure how far he would take this but the fever in his blood was too violent to let it go now. From the moment Lottie had stepped off the coach the complicated, contradictory emotions had driven him. He had asked for Lottie to act the shameless harlot. And yet he had wanted the sweet, trusting intimacy they had experienced before. He ached for it and the need in him drove him on.

He slid a hand around Lottie's waist and up to cup her breast.

"Ethan—" This time there was entreaty in her tone. "The window…"

"So modest," Ethan mocked.

He leaned past her and whisked the curtains closed then pushed her gently down so that her palms were braced against the lid of the rosewood piano. He pulled the neck of her gown down the last inch so that her breasts tumbled out, full and round, into his palms. He kneaded the soft flesh, pulling on her nipples, and felt her shiver.

The lust goaded him, spurring him on. Without further ado he drew up Lottie's skirts, unbuttoned his pantaloons with fingers that shook so much they could scarcely function and took her with one thrust.

It was hot, mindless, utter madness. He felt her body sheathe him, tight and close, and he thought he would shatter there and then. She clenched him, a deliberate movement that tore a groan from him. He held her hips and plunged into her, over and over, with a violent pleasure that spiraled into unbearable bliss. The piano creaked and rocked, Lottie's breasts bouncing extravagantly with each hard thrust. Ethan felt himself fly over the edge of the precipice as his climax exploded within him and he shouted aloud.

And then it was over. The pleasure ebbed like a draining tide and he felt an extraordinary regret, almost a shock, at what he had done and the way he had used her so ruthlessly. He was empty of desire and there was a cold ache within him that was deeper than the physical. He straightened his clothes and noted dispassionately that his hands were still shaking a little.

Lottie straightened up, too, adjusting her bodice and smoothing her skirts as calmly as though she had been paying a morning call and had risen to depart. When she turned to look at him her face was expressionless, the mask of the sophisticated courtesan. She even smiled politely, as though he were a stranger.

"I trust that was to your satisfaction, my lord?" Her voice revealed nothing, either.

"I…" Ethan found that he was at a loss, groping for words that simply did not come.

It had been perfect in the sense that it was exactly what he had thought he wanted. Even now, word would be winging around the town of his outrageous behavior with his equally shameless mistress. Everyone would know what they had been doing behind the drawn curtains. Everyone would be talking. He had created a storm of gossip and Lottie had played her part precisely as he had wished. Moreover, it had been exactly the emotionless, physically satisfying coupling that he had envisaged from the moment he had sought Lottie out. He had been afire with need and she had acted as the ideal complaisant mistress, accommodating his bodily requirements and making no awkward emotional demands upon him.

So why did he feel cheated? Why did he want to pull her into his arms and kiss her until her body softened against his and she responded with true passion? Why, when she was everything that he had required, did he want her to be different? Instead of triumph he felt a sort of hollow exhaustion. Instead of satisfaction he felt robbed in some way.

"I am going out," he said abruptly.

He saw a tiny frown mar the perfect composure of her expression. "Will you be back later?" She spoke in tones of the gentlest enquiry. There was no begging, no expressions of pleasure in his company.

"I don't know." He knew that he sounded ungracious and also that she would not reproach him for it because perfect mistresses never rebuked their lovers. "I have rooms at The Bear in the marketplace," he said. "I may dine there tonight."

He threw some coins onto the table. They fell with an empty clatter.

"For my services?" Lottie's voice was smooth. "Why, thank you. And I did so little, too."

"For your expenses," Ethan snapped. "I have engaged a maid for you. Send her out to buy some food."

"I have run a household before," Lottie said. "I expect I can manage that."

The tartness was back in her voice. Not such a perfect mistress, then. Contrarily, the flash of spirit pleased Ethan. He did not want a cipher. It appeared he did not want a complaisant woman, either. His mind whispered that he wanted the Lottie Palliser he had known in London, the warm vulnerable woman who had argued with him, challenged him and responded to his lovemaking with a passion that had been sweet and unfeigned. But that woman was dangerous to him in a way that he did not understand. It would be far better to avoid that emotional intimacy, even if he were claiming her body with a physical intimacy that could not have been closer.

She was still watching him with those dark, expressionless eyes. Ethan shook his head abruptly and went out, closing the door behind him with an exaggerated care that belied the odd feeling of violence in his soul. He needed brandy. Good French brandy would solve most problems or at least numb them until he no longer cared. Unfortunately the Wantage inns only offered villainously poor brandy at inflated prices, another betrayal of the country he had adopted as his own. Nevertheless, just this once, it would have to do. Perhaps the drink would bring some clarity so that he could work out what he truly wanted from Lottie and why the simple, pleasant liaison he had envisaged as a disguise for his more covert activities was proving to be so damned complicated.

LOTTIE WAITED until the sound of Ethan's footsteps had died away on the cobbles outside and then she threw open the parlor curtains and let the sunshine in. The street outside was empty. The crowds had gone, no doubt to spread the word of her utterly shameless and immoral behavior. She hoped that Ethan would be pleased. She had behaved as he had wanted. She had flaunted herself like a whore. She had created the scandal Ethan had desired. And she had only been here a half hour.

Lottie went down the corridor, through the kitchen and out into the tiny garden at the back of the cottage. It was shady and cool there. The sun beat down on the spread leaves of an ancient apple tree. There were old roses in pale pink and creamy gold entangled with honeysuckle on the tumbledown stone wall that separated the gardens from the priory lands beyond. The air smelled heavenly of hot grass and flowers, but Lottie did not seem to be able to smell or feel its beauty. She felt completely numb.

In a corner of the garden was a well. She turned the handle and heard the bucket splash down, then wound it up again, the chains slipping a little and grinding as the bucket rose, the water slopping over the brim. Lottie knelt down on the grass and scooped it up in her cupped hands. She gasped at the shock of the cold springwater against her face but it was so refreshing that after a moment she picked up the bucket and emptied it over her head. She refilled it and did the same again. The white dress now clung like a limp rag. Her hair was in rats' tails. She shivered. Suddenly the sun did not feel so hot.

The cold sting of the water had cut through the strange lassitude that had possessed her after Ethan had gone. She felt clean and alive again but her feelings were now awake, too, and they felt bruised and sore, as did her body. She had not wanted to be taken like a strumpet. Until Ethan had used her and discarded her with such ruthlessness she had not realized that she had secretly been hoping for the sort of passionate and emotional reunion that their lovemaking in London had promised. Despite telling herself that it was merely business, that Ethan was cold and detached about their liaison and she would be, too, in her heart she had wanted more. She had wanted to curl up in bed with him, to talk, to feel, if not loved, then at least a little cosseted and indulged. She had wanted Ethan's company in other ways, too, to eat together, to go out together in this godforsaken town and share whatever entertainment it had to offer.

She felt naive to have longed for so much when Ethan's ruthless possession of her had made clear exactly what he desired of her.

Shivering again in the summer breeze she hurried back across the grass and into the cottage. It was not such a poor place, she thought. It was light, well appointed and quite comfortably furnished. She should count her blessings. It was not something she was accustomed to doing but she refused to mope around like a poor-spirited creature with no backbone. What Ethan wanted from her was in truth very similar to what Gregory had wanted—except that Gregory had never wanted sex, at least not with her. But the other aspects—to be at Ethan's beck and call, to do as he desired, to be an ornament and a trophy, to be abandoned on whim when he went out—that was *exactly* like her marriage. How ironic. But at least she should be able to do this with her eyes closed.

The house was silent. Lottie paused in the kitchen and watched the sun chasing shadows across the wall. What she really wanted now was a cup of tea. Or several. And a plate full of pastries would not go amiss. There was something very comforting about tea and pastries when one felt bruised by life. There was only one problem. She had never made a pot of tea, never cooked or cleaned and had only recently learned how to dress herself without assistance. She had never been without servants in her life, and the kitchen was an alien place—the fire unmade, the utensils hanging on the walls strange implements with mysterious functions she could not even guess at. She could see a kettle but she had neglected to bring any water in with her from the well.

Sighing, Lottie went out into the hall to hunt up one of her new outfits from amongst the five portmanteaux. She was not going out in this harlot's garb. She doubted she would ever wear it again. She had chosen it in order to make an entrance, at Ethan's desire, and it had done its job all too well.

As she stepped over the first suitcase, wondering how on earth she was to get all her luggage up the cottage's narrow stair, there was a gentle knock at the front door and a head poked around followed by a slip of a girl in maid's uniform. She came in and dropped an awkward curtsy.

"Good afternoon, my lady."

"Thank goodness," Lottie said. "You must be the maid that Lord St. Severin engaged."

She straightened up. The girl was staring at her with ill-concealed curiosity, which was hardly surprising given her appalling reputation. She wondered what the girl was thinking and how Ethan had persuaded anyone to take on the role of her maid. This poor creature looked malnourished and barely more than a child. She had hair the color of straw, drawn back so severely that it only seemed to accentuate the thinness of her face, and big gray eyes that were currently riveted on Lottie with fascination.

"You have weed in your hair, my lady," the girl ventured.

"*Madam* will do," Lottie said. "There is nothing of the lady about me." She reached up and retrieved the offending piece of greenery. "What is your name?"

"Margery, madam." The maid dropped another curtsy. "I have references," she added, proffering a piece of paper. "From the employment agency."

"Marvelous," Lottie said. "I was not sure that anyone respectable would be prepared to take a post in this deeply disreputable household."

"There are a lot of people out of work in Wantage, madam," Margery said. "The tanneries are closing. Two of my brothers have no trade now so I have to take what jobs I can find."

"That would explain it," Lottie said with a sigh. "Could you make a pot of tea please, Margery, and then go into town to buy us some foodstuffs?"

"I'll try, madam," Margery said uncomfortably. "The stallholders have been saying that they will not serve you."

Lottie put her hands on her hips. "Because I am an immoral hussy, I suppose," she said.

"No, ma'am," Margery said. "Well yes, ma'am, but mostly it is because you consort with the Enemy." She glanced over her shoulder as though she expected Napoleon's army to be creeping up on them even as she spoke.

"The Enemy!" Lottie said. "Am I to suppose that if I was the mistress of an English officer that would win greater approval?"

"Yes, ma'am," Margery said, taking the rhetorical question literally. "Most people would prefer that."

Lottie sighed. "Not that it is any of their business.

Anyway, Lord St. Severin is Irish, not French, and I understand that some of his fellow prisoners are American. Do the people of Wantage show the same prejudice against all foreigners?"

"Oh yes, ma'am," Margery said, nodding enthusiastically. "No one likes outsiders very much."

Lottie sighed again, threw open one of the portmanteaux and extracted a gown in lime green with white spots. It was a most fashionable cut, but decidedly more respectable than the white muslin she had barely been wearing when she arrived.

"That's pretty, ma'am," Margery said, staring. "Don't see gowns like that around here."

"All my gowns are from London," Lottie said. "Where do the ladies of Wantage shop for their clothes?"

"They make their own clothes, ma'am," Margery said.

"Make their own clothes?" Lottie sat down rather abruptly on the second step. "Good lord! From what?"

"Mr. Mattingley sells the material, ma'am," Margery said, as though explaining to a slow child. "He has superfine and satin and muslin and corduroy. And Mistress Gilmore in the Market Square sells ribbon tiffany and cambric bonnets. Ever so pretty, they are." Her gaze fell again on the lime-green gown. "Not so pretty as that, mind you. The ladies will be even more envious of you now, ma'am."

"Even more envious?" Lottie raised her brows. "I see little to be envious of in my situation."

"No, ma'am," Margery said, "but Miss Goodlake

of Letcombe Regis—she's the daughter of the Justice of the Peace, ma'am—well, she wanted to marry Lord St. Severin before you came along. Proper put out she was to discover he was setting up a mistress."

"Well, she can still marry him," Lottie said. "A mistress need not interfere with the taking of a wife. Indeed in some circles the two work closely together so that neither has to endure too much of the husband's company."

"That sounds like London talk to me, ma'am," Margery said incontrovertibly. "All clever words and no morals."

Lottie smiled to be so neatly put in her place by her new maid. "Yes, well it is," she conceded. "But in any language, I doubt that Lord St. Severin is the marrying kind. And anyway, I thought that he was vastly disapproved of? Is he not the Enemy?"

"Oh, he is, ma'am, in a general way," Margery nodded. "But he is also rich and titled and handsome, and all the ladies have a *tendre* for him. And the officers are gentlemen, after all, and dine with the best families in the neighborhood and the war cannot last forever, can it, ma'am?"

"An admirably practical approach," Lottie said, "by which the gentry of Wantage can enjoy some new society and catch rich husbands for their daughters. What is the small matter of a war between friends, after all?"

She rested her chin on her hand. She was beginning to see how it would be now. Ethan would be out dining with the local gentry—as a rather dashing and dangerous character he was a positive addition to slow country society—whilst she would sit here alone because she was a fallen woman and no one would take her money, let alone speak to her. Society in the provinces was very much like society in London, only more narrow-minded. Lottie thought of Lady O'Hara administering the cut direct to her when they passed in the street in London and knew that the malice of a small country town would be even more concentrated and poisonous. In Wantage one could not be anonymous and melt into the crowds for there were none. There would be no escape and nowhere to hide.

Ethan had brought her here but he could not protect her. He probably saw no need to do so. After all, she was Lottie Palliser, brazen and worldly. And if that were merely a defense, a facade she hid behind, then it was a facade she would need every day of her time here in Wantage. She had to protect herself not only from the small town disapproval of her new neighbors but also from her stubborn desire to ask more of Ethan than he was prepared to give. She knew how undemanding the perfect mistress had to be.

She thought of her brother, Theo, and the commission he had placed on her to spy on Ethan for the good of her country. She tried to think of Ethan's callous usage of her as justification for her betrayal of him, but still it was unexpectedly difficult for her to excuse, even with her rather flexible sense of morality. Theo's last note, left at her lodging on the morning she had quit London, burned a hole in her conscience if not her pocket. She had sewn it into her cloak lining be-cause that was the sort of thing she imagined spies and conspirators did. Unfortunately her sewing was so wayward that the lumpy stitches would soon give away the fact that something was hidden there should anyone be suspicious. There was little incriminating in the note anyway. It was merely a contact address for her to send any information, a post office situated in the town of Abingdon some ten miles away. Theo wrote that he would keep in contact, and Lottie clung to this small flame of comfort and tried not to let the disillusionment creep in, tried to block her ears to the little voice that whispered that her brother was only staying close to her because he wanted something from her and if she did not prove useful he would discard her.

She got to her feet and picked up the first portmanteau, dragging it up the stairs. She could hardly ask Margery to move such heavy luggage. The poor child looked as though a breath of wind would knock her over. She needed feeding up. Looking down at her own generous curves Lottie made a mental resolution to make sure there would always be some spare food for poor Margery to take home to her family. If her brothers were out of work they might all be depending on her wages in order to survive. Lottie knew—none better—how frightening it was to be so close to the edge of despair.

She wondered if Ethan would return later to dine with her and share her bed. She knew she had to please him, to be the mistress he desired. She had to try to please Theo, too, and pass him any useful information that came her way. She felt chilled when she thought of the price of failure. She was trapped, pulled between an unexpected loyalty to Ethan and a desperate need for self-preservation. In the end she had been used again. It was the only life she knew.

CHAPTER NINE

"THERE IS A DISTURBANCE in the marketplace," Jacques Le Prevost said to Ethan as he slid into the booth beside him in The Falcon and Globe, Wantage's roughest and dirtiest inn. "I thought that you should know." He looked around the slatternly taproom. "*Mon dieu,* you choose low company, my friend. Is this not the place where a woman was murdered a few years ago and they made the crime into a freak show to entertain the visitors?"

"She probably complained about the quality of the brandy," Ethan said, gesturing to his glass. "That really is a crime." He shrugged. "A disturbance, you say? Not the junior officers having a mill with the townsfolk and canal workers again? Have they not learned to bite their tongues or lose their allowances?"

He did not really wish to be troubled by the ongoing warfare between the younger officers and some of the rougher elements of the town. The apprentices and mill workers had an ancient and rabid hatred of the French and it frequently spilled over into quarrels and occasionally into outright violence. Then there were the navvies who worked on the canals, tough men with a swagger in their step and money in their pocket. It did not pay to get on the wrong side of them, either.

Generally, though, the different groups all managed

to rub along tolerably well, for the prisoners spent a vast amount of their allowance in the town—there was little else to do—and the town was suitably grateful. In some cases the French prisoners also offered tutoring in music and dancing and languages to the socially ambitious daughters of gentry families. And the rich, well-connected senior officers like Le Prevost and Ethan himself were always welcome in the higher echelons of county society. Sometimes, Ethan thought cynically, when one was dining on the lawn with the Earl of Craven or Sir Roger Goodlake, it was easy to forget that there was a war on. Except that he never forgot.

"The boys are young and hotheaded," Le Prevost said philosophically, "and so are the youths of this town. It was ever thus. But no, that is not the problem this time."

"What then?" Ethan asked. He wondered whether to purchase another brandy. He did not really wish to. He had barely touched the first one because the spirit was too rough and too sharp. He knew he should be working on the next, delicate stages of the escape plan. Matters were reaching a critical point where he had to draw together all the threads. He had messengers out across the country, bringing together dates, times, details. A mass uprising of prisoners was an enormous task requiring endless planning and vast resources of money. He could afford no mistakes.

And yet at this moment when he most needed to focus on his strategy, he was distracted by thoughts of Lottie, which was ironic, he thought, since his plan had been to bring her to Wantage to distract everyone else, and leave him free to concentrate.

He knew he had treated Lottie badly that morning. Not only had he used her to create a scandal, he had taken her with scant consideration for either her feelings or her response. Ethan was not accustomed to reproaching himself for his actions. Regrets had always seemed pointless to him, a demonstration of weakness. But when it came to Lottie nothing seemed that simple and he did not understand why.

"It is your *chère amie*," Le Prevost said now. "*Madame* Palliser. It seems she wishes to go shopping but many of the stallholders do not want to take her money. A few moments ago it looked as though there might be a riot in the marketplace." He smiled. "She is determined, that one. Most women would have backed down and slunk ignominiously away. But not *Madame* Palliser. She is courageous."

"You mean she is foolhardy." Ethan felt a pang of apprehension. He put his glass down with a snap and got to his feet. "Why could she not send the maid and avoid a confrontation?" he demanded.

Le Prevost looked at him with pity. "Why do you think? Because she has pride, *mon brave*. She will not accept such shabby treatment. You, of all people, should understand that."

Le Prevost had a point, Ethan thought, as he grabbed his jacket and set off down Grove Street toward the market. He had run away from home at the age of fifteen because he was sick of the slights and the insults habitually handed out to him as the Duke of Farne's bastard child. He had never accepted that he was less worthy than his siblings simply through an accident of birth. So why should he expect Lottie quietly to accept the treatment meted out to her? Admiration and exasperation warred within him, his fear for her razor sharp now.

Grove Lane opened into the marketplace at the western end, opposite The Bear Coaching Inn and Hotel. Ethan was shocked to see a crowd gathered, far greater than any normally seen on market day. Gentlemen loitered, ladies hung at the back of the crowd wanting to exercise their curiosity without seeming ill-bred. Apprentices and ragged children, with a scent for trouble, were pushing to the front to join in whatever strife was brewing.

Ethan quickened his pace, pushing through the crowd. Anxiety gripped him by the throat. Whilst he had wanted Lottie's arrival in Wantage to create a stir, having an angry mob pelt her with rotten vegetables had not been part of the plan at all. He had not anticipated such outright hostility. Gossip and commotion, yes—a public lynching, no. This, he thought, was largely his fault. He had brought Lottie here, deliberately exposed her to scandal in order to create talk and then left her to deal with it all on her own. Remorse gripped him hard and he forced a way through the crowd, suddenly desperate to reach her. He had nothing other than his fists to protect her with. The prisoners were not allowed to carry arms for obvious reasons. Glancing around, he sensed that the mood of the crowd was volatile, not wholly ugly but on a knife-edge. He knew it could turn in a moment. He had seen it happen. Beside him he could feel Le Prevost stiff with the same tension

that ran through his veins. Between them they could
probably deal with at least half the men in the crowd—
bare-knuckle boxing was not exactly his favored sport
but he knew the principles well enough. However, that
would end with he and Le Prevost clapped in gaol and
probably on their way back to one of the prison ships,
which did not suit his plans at all.

Ethan reached the front of the crowd and saw Lottie
standing by a trestle laden with fresh fruit and vegetables. She looked both respectable and exceedingly
pretty. She was wearing a green-and-white dress that
was fresh and bright with a green spencer over the top
and a smaller straw bonnet than the one she had arrived in. She could have been any wife out doing the
marketing. A small girl in maid's uniform was standing
beside her holding a basket and looking scared. The
stallholder, a big man with high color and a mean look
in his eye had his arms folded tight across his chest and
was evidently refusing to serve them.

Ethan stepped forward. He felt an extraordinary urge
to protect Lottie, who looked so vulnerable and defiant
in the face of such outright hostility.

"Lottie," he said, taking her arm and trying to draw
her behind him, trying to shield her from both the hostile gaze of the crowd and the potential danger of flying
objects, "this is foolish. Come away and let the maid
do your shopping for you—"

"I will thank you not to intervene, my lord." Lottie's
tone was fierce. Her look warned him not to interfere.
She shook his hand off her arm and deliberately stepped
out from behind him. "This gentleman—" she indicated
the stallholder "—and I were having a conversation."

"You are about to cause a riot," Ethan said tightly. Could she not see the danger she was in? Could she not accept his protection?

"Well—" Lottie shot him another glare "—that was what you wanted, was it not? To cause a stir?" She turned to Jacques Le Prevost. "*M'sieur* Le Prevost," she said, "may I trouble you to lend me a shilling?"

"Of course, *madame*." Le Prevost stepped forward. He presented the money to Lottie with a bow. The exaggerated chivalry of the gesture made some in the crowd smile. Ethan could feel the tension easing very slightly though the mood of the crowd was still unpredictable.

Lottie took the proffered coin with a word of thanks and turned back to the grocer.

"Do you observe any difference between these two coins?" she asked the man sweetly, holding up two shillings, one in each hand. The stallholder looked at her suspiciously and then grunted a negative.

"They are identical," Lottie said. "Of equal value. And yet—" she smiled "—you will accept the one and not the other. Do you see my point?"

The crowd was silent.

"I think," Ethan said, trying not to smile, "that you may be attempting to explain too complicated a philosophy."

"I am explaining some simple economics," Lottie corrected. "My shilling is worth…a shilling."

"It's not your shilling," someone in the crowd shouted. They pointed at Ethan. "He's the one paying you!"

"And I assure you that I earn every penny," Lottie

said. The appeal to the bawdy humor of the crowd seemed to work. A ripple of amusement ran along its ranks.

"We know!" Someone else shouted from the back. "We *saw* you earn it!"

This time the laughter was louder still.

Lottie tossed her shilling in the air and there was a scramble as a couple of ragged children rushed forward to grab it. "Some," Lottie observed, "are not slow to see the value of my money."

The crowd was smiling now, the mood turning. The stallholder sensed it. His frown deepened. Lottie turned back to him. "So all I have left is this coin that is not mine. Will you take it in return for the fruit and vegetables I requested?"

"I'll not take anything from the likes of you," the man muttered.

"For shame, Sam Jones!" someone shouted. "Pretending to be so righteous when you're no saint yourself! Who was that woman we all saw you with in The Horseshoe last week? Not your wife, and that's for sure!"

This time the whole throng erupted into mirth and the stallholder rounded angrily on the heckler. A thin woman pushed through to the front and caught Lottie's sleeve.

"I'll serve you, ma'am," she said. She shot Jones a look. "Men can be such hypocrites. My vegetables are fresher than his, too, and I won't try to cheat you on weight. This way, ma'am."

"Thank you," Lottie said, smiling as though the

sun had burst through the clouds. "Thank you very much."

Ethan released the breath he had been holding and felt the tension slide from his shoulders. He could see that Lottie was relieved, too. For a moment her mask slipped and he saw the look in her eyes. For all her bravado, she had been afraid; afraid of humiliation, afraid of being shamed in public again. Her hands, he saw, were shaking. She saw him watching and folded them tightly together, turning away from him, the tilt of her head defiant. Nothing could have indicated more clearly her independence and her rejection of his efforts to defend her.

Ethan felt something cold and hard twist inside him. He knew he was a scoundrel to inflict this notoriety on Lottie for his own gain. When he had made his plans, Lottie's feelings had not come into his calculations once. He was paying her, after all; he had a right to demand whatever he wanted from her in return. Yet now, seeing her bright gallantry in the face of the hostile crowd, he felt remorse and regret, bitter and sharp. To use Lottie like this suddenly seemed shabby and dishonorable.

He shifted, trying to shake off the feeling. He had his plans to fulfill, a clear, cold strategy that allowed for no sentiment. He could not falter now. Nothing must come between him and his scheme to free his son and all the other men locked in the hell of the British prisons.

"*Mon Dieu,*" Le Prevost said in his ear, "that was a close run thing. *Madame,* she takes some risks but she is clever. I like her style."

The crowd was dispersing now, returning to their

shopping, murmuring amongst themselves over this latest piece of entertainment. In a town with no theater, Ethan thought, Lottie's arrival was proving as good as a play. The idea should have amused him. Instead he felt protective and oddly unsettled by the whole experience. He looked around for Lottie and saw that she had moved away to another stall, where she was choosing fresh fruit, strawberries that smelled sweet and were jewel bright, plums that were a deep velvety purple.

"Thank you," she was saying to the vendor, "I do not need any apples for we grow them in our own orchards. May I try the apricots?" She laughed as the juice ran over her chin and wiped it away with sticky fingers. Ethan could sense her heady relief. Her eyes were vivid and her cheeks bright pink with the release of tension. "Oh, those are delicious!" she exclaimed. "I will take a half dozen."

Her easy charm was drawing everyone to her. In the space of ten minutes, Ethan thought, they appeared to be eating from her hand. Some other stallholders pressed forward now with produce for Lottie to try. She was haggling good-humoredly over the prices, laughing with them, the maid's basket now weighed down with fresh bread, fruit, vegetables and meat. Suddenly it seemed that Lottie's money was in great demand after all.

"You were splendid," Ethan said, falling into step beside her as she and Margery finally finished all their marketing and, scattering thanks and smiles on the stallholders, Lottie turned for home.

She smiled coolly at him. "Thank you, my lord," she said. Her tone was formal and the smile did not reach her eyes. For a moment her dark gaze searched his face and Ethan felt a disturbing stir of emotion, as though she was seeing far more than he wanted her to see, more than he understood himself.

"Why did you seek to protect me?" she asked. "That was not part of our arrangement."

"Nor was it part of the agreement that you would be lynched in the street," Ethan said, a little grimly.

"I did not think you would care," Lottie said. "Money for scandal was what you wanted." She gave a quick shrug. "They could have put me in the stocks, could they not? Shown their disapproval for my appalling morals with their rotten vegetables. That would have set the town about the ears—"

Ethan caught her arm. He had seen the sheen of tears in her eyes and heard the quiver in her voice. She was trembling still. He drew her close. She felt so vulnerable in his arms, small and defenseless, and yet he had seen the strength and courage with which she had faced the crowd.

"Hush," he said, pressing his lips to her hair. "I would not have let that happen."

She wrenched herself away from him. With a shock he saw that the tears in her eyes were of anger not fear.

"How singular of you," she said scathingly. "How singular of you to wish to defend me when surely you seduced me in full public view this morning in order to provoke outrage?" She turned away. Her tone flattened, the anger draining from it. "We should not forget that our association is only business," she added. "Your money in return for my notoriety. Surely you recall that was our agreement?"

She started walking but Ethan caught her arm again to stop her. Margery, sensing the palpable antagonism between them, cast one frightened glance from Ethan's face to Lottie's and scuttled past them, away down the footpath.

"You are angry with me," Ethan said evenly.

"Why should I be angry?" Lottie maintained a clipped, cool tone. Her profile, still turned away from him, was charming, ruffled and pink with annoyance. Ethan felt a sudden violent urge to untie the bonnet ribbons and throw it aside, grab her and kiss her until he had wrenched a response from her that was neither cool nor unemotional. He wanted to kiss her until she was breathless and flushed and tousled in his arms just as she had been before.

"You are angry because this morning I treated you badly," he said. He kept his voice low, very aware of Margery, scurrying away as fast as her legs could carry her. "I apologize," he said. "It was very wrong of me to use you as I did."

Lottie bit her lip. "You pay my bills," she said. "You are entitled to behave as you please."

"That is nonsense," Ethan said. "You do not believe that and neither do I." He was surprised at how angry he was starting to feel. He could scarcely deny that he had told Lottie theirs was no more than a business agreement. Those had been his precise words to her in London. And as recently as that morning he had thought he wanted their relationship to be that simple, wanted no more than an emotionless arrangement with

her, sex and scandal in return for his cash. Use her, pay
her and discard her. That was the way he had planned
it. It should have been straightforward. Yet it was not.
The notion of a business arrangement repelled him now.
And if he were honest, he had wanted more than that
from her from the very start.

"How you feel is important," he said. "Do not pretend otherwise."

"How I feel is of no consequence," Lottie corrected.
She was striving to sound indifferent but there was a
spark of pure, hot temper in the look she gave him. "A
complaisant mistress does as she is told, as she is paid
to do. A complaisant mistress would never reproach
you, no matter how you used her."

"I don't *want* a complaisant mistress," Ethan ground
out. He was aware of feeling immensely frustrated and
immensely aroused, both at the same time, and equally
unable to explain either reaction.

"No?" Lottie challenged. She spun around on him.
"Then what *do* you want, Ethan?"

For one long, furious moment they stared at one
another, dark eyes locked with blue and then Ethan
swore, pulled on Lottie's bonnet ribbons, cast the hat
aside and kissed her hard. Lottie gave a little muffled
squeak. Ethan backed her up against the wall of the
passageway and kissed her again, his mouth gentling
on hers this time, wooing a response rather than demanding one. He felt Lottie's lips soften against his as
she yielded to him and a hot, sweet tide swept through
him. This was what he wanted; Lottie Palliser in his
arms and in his bed for as long as he needed her.

He deepened the kiss until they were both breathless,

running his hands into her hair, holding her face up to his as he ravished her mouth with his own. His body instantly hardened. Once again, as in London, he felt the profound need he had for her sweep through him like a tide washing into all the dark corners of his soul. It was inescapable, all consuming.

"What I want," he said, as his lips left hers, "is you, Lottie Palliser."

For a moment her gaze searched his face again and he could not read what she was thinking. Then she sighed. "For an apology, that lacked contrition," she said, "but I will accept it." She shook her head. "Damn you, Ethan. I tried to be accommodating and obedient." She said the word as though it had a bad taste. "I tried very hard. But you *will* provoke me."

Ethan reached for her bonnet and tied it haphazardly under her chin. He dropped another kiss on her lips. Her mouth was soft and full, clinging to his. She raised her hands to his forearms and held him gently, leaning into him this time. Ethan could feel the whole length of her body pressed against his and his desire for her tightened like a ratchet, inexorable need possessing him.

"Just so we are clear," he said, "I do not want a meek mistress." His tone was a little rough. "I want you just as you are, Lottie." He kissed her again, unable to resist, feeling his blood heat and quicken. "Be open with me," he said, against her lips. "If I anger you, tell me. Be honest. Don't pretend."

He felt her lips curve into a smile. "Very well," she whispered. "Then I must be honest and confess that there is something I want from you now."

Ethan released her and looked into her eyes and saw the flagrant invitation there. The lust within him was so sharp now that he ached with it.

"You are the most perfect mistress, Lottie," he said. "Never doubt it." He put his hands on her shoulders. "Did I tell you how beautiful you look in that gown?" he continued. "Like the most respectable housewife out to do her marketing?"

"False pretenses." Lottie's smile was warm and wicked now, her eyes knowing, tightening his desire notch by notch. She knew he wanted her and it pleased her to be desired. Ethan could see the triumph in her eyes. She ran her tongue over her lower lip and he almost groaned aloud. She was playing him now, toying with his responses, and he was more than willing. She was his weakness but for now he really did not care.

"Do you want to strip my charming gown off me and make love to me like the Cyprian I am?" she asked lightly. "I thought the idea might appeal to you."

Ethan's breath caught. The dimensions of his world seemed to have narrowed to Lottie and his driving need to remove all her clothes and plunder her lush, curvy body beneath his until he had had his fill. He could not understand her power over him, nor did he like to lack so much control, but he could not fight it, did not wish to.

"Your gown does arouse me," he rasped. "It is so very modest."

"Unlike its wearer," Lottie said, "who is, I fear, so very brazen."

Ethan grabbed her hand and pulled her the remaining hundred yards down the street, crashing through

the door of Priory Cottage and letting it bang shut
behind him, catching a fleeting glimpse of Margery's
shocked face as she dived for the safety of the kitchen.
He started to kiss Lottie again with feverish intensity,
overwhelmed by the taste and the touch of her, of the
sensation of her skin against his fingers and his mouth.
He felt drunk with need, desperate, while she laughed
at his haste and his clumsiness. He picked her up and
carried her up the stairs to the pretty bedroom beneath
the eaves, which he had made sure was furnished with
an enormous four-poster bed. At this moment, feeling
as he did, he could only congratulate himself on his
forward planning. Here at last he could strip the elegant
green-and-white gown from Lottie's opulent curves and
bury himself inside her. Even as he did so, even as he
felt the pleasure cascade through him and burn through
to his soul, he knew that he was lost in some way that
he did not understand, did not *want* to understand and
could never analyze, for in doing so he would be finally
undone.

CHAPTER TEN

LOTTIE HAD HIRED a coach from the livery stables in Back Street to take her all of the two hundred yards to The Bear Hotel that night to dine with Ethan and the other French officers. It was the best carriage that the stables had to offer. Admittedly they did not have an enormous choice, but it met Lottie's exacting standards of quality. Ethan had no idea how expensive she was going to be, she thought, as the footman held open the door and she ascended the steps. One simply had to arrive in style even in a little backwater like Wantage. She was amused to see, however, that the livery owner, evidently having heard of her reputation, had sent what appeared to be the oldest coachman in the world, a man who could have passed for her grandfather, and a footman who looked barely a day younger.

The hotel was quiet and she was led to a private dining room on the first floor. The only occupants were Ethan and his fellow officers, resplendent in their blue uniforms. Lottie had never seen Ethan in his hussars' uniform before and the deep navy blue with striking splash of red at the shoulder almost stole her breath. He had the broadness of chest and thigh to carry it off, she thought, unlike some of his comrades whose spindly little legs looked rather like frogs in their clinging buckskins.

"Dear me," she said lightly, as she approached Ethan and his colleagues, "you are a sight to raise certain emotions in the British, gentlemen. A strong patriotic dislike on the part of the men, I imagine, and something rather different in the ladies."

As Lottie had swept in, the officers had fallen silent, then they rose to their feet with remarkable alacrity and a fine show of respect. Everyone vied to bow to her, kiss her hand, find her a place at the table. Lottie's lips twitched.

"Never have I entered a room to such a rapturous welcome," she said dryly, "or at least not since I was about eighteen years old. You quite turn my head."

She felt a certain self-satisfaction that their response was not entirely feigned in order to please Ethan. She had dressed with care that night in a gown of vivid midnight-blue that complemented Ethan's uniform perfectly. It was an elegant gown and yet somehow not quite suitable for a respectable matron. The décolletage was modestly low and edged with sheer transparent lace that lay over her skin like a caress. The silk skirts rustled sinuously about her ankles. Her hair was swept up into a sapphire clasp leaving the nape of her neck exposed but for one curl that fell over her shoulders to nestle between her breasts. The good people of Wantage would be hard-pressed to explain just why this latest outfit was not quite decent, she thought, but it would make them hot under the collar, nevertheless. Indeed, the eyes of a couple of the younger officers were almost popping from their heads and one or two surreptitiously ran their fingers around the inside of their collars as though they were suddenly too tight.

Ethan introduced her individually to his colleagues. Le Prevost she knew already, of course, and there was another face at the table she recognized. Captain Owen Purchase, late of the ship the *Sea Witch,* came forward to greet her with his familiar laconic grace.

"Captain Purchase!" Lottie stood on tiptoe to kiss his cheek, lingering over the embrace a little longer than was strictly necessary, watching Ethan's reaction out of the corner of her eye. Owen Purchase, she thought, was as handsome as ever. She had known him before her divorce and would not have been averse to a dalliance with him in those long-ago days. It had not happened, for Purchase had had eyes for no one but her friend Joanna Grant.

Ethan was watching her with his mocking blue gaze. Lottie knew he was too cool to be thrown out of countenance if she flirted with another man. Nor would he be jealous even if Purchase had indeed been her lover. She had seen that in London, in Ethan's reaction to James Devlin. He was too confident of himself, too self-assured, to be threatened by anyone. She felt a tiny stirring of chagrin that she could not seem to arouse any possessiveness in him.

There was a glint of wicked amusement in Owen Purchase's eyes as he released her and stepped back. "I hesitate to plead a prior acquaintance with you, ma'am, in case St. Severin calls me out," he said in his rich Southern drawl, casting Ethan a droll sideways look, "but it is a pleasure to see you again."

"You, too, Captain Purchase," Lottie said, smiling, "although I believe your much-vaunted good luck must have failed you if I am to find you here in this company of miscreants."

"You are not mistaken, ma'am," Purchase said ruefully, drawing out a chair for her to sit beside him. "I was captured on my first engagement. Dashed poor seamanship."

"What Purchase does not tell you," Ethan put in, "is that he took out two British frigates before they dismasted his ship, and then only with a lucky shot."

"But surely you fought *with* the British against the French at Trafalgar?" Lottie said, accepting with a smile the glass of wine that a blushing younger officer was offering her. "Why did you change sides?"

"I wasn't fighting for the *French*, ma'am," Purchase said, scowling at Le Prevost as he raised a mocking glass in tribute. "I may be an adventurer but I do have some principles. No, I was fighting for the Yankees off New York against Brooke's British squadron." He rubbed the back of his neck. "The Brits have become too arrogant at sea, ma'am, and I don't care who hears me say it. We Americans don't like them telling us whom we can and cannot trade with, or pressing our citizens into their Navy."

"So as a result you end up here rubbing shoulders with the French," Lottie said. "And the Irish," she added, looking at Ethan.

"A good job we're all gentlemen," Purchase said, smiling sardonically, "or I'd be having one hell of a time."

"There's a Danish sea captain on parole in Tiverton," Ethan said. "A famous privateer. All nations unite against the British these days."

"Does no one like us very much?" Lottie asked, a little plaintively. Politics had never been a passion of hers but she was beginning to feel like an oppressed minority. She was also remembering Theo's instructions to gather what intelligence she could. It was decidedly difficult when she had no grasp of the issues involved and even less interest. Really, she thought crossly, Theo should have thought of that before he gave her such an impossible task.

"No, ma'am," Purchase said gravely, "no one likes the Brits very much, but we will make an exception for you tonight."

The officers fell to talking about the current state of the war and Lottie tried to listen even though it sounded both complicated and boring. It also sounded as though the French were losing, though Le Prevost contended hotly that that was simply the bias of the British newspapers.

"Since we receive the London papers about three days late, it will all be over before we hear," Purchase commented dryly.

Lottie looked up to see Ethan's gaze resting on her with amusement. There was something in his eyes that made her feel hot and guilty. It was not as though she had even done anything to betray him, she thought. Not yet. She had intended to write to Theo that very afternoon but Ethan had kept her in bed for several hours and after that she had needed to bathe and wash her hair and dress and prepare herself for this evening. That had taken her another three hours so there was no time for any spying, which was a good job as she had precisely nothing to report to her brother.

She cast Ethan another glance under her lashes. She had been so angry with him that morning and in the end so incapable of hiding it. For so long she had tried to be what people demanded of her: the good child, the trophy wife, the obedient sister, the conformable mistress. Perhaps it might not have mattered had she liked Ethan less—she could have pretended to be whatever he wanted—but though she struggled with her feelings she could not help herself. She wanted his respect even if she could not have his love. Yet she was prepared to betray him to the British authorities. She knew she was a hypocrite and she hated herself for it.

As she picked over a dish of frogs' legs sautéed in butter—utterly revolting but added to the menu at The Bear in tribute to their French guests—Lottie struggled with her feelings of guilt. It should have been easy to inform on Ethan, she thought. Theo was offering her everything that she had lost, or as much of it as she would ever be able to recover—money, a home, the chance to regain a place in society. She ached for that, ached to escape the trap into which she had fallen. In contrast, Ethan offered her nothing but a temporary place in his bed. He promised nothing and she owed him nothing. There was lust between them but little else, no trust and no honesty. That morning when they had quarreled Ethan had told her that he wanted her to be open with him, but of course she could not be, not with Theo's commission hanging on her conscience like a lead weight.

And yet despite the fact that she knew their association would be over in a few weeks, a couple of months at the most, it still felt damnably difficult to play Ethan false, and she did not understand why. Nor did she like the guilt and the strange feeling of loneliness her duplicity brought with it.

Ethan smiled at her and raised his glass in silent toast, and Lottie felt herself go as scarlet as a debutante swept off her feet by a handsome suitor. Her heart skipped a beat. She smiled at Ethan, saw the heat and the promise in his eyes and felt a little breathless. Gracious, she was degenerating into a green girl at the mercy of her feelings. If she were not careful she might regress to being a virgin.

"Miss Palliser does not care for political or military talk," Ethan drawled, "so let us not bore her with our usual conversation tonight, gentlemen."

"Lud, I do not mind!" Lottie said hastily. "If you wish to discuss gun emplacements or cavalry formations, pray do not let my presence inhibit you."

"We would not dream of it, my love," Ethan said, the laughter deepening in his eyes. "You must forgive us. We have little society or entertainment here and so tend to fall back on politics for our discussions."

"Speaking of entertainment," Le Prevost put in, "perhaps *madame* would like to join us for our morning *sortie?*" He turned to Lottie. "We ride the boundaries of the town each morning, *madame,* at eight of the clock. It helps to force us from our beds and maintains some sort of discipline, though it is frustrating in the extreme not to be permitted to go beyond a mile of the town without breaking our parole." He glanced at Ethan. "I imagine St. Severin will have some trouble in joining us early now."

Lottie laughed. "I do not imagine Lord St. Severin the type to lie late abed."

"Not as yet, perhaps," Le Prevost said, smiling at her, "but he has a greater incentive to stay with you than he ever had to ride out with us." He took her hand. "Who would not choose to lavish his time and attention on a beautiful woman in preference to his colleagues?"

"Jacques," Ethan said, sounding resigned, "if you wish to try to seduce Miss Palliser pray have the grace not to do so beneath my very nose."

Le Prevost shrugged fatalistically. "They say that all is fair in love and war, my friend." He kissed the back of Lottie's gloved hand. "I am richer than St. Severin, *madame,*" he added provocatively. "Think about it."

"Alas, *m'sieur,* I am not in the market for a protector," Lottie said, smiling demurely, "but I shall keep your generous offer in mind."

The arrival of a rather tough fowl interrupted the conversation at that point. It was obvious that the staff of The Bear, and in particular the pretty maidservants, were absolutely charmed to have such a group of handsome, well-mannered and extremely wealthy officers billeted on them, regardless of their nationality.

Lottie chatted to Lieutenants Marais and Duvois, both of whom were so young they looked to be barely shaving. They were so attentive to her and seemed so struck by her charm, beauty and conversation that Lottie wryly concluded that they must believe that the way to Ethan's approval was through flattering his mistress. Certainly he seemed something of a hero to them.

"You should have seen the charge Lord St. Severin led at Fuentes de Onoro, ma'am," Marais said. "Such daring and consummate horsemanship! If I had a quarter of his skill I would be a happy man!"

"It cannot have been so very marvelous," Lottie pointed out, "since Lord St. Severin was captured an hour later."

Marais spluttered into his wine. "Only because Colonel Benoit was a fool and lost the advantage St. Severin had gained—"

"It wasn't Benoit's fault," Duvois put in hotly. "He was under pressure on his left flank…" And they fell to re-enacting the battle with the salt bowl and pepper cellar as props.

"Are you still enjoying the military chat, my love?" Ethan enquired, leaning forward to fill Lottie's wineglass. "In truth that was why we lost," he added dryly, lowering his voice. "Because no one could agree on tactics."

"It must be very tedious for you all sitting here discussing old battles," Lottie said. "Does no one ever break parole in order to return to the fray?"

"It is the responsibility of every gentleman to try to escape," Marais piped up.

"You are a fine one to talk," Duvois said. "You did not even get as far as the coast and ended in the prison hulks for your pains."

"Better to have tried and failed," Marais said huffily, "than to have sat here on my derriere for the past six months doing nothing!"

"What do you think, Colonel Le Prevost?" Lottie asked. The senior officers, she noted, had been silent on the subject whilst the younger ones squabbled amongst themselves. Owen Purchase was toying with his wineglass, tilting the liquid so that it caught the candlelight. His expression was pensive. Ethan sat back in his chair, long and lean, ostensibly at ease, but Lottie sensed some tension in him. She wondered if he was thinking of Arland. She had heard of breakouts from the prisons but they were rare; the British authorities ruled the gaols with a rod of iron.

"*Madame,* I try not to think of anything as strenuous as escaping," Le Prevost said easily, smiling at her. "*Enfin,* it would disturb the set of my coat."

"For shame, Le Prevost," Purchase said, laughing. "You fought strenuously enough at Marengo by all accounts!"

"I cannot deny it," Le Prevost said, shrugging, "but now I have lost my hunger for bloodshed. I am comfortable enough here."

There was a murmur of dissent around the table. Lottie watched Ethan lean back and take a long drink of his wine. He did not say a word. And then his eyes met hers and there was something quizzical in the deep blue of his gaze and she was certain—absolutely sure—that he knew exactly what she was up to.

"Ah, well…" She gave a little shrug of her own. "It seems that my time here will not be enlivened by any attempts at escape. A pity—it might have been amusing."

She turned an ostentatious shoulder to Ethan— anything to block out his too-perceptive gaze—and started to talk with Captain Le Grand, a thin, dyspeptic elderly man who had the entrée to all the local houses in his role as dancing tutor.

"The young ladies are eager to learn," he confided

in Lottie, "but the young men! Pah! Two left feet and no talent." He threw up his hands. "The parents blame me but truly these boys were born with no sense of rhythm!"

"I'm afraid it was ever thus," Lottie said sympathetically. "I remember having my feet stepped all over when I was a debutante at Almack's. I thought I would not walk for a week."

The fowl was followed by the pudding course, a thick potato dessert with wine sauce. It was dense and sugary, like a spiced curd tart, not unpleasant but extremely heavy on the stomach.

"Dear me," Lottie said staring, "Wantage truly is still in the last century. I haven't eaten potato pudding since I was a child!"

She turned to speak to the officer on her left, a thin quiet youth called Paul Santier, who had taken no part in the conversation and was easily the youngest and most junior soldier present. He was shy and evidently terrified of her, but gradually she drew him out until he was telling her that he wrote the theatrical entertainments with which some of the officers passed their time. He composed the words and music, Le Grand arranged the dances and they had already put on one performance for the people of Wantage, which had been very well received. He lost his self-consciousness when Lottie spoke to him in French, and soon she was hearing all about his widowed mother, his two young sisters, their farm in Brittany and their pride that their son and brother had fought for his country.

Lottie, who several years before would have deplored

the role of confidante to a youth barely out of short trousers, tried not to yawn and to appear sympathetic.

The pudding was taken out and the port came in.

"You will forgive me if I do not withdraw, gentlemen," Lottie said. "Since there are no other ladies with whom to take tea, and since I have always enjoyed a glass of port, I shall pretend to be a man for the purposes of this course."

It seemed that her presence did not inhibit the officers in any way, for they enthusiastically passed her the decanter, sat back in their chairs and allowed the drink to flow. The port was followed by a poor quality brandy, about which there were many complaints. The conversation became broader and rather more scurrilous. One of the maidservants came in and sat on Duvois's lap and another next to Marais with her hand on his thigh. Santier looked terrified, Le Grand scandalized.

"Time for me to leave, I think," Lottie said, as Marais's doxy started to kiss and fondle him. "After all, I am a far better class of courtesan than these. I am surprised that the proprietor of The Bear allows such license in his hotel," she added as Ethan escorted her down The Bear's grand staircase and out to the carriage. "This is supposed to be a respectable house."

"As always, money talks louder than disapproving voices," Ethan said. He handed her into the coach then joined her. "Despite the willingness of some of the maids," he added, "there is not one of my colleagues who does not envy me now."

"Apart from Monsieur Le Grand, perhaps," Lottie said. "He thinks you all depraved. And poor little Lieutenant Santier," she added. "He would be terrified if a woman tried to kiss him!"

"You were very kind to young Santier," Ethan said.

"Kind!" Lottie said, revolted. "I am not kind!"

"I do believe," Ethan continued, a spark of humor in his eyes, "that he sees you quite as a motherly figure."

"A mother!" Lottie exclaimed. "Have you given up all attempts to flatter me, my lord?"

Ethan laughed. He took her hand and stripped off the glove, kissing her palm. "You know that you relish the role really," he murmured, his lips against her skin.

"I do not!" Lottie's hand tingled at his touch. She tried to sound outraged. "I assure you that you misjudge me, my lord," she said. "I am the least kind person in the world and have *no* desire to be anyone's mother!"

Ethan kept hold of her hand, toying with the fingers. "Very well," he said. "I accept your protestations as sincere." His voice changed. "You looked very beautiful tonight, Lottie. Everyone was dazzled."

"Thank you," Lottie said, mollified. She had known that Ethan was teasing her over Santier but at the back of her mind was the lowering thought that she *was* almost old enough to be the lieutenant's mother. She remembered Mrs. Tong's barbed comments on her encroaching age and shivered deep inside. Ethan might have no complaints of her as a mistress but it was not a secure career for a woman of her years. There was nothing more pitiful than a raddled old harlot and she was damned if she would sink that low. It was far more sensible to ensure a respectable future by working to help Theo.

Betrayal…

She repressed another shiver.

"Do you think it likely you will wish to ride out with us in the mornings?" Ethan asked. He was watching her, his face in shadow. "If so I will bespeak a mare for you from the livery stables."

"I should like it extremely, my lord," Lottie said, trying to shake off the blue devils. She made her voice light, unconcerned. "There is but one difficulty. I would have to rise from my bed at some intolerably early hour of the morning in order to join you and I fear that will be quite out of the question."

Ethan smiled. Her heart skipped a little beat at the warmth in it. "You could try," he said.

"Impossible," Lottie said. "There speaks a man who has *no* understanding of the complexities of the female condition!"

"Very well," Ethan said. "You do ride, though?"

"Indifferently, badly," Lottie said. "I last rode in Spitsbergen. That," she added, glancing at him, "was the expedition on which I met Captain Purchase."

There was the tiniest breath of a pause.

"Ah," Ethan said. "I wondered."

Lottie looked at him. His expression was impassive, his voice even more so. It was impossible to know what he was thinking.

"You did not ask," she said.

"We established in London that I have no desire to pry into your past *affaires*," Ethan said. There was the very slightest edge to his voice.

"Would you actually care?" Lottie hated herself for asking and hated herself even more for the pleading note she heard in her voice. She would have given anything to withdraw the question, but it was already out there.

Ethan laughed. "Oh, yes," he said, and suddenly there was an undertone of steel in his tone that simultaneously chilled her and excited her. "I would care, Lottie. Make no mistake." He gave a short laugh. "I don't care—much—about that puppy, James Devlin. He's no more than a boy. But Purchase…" He paused. "Purchase is my friend. So…" He turned to her and his gaze dwelled on her thoughtfully, sending a long shiver down her spine. "Would you like to tell me the truth? I would hate to put a bullet through him unnecessarily."

Lottie gulped. "You don't mean it," she said.

Ethan shrugged. The hot night air felt laced with his tension. He shifted a little, easing his long body more comfortably onto the inadequate carriage seat. "Perhaps I would forgive him for any transgressions before I met you," he said. "But you are my mistress now, Lottie, and it matters not if it is Le Prevost or Purchase or any other man. I bought your fidelity and I don't expect you to play me false."

There was a silence.

"You need not worry about Le Prevost," Lottie said truthfully. "He is not my type. Far too pretty."

"That's a mercy," Ethan said. "For him." He waited a moment. "And Purchase?" he asked.

"I like him," Lottie said. She had been half tempted to prevaricate. This possessiveness in Ethan was a new thing and it flattered her, made her feel wanted. On the other hand she had enough experience to know she would be a fool to try to excite Ethan's jealousy. That would be madness. She could feel something in him tonight, something dangerous, that it would be very unwise to provoke.

"We were never lovers," she said. "I know Captain Purchase because I sailed to Spitsbergen with him and for no other reason, so you need not challenge him outside of fencing practice, my lord."

She felt the tension in the carriage simmer down a little and let out her breath on a long sigh. "You do not show your feelings often," she said. "I could have sworn you did not care a rush for me and would do no more than laugh if I ran off with another man."

In reply, Ethan drew her close and kissed her with a thorough, sensual possessiveness that left her breathless. His mouth moved over her throat, pressing little kisses against her skin, seeking the tender hollow beneath her ear, brushing aside the tendrils of hair that curled against her cheek.

"I won't share you," he said softly as his tongue traced the line of her collarbone, flicking over the curve at the base of her throat with a wicked touch that left her breathless and trembling. "You are mine, Lottie."

It was not a declaration of love, Lottie thought, but it was the best that she would get. It had to suffice, even though it left her wanting more.

Ethan's fingers swept over the lace that edged her bodice. "Another modest gown," he said, and there was laughter in his voice. "How you tempt me."

His hand was against her breast and Lottie felt the

nipple harden against his palm. She gave a little gasp, and he covered her mouth with his again, kissing her deeply, sliding the lace down so that his fingers could stroke and tease her breast, tormenting her into giving a response she could not control. So often her transactions with men had been driven by calculated sensuality; she had done it that very morning, seducing Ethan deliberately, making him want her because his desire reassured her and made her feel safe. Unlike most of her lovers, though, Ethan had the power to turn the tables on her and leave her the one wanting more. And now, suddenly, she understood. She knew that every kiss, every touch, was a demonstration of Ethan's mastery and her submission. He had claimed her with his words. Now he would possess her body and she would be helpless to resist. In truth she had no wish to. Sin, she thought, had never tasted so sweet.

Her head fell back against the carriage cushions as Ethan's mouth replaced his fingers at her breast. He licked gently, experimentally, tasting her, holding her still with his hands as she squirmed. Her skin felt intolerably responsive, aching for his touch. Her nipples tightened and the fierce longing inside her spun tighter still. But she knew that Ethan would not hurry to satisfy her need. The more she trembled for him the more it would please him.

A tiny moan escaped her as Ethan's hands slid down from her bare shoulders, taking the bodice of the gown down with them so that she was naked to the waist. Her arms felt chilled. She shivered. She felt so exposed. Odd, when she had flaunted herself so many times in gowns that were barely there, that this man's calculated

stripping of the clothes from her body should leave her
feeling so utterly vulnerable to his gaze and to his touch.
He bent his head to her breasts again, tugging, nipping
and sucking at the sensitive peaks until she groaned.
His mouth covered hers quickly, hot and open.

"Hush," he whispered and she could hear the laughter in it again. "Our coachman looks too old to sustain
the shock of hearing you come."

Lottie's mind splintered at his words even as she
felt his hand beneath her skirts, seeking out the hot
damp core of her. The pressure of his fingers against
her was unbearable delight, fleeting, tantalizing one
moment, a firmer caress the next until she wanted to
scream. The velvet of the coach seat was rough against
her bare back, the night air cool against her naked skin.
Ethan's touch now was frustratingly light but she knew
that there was no point in pleading with him. He would
allow her to come only when he was ready. The torment
was excruciating. Whenever she arched to his hand,
wanting surcease, he would slow his strokes to the
slightest touch that only drove her wilder with need.

She was shaking all over, the muscles of her stomach
tightening helplessly as her body sought the fulfillment
Ethan withheld from her. Her skin was feverishly hot,
her mind dark with need. She felt the first tremor inside
her. Ethan did, too, and drew back so that she cried out
to him in desperation, begging now, heedless of pride.
Her body was racked with another spasm, and Ethan
scooped her up into his arms then, kissing her with
triumphant possession as his fingers caressed her, and
her mind and body exploded into rapture so exquisite

that it was pleasure and pain mixed. She could not seem to stop the shudders of bliss that shook her, leaving her limp and exhausted in his arms.

"It is odd," Ethan said, against her hair. "With any other woman I would not give a damn. And yet with you, Lottie…" His glittering gaze fixed on her pensively. "I feel a spectacular degree of possession matched only by the spectacular degree to which I want you. No doubt," he added, "when one burns out so will the other."

Silence settled in the carriage. Lottie could feel the pleasure seep from her body like the ebbing tide. Her mind felt cold and blank, her heart shriveling.

"No doubt," she said. She pulled up the bodice of her gown. She hated to see that she was still trembling.

For a moment Ethan's jealousy had reassured her, warmed her because it burned so strongly. But this was not love, this primitive claim he made on her, and she should not confuse it with love. Ethan's desire for her was clear. It was also nothing more than a lust that would flare and die to ashes.

"I am glad," she said, "that we have that straight now." She put a hand out and touched his lightly. Not for a second did she want to show how hurt she was. "The horses will be growing chilled, my lord," she said. "Do you wish to come back with me tonight?"

There was a pause. "No," Ethan said, after a moment. She could hear the smile in his voice although she could not see his expression in the darkness. "I have work to do and you distract me from it."

"Work?" Lottie said. "How so?"

"Letters to write…" Ethan said. He sounded vague. She wondered if he was being deliberately so. "Matters to prepare to discuss with Mr. Duster, the Parole Officer." He kissed her a final time, brief and light, and let her go. "If you will excuse me…I will call on you tomorrow."

"Of course," Lottie said.

The short carriage journey back to Priory Cottage seemed inordinately lonely. Lottie sat in the darkness and thought about what Ethan had said, not about his feelings for her, but about his work. It seemed easier to concentrate on that, to block out the other words that scorned and hurt her. Letters, matters of business… Those were the things that Theo would be interested in hearing about.

Those were the matters that Ethan would never discuss with her.

She knew that with absolute certainty. Ethan was such a self-contained man. He would never give anything of himself away, least of all those secrets that he had to guard with his life. To expect it would be to misunderstand him completely. She knew that Ethan trusted no one, least of all her.

She thought back over the evening and remembered Ethan's cool blue gaze resting on her with such thoughtful appraisal. She shivered a little. She was almost certain that he suspected her and she had not even done anything wrong yet. When she did, she would have to be careful. She had every intention now of betraying him to Theo. Tonight had hardened her resolve. Ethan himself had spoken dismissively of the time his desire for her burned out. She would not wait for that to happen. She would be the one who took control. She would leave him first.

ETHAN STOOD ON THE STEPS of The Bear Hotel and watched the carriage roll out of sight. It had cost him a fortune to hire their best equipage on Lottie's behalf for a journey of a couple of hundred yards. Lottie was proving to be vastly expensive, just as she had threatened to be, but she was also proving to be worth every penny in entertainment value. Ethan's lips twitched into an involuntary smile. Gun emplacements? Cavalry maneuvers? If Lottie Palliser had any interest in those beyond what she had been told to pretend he would be astounded. Her artless questions about breaking parole had been equally transparent.

Ethan shook his head. All evidence suggested that Lottie had been bought by the British, another spy set up to report back on him to the authorities. It would have been easy enough for them to get to her during those two days she had been alone in London, and no one would be better placed to spy on him than she. A small smile curled his lips at the thought. Well, time would tell. And he would certainly derive a great deal of amusement from seeing how such a hopelessly indiscreet person, such a poor actress as Lottie Palliser, managed the role of English spy.

His amusement faded. The prospect of Lottie trying to deceive him was comical but he also felt an odd pang of regret. He had wanted to trust Lottie, which ran counter to common sense and went against all his experience, as well. Time and again life had taught him to trust no one. Lottie's betrayal would simply be the latest in a long line. Even so, it seemed to hurt more than it should. It proved that she had not a jot of genuine regard for him, not a scrap of loyalty. That was strangely painful to confront. It was one of the reasons—one of the many less-than-admirable reasons—why he had treated Lottie with such ruthless possessiveness that evening. Her duplicity had angered him. He had wanted to show her that she was his to command in every way.

He had wanted to go back with Lottie to Priory Cottage and ease the arrogance he had shown her with tenderness. He had wanted to hold her and make love to her with gentleness and passion, woo a response from her, not demand one.

Ethan gave an impatient shrug. It could not be. The truth was that Lottie was, in her own way, a mercenary. She sold herself to the highest bidder. There was no sentiment in her. If she was working for the British authorities then they must be offering her more incentive than he ever could. And now he needed to cease thinking about her perfidy, and about how much he wanted her, and concentrate on his work.

Ethan drove his hands into his pockets and strolled down the narrow, noisome passageway at the side of the inn. Here, amongst the rotting vegetables and scavenging cats, the empty beer barrels lay discarded, waiting collection by the local Wantage brewery. The wooden stoppers were scattered about, some pushed carelessly back into the casks, others lying on the ground. Ethan picked up the stopper that was lying nearest the wall and tossed it casually into his pocket before entering the taproom of The Bear by the side door and making his way back up the stairs to his room.

Once there he sliced the wooden bung in half and extracted the note that was inside.

August 3. Midnight. One tree hill.

As he watched the wood flare into flame and the paper blacken to ash in the grate, Ethan reflected that if Lottie were indeed an agent for the British he would have to be even more careful in keeping his secrets. There would be no confidences exchanged in the aftermath of lovemaking no matter how expertly and blissfully she pleasured him. He was too experienced a hand at this game to fall into so obvious a trap.

He smiled cynically. If Lottie really was a spy then she had most definitely bitten off more than she could chew. Beautiful, *treacherous* Lottie Palliser would rue the day that she had agreed to sell him out.

CHAPTER ELEVEN

THE DAYS SLIPPED past and nobody called. There were no invitations. Lottie did not really expect it. She knew that she was a social outcast as far as the respectable elements of Wantage society were concerned. She was welcomed amongst Ethan's military colleagues, of course, but she had no desire to spend her days in the alehouses or playing billiards at The Bear. Amateur theatricals appalled her and she could never manage to rise early enough in the mornings to join the officers on their daily ride.

Ethan came to visit her most days. Sometimes he stayed overnight. Physically they could not have been more intimate. In all other respects, though, Ethan held himself apart. He gave nothing of himself, his thoughts or his emotions. He never spoke of his childhood or his son or of anything of import. Lottie was no stranger to skating over the surface of life herself, but she wanted more from Ethan. The need for intimacy started as an ache and grew to a hunger, but it was never satisfied.

Nor was life in Wantage anything other than the dead bore she had predicted it would be. Lottie would dine with Ethan alone and occasionally with his colleagues at The Bear but it was hardly a social calendar to set the world alight. When Ethan had been given leave to visit Lord Craven at Ashdown Park to dine and to advise on his purchase of a couple of hunters for his stable, Lottie had not been invited to join the party. Naturally not—she was Ethan's mistress not his wife, and the Countess of Craven would never have countenanced it. Lottie understood, but the slight rankled with her. She was a woman no longer recognized in the world where once her place had been assured.

She imagined that the life of a courtesan in London would be vastly different from this. True, she had Margery to bring her a pot of hot chocolate in bed in the mornings, and to draw her bath for her, but Lottie secretly felt unkind making the poor little maidservant haul heavy buckets of water in from the well to heat up, then drag them up the stairs, as well. There were no newspapers to read over the breakfast table unless she took the *Wantage Chronicle* and she had tried that once only to find that it was full of reports of a sale of farmyard animals, articles on the building of the local canal, and very little else. There were no reviews of plays, or accounts of balls or exhibitions, or gossip about her friends as there were in the London papers.

There *were* the shops, of course, poor as they were in comparison to London or even Oxford. There were three drapers in fierce competition with each other, and Lottie considered them all hopelessly old-fashioned, though John Winkworth's emporium, the windows draped with velvet and silk, was the one patronized by the more well-to-do families of the town. Mr. Winkworth had greeted Lottie's first visit with nervousness; she could see that it was a delicate problem for him. On the one hand she was likely to spend a great deal of money. On the other, her presence in his shop might drive away more respectable customers. Whenever she called he danced around her like a large moth to a flame, trying simultaneously to serve her and hide her from the other patrons.

Disaster occurred on her fourth visit. Whilst Lottie was browsing behind several large bales of silk, Mrs. Ormond, the wife of the richest lawyer in town, arrived with her daughter, who was intent on purchasing some material for summer gowns. Lottie saw Mr. Winkworth throw her an agonized glance. She wondered if, given the chance, he might roll her up in a carpet to hide her until Mrs. and Miss Ormond had left.

"What do you think, Mama?" Miss Ormond, a young lady with a bright, expressive face and brown ringlets, was holding up two different bales of muslin. "The blue with white spots or the pink?"

"The blue," Mrs. Ormond said decisively. "It vastly becomes you."

"I apologize for interrupting," Lottie said, unable to hold her tongue, "but I advise you to choose the pink, Miss Ormond. I fear the blue is too pale for your complexion. It will make you look sallow, whereas the pink is very pretty indeed."

Both ladies turned to look at her, appearing as startled as though the bales of cloth themselves had spoken. Mrs. Ormond, who was a thin woman with a tightly pinched mouth gasped aloud and looked as though she was not sure if she ought to faint with shock at being addressed so impertinently by a fashionable impure. Lottie checked her reticule for sal volatile just in case. Mr. Winkworth, who was showing another lady a selection of kid gloves at the counter, froze as though he were playing a game of statues.

"Come, Mary Belle, we are leaving!" Mrs. Ormond snapped.

"Oh, Mama, not without my dress material!" the young lady protested. "Besides, we have only just arrived, and I have my entire allowance to spend!" Her bright brown gaze was fixed thoughtfully on Lottie and there was amusement lurking in her eyes. She had the sort of face that looked as though she were perpetually smiling and now it seemed she was finding it difficult to keep her face straight. "You know that Miss Palliser is correct, Mama," she added. "The pink is a great deal more flattering."

"It would look divine with this silver-gray spencer," Lottie added, catching Mr. Winkworth's eye, "and perhaps a little of this lace for the hem?"

"Oh yes!" Mary Belle clapped her hands together appreciatively. "You have quite the eye for color, Miss Palliser! And if I could achieve a quarter of your style I would be most happy. That bonnet is so sweetly pretty—"

"Mary Belle!" Mrs. Ormond's neck and face were a mottled purple. "You must not *speak* to such a creature as Miss Palliser—"

"Oh fie, Mama, I doubt that I shall become corrupted simply by *speaking!*" Mary Belle said blithely. "It takes a great deal more than that, or so I believe! Besides—" she shot her mother a swift, teasing glance "—you yourself said that Miss Palliser is the cousin of the Duke of Palliser."

"Yes, but I fear that I do not acknowledge Cousin

James," Lottie said, smiling. "He is quite beneath my touch, Miss Ormond." She smiled at the girl to soften her words. "Your mama is correct, you know. It could damage your reputation to be seen to speak with me."

"Thank you, Miss Palliser," Mrs. Ormond said stiffly. "I am glad that you possess the sense of propriety that my daughter clearly lacks. Come, Mary Belle!"

"But my purchases, Mama!" Mary Belle wailed. She hurried over to the counter with the bale of pink muslin, scooped up the Brussels lace that Lottie had indicated and gestured to the silver-gray spencer with pearl buttons.

"If you please, Mr. Winkworth," she said, with a very pretty smile. "Oh, and I would like a pair of silver-gray gloves to go with the spencer, and a straw bonnet with a silver ribbon!"

"You will exceed your allowance, Mary Belle!" her mother said. "She is ungovernable," the matron complained in an aside to Lottie. "I fear she gets her headstrong nature from her father."

"Miss Ormond does indeed have a most independent spirit," Lottie agreed, very diverted that Mrs. Ormond had briefly forgotten her disapproval of her in a greater displeasure with her daughter's waywardness. "However, that can be a good thing under some circumstances."

"The sooner we marry her off the better," Mrs. Ormond said darkly.

"Oh, pray do not be in too much of a hurry," Lottie said, looking across to the counter where Mary Belle was dazzling Mr. Winkworth with her dimpling smile.

"I was married off at seventeen and look what happened to me!"

Mrs. Ormond blushed. She gave Lottie a doubtful look. "Well, that's as may be," she said. "My prime concern at present is to thwart an elopement between Mary Belle and any of those *appalling* French officers who hang about the town!"

"I fear they have no choice other than to hang about," Lottie said, "if they do not wish to break their parole. And they are very rich and charming, you know. Miss Ormond could do worse."

"There are more than sixty thousand of them in the country, Miss Palliser," Mrs. Ormond said. She swelled with indignation. This was clearly a familiar refrain for her. "*Sixty thousand* of the enemy, living amongst us! We could be murdered in our beds at any moment!"

"Most of them are locked up," Lottie pointed out.

"That's as may be," Mrs. Ormond said again. Lottie saw Mary Belle cast a quick glance in their direction, note that her mother was preoccupied, and slip another pair of gloves onto her pile of purchases. "And I know what you will say, Miss Palliser," Mrs. Ormond continued. "You will say that the officers are gentlemen and that they are welcome in all the great houses and that they are no true enemy of ours…."

"I would not dream of saying so," Lottie said promptly. "I feel your concerns are most justified, Mrs. Ormond. I remember my cousin, the Duke of Palliser, saying much the same thing about giving prisoners of war parole after Trafalgar."

"Oh!" Mrs. Ormond looked taken aback. She looked at Lottie, curiosity and reticence at war in her eyes.

Curiosity won. "Is it really true, Miss Palliser, that your family has cast you off?" she demanded.

"I fear so," Lottie said, sighing. "And who can blame them when I am such a black sheep? But who knows—" she smiled "—now that I am living so near my family home perhaps my relatives may be persuaded to welcome me back."

"Pray do let us know if they do," Mrs. Ormond said, her face brightening. "You would then be most welcome to take tea with the ladies of Wantage."

"Oh, I could not possibly," Lottie said, trying not to laugh. "You yourself pointed out a few moments ago that I am quite beyond the pale, Mrs. Ormond, my reputation shattered, my respectability blown to pieces—"

"Well, of course, we could not entertain you to tea *now*," Mrs. Ormond said, blushing. "That would be most inappropriate. But where the Duke leads…"

"Of course," Lottie said. "I quite understand."

She did. Mrs. Ormond could not be seen to give so notorious a woman as herself countenance by receiving her publicly, but oh, the lawyer's wife ached to be first with the gossip.

"You could not be persuaded to give up Lord St. Severin, I suppose?" Mrs. Ormond pursued, her eyes gleaming with the excitement of the *on dit*. Now she had started gossiping she could not stop, not even with a Cyprian.

"Oh, I could not!" Lottie said, casting down her gaze. "I have the greatest regard for Lord St. Severin."

"He is a dangerous renegade, so I hear," Mrs.

Ormond said, leaning closer. "Ungovernable as a boy, ruthless as a man."

"I heard that, too," Lottie said.

"A man who is drawn to danger, Miss Palliser," Mrs. Ormond said darkly, "will pursue it whether he is confined or not."

Lottie began to wonder whether the Wantage circulating library had a big collection of Gothic novels. Mrs. Ormond certainly seemed to have fallen under their influence at some point.

"I confess that my regard for Lord St. Severin has nothing to do with his personality," she said, "dangerous or otherwise. It is based solely on the enormous size of his—"

Mrs Ormond drew back with a gasp.

"—fortune," Lottie finished sweetly.

"Oh!" Mrs. Ormond straightened, seemed to recall precisely whom she was addressing and took a hasty step back. Her hands fluttered. "Well, Miss Palliser..." She seemed at a loss.

"It was a delight to make your acquaintance," Lottie said, smiling, "though you need not fear that I will boast of it amongst the more straitlaced ladies of Wantage. I would not wish to put you to the blush."

"You are very good, Miss Palliser." Mrs. Ormond hesitated. "I wonder...before we go... Do you think the puce or the maroon silk would suit me best? With my complexion?"

"Either," Lottie said, smiling broadly. "Both. They are equally flattering."

"Thank you," Mrs. Ormond gushed. "Mr. Winkworth? Mr. Winkworth! I would like to place an order for material for *two* gowns...."

A couple of hours later, as Lottie was sitting alone at home taking tea, a letter arrived:

Dear Miss Palliser,

Pray excuse me for not being able to call in person. I appreciated your advice a very great deal this afternoon. You have such splendid style! I wonder if you would be even kinder and settle for me a disagreement that I have with my friend Millicent Bennett? She says that it is quite acceptable for me to wear my striped red-and-white spencer with my spotted blue-and-white gown, but I am not sure. What do you think?

This missive was signed artlessly, "Your very great friend, Miss Mary Belle Ormond."

Highly entertained, Lottie sent for ink and paper and composed her reply.

My dear Miss Ormond,

Thank you very much for your letter. It was a great pleasure to meet both you and your mother, and I am happy to have been of service. It is difficult to tell without seeing the gown and the spencer, but as a general rule spots and stripes should not be mixed. A plain spencer will look nice with a spotted dress and a striped one with a plain dress provided the colors match.
Very best wishes, Lottie Palliser.

She sent Margery off with the letter and a half hour later the maid returned carrying a large parcel wrapped up in brown paper.

"Miss Ormond was very grateful for your help, ma'am," Margery said, starting to untie the string. "She asked if she might trespass further on your kindness and beg you to take a look at the enclosed material. Her mama wishes it to be made up into an evening gown for Miss Ormond but the young lady is afraid that it will make her look like an old maid."

"Oh dear," Lottie said, holding up the material. "Oh dear me, no. Poor Miss Ormond! She should wear cream, not white, with her coloring, and not this shiny satin! This will not do at all!"

"Dear Miss Ormond," she wrote, ten minutes later:

I really cannot recommend that you go out in public tricked out in this material. I fear it will make you look a frump. I did notice some pretty pale lilac gauze in Mr. Winkworth's shop when I passed by. That would be most becoming for you. If you have not outrun your allowance, or if you can persuade your mama to exchange the material, I am persuaded that you would look a great deal better in a color than in this bright white.

It was the start of a considerable correspondence. Mary Belle Ormond wrote every few days for advice on everything from how to match a reticule to a hat, to whether or not unmarried ladies should wear jewelry. Every so often she would include a little thank-you gift with her letters such as a hand-painted card—very *badly* painted, Lottie noted, art evidently not being Miss Ormond's forte—or an embroidered handkerchief. After a week Miss Ormond's friend Miss Bennett also started to write for advice on clothes, and then Miss Bassett of the Letcombe Bassetts, and then Miss Goodlake, daughter of the Justice of the Peace, who had evidently overcome her jealousy that Lottie was Ethan's mistress. Lottie referred a couple of the young ladies to the goods she had seen displayed in Mr. Winkworth's shop; after a week or so, Mr. Winkworth sent round a pair of leather gloves as a thank-you for increased sales. A few days after that Mrs. Gilmore, the milliner, sent some sample ribbons around and an extremely becoming bonnet, with a carefully worded note to the effect that she hoped Miss Palliser would like her goods sufficiently to recommend them to other ladies. A day later Mr. Mattingley, the other draper, sent an embroidered shawl.

"You are getting quite a reputation around town, ma'am," Margery commented one morning, as each day brought new letters from ladies and even gentlemen on occasion, requiring sartorial guidance.

"I thought that I already had one," Lottie said, sighing.

"No, ma'am," Margery said. "I meant a reputation for the best advice."

Within a few weeks, however, it seemed that the nature of advice the townsfolk of Wantage required from Lottie was changing. No longer were their requests merely about gowns and accessories. The ladies were moving on to matters more delicate.

"Dear Miss Palliser," Lottie read aloud from her pile one Monday morning, "I understand that you are experienced in matters of the heart, so I beg that you will help me."

"Experienced in matters of the heart," Lottie said to Margery. "That is certainly one way of putting it."

The letter continued:

> I have been married to a very worthy gentleman for the past ten years. He is kind and benevolent and a good husband.

"Poor woman," Lottie said. "How dull."

"However—" the letter was warming to its theme, the writing becoming even loopier "—he has no idea of my womanly needs." The last two words were underlined. The final line contained a request:

> I wonder if you might proffer some advice on how I might attract his attention and help him to understand what I desire of him?

"I admire her for wanting to try," Lottie said, sighing, "but husbands are the very devil to retrain."

"That sounds as though it will be from Mrs. Duster, the Parole Officer's wife," Margery said. She had come in with a pot of tea and some freshly baked walnut cake. "Everyone knows he is a stuffed shirt and that he has been plagued with digestive problems since the French came to the town. Lives on his nerves, they say."

"I thought him a very kindly man when Ethan introduced us," Lottie said, "though most frightfully embarrassed to have to acknowledge my existence."

"Mr. Duster doesn't approve of mistresses," Margery said with a giggle.

"He will approve of his wife behaving like one once I have given her some advice," Lottie said. "And we shall send some soothing pastilles for his stomach problems, too."

The final missive of the day was from a young and impressionable lady who was apparently in love with one of the prisoners at Whitemoor gaol.

"These Frenchmen," Lottie sighed. "They cause so much trouble."

"Well, you would know, ma'am," Margery said.

"I was not aware that one could visit Whitemoor," Lottie said. She tapped her quill pen against the letter. "It seems quite odd to allow the townsfolk to mingle with the prisoners."

"There is a market at the gaol every third Tuesday in the month, ma'am," Margery said. "The prisoners sell items that they have made—carvings from wood and bone, ships in bottles, dominoes and suchlike—and us Wantage folk go along to buy it. Well—" she corrected herself "—no one goes to buy the goods, to be fair, but to gawp at the prisoners, ma'am."

"Like a freak show," Lottie said.

"Not really, ma'am," Margery said, staring. "Many of them are quite handsome, ma'am, and not freakish at all."

Lottie refilled her teacup and wandered out into the garden. She wondered if Ethan knew of the Whitemoor markets. Surely he must have heard of them. One thing that was for sure was that the officers on parole would never be permitted to visit the gaol and see their fellow countrymen. She was beginning to appreciate the true nature of Ethan's punishment the longer she was here in Wantage. He was penned up within three miles of his son. He could see the prison but never visit it. He would be tormented each and every day by the knowledge that Arland was so close and yet out of reach to him. Lottie's heart twisted with compassion. Perhaps Ethan never spoke of his son because the hurt was simply too great. She understood that, understood how one might lock the pain away somewhere deep and never access it because to do so could be soul destroying. She looked at Whitemoor's towers, so dazzling in the sun, and felt a long shudder down her back.

When Margery had gone out to take her replies to the post office, Lottie turned to the one remaining letter on the pile. It was from her brother, Theo, writing under the guise of an imaginary friend called Clarissa Bingham and it was somewhat plaintive.

My dear Lottie,

I hope that you are well and enjoying your new situation. Do you have any news for me? I have been awaiting your letters with impatience but so far you have neglected to write about our mutual friend. I am hoping to hear the most exciting reports. Send to me at your earliest convenience.
Your dearest friend, Clarissa Bingham.

The phrases *mutual friend* and *earliest convenience* were heavily underlined.

Lottie sighed. She had secretly been hoping that Theo might have forgotten about her commission. She had nothing to tell him—not that she had tried very assiduously to spy on Ethan—but there had been no letters left lying carelessly around and no mysterious strangers calling by with clandestine intelligence, so what was she supposed to do? Theo had told her simply to keep her eyes open, and she did, but she saw nothing. It was almost as though Ethan knew her game and was at pains to thwart her.

Lottie felt the panic and guilt rise up in her throat. Theo's reminder meant that her time was running short. If she did not come up with something for him soon he might be inclined to cut his links to her and her hopes for the future would be extinguished. For once Ethan left her she would have nothing other than the assistance that Theo could give. His pledge to help her in return for information was her lifeline now. Besides, she had promised herself that she would be the one to leave, taking her pride and her self-respect with her. She would not wait for Ethan to dismiss her.

She grabbed the last remaining piece of writing paper and wrote quickly:

My dear Clarissa,
    How delightful to hear from you! I trust that you are well and not too bored with your current post. I fear I can add nothing to the sum of your entertainment for now. Our friend leads a most exemplary life and indulges in nothing that would arouse your curiosity. In fact I sometimes wonder if you are quite mistaken in your opinion of him.

If anything should occur to capture my interest I
shall be sure to pass it on immediately. I hope to
have better news for you soon. In the meantime
I remain your devoted friend…

She sealed it, added the address that Theo had given
her and took it to the post herself.

She felt the most abject traitor.

THERE WAS A REWARD of ten shillings for any member
of the public who caught a prisoner breaking his parole,
so on those nights that Ethan slipped away to meet his
contacts he was always extremely careful. The British
habitually set a man to spy on him, a man who claimed
to be a gentleman called Ponsonby and had rented the
manor of Stirlings for the summer. Ponsonby had British Army stamped all over him, Ethan thought, and
stood out like a sore thumb loitering in the marketplace
as he tried to keep an eye on what the French officers
were up to. Ethan had some sympathy for him. Ponsonby was easily outwitted and could not have garnered
a single useful piece of information to feed back to
his paymasters. It was no wonder, Ethan thought, that
they had upped the stakes by recruiting Lottie, as well.
Very possibly they had other spies and informers, too.
Betrayal was rife. It paid to trust no one.

On this particular night, Ethan waited until the parish
clock struck midnight and then slipped out of The Bear
and headed in the direction of Lottie's cottage. There
was a curfew on the prisoners—the bell rang at eight
in the evening to call them back to their lodgings—but
Ethan knew that Duster, the Parole Officer, would not

make a fuss over him spending the night with his mistress. In the past few weeks Ethan had deliberately set up a routine of visiting Lottie after curfew and Duster was far too buttoned-up and embarrassed by the whole business to have raised it as an issue with him.

It was a warm night, clear with a bright sickle moon. The shadow that was Ponsonby—a somewhat substantial shadow—detached itself from the darkness and followed him at a discreet distance. Ethan could hear the echo of his steps on the cobbles. Ponsonby did not have a talent for passing unseen or unheard. Ethan smiled to himself and strolled along casually, hands in pockets, with the self-satisfied demeanor of a man contemplating a night of erotic pleasure.

When Ethan reached the corner of Priory Lane he quickened his pace suddenly so that Ponsonby, taken by surprise, missed the actual moment he slipped through the garden gate of Priory Cottage. Instead of entering the house he trod softly round into the orchard at the back. Here he paused for a moment to listen for sounds of pursuit—but there were none. Ponsonby would, he thought, be loitering in the lane wondering if it was worth waiting for Ethan to reemerge or whether he would be exercising his sexual prowess all night. Poor Ponsonby. What a tedious job he had.

There were lights in Priory Cottage. Ethan paused for a moment and realized that he could hear music faintly on the summer air. Lottie must be playing the piano in the parlor. He had not even known that she could play. He felt a little odd to realize it. There were so many aspects of Lottie's life and character about which he knew nothing at all. The piano had been part of the furnishings of the house when he had rented it; he had not provided it for Lottie's pleasure. Now he wished it had been a conscious choice, not simply part of the fittings.

He listened to the lilt and fall of the music. There was a descant there, a rich, golden cascade of sound. The canary, he thought. Day after day it had sat mute in its cage until he had almost stopped noticing it. Now it was singing. How extraordinary.

Ethan almost turned and went back to the cottage door. He wanted to see Lottie. The lure of the lighted windows and the sound of the music drew him. He knew that he habitually withheld something of himself from her when they were together. Sometimes he could feel himself slipping closer to confidences and drew back. He was a man who had never given away a part of himself to any woman and had never seen the need to do so before. Yet with Lottie he felt the urge to draw close, as he did tonight, and he had to make himself fight it. In bed he demanded that she be as uninhibited and unrestrained as he wanted and she never refused him. Their sexual relationship was intense and exciting. But something was lacking, something that had touched him briefly during those two days in London when they had first met, something that was deeper than the merely physical, something that even now he wanted back….

The music seemed to change, picking up speed, the notes dancing across the night air like the gaudy tune of a barrel organ. Suddenly the sound in Ethan's ears was the raucous, brazen blare of the traveling circus and he was back without warning in the days of his childhood. He could smell the horses and see the vivid costumes of the tumblers, the clowns with their white faces, the acrobats turning cartwheels. And there was his mother holding out her arms to him and she was warm and smelled of flowers and she was smiling.... When he had run away from Eton at the age of fifteen he had searched halfway across Europe for her, following the circus from town to town, always running to catch up, chasing her shadow, never quite finding her. Where she was now he had no notion. He did not know if she was even alive.

The music jarred to a stop and Ethan shuddered, released from his memories. He could hear Lottie speaking laughingly to Margery; lamplight pooled by the window. Quickly he slipped across the bridge that spanned the brook, away across the priory fields, keeping in the lee of the hedges. The ease with which he could reach the open country was another of the reasons he had chosen Priory Cottage for Lottie. Her role as decoy and distraction was not simply about creating scandal; she was his alibi, too, a tool to be used.

He had almost reached the place where he was to meet his contact when his luck ran out. In the lane that led westward across the Downs, a hay cart was rumbling downhill late, without lights. The horse saw his shadow and shied. The driver drew rein and jumped down, and Ethan felled him before the man had a chance even to see him. The laborer went down with a grunt to slump at his feet, and Ethan hauled him into the back of the cart and led the horse off the road to tie up in a nearby field.

"You didn't kill him, did you?" a voice said, behind

him. Ethan turned to see a man in the red of a British
Army uniform step out into the moonlight.

"I hope I'm not such an amateur," Ethan said. "I
don't agree with senseless killing." He held out a
hand. "Good to see you again, Chard. You had a safe
journey?"

The other man grinned. "The best. A uniform and
set of false papers eases the way."

"You have messages for me?"

"Of course. You have the money I need?"

"Naturally."

The exchange took place.

"Where do you go next?" Ethan asked.

"I travel south," Chard said. "I'm for Portsmouth,
and then Plymouth." He grinned again. "I need to speak
to a few smugglers, grease a few palms."

Ethan nodded. Smugglers had always been great
allies in helping the prisoners of war to escape—if the
price was right. They also passed intelligence across
The Channel and just now he had plans he needed to
communicate to the French generals if they were to
coordinate an invasion with an uprising of prisoners.

"Be careful," he said. "Those places are crawling
with troops."

Chard gestured to his uniform. "I am just one
amongst many, hidden in plain view."

Ethan nodded, unsmiling. "Two weeks?" he
asked.

The other man nodded, too. "I'll send word." He
stowed the money in a battered leather satchel. "What
will you do in the meantime?"

"What I always do."

"Kick your heels and wait for news?"

"Ostensibly so."

"Keep your mistress's bed warm? I heard rumors."

"Good," Ethan said. "That is exactly what I want people to hear."

Chard laughed. "Good luck, St. Severin."

"And to you."

The trees shifted in the breeze, the moon dipped behind a cloud and then the night was still again. Ethan waited. Nothing moved in the quiet landscape. And yet he felt sure he was being watched. The hairs rose on the back of his neck and the wind breathed gooseflesh down his spine. There was danger here. His instinct told him so.

He dropped down into the lane. There was no one in sight. He started to walk quickly downhill toward the town. He heard no footsteps behind him. He saw nothing. He wondered if he had imagined the watcher. He passed the tollbooth and turned into the end of Priory Lane, then quickly doubled back on himself around the back of the tollhouse in time to see the cloaked figure that dipped into the shadows at the corner of the road. She was gone before he blinked but he knew he had seen her. And he knew who she was.

Lottie had been following him. She had been spying on him.

Ethan's first reaction was one of shock. He had suspected Lottie from the first, guessed that she was being paid as a British spy. Now he actually felt surprise to have been proved right because she had been so conspicuously lazy that she had lulled him into a false sense of security. Evidently he had underestimated her.

He walked down the lane and turned into the gate of Priory Cottage. The house was locked. It was a couple of minutes before Margery came to the door, a shawl over her nightgown, rubbing the sleep from her eyes. She did not seem particularly surprised to see him.

Ethan took the stairs two at a time and walked straight into Lottie's bedroom.

He was not quite sure what he was expecting to find. He had given her precious little time to return ahead of him, even less to strip off all her clothes and leap into bed. Yet there she was, arranged prettily against the pillows in a fetching lace confection, reading by candlelight. He could see it was one of the many letters that these days the townsfolk sent to her on everything from matters of dress to problems of the heart. Really, he thought, there was no end to Lottie Palliser's talents: scandalous mistress, purveyor of advice, British spy....

"Ethan, darling!" Lottie put down the letter and gave him her most brilliant smile. "How marvelous! I thought you had work to do this evening, and here I am, so very bored, although I do hope that now my night will take a more exciting turn."

"Oh, it will," Ethan said, smiling at her. "It will."

He walked over to her wardrobe and pulled open the door. There was a dark cloak folded on a shelf. It felt cool to the touch and smelled of fresh air underlying the stronger scent of jasmine perfume. In the farthest corner lay a pair of slippers. They were clean but for the tiniest trace of white dust on the soles. Ethan touched it;

it had the dry, chalky smoothness that was character-
istic of the local roads in the summer. He straightened
up. Lottie had done well to hide her tracks but not quite
well enough. He felt anger at her perfidy mixed with
reluctant admiration that she had so thoroughly duped
him.

"What on earth are you doing, darling?" Lottie enquired, from the bed. "I would not have had you down
as a man who wanted to try on my clothes."

Ethan sat down on the side of the bed. He looked
into her eyes and saw nothing but guileless innocence
there. He wondered if she would tell him the truth.
There was only one way to find out.

"Why were you spying on me?" he said.

CHAPTER TWELVE

LOTTIE JUMPED. Ethan's tone was mild but there was something else in it, something beneath the surface that was as cold and cutting as ice.

He was watching her. She felt anxious, flustered. She had only followed him this one time and she thought she had covered her tracks exceptionally well. Yet he had found her out. Damn him.

"Well?" This time Ethan's voice was harder. She looked in his eyes and felt her heart give a little swoop of apprehension. He was angry and he was cold. She would not be able to cajole him out of this, or seduce him into forgetting.

She thought about denying it and pretending that she did not know what he was talking about but she quickly dismissed the idea. She had already discovered that lying to Ethan, cheating him, was not a good option. She had learned that in London. Besides, he had an uncanny and inconvenient way of knowing if she was not telling the truth. He was too quick and too perceptive.

"Devil take it," she said, after a moment, "how did you know?"

She saw him relax a little and his voice warmed into amusement. "For a moment there I thought you were going to deny it," he said. "Then I would have been disappointed in you."

"How so?" Lottie said.

"Because generally when I confront you, you tell the truth," Ethan said. "Even if you try to deceive me first."

Lottie winced. His assessment of her character was unflatteringly accurate.

"This time I didn't have a choice," she said. She found that she wanted to explain, to justify her betrayal of him, but she had the lowering feeling that none of her excuses would impress him.

"You always have a choice," Ethan said. "I suppose they got to you that day I left you in London? You said you had a brother in the British Army."

"You are too quick," Lottie complained. "I hoped you had not remembered that."

"I have been playing this game a lot longer than you," Ethan said. He kept his gaze on her. It was shrewd and watchful and she felt very small, like a child caught out in a misdemeanor.

"I suspected you several weeks ago," Ethan continued, "when you plied us with those hopeless questions about gun emplacements and cavalry maneuvers. That was very clumsy of you."

"I know," Lottie said. She gave a little exasperated shrug. "It was the best that I could think of under the circumstances," she said. "I am not accomplished at this, you know. Theo should have thought of that before he asked me to be a spy. I have no talent for it."

Once again she felt Ethan's cool blue gaze search

her face. "Oh, I don't know," he said. "Tonight you impressed me. You almost got away with it."

"Did I?" Lottie felt ridiculously flattered when she knew she should actually be afraid. Would he turn her out into the street now or would he give her a chance to try to explain? Not that she could. She had betrayed him. Ethan was right; she had had a choice and she had not chosen him.

"You were very good at following me inconspicuously," Ethan said. He leaned back against the wooden rail at the head of the bed. "You were quick and you were quiet." He paused. "Tell me how you gained such skill."

Lottie toyed with the bedclothes, averting her gaze from his. "I have no idea," she said. "I suppose I had to be good at *something*."

"You have had practice," Ethan said. He put his head on one side, his gaze quizzical. "Your husband?"

Lottie's heart jumped. She looked up, frowned at him. "I do not know how you guess these things," she burst out. "You are too shrewd." Just as Ethan had not confided one whit of his past life in her, so she had had no intention of telling him about her history. But now he was waiting for answers.

"I used to follow Gregory sometimes," she admitted. "When we were first wed—"

She stopped. It was painful to talk of this, even now when the bonds that had held her to Gregory had been severed for good.

"Was he unfaithful to you?" Ethan asked.

Lottie made a slight gesture. "Oh, not in the way that you mean! I think I told you that I was seventeen when we married and he a great deal older?" When Ethan nodded she continued.

"On our wedding night Gregory told me that he did not desire me, would never wish to sleep with me nor to have children by me, and that I was free to have *affaires* as I chose so long as I did not foist any of my bastards onto him." The words slipped from her lips with as much bitterness as she had felt when first Gregory had uttered them. She had been so young and unprepared. The shock of Gregory's repudiation of her had been devastating. And even now, with all that had happened since, time had barely started to heal her hurt.

Ethan was silent, waiting. Lottie looked at his still face and swallowed hard.

"Naturally I thought—" She stopped, started again. "I thought that he had a mistress," she said, "and that he had only married me for the dowry the Pallisers had provided and for the connection to a ducal family. He was an ambitious man, a self-made man with no title nor estate to pass on after all."

"The wonder is," Ethan said, "that you chose to marry him in the first place. A man old enough to be your father?"

"He was rich," Lottie said, a little defiantly. She hugged the bedclothes closer. No one had understood her need for the security that she had thought Gregory would provide.

"Money is your answer to everything," Ethan said.

Lottie shrugged. "He was rich," she repeated, "and I had nothing." She strove to keep the bitterness from her voice but it seeped through like water through sand. "All I had," she said, "was a father who ran off when I was six, a mother who cried forever after and a family who did not wish to be burdened with me. So of course I chose to escape through a rich marriage."

There was quiet in the room. The candle flame flickered in the breeze from the open window.

"Did you love him?" Ethan asked.

"Yes," Lottie said. She smiled sadly. It was true; she had. She had always been looking for love. "I thought I did," she said. "Gregory seemed like a father figure, a man to respect." She shifted against the pillows. "So when he did not want me I was shocked and angry. On our wedding night after he had dismissed me I heard him go out, so I followed him. It was easier in London," she added. "The streets were busier so there were more people to hide amongst."

"Where did he go?" Ethan asked.

"He went to a private house in Prentice Street," Lottie said. "I peeped through the window. There were men there—with other men. Some were dressed as women, in petticoats. Some had their faces painted. There was at least one man I recognized, a member of the government." She stopped. "I used to follow Gregory sometimes after that…."

"You were curious?"

"I wanted to understand," Lottie said fiercely. She gripped the bedclothes tightly. "I wanted to understand why he wanted them yet he never wanted me."

"There is no explanation," Ethan said, "other than that is the way some men are." His tone was rough. "It was not your fault, Lottie."

Their eyes met. There was something in Ethan's gaze that comforted her and made her feel whole. Lottie had

known that it had not been her fault; she had told herself
that time and time again, and yet she had never truly
believed it. But now, with Ethan's hand resting on hers,
she finally felt the truth of it.

"I do know," Lottie said. "I understand that now. But
I was naive." She shook her head slightly. The emotions
tumbled through her, all the fear and confusion and
dismay she had felt as a seventeen-year-old bride adrift
in a world she could barely understand.

"I was frightened for Gregory, too," she admitted,
"in the beginning, when I still cared for him. If anyone
had found out, he could have been hanged."

"You held his life in your hands," Ethan said. His
gaze narrowed on her. "I am surprised that when he
threatened to divorce you, you did not threaten in return
to expose him."

"Oh, I did," Lottie said. She gave a mirthless laugh.
"It proved to be a huge mistake, for it only made him
more anxious to be rid of me. He told me that no one
would take my word against his for he had the power
and the influence and I would merely be seen as no
more than a vengeful harpy. He said that if I spoke a
word of it he would have me locked up in Bedlam."

She knitted her fingers together. "They call me a
whore," she said slowly, "but it was five years before
I took Gregory at his word and had an affair with another man. And then I only did it because I was so very
lonely. And after I had started it became…" A frown
wrinkled her brow. "It became an escape, I suppose,
because I did not know how to endure otherwise."

She had lived like that for eleven years. She had

taken lover after lover. She had been searching for something she had never found.

"I was good at it, too," she said, defiant again, even though Ethan had not uttered a single word of condemnation. "I had always been very mediocre at my studies, apart from the French. Suddenly I discovered that I had an aptitude for something else. It was very pleasing to be so good at sex."

A smile shadowed Ethan's lips. "And so you practiced?"

Lottie smiled, too. "I enjoyed developing my skill. My first lover was an excellent tutor." She paused for a moment. "Over the years my talents have gained me a great deal of appreciative masculine attention," she said.

"And was that what you wanted?" Ethan was very still. The candlelight reflected in his eyes, very dark, very steady. His question gave Lottie a hollow feeling beneath her breastbone. Yes, she had craved attention, the interest that Gregory had failed to show in her. But it had never been enough. For some reason, a reason that slipped through her fingers like water, her sexual adventures had given her pleasure and excitement in the moment but had always left her feeling empty and dissatisfied, grasping after an illusion. She did not know what it was that she truly wanted.

"It was most gratifying," she said.

Ethan took her chin in his hand and turned her face to the light. Lottie thought of the way that it would show up all the wrinkles about her eyes and tried to pull away, but he held her still.

"I am sure that it was very enjoyable," Ethan said

softly, his voice sending prickles of sensual awareness shimmering along her skin, "and yet it was never
enough, was it, Lottie?"

Lottie's eyes locked with his. "I don't know how you
could know that," she whispered.

"I know it because I have been to all the same places,
searching for all the same things." Ethan touched her
cheek in a brief caress and then his hand fell away. "I've
sought escape in women," he said wryly, "and in drink
and plenty of other vices, as well."

"And you enjoyed it," Lottie said. "Admit it."

Ethan laughed. "I enjoyed it. But in the end a man
needs more than transient pleasures."

"You have your cause," Lottie said. "You have principles. You fight for what you believe in." She felt cold.
She had nothing to compare with Ethan's sense of purpose or his ideals. She had flitted along the surface of
her life, shallow, superficial, searching for entertainment and enjoying excess.

"So I do." Ethan got to his feet and walked across
to the window, drawing the curtain aside to look out
onto the moonlit orchard. "I was only a boy when I
heard Wolfe Tone speak for Irish freedom and praise
the principles of liberty and equality embraced by the
French," he said, "but I knew from that moment that it
was a cause I could believe in."

"You have other things to believe in, too," Lottie
said. "More personal things. Your son—"

Ethan's brows snapped down and she knew at once
that she had trespassed. "My son would have been infinitely better off without me," he said harshly.

There was such unhappiness in his voice that Lottie could feel his pain as powerfully as a physical touch.

"That cannot be true," she said.

"I assure you it is." Ethan looked at her and Lottie saw that his eyes were blind with pain. Her heart jolted. "Arland came looking for me when he was fifteen," Ethan said. "I should have protected him. Instead I let him fall into the hands of the British and now he is a prisoner."

He gave a shrug, as though trying to slough off an unbearable burden. It was the only time he had ever spoken to her of Arland, and now his expression closed and Lottie knew he would not speak of the boy again. Ethan's next words confirmed her suspicions. He had shut himself off from her. That moment when she had seen into his soul was gone.

"How did you know that I was out tonight?" Ethan asked. He let the curtain fall back into place and turned to face her.

Lottie played with the edge of the counterpane. "I saw you in the garden," she admitted. "I had been playing the piano in the parlor and got up to close the window because the breeze was getting cool." She looked at him. "I saw you standing under the apple tree. It looked as though you had seen a ghost."

Watching him, she saw in his eyes the same withdrawal and the same loneliness that she had sensed in him in the gardens. He looked as though he was looking through her.

"It was careless of me to be seen," he said. He spoke so quietly Lottie had to strain to hear him. "I heard the music you were playing. It reminded me of my childhood."

"I was playing '*Au Clair de la Lune*,'" Lottie said. She hummed a few bars softly and saw Ethan shiver as though someone had walked over his grave. "You never speak of your childhood," she said.

"My mother used to sing to me," Ethan said. "I lived with her until I was five years old. I travelled with the circus. And then my father decided that despite my low birth, I should be brought up as a gentleman."

"Your mother gave you up?" Lottie's heart felt chilled. In her mind's eyes she could see a golden summer morning twenty-seven years before and another parent saying goodbye to his child, never to see her again.

"My mother thought it would be for the best," Ethan said. There was an odd note in his voice as though he wanted to believe it but did not quite do so. "She wanted me to have a place in life," he said, "and an education. Even though I wanted to stay with her she thought it better that my father should take me away."

"So you went to Farnecourt," Lottie said. She was watching his face, the chase of light and dark across his features that mirrored the memories. "That must have been a shock for a child brought up in the traveling circus."

"I loved it," Ethan said, surprising her. "I loved County Mayo and the sea. The house was huge and sprawling and full of secrets. And the land was beautiful, fierce and free. But for the rest…" He shifted, as though the memories and ghosts were pressing on him. "Well, you have heard all the tales. My father

disapproved of my wildness from the very start and
the servants took their cue from him. Naturally the
Duchess hated me—how could she not, when I was
the living proof of my father's infidelity? She brought
up her children to detest me, all except Northesk, who
had his work cut out trying to stand between me and
trouble." He sighed, shrugged. "And there always was
trouble—at Farnecourt, at Eton, wherever I went."

"Is it true," Lottie asked, "that when you ran away
you went to Newmarket and stole one of your father's
racehorses?"

"Quite true," Ethan said. He gave her the shadow of
a smile. "Wild Darrell was a beautiful creature—and a
damned sight nicer natured than most of my family."

"And that you worked in Ireland for several years as
a jockey before you went to France to join Napoleon's
army?"

"You have been assiduously listening to the gossip,"
Ethan said.

"Margery told me," Lottie said. "You must know that
everyone talks about you, my lord. There is nothing
better to do in this provincial little place."

"Oh, but there is," Ethan said. He came back across
the room toward her. "There is spying."

Lottie's heart jumped and started to race. The brief
moment of intimacy was over, the tiny window into the
past closed. It had been an illusion to think that when
they had shared confidences for the first time it had
bound them closer together. She was still the betrayer
and Ethan the man she had deceived.

"Tell me about tonight," Ethan said. "You saw me
in the garden and you followed me."

Lottie gave a little shrug. "I thought you might be going somewhere interesting," she said. "It was a spur-of-the-moment decision to follow you, I swear. And I had promised Theo that I would try…." Her voice trailed away. She was trapped. It did not really matter what she said. Ethan could see all too clearly the depth of her deceit.

"We'll come to your brother in a moment," Ethan said. He caught her shoulders, turning her so that she faced him. "Did you see where I went?"

"No!" Lottie protested. "I only caught up with you by the time you were walking down the toll road back into town," she said, "and by then my feet hurt and I had torn my gown on some brambles and I was wishing I had not bothered to go out at all."

Ethan scanned her face. She could feel herself flushing beneath his scrutiny even though she had been telling the truth. There was something so keen and hard in his gaze that it seemed to cut right through her.

"Someone else was out tonight," he said. "If it was not you, then—who was it?"

Lottie winced as his hands tightened on her shoulders and he loosened his grip at once. "Did you see anyone else?" he questioned, more softly.

Lottie shook her head. "No one."

"Are you sure? This is important."

Lottie looked up and met his eyes. "There was a man turning into Newbury Street as I returned," she said. "He was one of your fellow officers, I think. I did not see him clearly but there was something familiar about his gait." She frowned, trying to recall more of the shadowy figure she had seen for just a moment.

Ethan was looking pensive. "A French officer," he said. "I wonder…"

"Surely no one would betray you," Lottie said. She blushed bright red under his quizzical gaze. "On your own side, I mean."

"Everyone has a price," Ethan said. He sat down on the edge of the bed. "Don't they, Lottie?"

Lottie bit her lip. "I am British," she said. "Most people would see my actions as patriotism."

Ethan laughed. "Then they would give you too much credit. You do not act out of principle. What did your brother offer you? Money, I suppose, as is traditional."

"Theo offered me what I had lost," Lottie said.

Her words fell softly into the candlelit room.

She had not meant to tell Ethan, had not meant to expose more of her weakness to him, but his words had wounded her. The regret was like sawdust in her throat, rough and choking. Ethan was right, she thought bitterly. Her principles had been for sale. The thing that mattered to her, the thing that she wanted more than any other, was not to save her country or any such high-minded sentiment. She had wanted to go back; back to the past when she had been rich beyond dreams and had not appreciated quite how fortunate she was.

She looked at Ethan and saw that there was under-standing in his eyes and something that looked like sympathy. Emotion shivered between them, like the tightening of a gossamer thread.

"I am sorry," he said. "But you know you can never go back to your old life, Lottie. What they offered you was an illusion."

"I can try," Lottie said stubbornly. She felt stripped bare of pretense. "It is not all about the money," she said, struggling to explain. "I love Theo. He is my brother. He was the only one who cared for me after our father left and our mother proved such a broken reed." She spread her hands in a gesture of appeal. "Is it so strange that I would want to help him—and for him to help me in return?"

She could not bear the pity in Ethan's eyes. She knew he thought Theo was using her and she tried fiercely to push the idea away. She wanted Theo to be her white knight. Yes, there was a price to be paid for his help, but that was the way of the world. It did not mean that Theo loved her any the less.

"Oh, I wish you had not guessed!" she burst out. She pulled away from him. "I do not know what I shall tell Theo now."

"You'll tell him what I give you to tell him," Ethan said.

For a moment Lottie was confused and then her heart started to slam through her body in powerful strokes. "You mean that you want me to lie to him?" She gasped. "To pass on information I know to be false?"

"That will be very useful to me," Ethan agreed. The sympathy had gone from his face now as though it had never been. He looked hard and implacable. Lottie stared at him. Mrs. Ormond had called him ruthless, and she had visualized Ethan cutting Napoleon's enemies down in battle. But there were different sorts of ruthlessness and now she was looking straight into its cold heart.

"Theo will guess," she said, speaking as dispassionately as he, as though they were merely discussing the weather or the events of the day. Her heart beat hard and fast but she kept her voice steady now. "I could not fool *you* for one minute—I would never be able to convince him."

"The information I will give you will be very convincing," Ethan said gently.

There was a silence.

"What alternative do I have?" Lottie said. "You said that there are always choices."

The hint of a smile touched Ethan's lips. "I confess I cannot see many choices for you now." He shrugged. "Either you work for me as penance for your deceit, or you go to your brother, tell him that you have failed him, and see if he will still help you. But without having anything to offer him…" Ethan's voice faded away. "Unless you think he might help you out of family loyalty…"

"Perhaps he would," Lottie said. She felt cold in her bones, the doubt gnawing at her even though she tried to keep it out. Theo had sworn that he cared for her. Surely he would not turn her away, even if she had failed him.

"I could ask him," she said. "I *will* ask him."

Ethan smiled. "By all means," he said gently.

"But that is a risk…. He might turn me away…." Lottie knitted her fingers together. They were shaking. She loved Theo and wanted to trust him but he had made it plain in London that there was a price for his help. Now she had failed so abysmally in her role as spy, would he reject her, wash his hands of her as so many men had done before him? She did not want to put him to the test.

"You have no other choice than to throw in your lot with me," Ethan said. He waited, watching her. "Unless you wish to end up on the street."

Once again there was a silence in the hot little room. Ethan was watching her with amusement and Lottie realized that her struggles must be clear on her face. Her choice was no choice and Ethan knew it, she thought bitterly. She could work for him and betray her country or she could throw herself on Theo's mercy and risk rejection. If she turned Ethan down or if Theo discarded her, she would be alone and ruined.

The shadows of the past pressed close and she shuddered.

"I'll not become a spy for the French," she said. "Even I have a sticking point. You ask too much, my lord."

She saw the glimmer of amusement in Ethan's eyes and something else, too, something that might have been admiration. His gaze examined her face and she pressed her lips together tightly to keep herself from going back on her word, from caving in, compromising, to save her own skin. It was more difficult than she had imagined. Her instincts were screaming at her to agree to Ethan's suggestion. Anything to avoid the risk of Theo rejecting her, anything to escape being out on the streets once again…

"I thought we had just agreed that you had no choice?" Ethan said.

"It's wrong," Lottie said fiercely. "It's treason. They would hang me if they found out."

"For a moment I thought you were having a crisis of conscience rather than concerns about your self-preservation," Ethan said dryly, "but I should have known better." He shrugged. "If the British find out what you are doing you can always plead that you were under duress."

"No," Lottie said. She raised her chin and looked him straight in the eyes. "I will not plead for anything or with anyone, anymore," she said. "I am done with begging." She remembered the way in which she had implored Gregory to take her back and the way she had pleaded with Mrs. Tong for a place under the bawdy-house roof. She thought of the desperation with which she had wanted Theo to save her. None of it had served. All it had done was rob her of her self-respect.

"You will not spy for me and you will not go cap in hand to your brother," Ethan said thoughtfully.

"No," Lottie said again. She felt a desperate mixture of bravado and uncertainty. What would she do if Ethan called her bluff and threw her out? She could not sell her favors like those maidservants at The Bear. She would rather starve now than sink to that level. Nor would she walk twenty miles to Palliser Hall and throw herself on the mercy of relatives who had already proved they had none. That would be more begging, and she wanted none of it.

"No," she repeated more softly.

Ethan shifted on the bed. The candlelight flickered across his face.

"Now you *have* surprised me," he said slowly. "How interesting. I did not think you had the courage to defy me."

"You can throw me into the street if you wish," Lottie said, hoping that he would not take her up on this, "but I will not change my mind."

Ethan laughed. "I doubt there is any need for such melodrama," he drawled. He reached forward, touched her cheek. His fingers were seductively gentle though that tenderness was at war with a kind of conflict she could see in his eyes. "I find I have no desire to part with you just yet," he said, "though you richly deserve for me to send you packing for your treachery."

The relief swept through Lottie in an engulfing wave. "So what do we do now?" she asked, after a moment.

Ethan smiled at her and her heart did a little leap.

"What we did before," Ethan said. "You are my mistress. You perform that role admirably."

"But my commission for Theo—" Lottie began.

Ethan laughed. "Tell your brother whatever you wish," he said, "if it will secure your future." His laughter died. "Just make sure it is not the truth, Lottie. Do not betray me again." His hand came up to cup her cheek again. "Please," he said. The word was gentle but his tone was hard. "Do not put me to the test on that. I mean it."

Their eyes met and held. Lottie shook her head. "I don't understand you, Ethan," she complained.

Ethan laughed. "You don't need to understand me," he said. "I like you, Lottie," he added. "I like you very much. That is all there is to it."

"But you don't trust me," Lottie whispered. Her mind was spinning. Ethan would let her stay. He would not throw her out into the street. She was safe, for now. And Theo need never know…. She felt relieved, confused, utterly torn by the conflicts of loyalty and self-interest.

"I don't trust you in the slightest," Ethan said. "And you do not trust me." He shrugged. "It is a fine basis for a relationship between the two of us."

There was a pause. "Will you stay?" Lottie said.

Ethan hesitated. She could see the candlelight reflected in his eyes. "Yes," he said. "Damn it, Lottie Palliser, I am so angry with you for betraying me and thwarting me, but I will stay because I want you."

He leaned forward and kissed her. Lottie could feel the temper in him, hot under the surface. He eased her back against the pillows and she shivered in response to his touch. Ethan was kissing her with barely leashed passion, his hands already moving over her, stripping her of her nightgown, exposing her nakedness to his gaze and spreading her for his pleasure. She understood what would happen now. He would ask her to surrender everything and to give herself up to his will. It was his price. She had forced him to concede and he was furious with her, so now he would make her pay, exacting his revenge in the sweetest, most decadent ways she could imagine. It would be like the time in the carriage when he had asserted his absolute mastery over her. She would have to submit to his will. This was what he demanded of her. And in the past she had paid.

Not this time.

Defiance flickered within her. They had engaged in a battle of wills and for once she had won.

And now he would dance to her tune.

Quick as a flash she moved to straddle him, catching him off guard as she grabbed a scarf from the chair, wrapped it around his wrist and tied it to the wooden headboard. She could do knots. Theo had shown her how when they were children.

"What the devil—" Ethan rolled over to see what she had done and she took advantage to grab his other wrist and tie that one above his head, too, this time with her discarded nightgown.

"Don't tear my silks," Lottie said sweetly, "or you will have to buy me some more."

She saw the muscles in Ethan's shoulders bunch beneath the cotton of his shirt as he jerked against his bonds. The silk held. He cursed, turning his incredulous blue gaze on her.

"What the hell do you think you are doing?"

She knew that the bonds might not hold him if he became really angry so she straddled him again, running her hands beneath his shirt so that she could press her palms against his chest. She leaned over him, sliding her tongue between his lips, parting him, nibbling his bottom lip, flirting her tongue against his. She could feel his response—and his resistance.

"I'm a little tired of being at your mercy, Ethan," she said, "so I thought it was about time you were at mine."

Ethan's reply was couched in some very colorful, very idiomatic French. Lottie laughed.

"That is physically impossible, my love," she said. She slid down his body, brushing her nakedness against him. The rub of his breeches was rough against her skin. He already had an enormous erection, which she was careful not to touch.

"I think," she said, sitting back and looking thoughtfully down at Ethan's straining body, "that I am going to have trouble with your boots. I cannot really call Margery to help…." She paused. "So perhaps we shall just have to leave some of your clothes on."

"For pity's sake, Lottie," Ethan said hoarsely, "let me go."

Lottie's only reply was to graze another kiss across his lips. He groaned.

"How interesting that you do not like surrendering control," Lottie said, pressing her lips to his lean stomach and tasting the skin hot and salty against her tongue.

"Of course I do not…" Ethan's voice was even tighter now, as though he was in physical pain. "I have been in control since I was fifteen years old. No one takes that away from me."

No one takes that away from me….

This was Ethan's strength. Lottie could see that now. Even in captivity when every freedom had been taken from him there was a power about Ethan that was untouched because he would never willingly surrender it to any man. The authorities had recognized that in him and had tried to break him but he had not capitulated. It was why they hated him and wanted to bring him down. He had taken control from his father when he had run away from home and he had been his own master ever since. No one had brought him to his knees. But now Lottie had stripped that power from him and made him her captive, and she could see that he was simultaneously angered at his loss of control and fascinated by it.

"Let go. There is nothing you can do." Lottie trailed

her lips up over his chest and pressed little openmouthed kisses over the muscular hardness of his shoulder. Ethan moved restlessly against his bonds.

"I want you to beg," Lottie whispered. She bit him gently. A jolt shuddered through him.

"You're punishing me." Ethan's blue eyes were narrowed to a fierce glitter. "Release me, Lottie—"

"This isn't about punishment," Lottie said. "You said that you wanted me."

"I did," Ethan said through gritted teeth. "I do."

"Then…" Lottie's hand brushed his erection through the material of his breeches and he jerked once again against the ties that held him. "Then there is no difficulty, is there?" she finished.

Ethan swore again. "How do you know how to tie knots?" he demanded. "No woman knows how to tie knots."

"I do…" Lottie said vaguely. She felt wonderful. Triumphant and feminine and very, very pleased with herself. She set her hand to the fastening of his breeches and felt him tense. The buttons came free and his cock sprang out, hard, hot and aroused. She deliberately did not touch it.

"You can't do this," Ethan said. His eyes glittered. His jaw was tense. He shifted restlessly on the bed.

"I am doing it," Lottie said. "Always we play by your rules, Ethan. Well, not this time."

Once again she leaned in to kiss him, her hair falling about them like a soft waterfall, and Ethan turned his head fiercely to capture her lips but already she was withdrawing from him, licking her way down his body, teasing with her tongue, exploring every hard line and contour of his body.

There were two scars on him. She had noticed them before. One was a shallow slash across the ribs. The other looked like a deep saber cut to the leg that must have taken months to heal. Even now the skin was puckered and uneven. Lottie rested her hand below it aware that it was probably too raw and sensitive to be touched.

Ethan opened his eyes and looked directly at her. Beneath the shimmer of desire in his eyes she saw something else, something so vulnerable that her heart seemed to stop for a moment.

"The Battle of Busaco," he said. "I almost died."

"I'm sorry," Lottie said. She hesitated. "You don't have nightmares?"

The glitter in his blue eyes intensified. "Sometimes."

Lottie kissed him with gentleness and compassion and he responded to her hungrily. Her world tilted and teetered on the brink. She could feel that Ethan wanted to hold her. He needed her. That was no pretense. It was in the way that he lifted his body toward her, straining at the bonds that held him. It was in the desperation of his touch as his mouth met hers.

"Release me," he whispered against her lips.

"No." Lottie drew back, smiling. "A good try, Ethan, but I am not so softhearted."

Ethan cursed. The sweat stood out on his brow and the ravenous gleam in his eyes deepened to a fierce blue. "Then touch me."

"In my own good time."

She was tormenting him but she was tormenting herself, too. The low sweet ache of desire in her belly was like a tightening spiral. She wanted to take him inside herself but they both had to wait. Instead she ran her hands over him, loving the feel of his skin, the heat of it, the roughness of the hair that ran in a line down below his navel. She bent her mouth to his cock and licked the tip. He gave a harsh groan. She took him and tasted him and felt him harden further beneath the slide of her mouth. Her senses were spinning with the scent and the flavor of him and his moans of pleasure filled her ears and drove the tense need inside her to fever pitch.

She raised her head. Ethan was lying still within his restraints now, his hard powerful body so taut with desire that he looked ready to explode. Lottie straddled him again, sliding down so that his erection was nestling between her opulent breasts now. He felt the yielding softness of her cradling him and a deep shudder shook him. He groaned aloud.

Carefully Lottie began to ease herself backward and forward, his taut cock squeezed between the softness of her breasts, her nipples brushing his stomach. Ethan's breath came in a harsh gasp now, his face fierce with arousal.

"Don't come," Lottie whispered, slowing the movement to the gentlest of strokes. "Don't come before I give you permission."

Another groan was wrenched from his as he struggled in his bonds. "For pity's sake, woman, where did you learn such wickedness?"

"I told you," Lottie said. "I practiced. I have always been an apt pupil."

She released him, arching over him now, allowing the tip of him to touch her intimately, drawing away when he thrust upward to try and enter her more deeply. She saw the flash of frustration in his eyes again as he strained against the ties, and then she took him deep inside her, meeting the drive of his body with the pulse of hers again and again, hearing him cry aloud, over and over, as relief and desire and anger fused into one blinding sensation that drove them both over the edge into the darkness below.

Very slowly Lottie became aware of reality again. The room was quiet, filled with candlelight and the dying embers of the fire. Outside an owl hooted in the wood. The house creaked and settled. She looked at Ethan. He was unmoving, his eyes closed, his breathing still a little ragged. The silk was hopelessly tangled about his wrists. She reached up to unfasten the knots.

"Ethan?" Suddenly, as the silk slipped through her fingers, she felt a little wary.

He rolled over so suddenly that she cried out. His arms went about her and he bent his head to her breast, taking her in his mouth. The pleasure swept her again like the drag of the tide and she cried out in shock and delight as the echoes pulsed through her body. His mouth gentled on her and the sensation softened into the sweetest aftermath of bliss.

Ethan pulled her close, dropping kisses on her hair.

"Are you angry with me?" Lottie whispered, reaching

up to press her palm to his cheek. In the candlelight she saw the shadow of his eyelashes against his skin, so spiky and hard, yet so soft that her heart did an odd tumble. Strange that it should be that one small thing that pushed her over the edge into love and yet she could no longer deny it. She had wanted to keep her distance, to protect herself, and yet this act that had torn away Ethan's defenses had also shattered her own.

"Very angry." But something had changed between them. Lottie could not name it but she could feel it. There was humor in Ethan's voice and no undertow of anger at all. He sounded on the edge of sleep. "I would show you how angry I am," he continued, "if I had any energy left. But that—" his tone changed "—was like nothing I have ever experienced before."

He drew her closer and Lottie rested her cheek against his chest and listened as his breathing changed and he fell into sleep. This, she thought, was like the intimacy of their first night in London. There was tenderness in the way that he held her so close. For a little while at least, here in his arms, she could succumb to the illusion of loving and being loved in return. For there was no doubt that she loved him. Her heart was spilling over with happiness, so full and fulfilled. And for once she would stave off all thoughts of the future and simply accept it. There would be time and plenty for regrets in the morning.

WHEN ETHAN WOKE, the bed was cold and empty and Lottie had gone. He sat up, shaking the last warm dregs of sleep from his mind. He felt bereft and alone in a way that he did not really want to analyze. It was odd, he thought, that he needed Lottie to be there. He never needed anyone. It was his need for her that had made him so furious at her treachery and betrayal. He had not wanted Lottie to deceive him. It had hurt to know that his enemies had bought her, that her desire for money was stronger than her loyalty to him.

Such vulnerability to his feelings for Lottie was deeply disturbing.

Shrugging off the unwelcome thoughts, Ethan eased himself from the warmth of the bed and walked across to the dresser. He washed in the water from the jug, wincing a little at its cold sting. His body felt unfamiliar in some way, not aching exactly but physically tired, worn out with pleasure. His mind too felt cloudy, returning once again to the question of where Lottie had gone. She could not be far away, he thought. She had nowhere to go. Despite her defiant words the previous night and her even more defiant actions, she was dependent on him for a roof over her head and indeed for money, the thing that had always mattered to her the most.

He drew on his clothes and walked over to the window, where the morning light was strengthening with each moment. Downstairs he could hear Margery crashing around in the kitchen. The rather unappetizing smell of bacon was wafting on the air. The church clock was chiming seven and he could see Lottie now, down in the orchard, picking apples and placing them in a basket at her feet. She was dressed in an old, faded gown with an apron over the top and a ridiculous mobcap on her head that should have made her look like an old maid but for some reason seemed to make her look even more young and pretty than usual. She looked up at the window and he saw her smile and she waved to him. The smile, the wave, the open uncomplicated pleasure in her eyes... Something shifted in Ethan; something warm and sweet, something that felt infinitely dangerous.

Ethan drew back from the window. He did not want to return to his Spartan room at The Bear. He wanted to stay with Lottie, to spend the day with her, to talk to her, take her driving, maybe even take a picnic out into the fields. This vision of domestic bliss simultaneously attracted and appalled him. Hell, he found he was even prepared to endure Margery's inexpertly cooked English breakfast with cold eggs and congealing bacon fat, if he could sit across a table from Lottie and simply look at her. There was no explanation for this weakness in him, but he did not like it and he was not going to succumb to it. He ran down the stairs and went out into the street without saying goodbye. He felt guilty. And then he felt annoyed with himself for feeling that way. This was becoming intolerable.

The streets of Wantage were starting to fill up with the market traders setting up their stalls. A few drunkards littered the shop doorways. The Bear Hotel was not locked but the night porter was still asleep. Ethan did not wake him. He trod softly up the stair, taking care to avoid the treads that creaked, and entered his room.

All was exactly as he had left it the night before and yet Ethan knew, as soon as he stepped inside, that someone had been there. Once again he felt that brush of gooseflesh over his skin and the sense of being watched.

He checked methodically through all the drawers and cupboards, looking for the slightest hint that someone had been searching for something. He knew what they sought. He knew they would not have found it.

Finally, reassured that everything was exactly where it should have been, he sat down at his desk to compose a letter.

He had been writing for less than two minutes when he heard Mr. Duster, the Parole Officer, hammering on all the doors, shouting that a man had been found murdered at the inn at Lambourn Cross and demanding to know where all the French prisoners had spent the night.

CHAPTER THIRTEEN

LOTTIE SAT AT HER ESCRITOIRE and looked at the pile of correspondence that the day's post had brought her. The first letter was from Mary Belle Ormond's brother John, a young gentleman who prided himself on the style of his linen cravats, asking for advice on how to get the points to stand up correctly. The second letter was from a Miss Butler, asking whether or not she should elope with one of the parole prisoners. A third was from the doctor's wife with an enquiry about the best way to remove damp spots from kid gloves and yet another, worded with such circumlocution that Lottie could barely understand it, appeared to be from a widow asking how to find a lover who would be better in bed than her husband had been.

"I do not wish to die in ignorance," Lottie's correspondent had written, "and I do wonder if you might recommend someone to me, Miss Palliser. I am able to travel to London," she had added, "if the choice there would be greater."

Lottie pushed the pile to one side with a bad-tempered sigh as Margery entered with tea and arrowroot biscuits.

"Blue-deviled, ma'am?" Margery asked sympathetically.

Lottie was more than that. She had spent the morning

lying to Mr. Duster, the Parole Officer, on the subject of Ethan's whereabouts the previous night. As soon as Duster had stepped over the threshold of Priory Cottage he had looked around nervously, as though the evidence of sin, whatever that was, should be apparent for all to see. Margery had shown him into the parlor and its neat respectability seemed to have made him even more uncomfortable. He had perched on the edge of a chair as though expecting something scandalous to occur at any moment.

The only scandalous thing that had happened was that Lottie had perjured her soul by swearing that Ethan had been with her all night. And Ethan had not even thanked her for it. Instead he had sent a message that he would be dining that day at Letcombe Park and would see her on the morrow. Lottie had been furious.

She shredded her quill pen between her fingers with quick, angry tugs. She had no future with Ethan. She knew it; how could it possibly be otherwise with a renegade Irish prisoner who had promised her nothing? And yet that had not prevented her from falling in love with him. She had known it the previous night when she had seen the scars on him and looked into his eyes and seen his nightmares reflected there. No longer were they a man and his paid mistress who met merely for mutual pleasure and avoided any other intimacy. Something had changed between them, and those flimsy barriers she had placed about her heart which had been under siege from the first night in London, those had given way and she had been forced to let her love for him flood in. It had always been an unequal battle anyway; Lottie knew she fell in love very easily,

seeking a closeness she desperately craved, wanting to
build something she had never had.

Ethan did not share her feelings.

She had been so happy when she had woken that
morning. She had waited for Ethan in the garden until
her basket was full of apples and her bare feet were cold
with the dew. Then she had gone back inside the house
to find that he had left without saying goodbye. In the
night he had held her close but in the morning he had
not wanted that intimacy and she understood then that
he never would. So once again there was a man and
she loved him and he would leave her. It was a pattern
she knew all too well.

She thought of the way Ethan had walked away from
her that morning, deliberately rejecting the intimacy of
their night together. Ethan would never trust her and
he would certainly never love her. And tonight he was
dining with the local gentry, a French prisoner who was
nevertheless accepted in society because he was rich
and titled, nominally if not very actually a gentleman.
After all, the war could not last forever. Whilst she, the
cousin of a Duke, moldered away here on her own, cast
out and disgraced.

Last night she had promised Ethan she would not
sell him out to her brother. This morning, alone and
rebuffed, lonely, heartsick, she saw matters a little dif-
ferently. Who was the fool here, if she did not look out
for her own interests? She grabbed her quill and wrote
a few slashing lines to Theo:

Dearest Clarissa, news at last! It may interest you
to know that last night there was a murder....

Five minutes later, angry with Ethan, even angrier with herself, she threw down the shredded quill and looked at Margery, who was bustling about the parlor opening the windows to the afternoon sunshine and plying her feather duster to great effect.

"Margery," she said, "pray go and prepare a bag for me, if you please. I am going to London."

Margery's mouth fell open. She put the feather duster down slowly. "London, madam?" she said, as though Lottie had mentioned a trip to the moon. "Why would you want to go to London?"

"Because I can," Lottie said defiantly. What did it matter if she hated London now that the *Ton* had turned its back on her? Damn Ethan Ryder. He might be accepted to dinner at Letcombe Park, but he could not travel more than a mile out of Wantage without permission of the parole officer, whereas she could come and go as she pleased. And go she damned well would. The idea started to take hold and grow inside her. She would go shopping and send all the bills to Ethan. She would attend the theater, perhaps even go to a masked ball if she could arrange it. There was plenty of money to take with her. Ethan had been exceptionally generous with her allowance. She would make a stir and cause a scandal. That should please her neglectful lover.

A little smile curved her lips. She lived for pleasure and there was precious little to be had in this godforsaken town.

"London," she repeated. "And pray call me a carriage from the livery stables, Margery. This time I shall travel in style."

ETHAN STOOD IN THE SHADOW of the refreshment room
doorway of Gregory Cummings's town house in Grosvenor Square, sipping a glass of very fine champagne
and watching Lottie as she chatted animatedly with a
gentleman in a green domino. He had recognized her
immediately even though she was cloaked and masked.
What Lottie was doing at a masquerade ball at her
former husband's home was anyone's guess, Ethan
thought. Only she would have the sheer audacity to
walk out on *him* and then walk in here and mingle with
Cummings's guests, hiding the secret of her identity
behind the anonymity of a scarlet domino and a matching bejeweled black silk mask.

Not that Lottie was hiding, precisely. The candlelight
caught the sparkle of the rubies each time she turned
her head with those expressive gestures Ethan knew so
well. She had on scarlet gloves and a huge ruby ring
that fractured the light into a hundred rainbows. Ethan
wondered where the ring had come from. Perhaps he
was paying for that as well as everything else.

On Lottie's feet were tiny high-heeled scarlet silk
evening slippers. She drew all eyes. She looked ravishing. Her companion certainly appeared to think so,
pressing closer with gallantry as he tried to coax her
into divulging her identity. Ethan itched to intervene,
take the man by the throat and toss him aside. He stayed
where he was, watching. He and Lottie would have a
reckoning soon enough.

He had been furious when he discovered that she
had left Wantage and gone up to London. She had left
no note for him and no word of explanation; there was
nothing but Margery's confused statement that madam

had decided she wanted to visit Town, because she could, because she was bored and lonely, because he was away entertaining himself at some house party or dinner from which she had been excluded. Ethan was not sure if his fury had sprung from frustration that Lottie had the liberty he lacked and was displaying it ostentatiously in his face, or a rather more disturbing fear that she had left him for good. On reflection he had decided that it seemed unlikely she had traded him in, for she had left almost all her clothes behind and Ethan suspected that were she to decamp, Lottie would take with her every last thing she could fit in a portmanteau, whether it belonged to her or not.

Cummings's butler had not been keen to admit him to this most exclusive of masquerades. He had demanded to see Ethan's invitation, to which Ethan had replied coldly that no one revealed their identity at a masked ball since that was the whole point of the disguise. The butler had waited, stubborn. Ethan had looked at him. The man had waved him inside. Now Ethan watched as Lottie slipped away from her persistent suitor, one consoling hand placed charmingly on his sleeve to soften her rejection. She paused by the overloaded refreshment table; quick as a flash she had swept half a dozen of the salmon and prawn patties into her bag. Ethan raised his brows.

"All alone, my lord?" A striking redhead with bold eyes and a sultry voice claimed his attention. There was no mistaking her interest. Her gaze slid over him with the sinuous intensity of a predator.

"I fear not," Ethan said, removing the hand that

was already trailing suggestively over his chest. "Pray excuse me."

"Another time," the redhead said, pouting. Evidently she was not accustomed to rejection.

Ethan followed Lottie unobtrusively from the refreshment room and out into the hall. Here the crowd was thinning because a lively mazurka was taking place in the ballroom. He could see the swirling dancers through the open doors. Lottie slipped across to two three-foot-tall blue-and-white urns resting on pedestals beside a closed door. A flick of the wrist and the fish patties were consigned to the depths of the vases, one after the other. Ethan watched in admiration.

He strolled over to her and spoke in her ear. "Masterly, madam. I congratulate you."

She jumped, catching her breath on a gasp, and the ruby-studded evening bag slipped from her fingers. Ethan bent to retrieve it, offering it to her with a mocking bow.

Her eyes, a wary brown behind the mask, were fixed on his face. "What are you doing here?" Her voice was a whisper edged with something fierce. Anger? Fear? He was not sure.

"I could ask the same of you," he said coolly. He placed an arm against the doorjamb, trapping her between the heavy mahogany panels and his body. No one paid any attention; conduct was always a little more open at a masked ball.

"You saw what I was doing," she hissed back.

"Revenge?" Ethan said. "Rotting fish in the hall? You are original, I will say that for you."

Her gaze sparked. "It is no more than Gregory

deserves. The servants are all slovenly." She dismissed
them with a flick of a bejeweled wrist. "They will not
discover the source of the stink for months. Very likely
Gregory will have dug up the sewers by then in a desperate attempt to find out what is wrong. Nobody will
want to be a guest here in the meantime." A smile
slipped behind her mask, lighting her eyes. "Rotting
fish for a man rotten to the core. Appropriate, don't you
think?"

Her chin tilted up defiantly toward him. Beneath the
mask her lips were a luscious red bow. Ethan wanted
to kiss her. He leaned a little closer.

"What else have you done?" he asked.

"Oh…" Again her eyes smiled at him behind the
mask. "Not much. Gregory's expensive Spanish cigars
are making a delightfully scented fire in the library
grate. And I fear that the sleeves are missing from a
couple of his favorite jackets and greatcoats…. Weston
never thought of such an unusual style, believe me."

"You cut off the sleeves of his jackets?" Ethan
repeated. It was practically treasonable to desecrate
Weston's work. His admiration for her creativity was
growing.

"Only one sleeve on each," Lottie corrected. Her
gaze flickered to his, wicked and amused. "Better
than cutting off something else of his, tempting as that
was."

"Is that all?"

She ran a finger thoughtfully along Ethan's arm,
leaning so close that the feathered edging on her mask
brushed his cheek. "I gave the servants the keys to
Gregory's private wine cellar," she whispered. "The

one with all the bottles he does not wish to share. They are serving his priceless champagne to the guests now. Oh, and I put nettles in his bed, under the sheets, so more than his pride will be stung."

Ethan laughed. "It is a very fine wine. I must remember to compliment Mr. Cummings on it on my way out." He shifted. "And this was why you came to London? For revenge?"

Her body tensed a little. She tried to move away from him but he held her close now, a hand on her wrist.

"No." She sounded sulky. "I only heard of Gregory's masquerade from gossip in the gown shop yesterday. That was when I decided to attend uninvited." She straightened. "I came up to London because I was bored. I told you—I need to be entertained. I require it. You neglected me."

"Nonsense," Ethan said. "I have been most attentive to you."

"Oh, in bed…" Her tone was dismissive. "I cannot fault your attentions nor indeed your style, my lord." Her mouth curved into that provocative smile. "But alas, not even you have the stamina to keep me occupied all the time."

"And Wantage did not provide sufficient entertainment for you?"

"Of course not," Lottie said. "How could it?" She flicked him another look. "There is no theater or concerts but for those ghastly musical displays that Captain Le Grand organizes, and no balls and parties, at least not the sort that I am invited to attend. You can go to those tiresome gentry dinners whilst I am considered too decadent." Her scarlet fan tapped his chest. "Well,

I can come up to London, whilst you cannot. At least you *should* not." She frowned. "How comes it you are here? Do you have permission from the Parole Officer? And how did you find me?"

"So many questions," Ethan mocked, "now that your thirst for revenge is quenched."

He saw the temper flare in her eyes. "At least I am *free* to come here and take my revenge on Gregory." Now her tone mocked *him.* "I went to the most delightful play last night, my lord. Incognito, of course, but even so I was in no danger of arrest. Unlike you. And tomorrow—"

"Tomorrow you will be back in Wantage with me," Ethan said.

"Not if I find myself a new protector before then," Lottie said sweetly.

Ethan bit back the instinctive repudiation that sprang to his lips. God help him, he had been about to forbid it, claim her, say: "You are mine, I want you, I refuse to cede to another man…."

Masculine pride, primitive possessiveness, jealousy… He had never been motivated by any of those emotions before. And she was testing him, pushing him a little to see how far she could go. He was not going to rise to that provocation just to please her. He smiled down at her.

"How busy you have been in the couple of days since I have seen you, madam. Any success in that direction yet?"

Her lips pressed together in temper. "Do you think that I would tell you if I had?"

"No," Ethan said. "I think you would fleece me and then run off with another man without a word."

She laughed. A couple of heads turned in their direction at the sound, so full of genuine amusement, and she quieted at once, as though aware that someone might recognize her.

"It is true that you know me very well, my lord." Her voice had quieted, too. "But you offer me nothing." She sounded disdainful. "Other than this—" Her hand slid to the band of his pantaloons and he stopped her with an iron grip.

"Enough, madam. Not here, now. Unless it pleases you to make love with me in your former husband's house?"

Again that little smile played about her lips. "I'll allow that the idea has some appeal, but... No, on balance, I think not."

"Then come and dance with me instead." The lilt of the waltz was calling to them from the ballroom.

He could see that the idea intrigued her. She had never thought that they would waltz together in a London ballroom. Neither had he, for that matter.

"Dance?" she said. "In there—in front of everyone?"

He drew her toward the ballroom doors. "Of course. Are you nervous that someone will recognize you?"

She was. He could feel her hesitation even as she denied it. "No, of course not. I have been here a full hour and no one knows who I am." She paused. "Except your brother, Northesk. He gave me a very searching look when we met in the library."

They stepped into the dance. It was a risk, a dare,

and he knew that Lottie would not shrink from it simply because that would prove she was afraid, prove that he had won the challenge. Her scarlet domino flared out to reveal a gown of silver beneath. The silk brushed his thigh, rippling, smooth and sensuous as Lottie herself. The other dancers swooped past as the rhythm of the music swept them up and spun them around, and Lottie smiled with exhilaration, as light as thistledown in his arms.

"You dance well," she murmured. "I would have expected a cavalryman to thunder around the room as a horse would."

"You do the cavalry an injustice," Ethan said. "Our leg muscles are very well developed. It makes us the best of dancers."

"I had noticed your well-developed muscles." Her voice was dry. She tilted her head to look at him. "So how *did* you find me, my lord?"

"You had told Margery you were coming to London," Ethan said.

"It is a big place."

"It was not so difficult."

It had not been. He had a network set up to gather intelligence about the war, about prisoners and escape routes. Such an intelligence service could also gather information of another sort and find a wayward mistress who was flitting about London incognito and causing quite a stir in the process.

"And why did you trouble to follow me?" Her voice was soft. "Did you miss me?"

That, Ethan thought, was a very good question.

"I wished to ascertain whether or not you would

come back," he said. Half truths, he thought. Actually she deserved better than that. He had come to find her, to claim her, because he did not want to be without her.

"Did it matter whether I came back or not?"

That was another good question. Ethan had forgotten her penchant for putting him on the spot. He hesitated. What had she said?

You offer me nothing....

He thought about it. It was true that he had given her nothing but money. That had been their agreement. He had bought her for her scandalous name. He did not trust her. He had barely confided in her, other than a few insights into his childhood and a brief painful mention of his son. He had rejected her attempts to draw closer to him. He had even turned from her after the intimacy of making love with such profound and tender passion.

He was using her—even tonight, on his way to find her, he had stopped in some smoky tavern in the rookeries off the Radcliffe Highway to exchange information, letters, plans and news, sending out more spies, more instructions as the day grew closer when the conspiracy would come together. That would be the day he would leave her, with the pile of cash that would be her final payoff.

Except...

Except that he did not want to lose her. He knew that now. He had known it when he had returned to Priory Cottage and found her gone. They were two of a kind, he and Lottie. They understood one another.

For the first time he considered taking her with him. And wondered if she would be prepared to go.

"Yes," he said. "It mattered whether or not you would come back to me."

Something shimmered in her eyes behind the mask, an emotion that gave the lie to all her claims of indifference. He felt it, too, the tug of emotion that went deeper than lust. He remembered the times he had made love to her and lost himself in that sense of rightness, of recognition. Such a dangerous affinity, for a man who had never loved and who wanted no ties to bind him. He had been fighting this feeling for weeks. Now he admitted that it had finally caught up with him and it showed no signs of letting him go.

Lottie did not speak. Ethan wished that she would, to break that moment. It felt like a strange magic, the music, Lottie in his arms, and the candlelight and her scent of flowers and summer leaves. He felt like an untried youth who had never had a woman before. Bizarre. Impossible…

There was a clatter of noise in the ballroom doorway and a splash of red uniforms. Candlelight struck metal. Pistols. Someone screamed. The music faded, discordant, and died away. There was a silence with an odd quality of tension to it.

"We have come to arrest the parole breaker, Ethan Ryder." The captain had stepped forward. "We have information that he is here."

The crowd gasped with a mixture of fear and excitement, rippling like corn in a storm. A corpulent man in a blue domino, whom Ethan assumed to be Gregory

Cummings, had ripped off his mask and was advancing on the posse of soldiers.

"Ridiculous!" he sneered. "Ryder, here? How dare you disrupt my ball on such a foolish basis, sir!"

Lottie's hand was in his, tugging at him. "This way," she whispered in his ear. She was drawing him stealthily through the shifting crowd with a murmured "excuse me" here and an apology there as she stood on someone's foot. But it was impossible to be surreptitious in scarlet. Heads turned, people pointed. The captain broke off his apologies and explanations to shout an order. And then Lottie was running, dragging him with her, through the door into the refreshment room, pulling the cloth from the table to scatter silver dishes in the path of the pursuing soldiers. One of them raised his pistol, and Ethan saw a man in a domino stumble heavily against the soldier just as he was about to take the shot. It flew wide, smashing a bust of Cummings himself on a marble side table.

"Frightfully sorry, old chap," the man said. Ethan recognized Northesk's voice. He raised a hand in brief thanks and Northesk nodded acknowledgement.

Then Lottie was bundling him through the refreshment room door, into the library—which smelled deliciously of burning tobacco—over to a spiral stair in the corner. She grabbed an antiquated sword from the wall and threw it to him, by which he realized she meant him to fight on the stairs. Ethan wondered if the sword was even serviceable. Well, he would find out. The soldiers were bursting into the library now and piling toward the spiral stair. Lottie was dragging him backward up the steps. It was the devil of a job to fight at the same time, though there was only room for one man to challenge him at a time and the turn of the stair gave him the fighting advantage. He really did not want to kill anyone because then he would be in genuine trouble, so he had to very careful. He nicked one man in the arm, slicing through his sleeve if little else, and caught the next in the shoulder. The whole posse fell back in dismay at the sight of blood. Really, Ethan thought, if this was the way the British fought they did not deserve their reputation. And the antiquated sword was proving rather good. It had excellent balance.

He and Lottie fell backward into an upstairs bedroom and Lottie slammed the door in the faces of their pursuers, turning the key in the lock. Ethan put out a hand to steady her, slow her down, but she was in full flood now and could not be stopped. She had torn off her mask and her eyes were alight with excitement and fervor. Her hair streamed from beneath the hood of the domino, chestnut and gold, adorned with glittering rubies.

"The servants' stair!" she gasped. "Come on!"

With a philosophical shrug, Ethan followed her through a maze of connecting doors, bedroom to bedroom, down the servants' stair, flight after flight until they reached the kitchen, the servants jumping back at the sight of the naked blade, a scullery maid screaming with her apron over her head, a potboy leaping for cover and Gregory Cummings puffing through the door with the Captain in his wake. Ethan was willing to bet that it was the first time Cummings had ever visited his own kitchens. The Captain raised his rifle and missed Ethan completely, the bullet ricocheting off a large iron cooking pot and smashing through a window. A man came at him from the left with a kitchen knife. Ethan disarmed him with a quick twist of the wrist. Out of the corner of his eyes he could see Lottie taking advantage of the moment her former husband's attention was distracted to break a flan dish over his head. Gregory Cummings slumped to the floor.

"The *Ton* will be talking about this for years to come," a voice said in his ear, and then Northesk had taken his arm and swept Lottie up, too, and was ushering them out into the Mews where there was already a closed carriage put to with horses, waiting.

"Give me your papers," Northesk said, holding out his hand. "I'll sort this out for you."

Ethan reached into his breast pocket and handed over the letter from Mr. Duster granting permission for his trip. He shook Northesk's hand. "Thank you."

Northesk nodded. "Godspeed."

Lottie was looking at him, her eyes wide and dark. To forestall the questions he knew were coming, Ethan bundled her up into the carriage, slammed the door and tapped on the roof. The coach sprang forward.

Lottie took a deep breath. "You had permission to be here *all along?*"

Ethan grinned. "Of course."

Lottie's face was working like milk coming up to the boil. "Then what the *devil* was all that about?"

"When a detachment of soldiers come at you with rifles, you tend to fight first and ask questions later," Ethan said mildly. "Otherwise you may end up dead before you get the chance to ask anything. Besides," he added, "you were having such a good time. I did not want to spoil it for you."

"I? I was terrified!" Lottie looked furious. "I thought they would arrest you—or kill you!" Her eyes kindled. "Not that you do not deserve it! I wonder why I tried to help you! Clearly I am completely misguided."

Ethan caught her angrily flailing hands and placed a kiss in her palm. "You enjoyed it," he said. "Admit it."

Her fingers curled over to trap the kiss. "I enjoyed besting Gregory with a cooking dish. That is true." She hesitated. "I suppose it was rather fun…." A reluctant smile tilted the corner of her lips. "You do fight awfully well, Ethan Ryder. I am glad I have seen it or else I might never have believed your legend. How you managed not to kill any of those soldiers is beyond me."

"It was difficult," Ethan said. "I am afraid that I seem to have stolen this rather excellent sword," he added. He placed the rapier gently on the floor of the carriage. "Perhaps I should return it?"

"I wouldn't bother." Lottie raised one shoulder in a light shrug. "Gregory could never use it anyway. He could not fight his way out from behind a newspaper." Her eyes narrowed. "If you had permission to come up to Town, Ethan, why would the authorities think that you did not?"

"A fair question," Ethan said. "I imagine that someone has been trying to stir up trouble for me."

He lay back against the seat. The smooth movement of the carriage rocked him, soothing the fever in his veins, blunting the edges of his bloodlust. Kill or be killed. Fight and escape. There lay the key, he thought.

Someone had set a trap for him. Someone had wanted him to fight and to be killed.

"I think someone sent word to the authorities in London that I had broken parole," he said slowly. "I think they were hoping that I would not have the chance to proffer my papers, that because I am considered dangerous they would come for me with swords or pistols, and I would not have a chance."

Lottie's gaze was narrowed on him. She sat forward. "A trigger-happy soldier, or a stray bullet..."

"Quite," Ethan said. "Yes, it would have been very easy to have been killed back there. My papers would have been found to have been in order, of course, but by then it would have been too late."

"Clever," Lottie said. Her eyes were bright on him in the darkness. "Who?"

Ethan shook his head. "Who knows? We have discussed before that there may be a spy within the ranks in Wantage." He hesitated. "It could be Purchase. As an American he is more the natural ally of the British than he is of the French."

Lottie shook her head stubbornly. "Purchase is an honorable man," she said. "He would not sell you out."

"Northesk, then," Ethan said. "He plays some interesting games."

Lottie's eyes opened wide in genuine shock. "You cannot believe that of him! He helped us! You said yourself that he was the only good one in your entire family."

Ethan shrugged. He felt tired. The taste of betrayal was in his mouth again and he hated it. This was such a dirty business, using people, trusting no one, not knowing who was friend or foe. He raised his gaze to meet Lottie's.

"Perhaps it was you," he said softly. "This London trip of yours—perhaps it was a suggestion of your brother's? You told him about Chard's death, didn't you? Even though you had promised me you would not, you wrote to him to tell him of my involvement in it."

There was such a long silence, stretching taut as a straining rope. The carriage was out of London now and rolling along at a dangerous pace. In the skipping lamplight he could not read Lottie's expression. She shifted restlessly on the seat.

"Yes, I did tell Theo," she said, and oddly, given that she was confessing to another betrayal, Ethan felt relieved. At least she did not lie to him.

She cleared her throat. Her voice was husky, underscored with some emotion he could not interpret. "Why should I not?" She sounded tired, too, and there was nothing of justification in her voice, merely a simple question. "You have offered me nothing, Ethan."

It was true. It was exactly what Ethan had been thinking earlier, before he had nearly—oh so nearly—asked her to come away with him. Lottie had no loyalty to him. He paid her to warm his bed, no more. So why did the realization hurt so much? He shook his head sharply to try to dispel the ache, but it was in his heart, not his mind.

"By the time Chard died," he said, "I was in your bed, not lurking in the jakes of some seedy inn with a knife. They will not be able to pin that one on me."

Lottie shrugged. "Then it does not matter, does it?"

But it did matter, Ethan thought. It mattered that she would promise him one thing and then so casually break her word to safeguard her future.

"And tonight—" He shifted. "Did you and Theo hatch this plot together? Did you tempt me up to London in pursuit whilst he called in the soldiers? Did you pretend to help me escape, thereby making it all the more likely that someone would try and shoot me…?" He waited. "No one but Margery knew where you had gone," he said gently. "You must be the one who betrayed me again."

She moved before he even realized what she was doing, grabbed the rapier from the floor of the carriage and held it to his throat.

"You think I seek your death?" she said. He could feel the anger in her, burning like brittle sticks on the fire. "Then what is stopping me from killing you now?"

Ethan spread his arms wide. "Nothing but your lack of courage, I would think. Or perhaps your desire to screw more money from me before you do the deed?"

The light shifted, the carriage jolted and the blade pricked his throat. "Have a care, sir." She sounded furious. "I am the one holding the weapon here."

"But you won't use it." Ethan raised his hand to flick the blade aside. He was rewarded by a cut to the palm.

"You were right," Lottie said. "It is a fine sword." She took a breath. "I had nothing to do with betraying you tonight. I have never sought to kill you. Spy on you, inform on you, yes. Kill you, no. Believe me."

"Believe you at the point of a sword?" Ethan said. He shrugged. "We have never trusted one another. Why does it matter?"

Lottie's expression puckered. He could sense both anger and distress in her now. "It matters," she said.

"Why?" He watched her face, the chase of emotions across it that betrayed every element of the conflict raging inside her.

"Why," he repeated softly.

"Because," Lottie burst out, "sometimes I do not know if I love you or hate you, Ethan!" She brought the sword down in a slice that cut through his jacket and the shirt beneath. He felt the cold blade against his skin, felt it drop to skewer his pantaloons and damn near skewer him. His beautiful handmade evening coat split apart. A button was cut free and rolled noisily across the floor of the carriage. His shirt was in shreds, his pantaloons gaping open. The cool caress of the rapier tickled his inner thigh.

"Oh…" There was a world of discovery in Lottie's voice. "I like this."

"Be careful with that blade," Ethan said, "or you'll get precious little more pleasure from me."

She laughed and raised the rapier to flick aside the tattered rags of his once-pristine neck cloth. The blade caressed his throat. Hell, the woman was mad. In the light of the carriage lamps he could see the vivid flare of excitement in her eyes and a wicked smile on her lips. The rapier menaced him again.

"Strip for me," she said. "Last time we were in a carriage you made me suffer your demands. Now it's my turn. Take off your clothes."

"You've done a pretty good job of that already," Ethan said. He kept a wary eye on the point of the sword. The lurching of the carriage and Lottie's inexpert aim threatened to take away more than his decency. He ripped the ruins of the cravat from his neck and shrugged off his shirt. The sword danced across his chest like a rain of kisses.

"Very nice," Lottie said. "Your pantaloons."

Ethan stepped out of them. There was no concealing his monstrous erection, no concealing anything.

"I do believe," Lottie said, staring, "that danger excites you."

Ethan moved fast then, wrapping the remains of his jacket about his hand, catching the end of the rapier and twisting it out of her hand with a strength and speed that left her gasping.

"Never point a sword at a trained soldier," he said pleasantly, reversing the rapier into his own hand. "It is asking for trouble."

With a swift slash he cut the ribbons of the domino and sliced straight down the front of the silver gown. Lottie screamed.

"Ethan, no! This was made by Madame Celestine and cost you a fortune—"

Too late. The gown crumpled from her like a broken shell, leaving Lottie, lusciously curved and indecently clad, bursting out of her chemise in all her beautiful opulence. Ethan lost his powers of concentration completely. He dropped the rapier with a clatter and caught hold of Lottie about the waist, pulling her to him, kissing her fiercely until everything dissolved into heat and blinding light and driving lust. They tumbled down onto the seat where the roll of the carriage and the urgent press of their bodies came together in a spectacular explosion that had them both crying out in ecstasy. It was over in seconds.

"So," he said, when his breathing had steadied sufficiently to speak, "have you decided? Do you love me or hate me?" He drew her closer and pressed his lips to the silken swathe of her hair.

He felt her smile against his neck. "Oh," she said. "I hate you. Most definitely."

He wrapped them both in the scarlet domino and also a black cloak, which Northesk had thoughtfully provided in the carriage and which had fortuitously survived Lottie's slashing blade. He drifted off to sleep, lulled by the rhythm of the coach and by Lottie's scent, and the feel of her body, soft and warm in his arms. There was a sense of rightness about it that troubled him, because beneath the surface of peace and contentment he knew that nothing had changed between them. One of them was always destined to be the betrayer and the other the betrayed.

CHAPTER FOURTEEN

LOTTIE WOKE TO DAYLIGHT and to the slowing of the carriage as it approached Wantage. She remembered the night like a flying dream: the journey; the inns where they had stopped to change horses; even a brief, blurred moment when, half-asleep, she had struggled back into the tatters of the silver dress and had wrapped herself in Ethan's jacket in order to go inside to wash and take a hasty cup of chocolate. The landlord and the sleepy hostlers had stared at her and little wonder. She peered into the speckled mirror in the ladies' withdrawing room and recognized that she looked a fright. For once she had not cared.

She raised the blind. Ethan was still sleeping like the dead. She had tried to make him respectable again by wrapping him in the remnants of his clothes but it was a lost cause. Both of them, she thought, looked utterly disreputable. Both of them *were* utterly disreputable. Soon people would be talking about their exploits this night from London to Land's End; the way in which they had secretly infiltrated Gregory's masked ball, the dramatic entry of the troops and their even more color-ful escape, the wild lovemaking in the carriage... That was what Ethan would want, of course. And though she had thrived on being outrageous for what seemed a very long time now, Lottie's heart felt bruised to think that there was no more than scandal between them.

Money for scandal... That had been their agreement. Nothing had changed.

She looked at Ethan's profile etched in the pale morning light. His cheek was darkened with stubble—she shivered a little as she remembered the brush of it against her bare skin—and his black hair was tousled. He lay a little uncomfortably, for the seat was too short to accommodate his height. She suspected he would be aching when he awoke, and not simply from the discomfort of his position.

Sometimes I do not know if I love you or hate you....

That had been a lie. She knew she loved him. She loved him not with the desperate pleading need that she had felt for some of her lovers, begging for their attention, wanting to matter to them, but with a deeper and more profound feeling she had never experienced before in all her thirty-three—not twenty-eight—years. She loved him so much that when he had accused her of conspiring to seek his death she had thought her heart would break in two with the pain of the deceit and betrayal that lay between them, with despair over her own perfidious nature and the desperate need for security that drove her always to put herself first. She knew it was impossible that they could ever trust one another. She could not even trust herself.

The carriage rattled over the cobbles of Wantage's market square, slowed and drew to a stop outside The Bear Hotel. Well, Lottie thought, this should be another arrival that the good people of Wantage could dissect and gossip over for a twelvemonth.

Then she saw that there was a welcoming party outside the coaching inn. Duster, the Parole Officer, was there, turning his hat around and around in his fidgeting hands. There was Jacques Le Prevost, looking urbane and handsome but also severe, and Owen Purchase, his fair open face set and dark for once. A sliver of apprehension touched Lottie's spine.

Ethan opened his eyes. The sleep in them fled. Within a moment he was awake and alert, his gaze riveted on her face.

"What is it?" he said.

"I don't know," Lottie said. "But I think that there is something wrong."

Ethan had a hand on the catch of the door before the coach had come to a halt and was jumping down onto the cobbles, and, despite his haste, turning to swing Lottie down before he turned from her with a word of apology to address Mr. Duster.

"Sir?" he said. "I did not expect a reception party."

Le Prevost stepped forward and put a hand on Ethan's arm. "It is your son, St. Severin," he said. There was regret in his voice, and compassion. "I am sorry, *mon ami*. He escaped from Whitemoor gaol last night. They are hunting him now. The orders are to shoot him on sight."

THERE WAS A SOLDIER ON DUTY outside the door of Ethan's room on the second floor of The Bear Hotel. He was slumped on a hard wooden chair but he straightened automatically when he saw Lottie approaching along the corridor.

"No visitors, ma'am," he said. "Orders of the Parole Officer."

"Yes," Lottie said, smiling at him, "I quite understand, Sergeant. But Mr. Duster did not mean that to apply to *me*, I assure you. Who better than I to provide Lord St. Severin with some comfort at this time?"

The soldier's eyes narrowed thoughtfully on her as he considered the type of comfort that she might be offering. "Well, ma'am, I suppose…"

"Oh, thank you!" Lottie said, breezing forward. She turned the door handle. It was locked. "Sergeant," she prompted, with a pretty gesture of appeal, and the man came forward eagerly enough to unlock it for her. Really, Lottie thought, as she knocked and entered the room, one could go a long way on charm and barefaced cheek.

She had never seen inside Ethan's chamber before, for he had never invited her. This, of course, was Ethan's prison. She realized it with an odd flutter of the heart. He might be given a nominal liberty as an officer on parole, but now she saw the shabby chamber with its bare wooden floor and frayed rug, the battered desk and narrow cot, she knew just how illusory that freedom was. For now he was penned in here as tightly as any inmate at Whitemoor. She could feel his tension and his frustration. The atmosphere was explosive with it as he paced back and forth across the tight boundaries of the room.

He looked up as she came in. His blue eyes were

shadowed and dark, impassive. But the muscles around his eyes were tight and his face pale and drawn with strain.

"What are you doing here?" He rapped the words out in a voice rough with pain. "Did Duster send you?"

"No," Lottie said. "I talked my way past the guard. Ethan—" She put a hand on his sleeve and felt him flinch.

"I don't want to talk to you." He turned his back on her.

This, then, was the ultimate rebuff, the ultimate expression of his lack of trust in her. He would never turn to her or let her offer him comfort. Lottie knew that the cause was lost.

Ethan's shoulders were rigid with rejection. The hurt tumbled over and over inside her. She could see every single one of her lovers walking away from her, Gregory delivering the crushing news of the divorce, and like a ghost behind them all, her father, leaving on that bright summer day so like this morning in this stiflingly hot little room under the eaves.

Little Lottie Palliser. No one wanted her. She should go.

Except that this time she was not going to give in. This time she would take one last gamble because she loved Ethan too much not to try.

She put out a tentative hand and touched Ethan's shoulder. It was the hardest thing she had ever done. His muscles felt tight and unyielding beneath her hand. He did not move.

"Tell me about your son," she said. She scarcely

recognized her own voice because it was shaking, but there was still a thread of strength in it. "Tell me about Arland."

FOR A MOMENT Ethan was afraid that he was going to explode with anger and frustration. Could the damned woman not leave him alone? How brutal did he have to be to get rid of her? Fury raked him and beneath it a pain so excruciating he caught his breath. He had never taken comfort from any other human being in his life. There had been no one to offer it. He had wanted no one. He was strong. He did not need protection, succor or consolation.

He strode over to the window and stared across the rooftops of the town to where the white chalk towers of Whitemoor soared against the blue sky. It looked so beautiful for such a hellhole. He could *see* the place where they had incarcerated his son but he could never see Arland himself. It was a deliberate torment that the authorities had inflicted on him and he had tried to ignore it, but each and every day it had fretted at him like the flick of a whip. And now his son was alone and unprotected, hunted like an animal, and he was penned here and could not help him. He was the ultimate failure as a father.

Tell me about your son….

Ethan closed his eyes. Almost he told her the truth. Almost he exposed all the grief and doubt that he had hidden for so long.

I am no good for him and I never shall be.

It is my fault that he was imprisoned and is now on

*the run in terrible peril. I could not protect him. I have
failed him.*

He felt Lottie's touch on his arm and threw her off.
The pain inside him spun like a Catherine wheel, spark
after spark of grief.

"I do not want to talk about him," he said. His voice
was so rough it did not sound like his own.

Her chin came up. "I understand that you must be
upset—"

Upset?

"You have *no* idea." He bit out the words, turning
on her, blind in his fury and desperation, wanting to
be alone. "Now go."

"No. Ethan, you need me."

"I don't want you here." He did not know how to
make her leave. She stood there stubbornly, holding her
ground with that damnable obstinacy he was beginning
to see was one of her defining characteristics, and she
would not leave.

He stepped back, raised his hands. "Go before I put
you from the room myself."

She walked right up to him. "Do it, then."

Slowly his hands came down to rest on her shoulders,
lightly, stiffly, as though he was afraid of what he might
do to her.

"Lottie—" It was her last chance.

She stayed still beneath his touch.

"I saw you in London after Northesk spoke to you
about Arland," she said softly. "I know you care for
him as a father should care for his child."

"I do not." His voice shook.

I cannot afford to care.

"We cannot always choose how we feel." She sounded as though she knew.

"I chose to bring him into the world," Ethan burst out. "And then I could not protect him." The anger flared in him, died. "I am just like my father," he said quietly.

"You are *nothing* like Farne." Now Lottie sounded angry. "When he took you from your mother it was an exercise of power. He cares nothing for doing the right thing! Whereas you—" She made a little helpless gesture. "Well, you would not be here now, would you, if you did not hold fast to your principles."

Something eased a fraction inside Ethan, like the very tiniest slipping of an intolerably tight knot. "You give me too much credit." His voice was rusty. "Let me tell you how it was and then you will see."

Lottie said nothing, but she moved away and sat down on the edge of his bunk, curling her legs up under her like a child settling itself for a bedtime story.

"I was nineteen when Arland was conceived," Ethan said, "twenty when he was born. His mother was older, a French aristocrat whose family had fallen on hard times during the Revolution. Most lost their heads. Louise survived through selling herself body and soul."

He saw a flicker of expression in Lottie's face. "Poor girl," she said softly. "Did you love her?"

Ethan shook his head. "No, I did not. I wanted her and I was flattered that she should choose me of all the gallants who flocked to her door, but I was young and careless and I loved no one but myself." He sighed. "Nevertheless, when I knew she was carrying my child

I swore to care for them both." He smiled faintly.
"Truth to tell, I could not be certain that Arland *was*
my child—until I saw him."

"Is the resemblance very strong?" Lottie asked.

"Undeniable." Ethan said. "The moment I set eyes on
him…" He frowned. How could he explain the sense of
bewilderment, the miraculous disbelief, that had possessed him when he, barely more than a child himself,
had seen the life that he and Louise had created? Except
that the emotion had terrified him, too, and in the end
it was the fear that had won.

"I loved him," he said with difficulty, "but I was too
immature to accept the responsibility. I behaved like a
coward. Louise had an aunt and uncle still living, farm-
ing in the Midi. When she said she was going south
to join them I—" he made a hopeless gesture "—I let
her go. To my eternal shame—" He swallowed hard.
"I did not offer to accompany her, to try to make a new
life with her and my son. I let her go alone and I let her
take Arland away."

"You were barely twenty years old—" Lottie began.
But Ethan brushed aside her attempt at comfort. "I was
old enough to father a child but not brave enough to
be a father to that child," he said scathingly. "Yes, I
was young and poor and dependent on the favor of the
Emperor. I had nothing to offer them but myself. But
that could have been enough."

There was a silence in the hot little room. Down
below came the shouts of the cellarer as he rolled the
barrels of the beer into the taproom.

Lottie sighed and stirred slightly. "What happened?"
she said.

"For ten years I told myself that Arland was better off without me," Ethan said painfully. "I told myself that he had a secure home, and a family, and that in contrast I could give him nothing. My behavior grew more and more reckless." He moved his shoulders restlessly beneath his jacket. The room was stifling. He wanted to be out in the fresh air, to try to clear his head of these feverish, desperate thoughts and come up with a cool, rational plan of how he might save Arland. But of course he could not leave. He was locked in, a prisoner, useless, emasculated.

"I took on suicidal missions," he said. "I felt as though I wanted to kill myself. I did kill others." He shook his head sharply. "Oh, they tell me it made me a hero, that it was for a cause worth believing in, that men die in battle…. Only I know that my reasons were dark and twisted, not always prompted by principle, as people credit me."

"You were punishing yourself," Lottie whispered.

"Perhaps," Ethan said. "Anyway, it did not serve. The need to see Arland grew stronger and stronger. It did not diminish. So once I had made a little money and bought some land I wrote to Louise." He stopped. He could remember every searing word of the letter he had received in reply, an indictment of his selfishness, tearing apart the defense he had carefully constructed, the belief that he had been doing the right thing in turning his back on his son.

Through your utter indifference toward Arland you have forfeited the right ever to call him your son…

He had known it for the truth it was. He was not worthy of the child. He had pretended it was best for the boy to let his mother take him away. He had soothed his conscience by thinking that he was a bad example, a man with nothing to offer, the wild, bastard son of a whore-mongering father. He had told himself that Louise and her family could offer Arland the home and the steady life that he never could. But it had all been lies to cover his weakness. The truth was that he had failed. He had failed as a father. He had failed his son.

"What did she say?" Lottie asked.

Ethan gave a faint smile. "She told me that I had left it too late. She had never told Arland his father's name and that as far as her family was concerned, I was dead to them all."

Lottie winced. "Like as not she did not really mean it," she said. "We all say harsh things in the heat of the moment."

Ethan shrugged. "Louise had justification," he said. "God knows, I deserved nothing from her. I had never sent them a scrap of money or anything else to help them, even though I knew that the Emperor's taxes were punitive and the harvests had been poor." He ran a hand over his hair. "I wrote to Arland." He had written, time and again, as reckless to regain his son as he had been to repudiate him. He had snatched moments in between campaigns, with the heat and the stench and the filth and the despair of battle all around. He had not known what to say to the son he had never met, and yet he had tried because it had been the only thing he could do.

"His mother only gave him the letters when she died," he said. "And then Arland came looking for me."

"He wanted a father," Lottie said softly. "I understand that."

Ethan's stomach lurched. "He lied about his age to join the Emperor's army," he said. "It was the only way that he could get to me."

"He sounds just like you," Lottie said. "I expect you did that twenty years ago."

"I did," Ethan admitted. "But that does not mean I wanted my son to do the same.

"I wanted to send him back to Angeville," he added, "but it was too late and Arland refused to go. The cavalry was already at Fuentes de Onoro. I tried to protect him, to keep him close. But I failed in that, too. We were captured. Then I tried to keep him out of the hands of the British. I offered a ransom, I offered myself…" He stopped. The despair had left him feeling hollow and drained. "You see how it is, Lottie," he said. "I have failed Arland every step of the way."

Lottie came across to him and put her arms about him. "All I see," she said, "is a man who has had to overcome so much, who has made mistakes and has tried to put them right."

Ethan tried to pull away from her. He did not want her sympathy because he did not deserve it. Nor did he want anyone to draw close to him. But Lottie would not be rejected now. She rested her cheek against his chest and kept her arms about him and he felt the resistance in him shiver and start to dissolve, like a veil parting, falling away as he reached out hungrily to her for comfort.

"I know what it is like to want a father to admire and respect," Lottie said. She gave him a fierce little shake. "There is much to admire in you, Ethan Ryder, and Arland recognizes that. You are all he has left. Do not deny him the right to love you if he chooses. Live up to his regard."

The crack in Ethan's heart gaped wider. There was a moment when he resisted, teetering on the edge, and then he pulled Lottie to him fiercely, holding her close, as though he would never let her go again. He spoke urgently, heedless of her loyalties now, heedless of what he might be giving away.

"I would have got him out of there, Lottie," he said. "I had a plan to help him. Twice I had tried to free him, only to be thwarted, but I would have tried again and again…."

Lottie hushed him like a child. "Shh, I know. I know you would." She rubbed her cheek against his chest. "I understand."

He wanted to sink into the feeling then, to grasp the comfort she offered and hold it tightly, never letting it go. Once, in London, he had felt this impossible grief for Arland, and he had taken Lottie and used her physically as a means to forget, as an escape, for a few desperate moments, from the torture. Now, though, the solace he wanted went deeper. He did not want to lose himself in her body only for the pain to reassert itself as soon as his pleasure was spent. He wanted her always to be there so that they could shield each other, giving and taking, so that he could protect her as well as draw strength from her.

It seemed impossible when there was so much to divide them.

He drew away from her a little and looked down into her face.

"Lottie…" he began, although he was not sure what he was trying to say.

"Hush." She pressed her fingers to his lips. She was smiling a little but her eyes swam with tears. "Don't say anything. Just hold me."

He did. They stood locked together for a very long time and he felt at peace and he knew that somehow this time he had crossed a line and there would be no going back.

CHAPTER FIFTEEN

IT WAS A SULTRY late-August night, heavy and dark
with the oppressive heat that precedes a thunderstorm.
Lottie could not sleep. Her mind ran like a rat in a trap,
scampering from thoughts of Ethan locked in his airless
little room under the eaves at The Bear Hotel to his son,
alone and friendless, being hunted through the length
of the kingdom. She rolled over, thumped the pillow,
then threw herself down again with a sigh. It was too
hot to sleep anyway but her thoughts gave her no rest.
Ethan's powerful frustration had communicated itself
to her along with a desperate desire to do something,
anything, to help.

   She had spent the afternoon in the markets and
shops, drifting from one place to another, listening to
gossip, trying to pick up the slightest hint that anyone
knew of the whereabouts of Arland Ryder. She had sent
Margery out to make discreet enquiries amongst the
servants and mill workers, dropping the delicate hint of
a reward for information. She had heard nothing. Most
of the gossip had been about her; everyone, it seemed,
had heard of her jaunt to London and now the *on dit*
was that she had shot her former husband with an an-
tique pistol before riding off bareback on one of Ethan's
carriage horses. Encouragingly, most people seemed to
applaud this imaginary action. Gregory Cummings was

a banker, and many people mistrusted the grotesquely rich in these times of war, food shortages and hardship for so many.

The bedroom curtains billowed in a sudden draft at the open window. There was a scrambling sound and then a man tumbled into the room and lay winded on the floor. Lottie grabbed the chamber pot and brandished it threateningly. He might be a very incompetent burglar but she was taking no chances.

"Don't scream!" The figure scrambled to his feet and raised a pleading hand. He staggered toward Lottie and grabbed her arm. He was panting hard, a long tear down his prison uniform sleeve and a slash to his face that oozed blood.

Lottie stared and dropped the pot with a loud clatter.

"Arland," she said.

The Marquess of Northesk had borne a similarity to Ethan in his features and bearing, but the likeness had been elusive and the coloring of the two men completely different. Arland, though, was the image of his father. There was no mistaking it. It was just as Ethan had said. Looking at Arland was like looking at a mirror image of Ethan. Except, on second glance, it was not. There was something so young and untried in the boy's face compared to the strength and watchfulness in the man. Arland was already tall and broad, but he still had the slight clumsiness of youth, a gangling quality as though he had not yet grown into his own body. And he looked emaciated, ill and exhausted beneath the disfiguring bruises and cuts of his face.

Lottie felt her heart jerk and start to beat harder.

"They said to come here," Arland gasped. His English was good but he had a strong French accent, almost exotic. He caught Lottie's arm, panting for breath. "Can you hide me?" he said. "Please?"

"Who—" Lottie began, but Arland shook his head.

"There's no time to explain! Please, they're close behind me—"

As though to underline his words there was a pounding of steps outside, wild shouts and a volley of knocks on the front door.

"They will find you if they search the house," Lottie said. Her mind was spinning, running from one plan to another, searching for an idea. It was impossible to give him up to the authorities. In the past she might have been prepared to betray Ethan but this was different. Ethan could take care of himself. Arland was a boy, too young to have been made a pawn in such a dirty game of war. He had already seen too much and suffered too much. Besides, Lottie knew that she could never betray Ethan again now, least of all through his son. Something had happened between them that afternoon when he had finally confided in her, something fundamental and profound, something that tied her to him more tightly than self-interest or greed or security ever could. She was not sure she cared for it. Selfless love was scarcely her specialty. But she did not seem able to escape it now.

"Take your clothes off," she said abruptly.

Arland recoiled violently from her. "I beg your pardon, *madame?*"

"Take your clothes off, hide them and get into my bed." The hammering at the door grew louder. Lottie could hear Margery's voice and the drawing back of the bolts.

"Do as I say," Lottie added sharply. "Hurry!"

She saw the understanding dawn in Arland's eyes and pushed him toward the bed. Grabbing her swansdown negligee, she ran to the armoire, pulled out some clothes of Ethan's and scattered them on the floor, entangling them with her own garments as though both sets had been discarded in a frenzy of passion. She hurried to the door. No need to disorder her hair; she had been roused from her bed by Arland's arrival and a quick glance in the pier glass told her she looked tumbled and rumpled, hopefully sufficient to distract the soldiers from their duty. She glanced again at the negligee and the transparent nightgown beneath. Oh yes, there was plenty there to distract the search party.

The hall was already seething with soldiers. Margery stood with a candle in her hand, looking small and frightened.

Lottie stopped at the top of the stairs.

"What is going on here?" She spoke with all the imperious authority of the Dukes of Palliser and saw the group of men freeze and turn to gaze up at her. She was incensed to see that they had already started to rifle carelessly through her possessions. The small table with its pretty flower arrangement had been overturned and one of the hangings pulled from the wall. She could hear raised voices in the parlor and the tramp of footsteps.

"Soldiers, madam!" Margery was trembling. "They say that the escaped prisoner is here." She cast Lottie a pitiful glance. "Are we all to be murdered in our beds, ma'am?"

"Of course not!" Lottie spoke bracingly as she came down the stairs. "I never heard such nonsense." She turned to the soldiers who were looking variously bashful, lascivious or nervous according to their dispositions. "Or do you mean we will be trampled to death by this mob of ruffians? Very likely!" Her eye fell on the officer who appeared to be in charge, a fair, tall young man who looked barely out of the nursery.

"Lieutenant, what is the meaning of this intrusion?"

The lieutenant blushed. "My apologies for disturbing you, ma'am. Your maid is correct in that a dangerous prisoner has been seen near here. It is my task to recapture him."

"How desperately dramatic," Lottie murmured. "And there was I thinking that nothing exciting ever happened in Wantage. I fear you will not find your fugitive behind my tapestries, however. Kindly ask your men to show more respect for my possessions."

"Yes, ma'am." The lieutenant blushed more deeply. "Careful there," he barked, as one of his men fell over his own feet and almost knocked over the bookshelf in the process. He turned back to Lottie.

"Permission to search upstairs, ma'am?"

"If you must." Lottie feigned boredom. "However, I have a small request, Lieutenant. Could you perhaps not search my room? I would be most grateful. I can assure you that no one has entered there without my permission."

The lieutenant looked grave. "Madam, I have orders

to search all of the house, without exception. Anyone could have climbed through a window and concealed himself whilst you slept. It is for your own safety—"

Lottie placed a soft hand on his arm and the lieutenant fell obediently silent.

"I have not been...sleeping, Lieutenant," she said truthfully. "Need I say more?"

For a moment it looked as though the lieutenant had not made the leap of imagination that she wanted him to and Lottie wondered if he really was fresh from the schoolroom. Then enlightenment dawned and he turned so fiery a red she was afraid that he might expire.

"Oh!" he said. He glanced down at her translucent nightgown, appeared to lose his nerve and fixed his gaze sternly on the picture on the far side of the hall. "I understood," he said, "that Lord St. Severin is with the other parole prisoners at The Bear, ma'am."

"Oh, he is," Lottie said. She held his gaze guilelessly. "I have quite a different guest tonight." She fluttered her hands. "I was lonely, you understand, and you know what they say, Lieutenant... A man who neglects his mistress creates a vacancy...."

"Madam!" The lieutenant's eyes were big as saucers. Lottie was not sure what appeared to be shocking him more; the fact that he believed that she was dallying with a man other than her protector or the terrifying thought of what a man like Ethan Ryder, as renowned with pistols as he was with a sword, might do if he thought that he had a rival.

"Then who..." he spluttered.

Lottie pressed a finger to his lips. "No questions, Lieutenant." She beckoned to him. "By all means come up with me and search the room, but pray do not disturb my…friend. He is—" she hesitated "—a young man from a good family in the neighborhood, and it would be the most *appalling* scandal were his identity to leak out. I am persuaded that you would not wish to be the one to blame."

"No indeed," the lieutenant said fervently. Lottie could see that he was running through a mental list of all the gentlemen in the neighborhood, trying frantically to imagine whom her visitor could be.

Lottie set off back up the stairs, beckoning him to follow her. After a moment he set his foot on the first tread with the air of a man undertaking a desperate mission.

Lottie knocked very softly on the bedroom door. "Are you awake, my dear?" she whispered, whilst the lieutenant blushed and shuffled at her side. There was no reply.

"I fear he is quite exhausted," she said truthfully. The lieutenant looked as though he was about to faint at the pictures his imagination was conjuring for him.

Lottie pushed open the bedroom door and, heart in mouth, led the lieutenant inside.

Arland had done well and she felt an enormous rush of relief. He had hidden his prison uniform and was sprawled in the big bed. The tumbled covers revealed only one shoulder, surprisingly broad, a part of an arm and a manly foot sticking out from beneath the sheets. He was lying on his stomach, face turned away, and he was snoring softly. As Lottie and the lieutenant looked on, he gave what sounded to be a heartfelt sigh in his sleep.

"Poor boy," Lottie said, smiling at the lieutenant. "He is very tired." She raised the candle to shine it around the room. "As you can see, there is no one else here, sir."

"The window is open," the lieutenant said, dragging his gaze from the man in the bed. "It is possible that the prisoner may have shinned up the ivy and climbed inside—"

"I opened the window myself a while ago," Lottie said, still smiling. "It is a hot night."

"I imagine it must have been," the lieutenant muttered. He gulped, his Adam's apple bobbing. He made a hasty check of the armoire and cupboard. It was clear that no one was concealed behind the curtains. "Do you wish to search under the bed?" Lottie asked helpfully.

The lieutenant shook his head. "That will be quite unnecessary, madam," he said.

"Then I hope that your curiosity is satisfied, Lieutenant," Lottie said sweetly.

"Indeed it is. I thank you, ma'am," the lieutenant stammered, backing toward the door like a man who had recalled a very urgent appointment on the other side of the town. "Most obliging of you."

He marshaled his men and Lottie saw them off from the front door.

"They've gone," she said to Margery, who was huddled beside her, a blanket clutched about her, shaking with nerves and reaction. "Get you to bed. You are safe now."

She gave the maidservant a brief, hard hug and sent her scuttling away up the stairs, then turned to bolt the door, almost leaping from her skin as Ethan stepped out from the shadows behind it.

"I thought that you were locked up," she said. "How did you get out?"

Ethan laughed. "I climbed over the roof." He caught her arm, urgency in his touch. "He is here?"

"Upstairs," Lottie said.

Ethan drew her into the house, bolting the door behind them. Then he turned to her, pulled her into his arms and kissed her. She could feel the relief in him, and the gratitude, and such sweet tenderness that she almost melted. Ethan had never before kissed her other than as a prelude to making love, and now Lottie almost smiled to see the comical look of confusion on his face as he let her go. This, she thought, was different for him, too, and her heart sang.

"Were you outside all the time?" she asked.

"Only for long enough to hear you shamelessly deceive a member of the British Army," Ethan said. "I hope you are aware that that is treason?"

Their eyes met and held.

"I knew what I was doing," Lottie said.

She saw a smile come through Ethan's eyes then like sunlight on water. "Thank you," he said. He did not ask her if he could trust her. He did not ask if she would betray Arland. He simply stood looking at her and Lottie felt as though her heart was being squeezed tight in a giant fist. There were tears in her throat, blocking her words.

You trust me….

Ethan gave her a dazzling smile. "Where is he?" he said.

"In my bed," Lottie said. "Where else would I hide a man?"

"That's my son you're talking about," Ethan said, laughing. He took the stairs two at a time. Lottie could feel the excitement in him, the blaze of happiness lighting him from within.

"Try not to wake Margery," she besought. "The poor child has been frightened half to death tonight."

Arland was awake, sitting on the side of the bed. He had managed to put most of his clothes back on and Lottie thought he looked younger than ever, the candlelight emphasizing the pallor of his face and the dark bruises on his skin. As the door opened he looked up sharply, saw Ethan and for a moment looked absolutely terrified. Lottie saw him swallow hard and open his mouth, but no words came.

There was a moment of utter silence as father and son looked at one another.

"You weren't supposed to do it all on your own," Ethan said. His voice sounded rusty with emotion.

Then Ethan put out his hand in an odd, hesitant gesture, and Arland scrambled up from the bed and he was across the room and into his father's arms faster than Lottie had ever seen anyone move, and she went out and closed the door softly behind her, leaving the two of them alone together.

THE STORM BROKE with shocking intensity an hour later, lightning ripping the sky and the thunder shaking the house. Lottie cowered under her blankets and thought of Ethan, even now guiding Arland to a safe house under the cover of the thick darkness and torrential rain. She had not wanted them to go although she knew it was not safe for Arland to stay at Priory Cottage for any length of time. She had stood on tiptoe to kiss Ethan on the lips, and she had felt such fear for him, and anguish, because she knew that Ethan would not want to leave Arland alone and unprotected ever again. She sensed, too, that the time was coming now when Ethan, too, would leave for good. He had said nothing yet, but she knew that his son's escape must have precipitated his plans, whatever they might be. He would want to ensure that Arland left British shores safely and so he, too, would go. It might not be tomorrow, or even the day after, but it would be very soon and then she would be alone. Ethan would be the father that Arland needed now, and she, the fatherless child, understood how important that was even whilst she greedily wanted to keep Ethan for herself.

Lottie burrowed farther under the blankets at the thought, pulling them up over her head, blocking out the drum of the rain on the roof and the grumble of the thunder as it receded over the hills, trying to block out thoughts that were not so easily banished. The air was cool now, scented with fresh leaves and rain. The chill of it against her face made her shiver. She was cold through and through and not even the heavy weight of the bedclothes could warm her. A mere two months before, standing under the apple trees in the orchard, she had acknowledged that the arrangement with Ethan was temporary, that she had always been alone at heart and that she always would be. Fathers, husbands, lovers came and went. She knew this. Men were an untrustworthy species.

Yet she would not write to Theo to tell him what had happened this night. Her decision had already been made when she gave Arland shelter. That was one betrayal she was not prepared to make, even to safeguard her own future.

She opened her eyes and stared at the billowing curtains. The thunder had gone now and the night was still. She had no idea what her future would hold with Ethan gone. She knew he would pay her off, as he had promised, but after that there was no certainty. Whatever her future would be, she would have to carve it for herself.

CHAPTER SIXTEEN

"You will have heard the *on dit*, Miss Palliser?" Mrs. Ormond whispered to Lottie behind the stacked bales of material in Mr. Winkworth's shop two days later. "Miss Butler, the vicar's daughter, has tried to elope with Captain Le Grand! They were apprehended on the Abingdon Road and he has been thrown into gaol and she is at home in disgrace. Such a shocking thing! Why, he must be three times her age and no great catch. And before all this dreadful business with the French officers occurred Miss Butler was engaged to a man who had patented a new form of stationary engine." She shook her head and the ribbons on her bonnet flapped mournfully. "Only think, Miss Palliser, to whistle down the wind a man who had secured a patent!" Her gaze sharpened. "Tell me, did you *know?*"

"But naturally," Lottie said. "I know *everything* there is to know in this town, Mrs. Ormond, and I tried to dissuade Miss Butler from so foolish a course of action as elopement, but…" She shrugged expressively, inviting Mrs. Ormond to join her in deploring the headstrong nature of youth. "Sometimes the young will not take our advice."

"I thought that you would know all about it, Miss Palliser," Mrs. Ormond said. "I know everybody writes to you even though they cannot speak to you publicly."

She grabbed Lottie's arm. "Now, tell me about this dreadful business of Lord St. Severin's son. There have been no further sightings?"

"None at all," Lottie said regretfully, shaking her head. "It seems that he has completely vanished."

"Extraordinary!" Mrs. Ormond opined. "Wherever can he have gone?"

"It is a mystery," Lottie agreed, smiling widely.

"These Frenchmen," Mrs. Ormond said. "They are so much trouble!"

Wantage that afternoon was only just returning to normality after the excitement of the unsuccessful hunt for Arland Ryder. The parole prisoners had been allowed out of their billets for the first time, the troops had been withdrawn from the town and the shops were full of customers eager to exchange the latest gossip.

"Good heavens, Miss Palliser, who is *that?*" Mrs. Ormond exclaimed, and Lottie looked around and realized that the shop was buzzing with a low hum of excitement and speculation. Mr. Winkworth had abandoned his place behind the counter to join several ladies in the bow window. They were staring past the drapes of silk at a black carriage pulled by four bay horses that had paused in the square outside whilst the coachman asked for directions. The sunlight gleamed on the polished paneling, and the family crest on the side almost blinded the eyes it was so bright.

"Oh!" Mrs. Ormond's voice was high and breathy with excitement. "Whose carriage can that be? Surely that crest… No, it cannot be! That looks like—"

"The Duke of Farne," Lottie said.

The ladies broke into the kind of chatter that occurred when a fox invaded the henhouse. "The Duke of Farne, here in Wantage, of all places? Whatever can he want?"

Mrs. Ormond swung around on Lottie, piercing her with an accusatory eye. "Surely Farne has not come to see Lord St. Severin? I had heard they were estranged!"

"I know nothing of it," Lottie said, staring despite herself as the coachman swung himself back up onto the box and the horses moved off. "For once I have to confess, ladies, that I am as baffled as you are. Though perhaps," she added, "the Duke has come because of Arland Ryder's escape from gaol. He is the boy's grandfather, after all."

There was an indiscreet rush out into the square as each shop emptied of its customers, all peering in the direction the carriage had gone.

"It has turned into Priory Lane!" Mrs. Ormond announced, like the Town Crier. "Miss Palliser, surely the Duke cannot be seeking *you?*"

"It seems that he is," Lottie said. "Pray excuse me." She picked up her basket, smiled her thanks to Mr. Winkworth and set off in the direction that the coach had gone. She wagered privately with herself that it would take no more than ten minutes for word of Farne's visit to be around the entire town.

Margery met her halfway down Priory Passage.

"Ma'am! Ma'am!" The girl fell into her arms panting as though she was being chased. She pressed a hand to her side. "The Duke," she gasped. "He's here! He wants to see you."

"Breathe slowly," Lottie instructed her, supporting

her along the pavement. "No man is worth choking over, least of all the Duke of Farne."

She had no cause to review her opinion when she reached the house and found His Grace waiting impatiently for her in the parlor. He was looking around with disfavor, as though, Lottie thought, he could not quite believe that he had stooped to enter such a lowly establishment.

She had never met the Duke of Farne before. They had not moved in the same circles even when she had been a London hostess. She thought that he and Gregory might well be acquainted, for Gregory had lent a great deal of money to the political classes and Farne was high in the government. Looking at him she could see the family resemblance that was stamped on both Ethan and his half brother Northesk. Farne's face was thinner and more gaunt, his hair a shock of white, his eyes very dark, his expression fierce, his mouth pinched thin like a man experiencing the pains of gout. But that might well be no more than disapproval, Lottie thought. He could not enjoy lowering himself to visit the mistress of his illegitimate son.

Those were, in fact, the Duke of Farne's first words to her:

"You are my son's mistress?" he barked.

"I am Charlotte Palliser, Your Grace," Lottie said politely. "I am not defined by my relationship to Lord St. Severin."

Farne's eyebrows snapped down into a frown. His dark gaze appraised her. "I heard that your husband divorced you for adultery," he said.

"I assume," Lottie said, holding on to her temper

by a thread, "that, speaking of adultery, you are here on a matter relating to your *illegitimate* son, Your Grace?"

There was a flash of flinty humor in Farne's eyes. "My, but you are pert."

"Your Grace," Lottie said, "you have been in my company no more than two minutes and already you have insulted me deeply. That is not the behavior of a gentleman. Was there something you wanted? Or are you leaving?"

This time Farne almost smiled. "I'll take a glass of wine, Miss Palliser," he said, "and thank you for the offer."

Lottie rang the bell and Margery, almost tripping over herself in her anxiety, brought two glasses of wine for them. Farne took a chair by the window and looked out across the orchard.

"You have a pleasant aspect here," he said, "though I cannot believe that a small town like Wantage provides the entertainments to which you are accustomed." He raised a dark brow. "Do you not find it parochial after London?"

"Everywhere is parochial after London, except perhaps for Paris," Lottie said lightly. She knew this could be no idle chat. The Duke of Farne would hardly drive to Berkshire simply to get to know his son's mistress a little better. She wondered what he wanted. She wondered if Ethan had heard by now of his father's visit, and what he would do.

"It suffices," she said. "For the time being."

Farne smiled. It was not a comfortable smile. "And yet you could have so much more, could you not?"

A shiver of premonition slid down Lottie's spine. She took a sip from her glass, buying time.

"Could I?" she said.

"If you are able to provide your brother with more information of the type that he requires."

Ah, so he had heard of Theo's recruitment of her to the British government's cause. Lottie was not surprised. Farne, she thought, was at the very heart of this web to trap his own son. The idea repelled her, and yet she wondered why she had not thought of it before. It was no secret that Ethan and his father were estranged and that for years the Duke had viewed his bastard son as no more than a thorn in his side.

Whilst she hesitated over her response, Farne spoke again.

"Such a conflict of loyalties," he said softly, "must be difficult to bear." He shifted. "I told Colonel Palliser that he asked too much of you and that I had an… alternative plan, one that would save you the difficulty of making such a choice."

The sun was playing in golden patterns across the carpet but Lottie could not feel its heat. She shivered. Farne sounded eminently reasonable, sympathetic even. But the room felt dark, shadowed with menace. Her instinct shouted to her to be very, very careful of what she said. And before her eyes was Arland's face with its bloodstains and livid bruising. *That* was the reality of what the Duke of Farne would countenance when it came to Ethan and to his son.

"You are most generous to consider my feelings, Your Grace," she said. "I thank you."

Farne made a slight gesture with his glass. "I believe that we are all on the same side," he said.

"Are we?" Lottie shrugged. "I have never pretended to an interest in politics."

"Perhaps not," Farne said, "but you do have an interest in money, don't you, Miss Palliser?"

Lottie met his eyes directly. He was watching her with the cold clear gaze of the predator.

"Always," she said.

Farne smiled. "So we understand one another."

"I am not sure that I *do* understand you," Lottie said. "What are you offering?"

Farne looked offended by such plain speaking. "My dear Miss Palliser—"

"And more importantly," Lottie finished, "what do you ask in return?"

Farne walked across to the fireplace, where he rested one arm along the mantelpiece.

"It has always been my desire to be reconciled with my son," he began.

"Has it?" Lottie said. "You astound me."

Farne flashed her a glance. "From the very beginning I did what was best for Ethan."

"Conceiving him out of wedlock," Lottie said, "taking him away from his mother, bringing him up with those who despised him, sending him to a school where his birth would be scorned. Yes, I can see how you tried."

The Duke gave her a thin smile. His gaze was sharp. "You are hot in his defense. I think you must care for him."

Lottie caught her lip between her teeth. She had been

too unguarded. She did not want the Duke of Farne, of all people, to know how much she cared for Ethan. But she did most heartily wish to know exactly what fate Farne planned for his son. She gave him a cool smile.

"At the moment Lord St. Severin offers me more than anyone else can," she said, "so naturally he has my loyalty."

"An eminently pragmatic approach," Farne murmured. "Perhaps what I should have said is that ever since my son took up his mistaken allegiance, first to the Irish republican cause and then to that of the French, it has been my most ardent desire to welcome him back into the fold."

"Yes," Lottie said. "I can see that he is a great blot on the Farne escutcheon and a great embarrassment to you."

"But if he could be…persuaded…to change his views…" Farne said. He let the sentence hang.

"Then the escutcheon could be polished to its former glory," Lottie finished.

"He is blocking my progress to hold Cabinet office," Farne said, suddenly vicious. Lottie could feel the anger and the ambition in him, as fierce and bitter as the swelling tide.

"There is only so far a man can rise when he has a renegade revolutionary as a son," Farne said, "and, equally as deplorable, an illegitimate runaway grandson. Soon my chance of high office will be gone."

"I can quite imagine," Lottie said. She narrowed her gaze on him, toying with the stem of her glass. "And yet a mysterious accident—a convenient death for either Ethan or his son—would not suit you, either, would it, Your Grace? Questions would be asked. Your enemies would seize upon it and use it against you, and then you would never achieve the heights to which you aspire. I suspect *that* is the only reason that Lord St. Severin is still with us—that and his own skill in self-preservation, of course."

"It pleases me," Farne said, eyes gleaming, "that you understand so acutely the dilemma that faces me, Miss Palliser."

"You could always let Ethan go," Lottie said. "Send him back to France. Death and glory on the battlefield would remove your dilemma."

"Alas, my son could not be relied upon to die appropriately," Farne said bitterly. "Instead I make no doubt he would go to America. His views match those of a country with such high-minded ideals." He shifted, leaning closer. "Tell me, Miss Palliser, do you have any knowledge of the whereabouts of my grandson?

You can see how important it is to me to find him first, before those dolts of soldiers shoot him dead and give me another problem to deal with."

Lottie felt chilled to the bone as she looked into the cold gray eyes of a man who calculated the worth of every member of his family in terms of what good, or harm, they could do to his political chances. It made her skin crawl to see Farne's total disregard for humanity. Oh yes, he would like to find Arland Ryder before the British troops did. He would take the boy and use him as another lever to try and force Ethan to his will. The thought repelled her. She felt sick, the nausea rolling through her.

"I have absolutely no idea," she said, "where Arland Ryder is now."

"A pity," Farne said. His piercing gaze did not waver. "But perhaps you may remember something useful in time. You understand, of course," he added, "that the boy *will* be shot if he is discovered? As will anyone aiding and abetting him. Under law—"

Lottie dismissed his words with a flick of her fingers. "I fear that the ramifications of the law bore me almost as much as politics, Your Grace." She moved to refill his glass. "I am, however, very interested in your other proposition." She smiled at him. "Let me understand you clearly. You wish me to exert any influence I might have to persuade Lord St. Severin to a different course?"

Farne nodded his thanks as she placed the decanter gently on the side table.

"You are, without a doubt, my best hope to persuade Ethan that he is on the losing side and that a discreet change of allegiance would be in all our interests," he said.

"And if I succeed?" Lottie pressed.

"A house," Farne said. He looked around. "Much bigger than this."

"Naturally. And?"

"Servants. A carriage, a certain sum of money settled on you in perpetuity…" Farne shrugged. "My man of business will take care of it."

"Of course," Lottie said. "Of course he will."

This, then, she thought, was the level to which the Duke of Farne would sink to manipulate his son. He would buy the support of Ethan's mistress; worse, he would seek to capture Ethan's son and use him as a pawn in his maneuvering. He was vile, utterly without loyalty or family honor. He was also wasting his time.

She looked at him. "I do not believe that you know your son at all, Your Grace," she said. "Ethan will never abandon his principles. He has fought for them all his adult life. Nothing I could say could make him change his mind whether I wished to help you or not."

There was a silence. Farne was watching her with those bright predator's eyes. After a moment he nodded slowly.

"Then," he said, "I believe there is only one further course open to me." He looked straight at her. "I offer you one hundred thousand pounds for any information you can give me about my son. Plus the house and the carriage and—" he sounded impatient "—whatever else you desire."

Lottie's mind reeled. Money had always been her only currency and one hundred thousand pounds was a huge sum. She need not worry about her future ever again. Those doubts and fears that had plagued her in the night, of where she would go after Ethan had left, of what she would become... They would all be gone. She would have no need to worry ever again. She would be rich. Her future would be assured.

All she had to do in return was to betray Ethan to his death, and Arland with him. Because that was what Farne was asking. The Duke would not be so indelicate as to say the words outright but he wanted information, her testimony that Ethan was committing treason. He wanted what Theo had asked for that day in London when she had agreed to betray Ethan for the sake of her future security. And Farne was offering her one hundred thousand pounds to sweeten the deal. One hundred thousand pounds to secure her future…

There was a knock at the front door. Farne looked acutely annoyed. "I do not wish to be interrupted until our business is agreed," he snapped.

"I can quite see why," Lottie said. Then, as Margery tapped anxiously on the door: "Who is it, Margery? Pray tell them that I am not at home."

"Begging your pardon, ma'am—" Margery gave a little terrified bob "—but I cannot. It is the Duke of Palliser, ma'am, and he demands an interview. Immediately, he said!" She gave an uncanny imitation of the Duke's authoritative tone.

"Palliser!" Farne snapped. "What does he want here?"

"I have no notion," Lottie said. "Since my cousin has been cutting me dead these three years past, the only way in which I find out the answer to that question is to admit him." She nodded to Farne. "If you will excuse me?"

"I will wait," Farne said. "I have invested too much time and effort in our conversation, Miss Palliser, to leave without your commitment to my plans."

"If you wish," Lottie said, shrugging. She turned to Margery. "Pray show his grace in here, Margery."

The Duke of Palliser was a big, fair fleshy man in his forties. He carried his weight well with all the innate confidence and self-importance of his rank. He strode into the room, saw the Duke of Farne and stopped dead.

"Your Grace!" he spluttered.

"Your Grace," Farne responded, bored.

"Cousin James," Lottie said, "what a most unexpected pleasure."

Palliser looked discomfited. "What is Farne doing here?" he demanded.

Farne stiffened.

"His Grace has been making me an offer," Lottie said. "Not of the amorous kind, you understand, of the pecuniary sort. So—" she fixed her cousin with a steely eye "—since I doubt that you have called on me to exchange family news, why do you not make your counteroffer, James, so that I may save us all time?" She walked across to the side table and poured wine into a fresh glass. "Let me guess," she mused, as she passed it to him. "My presence a mere twenty miles from your ducal family home is causing such social embarrassment to you that you have come to make me a proposition. You are prepared to welcome me back into the family fold, to restore me to respectability and give me in addition—" she shot Farne a look "—oh, a house—bigger than this one, of course—servants, a carriage, a sum of money…" She sighed. "Gentlemen, you do me so much honor." She looked from one to the other. "Which of you shall I choose?"

There was a knock. "Lord St. Severin," Margery said, from the doorway.

CHAPTER SEVENTEEN

"Your Graces…" Ethan strolled forward and sketched an elegant bow to the Dukes. "Your carriages have stopped the traffic in the street outside." He could feel his father watching him, his gaze cold and antagonistic. The hairs rose on the back of Ethan's neck even to be in the same room as Farne.

He had not seen his father within two years, not since he had been captured and his father had railed at him and demanded that he change sides and declare his allegiance to the British cause. His refusal then had driven the alienation between them to deeper and more painful levels than ever before. There was no way back for them.

But it was Lottie who drew Ethan's gaze. She looked cool and serene, the perfect hostess serving wine to her guests. But he could feel the tension in her, as tight and coiled as a trap.

He knew at once what must have happened.

His loving father had offered Lottie a huge bribe to betray him, or betray Arland, or both of them.

The thought turned Ethan's blood to ice. Would Lottie take the money? He wanted to believe she would not, could not, do such a thing, but he was desperately unsure of her. The terror cascaded through him, the fear for Arland and the damage that Lottie could do. True, she did not know where Arland was now, but if she were to breathe a word about last night's events, the authorities would surely arrest him and then Arland would be trapped, alone and abandoned again, whilst the British did their best to torture his son's whereabouts out of him. And what if Lottie were to mention his activities on the night that Chard had died? Her testimony would be enough to see him swing on the end of the hangman's noose for a murder he had not committed. That would please his father.

Yet if Lottie chose to sell him out, how could he prevent it? He had offered her nothing—how could he, as an enemy of the state, a prisoner. He could not hold her loyalty if others gave more. He had always understood her. Lottie was for sale. Men had used her all of her life and so she took; she took what was offered to give herself the security she craved. He ached for it to be different, for *her* to be different, but he knew it was not.

Three nights ago, when she had helped Arland, he had trusted her for the first time and she had not let him down. But this was not the same. This time his father would be offering her so much; a huge sum of money, he guessed, security, riches beyond her dreams, to put her back where she wanted to be, as a woman of consequence. The temptation to accept the bribe, the financial imperative to ensure her safe future, was surely too strong for her to resist. Her brother had offered to help her but the Duke of Farne was a hundred, a thousand times richer and more influential than Theo Palliser. Ethan could not see how Lottie could refuse.

He strolled forward with every indication of

nonchalance, not showing by the slightest flicker of expression, the fear that was in his heart.

"I came as soon as I heard, my dear," he murmured. "May I be of assistance?"

"I am so glad to see you, my love," Lottie said. She smiled at him but he could not read anything in her face. "Your father and my cousin," she said, "are both most generous, for both of them are offering me a very great deal to see matters from their point of view."

The Dukes both shifted uneasily.

"I see," Ethan said. So it was true.

"Two high bidders in one room," he said. "You are to be congratulated."

"So I think," Lottie said lightly. She looked at him. Her gaze was opaque.

James Palliser cleared his throat. "Cousin Charlotte," he began. "I really do beg you to accept my offer and sever your scandalous connection to this man."

Lottie looked highly entertained. "Cousin James," she said, "I fear I am too steeped in my dissipation to give it up now."

"You should think about it a little," Ethan said abruptly. The role of devil's advocate came easily to him and he understood why. He would far rather that Lottie accepted her cousin's protection because that would be no true betrayal. If she sold herself to Farne instead he would want to kill them both, his father for his craven-hearted treachery and Lottie for being the most conniving, duplicitous creature ever to have crossed his path.

He cleared his throat, forced the words out. "It is

what you want," he said. "Remember? You wish to be reconciled with your family."

Their eyes met. Lottie's gaze was pensive. "Is that what you want me to do, my lord?" She asked. "You want me to leave you?"

"This is nothing to do with me." Ethan tasted bitterness in his mouth and found that he was within an inch of begging her to stay with him, begging her to put principle and loyalty to him above money.

"You told me that it was your dearest wish to regain what you had lost," he said. "This is a way that you can do it with honor."

"Oh, honor…" Lottie smiled. "In truth you know that I have little truck with that."

She turned away and Ethan watched the gentle sway of her hips as she walked across the room. Odd that he could still want her with such an aching need when he also knew with a sick dread that she was going to abandon him one way or another. When he had told her about Arland and she had comforted him, then he had believed that matters might be different between them. He had allowed himself to think of a future where Lottie came with him, in poverty perhaps, in adversity certainly, hunted, running away, with nothing but each other. He was no green youth. He should have known better. Such dreams were in shreds with two rich men here offering her more money than she would know what to do with.

"You told me that I could never regain what I had lost," Lottie said. She had come to him and placed one hand on his sleeve. Her eyes were clear. "You were right, Ethan. I know I cannot."

"It is the best offer that you will get," James Palliser said stiffly.

"Taken back under the ducal wing to spare your blushes?" Lottie turned toward him with a rustle of silk. "A year ago, two years, you did not step forward to help me."

"That was different," Palliser said. He had the grace to look a little shamefaced. "A matter between husband and wife… I could not intervene—"

"You did not wish to be sullied by the scandal until I was practically sitting on your doorstep," Lottie said sweetly, "and even now you only come to see me because I have become too embarrassing to ignore."

"Take the offer," Ethan said, between his teeth.

But she shook her head. "I do not wish to be condescended to by my stiff-necked relatives for the rest of my life. How intolerable that would be! To be reminded every day with little slights and pinpricks that I am a fallen woman saved only by their generosity…" She sighed. "To be left to molder in some country village, denied all entertainment and pleasure?" She shook her head. "You know it would not serve, Ethan, darling. I would have run off with the curate within a week and be a fallen woman all over again." She turned to James. "Thank you, cousin, but I must decline."

The Duke puffed himself up. "You won't hear from me again," he said.

"Oh, good," Lottie said.

The air shivered with violence as the door banged behind James Palliser. Farne, who had stood quietly whilst his fellow duke was given his marching orders, smiled sinuously and moved forward. "So…" he said suggestively.

Ethan clenched his fists.

"Yes," Lottie said. "Your offer was both more interesting and more lucrative than that of my cousin, was it not, Your Grace?"

"I like to think so," Farne said, licking his lips. He looked from her to Ethan. "I quite appreciate that this is awkward for you, my dear. Would you care to come with me now and we may continue our discussions elsewhere? I am sure that you do not wish to prolong your farewells with my son."

Ethan waited.

"Oh, I don't think so, thank you," Lottie said briskly, whisking over to the door and opening it wide. "I am afraid that I cannot help you, Your Grace. I'll bid you good day."

The shock hit Ethan so hard he rocked back on his heels. For a moment he could have sworn that Lottie's eyes were full of tears, although there was a defiantly wicked smile tilting her lips.

Farne had also recoiled like a snake whipping its head back for the strike. "You make a grievous mistake, Miss Palliser," he hissed.

"Alas, I am renowned for it," Lottie said regretfully. "Do you think I would be where I am today if I had not made many mistakes?"

Ethan stepped in front of her. "If you have anything else to say, Your Grace, you can say it to me. Otherwise I suggest that you leave."

Farne's eyes narrowed to slits of fury. "I have nothing to say to you," he said.

This time the house shuddered so hard with the slamming of the door that some plaster fell from the ceiling to scatter on the rug.

"How very untidy," Lottie said, staring at it. She made for the door. "I must call Margery to sweep it up—"

"Leave it," Ethan said. He caught her wrist. "Why did you do it?" he said softly.

She evaded his eyes. The light went out of her face. Some sort of caution crept in, as though she was hiding something. "I meant what I said to James," she said. "Can you truly see me living quietly in a country village, Ethan, darling? You know how bored I get and how easily I am distracted." She freed herself and moved away from him. "Besides," she said, back turned to him, "I do have some self-respect, and to be condescended to by James's ghastly wife, to be perpetually reminded of my scandalous past with little gibes and sneers every day until I run mad…" Her shoulders hunched. "What sort of life would that be?" She turned aside, running her hand along the table and the exquisite little china figurines that decorated it. "Though no doubt I shall regret my stance in the morning," she said, on a sigh. "I am too impetuous and pride cannot feed me."

"Nor can principle," Ethan said. "So why did you turn down Farne's generous offer to betray me? I imagine that his terms were far more liberal than those your cousin was offering."

Lottie froze. He saw her fingers tremble a little as she withdrew her hand. "You gained no financial advantage from refusing to help Farne," Ethan continued. "You have betrayed me several times in the past. Why stop now?"

Lottie gave a little, light shrug. "Your father is a vile man. I did not care for him or his offer."

"True, he is," Ethan said, "but it shows damned poor judgment to let that sway you when he could have secured your future." He paused. "How much did he offer you?"

"One hundred thousand pounds," Lottie said. She shrugged again. "I thought he might cheat me," she added. Even though he was not touching her, Ethan could feel the tension in her. "I did not trust him and I did not wish to help him. And your son—" Her voice caught a little. "He does not deserve to be betrayed to such a man."

"Whereas I," Ethan said, with a lopsided smile, "am able to take care of myself?"

Her face lightened. She smiled that wicked little smile he knew so well. "Of course you are, Ethan, darling. You always have been." She came across to him and put her arms about his neck. Something had eased in her, as though she felt more secure again, on familiar ground.

"Come upstairs with me now," she whispered. "We can celebrate vanquishing the joint forces of the dukedoms of Farne and Palliser. We are both disowned twice over." She pressed closer to him. "We are renounced, rejected, cast out," she murmured against his lips. She was smiling.

"We are irredeemable," Ethan agreed, feathering kisses along her collarbone and down to the soft skin of her upper breasts that was exposed by the neckline of her pretty pink-and-white gown.

"Utterly disreputable," Lottie whispered. "Both of us."

Ethan released her. "Come riding with me," he said. "I want to talk to you."

She looked confused. "Talk? Now? I thought that we would go to bed." She started to pull him toward the door, tugging on his hand.

"No," Ethan said. "Lottie. We must talk." There was an odd sort of urgency in her, he thought, as though she were trying to deflect him—or to reassure herself. He wondered if it was because she had burned all her boats to be with him. He still did not understand why she had done it. She had not answered a single one of his questions, turning him away with light answers, attempting to distract him. It was true that he was easily distracted when presented with Lottie's body, so temptingly offered, but this time he had more urgent matters on his mind.

"We can talk later," she murmured, pressing her abundant curves against him in a blatant attempt to arouse. "Afterward. I want you now."

She kissed him again, and he knew that she was trying every trick, every artifice she knew, to seduce him so utterly that he forgot all that had happened before. He did not respond and after a moment she stiffened in his arms, and then took a couple of paces back. It was the first time that he had turned her down. Her eyes were bright with emotion, her mouth pink from his kisses and she looked terrified.

"What is it that you are hiding from me?" he asked.

Lottie spun away from him. "Nothing! I don't know what you mean!"

"Yes, you do," Ethan said. "Why did you choose me? Why did you turn down all the lovely material benefits offered by both my father and your cousin and settle for nothing but me?"

She shrugged a careless shoulder. He knew the gesture was false. "Your company amuses me," she said. "For now."

"You burned your boats for me."

She was fidgeting, another sure sign of her agitation. Her restless fingers were shredding the petals off the bowl of roses on the table. "Another boat will come along when I need it. They always do—for me."

"I think it is because you care for me," Ethan said.

For a second Lottie looked bewildered, then scornful.

"Oh no," she said. "You cannot order my feelings and emotions, Ethan. They are not for sale. You have bought everything else—" Her gesture encompassed the room, all it contained, her own body. "It is yours. Be satisfied with that. You cannot own me heart and soul." Her tone eased slightly as though she was still trying to please him, still trying to be the perfect mistress. "Why should you wish for more?" she added lightly. "You have all you wanted."

"I don't want those things anymore," Ethan said.

He saw her freeze like a rabbit trapped in the glare of the poacher's lamp. "You don't want *me* anymore," she said. It sounded like an accusation. "You are going to tell me it is over and you are leaving." For a moment he saw straight into her heart and saw the terror there.

Everyone leaves. Always. I am on my own.

It was the lesson that repeated itself for her time and again.

Then he saw her straighten and transform. Her chin came up with the courage and defiance he recognized.

"Ah well." She shrugged. "Save yourself the trouble of spelling it out, darling. I knew it would have to happen soon. As I said, I shall manage. I always do."

"Lottie," Ethan said. He put a hand on her arm, drew her back to him. She came reluctantly. "That was not what I was going to say to you," he said.

He could feel her trembling. Her body had gone soft with relief. "It was not?" she whispered.

"No." He pressed kisses against her hair. "Listen. I want you. I never stop wanting you."

She rubbed her cheek against his shoulder. "Sweet of you. Yet you will not make love to me."

Ethan loosed her. "Get ready," he said abruptly. "We are going out in ten minutes."

"Ready in ten minutes?" Lottie looked scandalized. "Are you mad? Where are we going?"

"We are having a picnic," Ethan said, "and we *are* going to talk."

"A picnic? Really?" Lottie threw him an appalled look over her shoulder. "Darling, only rustics have picnics! Think of the butter melting in the sun and the flies in the honey!"

"You mistake," Ethan said. "Only the rich have picnics. No one else can afford the time."

Lottie pulled a face. "It is a privilege I would happily forgo." She made it sound like torture. "And ten minutes?" She was already making for the door. "I will not even have selected my outfit in ten minutes!"

Ethan smiled slightly as he listened to her shouting desperately for Margery as she made her way up the stairs. She had denied that she cared for him, but it was the only rational explanation he could see to explain why she had sent both her cousin and his father packing. But of course she would never admit it to him of her own free will. All the men who had used and discarded Lottie throughout her life had hurt her badly. He could hardly blame her now if she had erected barriers about her heart.

So he would have to expose his feelings to her first. And the truth of it was that he was no better at showing such vulnerability than she. He smiled ruefully at the irony of it. Two of the most experienced lovers in the world, and yet the one thing that they could not expose was their hearts.

IN THE PRIVACY OF HER ROOM, Lottie stood with her hands braced against the chest of drawers, trying to regain her breath and her composure.

"What is it that you are hiding from me?" Ethan had asked, and how was she to answer him?

I love you. I've loved you for weeks. I would go barefoot for you, to the ends of the earth....

Well, perhaps not barefoot. One had to be practical. One had to preserve standards. But she had always fancied the idea of travel.

Only of course she could not tell Ethan that. Such

confessions were for love-struck debutantes not for an experienced divorcée who was rather farther into her thirties than she wanted to admit. She was a sophisticated woman not an ingenue. And she never ever wanted to be at the mercy of her feelings—or of a man's whim—again.

Ethan had wanted to know why she had rejected the more than generous offers made by her cousin and his father. Of course he had wanted to know. She wanted to know herself how she could have been so foolish as to put love before self-interest for the very first time in her life. It was inexplicable. And yet as soon as Ethan had walked in the room she had known what she had to do. She had looked at him and seen that he was twice the man his father was. A hundred times better than Farne if truth were told, honorable, principled, entirely admirable. She loved him for it. She loved him for being all the things his father was not. Actually, she loved him for being all the things that *she* was not. So for the first time ever she had let her heart rule her head and her wallet, and she had turned both Farne and James Palliser away.

She straightened and walked slowly over to the open window, gazing down on the leaves of the apple trees, stirred by the summer breeze. She had to admit that she had not suddenly discovered scruples, a moral code. That would have been doing it too brown. But to betray Ethan, and Arland, too, was something that she could not have lived with. The boy had already suffered too much, and the man… Her throat closed with tears as she acknowledged how much she loved him.

She had tried to put Ethan off with light answers.

They were her style so it was inconsiderate of him to remain unconvinced. Then when that had failed, she had tried to persuade him with her body. It was the most frightening thing of all that he could resist her. He had never withstood her seduction before. Previously she had not even had to try too hard. Damn his persistence. Damn him in general.

She vented her feelings by sweeping her silver-backed hairbrush from the chest onto the floor where it clattered to rest against the foot of the bed.

A mistress losing her allure…

Yet Ethan had told her that he still wanted her. He was not paying her off because he had tired of her. So there could be only one other explanation. This was the moment she had been dreading. He was going to tell her that he was leaving, taking Arland and escaping abroad.

Lottie could feel the breath tightening in her chest at the mere thought of abandonment. She knew that Ethan had to go. She had realized that when Arland had run away from Whitemoor and Ethan had taken him to safety. Arland would be in hiding now and his father eager to join him so that together they could leave the country. This, she thought, must be Ethan's farewell to her. He was going to tell her that he had to go and she was going to be the perfect mistress and say that she understood.

She went to the wardrobe and took out her riding habit, deep green velvet, buttoned tight over the bodice, with a full sweeping skirt. She always chose carefully when she selected the outfit that marked her parting from a lover. And even though her hands shook a little as she buttoned herself into the bodice, she kept her head high and a little smile pinned to her face because really there was no other way to save her pride. She wanted Ethan to remember her well. If that was all he could take away with him, she wanted the memory to be good.

She took a deep breath and went out and down the stairs. Ethan was waiting for her at the bottom. He smiled at her. Her heart cracked a little. She put her hand in his. Just a little longer to pretend.

CHAPTER EIGHTEEN

THE BUTTER MELTED in the sun and there were flies in
the honey but Ethan thought that Lottie had probably
enjoyed the picnic more than she had expected. They
had ridden a mile out of Wantage, to the edge of the
parole boundary, and had found an idyllic corner of a
field where a stream ran softly down toward the river.
They had spread a rug beneath the wide branches of an
ancient oak and ate bread and ham, cheese and honeyed
figs, and drank the strong local beer.

They did not talk, but it was a comfortable silence.
Ethan had been surprised. He had thought Lottie would
be on edge, demanding to know what it was that he
wanted to say to her. But from the moment she had
come down the stairs in her saucy green riding outfit
it was as though they had a pact not to spoil the peace
of the afternoon.

It was as though it was going to be their last
goodbye.

After they had eaten Ethan lay back in the grass,
jacket discarded, looking at Lottie. She was lying, eyes
closed, lashes a dark sweep against her cheek, her head
pillowed on one of the saddlebags. He knew she was
not asleep. A ladybird landed on her cheek and she
smiled and brushed it gently away without opening her
eyes. The smile was lazy and sensual, and the curve of

her cheek was rounded and freckling in the sun, and
Ethan felt an ache inside as he watched her. She turned
her head an inch to the left and opened her eyes a tiny
fraction and raised her arm to shield her gaze from the
sun.

"What are you looking at?" Her voice was soft and
slumberous, too, like the hot afternoon.

"You."

She smiled, contented, and closed her eyes again.
She moved her left hand to catch his, the fingers tan-
gling with his in the grass, and Ethan was shot through
with such strong emotion that he almost gasped aloud.
Not desire, this. It was too strong and too profound to
be mere lust. Besides, lust could be sated. He knew that
if he wanted Lottie she would not refuse him. She never
did. Anything he wanted he took. He had bought her
and so she acquiesced to all his demands. Yet strangely,
her giving, her subservience, had made him humble in
the end rather than arrogant. He looked at the sweet,
generous contours of her mouth and he felt the same
sensation, stronger than before. No, not desire, but
love.

Strange, so strange, that Lottie Palliser should be the
one to teach him about love. He had had many women,
too many, he supposed, and always they had bored him.
Lottie had been different from the start. He had felt an
affinity with her. He had felt recognition, instinctive,
primitive, and he had thought it was because they were
two of a kind. But they were not. Underneath the brazen
exterior Lottie had been softer and more vulnerable
than he had imagined, and certainly more vulnerable
than she had ever wanted to be. He wanted to protect

her and care for her though no doubt she would tell him she could look after herself. She had had to do so, as a child whose father deserted her, as a young woman seeking security in marriage, as a wife, deeply disillusioned and finally discarded. She had made mistakes but she had not let them destroy her.

"You are still looking at me." This time she did not trouble to open her eyes.

"I like looking at you," Ethan said. He took a deep breath. "I love you."

As soon as the words were out he felt anxious. It was a new sensation to him and he did not care for it, but the words were said now and he would not take them back.

There was a stillness, as though the day was holding its breath. Then Lottie opened her eyes very, very wide.

"I beg your pardon?" she said.

"I love you," Ethan said again. Even he could hear the note of desperation in his voice. "Say something," he added quickly. "Please. I am so damnably poor at this."

Lottie rolled over so that she was lying very close to him. He could see the flecks of gold in her brown eyes, see every little line about those eyes, every crease that deepened as she smiled, every freckle. He reached out to brush back her hair where the breeze teased it and saw that he was shaking a little.

"I never thought to be so happy," she said, and there was wonder and the surprise of discovery in her voice.

Ethan tumbled her into his arms and she came to

him, laughing a little, with eagerness and pleasure. "But do you love me, too?" he asked.

"Of course I do," Lottie said. "Of course I love you. That was why—" She bit her lip and fell silent.

"That was why—what?"

She raised her gaze to his. Her fingers fidgeted with his shirt. "That was why I did not accept James's offer," she said simply. "I knew it was the sensible thing to do, but I did not want to leave you because I love you."

"You should have told me," Ethan said.

She moved a little. "And expose my heart to hurt—again?" she said. "I thank you, but no."

"I can't offer to marry you," Ethan said.

He saw the bright light of happiness in her face extinguished like a fire stamped out. Her body stiffened a little. She pulled away from him.

"Of course not," she said. "Of course you cannot. I am a divorced woman, notorious, disgraced." She sat up and started to pick up the remains of the picnic, tidying it up with quick, jerky movements.

Ethan caught her hand, cursing himself for his clumsy words.

"Lottie—" He took her chin in his hand, raising her face to his. Her eyes were dull and determinedly blank. "I'm sorry," he said. "I did not mean—"

She tried to pull herself away from him. "I understand."

"No," Ethan said. "No, you do not. Lottie, listen to me. I want to marry you more than anything in the world."

Now she looked even more shocked. "Why?" she said. "When you sought me out three months ago you

wanted the most notorious woman in London to be your
mistress. The last thing you wanted was a wife."

"My ambitions have changed," Ethan said. "Lottie, I
want to marry you because you are my match, my love
and my heart. You complete me. Anything less than
marriage would never be enough."

A spark of amusement, of joy, had crept back into her
eyes, making them shine like stars. "Why, Ethan," she
teased, "you are a true romantic. It must be your Irish
heritage. I did not think you had it in you. So why…"
She tilted her head, looked at him quizzically. "Why
can you not wed me if you feel like that?"

"Because I have nothing to offer you in all honor,"
Ethan said. "I am a prisoner of war and even if I escape
I shall remain a wanted man, hunted throughout the
kingdom. It would be shameful of me to ask you to
share that, to risk all to be with me. And then there
are things I have to do. You know that I have plans.
Arland—" He stopped. He wanted to confide in her
very much, to trust her with his plans and his secrets.
Already she knew a great deal. But now she solved his
dilemma by pressing her fingers to his lips.

"Don't tell me," she whispered, "and then I can be
neither tempted to betray your secrets nor be forced to
do so."

He trusted her not to tell, and he would kill anyone
who tried to compel her to betray him but he kissed
her fingers.

"It is extraordinary that you think I am your match
when you have so many principles and I so few," Lottie
said. "Your scruples do credit to a man of honor, but I
assure you they are quite unnecessary with me. I am a

woman with absolutely no shred of reputation or good character left—" She stopped as Ethan leaned forward and kissed her.

"You are *my* woman of bad character," he whispered, "and if I wish to treat you with the greatest respect in the world you will oblige me by accepting it."

He felt her lips curve into a smile against his.

"Since I am *your* woman of bad character," she whispered back, "I shall do my ultimate to persuade you to overlook your scruples and to take me with you, and to marry me, too." She drew back, resting a hand against his chest. "I do not see," she added, "that you are entirely ineligible. You may be a prisoner of war, but you are rich and titled. And I think I would like to be Lady St. Severin. At my age one cannot turn down the opportunity of a comfortably wealthy old age."

"In that case," Ethan said, "perhaps we should celebrate our betrothal." He started to undo the tiny pearl buttons of her riding habit.

She smiled. "Not so honorable after all," she said. Then, as the buttons gave and he slid a hand inside her bodice she sighed, lying back.

"I do believe," she said, "that I am so reformed these days that you are the one wicked sin left to me, Ethan, darling."

THERE WAS THE WARMTH of the sun on her naked skin. She could smell the scents of summer, of hot grass and flowers, and then Ethan was kissing her and she forgot where she was, forgot everything and gave herself up to his embrace.

They had made love many times before, with lust,

with anger, even with gentleness. It had been sweet and it had been sensual and it had been fiery and heated. All of those things she had known before, the excitement of discovery, the wickedness of the flagrantly erotic. She had thought that she had nothing left to learn and nowhere else to go. She had been wrong.

There was love in the way that Ethan touched her now, love in each sweep of his hand against her skin, love in the reverence with which he kissed her.

"I love you," he said, as he pressed his lips to the hot hollow of her throat. He tangled his hands in her hair and kissed the vulnerable curve below her ear with exquisite tenderness. "I love you…" His lips moved against her skin, a breath, a torment.

She caught his face in her hands and brought it down to hers, kissing him urgently, fiercely, tearing at his clothes, reckless. For a moment she felt scared, as though if she did not capture this feeling now she would lose it and be cheated again, giving herself to a man only to feel lost and empty afterward. But it was not like that this time. Ethan drew back, steadying her and stilling her hands.

"We have all the time in the world," he said softly. "I will never leave you, Lottie. I swear it."

He kissed her slowly, thoroughly, tasting her, dipping his head to graze his tongue across her nipple, to suck and to bite, so that heat flared through her and set her shivering with need. She felt lost, afraid to surrender the last corner of her heart to him, but there was no escape. His touch was so sure, claiming her heart and soul as his alone. She trembled to possess him as much as she wanted to be possessed.

He lowered himself over her, spreading her open for him. The sun was blocked out, his face a shadow now against the light. And then he was inside her and her heart tumbled over and over and she ran her hands down his back to feel the play of his muscles as he moved within her.

"Look at me, Lottie… I love you…" His breathing was uneven. "I will always love you."

Lottie opened her eyes and smiled and arched up to meet the irresistible thrust of his body. The sunlight shimmered, scattering brightness through every last dark fearful corner of her soul. The spiral of light spun brighter and brighter, banishing all the bitterness of the past. Excitement pulsed through her, and helpless pleasure sweeter than anything she had known, exploding inside her, smashing her defenses, spinning through her, glorious, dazzling. Lust fused with love for all time.

It was some time before her shattered senses became aware of all the little things: the stalks of grass pricking her skin because they had rolled right off the rug; the buzz of the bees gorging on the honey because they had left the pot open; and the heat of the sun on her nakedness, which had passed the sensual and moved to the downright uncomfortable.

"I am burning!" Lottie said. "Literally."

She pulled Ethan to his feet and dragged him down to the stream. It was cooler here in the shadows. The water rippled over smooth brown stones and gurgled through pools and under the bowed branches of the willow. For a while they splashed and played in the water, then lay on the bank in the sun to dry off before making love again. Finally they dressed haphazardly, packed up the picnic and wandered back to the horses, hand in hand.

"This is very different from the first time I was betrothed," Lottie said. "Gregory gave me an enormous ruby ring that was too big for my hand and did not even kiss me." She smiled at Ethan. "I think that I prefer your style of proposal."

Outside Priory Cottage she stood on tiptoe to kiss Ethan. He put an arm about her waist.

"Be ready to go tonight," he whispered. "I will come for you after dark." He released her and smiled that earthshaking smile. "No more than one bag, Lottie."

Lottie saw the love in his eyes and her heart turned over. She stood by the gate for a long time after he had gone and then she went inside to pack.

CHAPTER NINETEEN

"MADAM!" Margery came into the bedchamber just as Lottie was folding the last of her gowns up and placing it in the third portmanteau. "You're leaving," the maid said flatly, sitting down on the edge of the bed.

"Yes," Lottie said. "I go with Lord St. Severin tonight." She picked the maid up and whirled her about the room, regardless of Margery's pleas to be put down. "We are to be wed, Margery!" she said. "I am to be Lady St. Severin!"

"And a good job, too," the maid said stringently, "given that you have been behaving as good as married these two months past."

"I have not!" Lottie said, stung. "I have been behaving like a mistress, not a wife, Margery. No wife sleeps with her husband. It is too, too bourgeois."

"Fiddlesticks!" Margery said. "You'll have to stop talking like a London lady now, ma'am," she added, "and simply admit you love your husband."

"Oh, very well," Lottie said, sighing. "I suppose I shall."

She looked more closely at the maid. Margery was fidgeting, her face full of unhappiness rather than pleasure. Lottie felt a swift rush of compassion. It was all very well to be so caught up in her own good news, she thought, but Margery could not be expected to share her joy. There was no chance that the maid could come with them. She would be left behind with no work in a town where jobs were scarce and poverty an ever-present threat.

"I am sorry," she said, putting out a hand to touch Margery's hunched shoulders. "I will write you a glowing reference, of course, although such words of praise from me may well do you more harm than good with the local matrons. And I will leave you money to tide you over for a good long time—" She stopped, a brush of fear touching her heart, for Margery had shaken her head, a little motion of denial that nevertheless spoke louder than any words.

"It isn't that, ma'am," the maid said a little awkwardly. She got to her feet, smoothing her palms down her apron. "You've been the best mistress to me a maid could ever ask for, ma'am. At the beginning," she gulped, "you told me that you were no lady, but it weren't the truth, ma'am. I worked for Lady Goodlake for over two years and she never once thanked me. I don't think she even knew who I was. But you, ma'am, for all your fancy London sayings you're a lady through and through."

"Margery!" Lottie said, feeling ridiculously affected. "You'll make me cry."

"Yes, ma'am," Margery said. She dived a hand into the pocket of her apron. "I think you should see this, ma'am. My brother gave it to me." She was pulling out a rather dog-eared piece of paper. "He works as tap man at The Bull, ma'am. Like as not he shouldn't have interfered, but curiosity killed the cat, they say,

and once he had got it out he couldn't put it back—"
She stopped.

"Margery," Lottie said, frowning. "I don't under-stand—"

The maid pushed the paper at her and Lottie took it a little gingerly. It was dirty and stained.

"It was in the bung of one of the beer kegs," the maid said in a rush. "It's in a funny foreign language, mind, so I knew it must be something to do with the prisoners, ma'am, and I didn't know what to do. I don't want John to get into trouble so I came to you."

"Of course," Lottie said automatically. "Don't worry, Margery. I'm sure we can sort it out." She took the paper. It felt smooth, as though it had passed through many hands.

Margery dropped a hasty curtsy. "I'll be in the kitchen, ma'am, if you need me," she said.

After Margery had gone out Lottie unfolded the letter and scanned it carefully. It was not in French, as she had expected. Margery's funny foreign language was Latin and it was also in code.

"Hodie mihi, cras tibi…" "Today to me, tomor-row to you…"
"Si post fata venit gloria non propero…" "If glory comes after death, I'm not in a hurry…"

Lottie frowned. She had seen these words somewhere before, glanced at them on a gravestone perhaps. She looked out of the window at the spire of St. Andrew's church piercing the blue of the sky. She grabbed her bonnet and spencer and the letter, and hurried from the door.

A half hour later, sitting chilled and hunched in the parlor, she wished that she had not remembered, wished that she did not have such a talent for languages, and wished that she had not, like Margery's brother John, had such an unhealthy curiosity. Her tea was cooling in a cup and on a piece of paper before her lay the code, transposed in all its chilling detail:

> "At Millbay Prison there is a tunnel of over five hundred yards leading out into the fields. The prisoners will overcome the guard and escape…."
> "At Forton Prison they have cut a hole in the wall…."
> "At Stapleton they have forged documents to enable the prisoners to effect an escape…."

The list went on and on. The prisons at Norman Cross, at Greenlaw and at Perth all had escape plans by road or river, overcoming the guards, taking their weapons, escaping en masse. And at the bottom of the page:

> "The night of 14th September 1813…"

Tomorrow night. Lottie shivered, drawing her shawl more closely about her shoulders as a long, long shudder crept down her spine. At last she could see the full grandeur of Ethan's plan. She had always known that he had planned something far bigger than his own escape and that of Arland, but lately she had not wanted to know. She loved Ethan. She wanted to run away with him. That was all that had mattered.

Not anymore. Now she could see that this was no small-scale plot to free Arland. It was an enormous conspiracy, magnificent in its scale, terrifying in its scope. Sixty thousand prisoners, French, American, Danish, Spanish, Irish, all nationalities would unite to rise up against the British on their own soil. No longer did Mrs. Ormond's panicked fluttering seem like a bat squeak in the dark. Her deepest fears would come to pass. All the prisoners would escape and overrun the country and people would fight and suffer and die as a result. The government would fall. The war would be lost. Hundreds, thousands, of her countrymen and women would be killed. It was no wonder that the British authorities had been watching Ethan so closely. This was what Theo and his colleagues had been waiting for.

She had to tell him. She had to take the letter to Theo and betray Ethan's plot.

She should not hesitate. This was treason. It was lethally dangerous. Yet still she sat staring into the fire, trying to feel its warmth, and she thought of all that she had heard, of the hell of the prison hulks with their torture and starvation and disease, of gaols like Whitemoor with their ragged prisoners, filthy and emaciated, the brutality of the guards, the cuts and bruises on Arland's face. She had seen the way that officers were treated in a parole town, seen the civilized face of captivity, not its violent, cruel underbelly.

She swallowed hard. It was not fair to expect someone like her to bear the burden for such a heavy moral decision, she thought bitterly. She was not equipped for it. Normally she only had to choose between red or green silk, not weigh the lives of her countrymen and her patriotic duty against justice and her overwhelming love for one man.

Intolerable choices...

She let the letter fall from her hand to the carpet. She knew what she had to do. She had to betray Ethan for the greater good. Not for money but for principle this time. It was the greatest irony that she admired and respected Ethan so much for his passion and his devotion to his principles. She loved him because of his certainty and his fierce loyalty to his cause and to the people he believed in. And now, finally, she had to sacrifice her self-interest and her love and try to find some of that deeply buried principle within herself because if she did not, her countrymen would die in their thousands. In the end it really was as simple as that.

She wrapped her arms about her. Only a few hours ago she had thought to be secure in Ethan's love. The world was a cold place without the strength of that love to draw upon. No doubt Theo would reward her for her loyalty to her country. She would not starve now. But life after love was going to be very empty.

She stood up and walked slowly over to her escritoire, dipped her quill in the inkpot, and started to compose a letter to Theo. When she had finished she sent Margery with instructions to find a post boy to take the letter directly to her brother, without delay. Then she sat down to compose a note to Ethan. She knew that she had to warn him, and give him the chance to escape. She would foil his conspiracy but the one thing she could not bear to do was to give him up to arrest and execution.

But what to say, when her heart was breaking?

I have betrayed you one last time. I love you, but it was not enough. I had to put my duty to my country first….

It sounded so pompous, so unlike her.

I found the principles I thought I lacked and unfortunately I discovered them at the most inconvenient moment….

There really was nothing that she could say, so she scribbled a few stark words of warning and left it at that. The last thing Ethan would want from her was words of regret or, God forbid, protestations of love.

Two hours later she was still sitting there, feeling stiff and cold, and twilight was starting to fall outside. Theo would have her message by now. He would be on his way. And so would Ethan. She prayed fiercely that he would be able to escape the net and take Arland to freedom.

The letter detailing the escape plans had slid from the table in a slight draft from the door. Lottie bent slowly, like an old woman, to pick it up from the floor. It fluttered, skipping out of her reach. She grabbed it and straightened up just as someone stepped into the room.

She had expected to see Theo, but it was Jacques Le Prevost who stood there. Lottie let out her breath on a gasp of combined shock and relief.

"Oh, *m'sieur*, you startled me."

For once Le Prevost made no showy bow and paid her no extravagant compliments. Instead, his gaze was so keen on her face that it made her feel quite uncomfortable. As she blushed and drew back he looked down at the piece of paper in her hand—and held out his own as though to take it from her.

"What do you have there, *madame?*" His voice was quiet and expressionless.

"I… Oh…" Lottie felt hot. Though Le Prevost was French she had no wish to confide in him that she had discovered Ethan's plans, for surely he would try to persuade her to hand them back. She felt trapped, torn. She crumpled the sheets between her fingers. "Nothing. A letter from a friend."

Le Prevost smiled but his eyes were cold. "You are a poor liar, *madame.*"

Lottie looked at him sharply. "What do you mean?"

Le Prevost did not take his eyes off her face. "I have looked everywhere," he said. "I should have known that St. Severin would hide it here. I thought of it—but then I thought he would not put your life at risk." His eyes gleamed cold. "It seems that I was mistaken—and that he cares nothing for your safety, *madame.*" His brows snapped down. "Where did you find it?"

Lottie's mind was whirling, full of darting thoughts and suspicions. Le Prevost, the foppish colonel who lavished those fulsome compliments on the ladies, who cared for no more than the set of his coat… Could he be an informer for the British? Had he been searching for Ethan's plans, too? Suddenly she remembered the night she had followed Ethan to his rendezvous up on the Lambourn road and the messenger who had died. She had known it could not have been Ethan who had

murdered him, but on that night she had glimpsed another man strolling out of town. She had thought it was
Le Prevost and had assumed that he was engaged in a
dalliance….

Perhaps he had had an assignation with death rather
than with a lover. She shivered.

"I don't understand," she said. The papers rustled as
she clenched her fingers about them. "*You* were looking for these? But I thought that you—" She stopped.
"You're French," she said foolishly. "Surely you must
support Ethan's plans—" But she stopped again before
she had finished the sentence because she could see in
Le Prevost's face how naive her words were. And then
she saw the pistol in his hand and the sword at his hip,
and knew that her worst suspicions were true.

"You are a renegade," she whispered. "You work for
no one but yourself."

Le Prevost shrugged. "I support whichever cause
offers me the most," he said.

"Because he has no honor and will sell his comrades
and his enemies equally if the price is right," said a soft,
deadly voice from behind them.

Lottie spun around to see Ethan lounging in the
doorway. There was a cold, hard light in his eyes as
he looked from Le Prevost's face to the pistol in his
hand.

"Isn't that right, Jacques?" Ethan continued. "British, French, American, it is all the same to you if the
money is good. I knew someone was betraying me."
He took a breath. "I should have guessed it was you."

The atmosphere sparked and tightened. Lottie

saw the flare of hatred in Le Prevost's eyes before he shrugged, an ugly smile on his lips.

"We cannot all be heroes like you, St. Severin," he mocked. "Besides—" he gestured to Lottie "—if you speak of betrayal then surely it is your *chère amie* whom you should be reproaching? She sold you out to her brother."

Ethan turned to look at Lottie and her insides shriveled. "I am sorry," she whispered. "I had to do it, Ethan—"

Ethan smiled then with such tenderness that she caught her breath. "I don't reproach you, Lottie," he said. "I would have done exactly the same." His smile deepened. "Though I confess I was surprised to discover that you possessed a moral code after all. And disappointed that you discovered it at such a confoundedly awkward moment." He turned back to Le Provost.

"Whereas you, Jacques…" His voice was ice-cold and level. "You possess neither principle nor conscience."

"Mon Dieu." Le Prevost was laughing. "My conscience is always quiet when I am paid enough." He spun around on Lottie. "The letter, if you please, *madame*. Your brother and I have gone to a great deal of trouble to try to obtain it."

"Theo?" Lottie said. She glanced at Ethan. His face was dark and set. She saw a muscle pulse in his jaw. "But I understood he worked for British intelligence," she said. Her world was falling apart, tearing at the seams. "Oh no, not Theo, too…" She could hear the pleading note in her voice.

"Madame is still such an *innocente* for all her experience," Le Prevost said contemptuously. "Your brother

and I have worked together secretly for several years, to our mutual benefit. We deal in information." He gestured toward the papers. "When there is intelligence like this to buy and sell we auction it to the highest bidder."

"No," Lottie said. She gripped the back of the chair more tightly, her fingers digging into the wood. "Oh no." She thought of Theo coming to her in London, claiming to represent the British authorities when he had in fact been planning to double-cross them all along. He had appealed to her to betray Ethan, offered her empty promises and dreams. He had exploited her most fundamental fears and desires to achieve his aims, but it had not been out of patriotic duty. He had used her for no more than his own gain. She felt sick and anguished to think of it.

"Theo lied to me from the first…" she whispered, and felt her last shred of faith in her brother vanish like mist when she saw Le Prevost nod.

"Your brother sought you out in London so that he could persuade you to help us with our plans," Le Prevost said. "He knew he could trade on your trust in him." He smiled unpleasantly. "And so it proved."

Lottie felt Ethan shift slightly. She glanced at him. There was compassion in his eyes.

"I wanted Theo's love," she said painfully, speaking directly to Ethan as though Le Prevost was not there. "He was the only one who cared for me since childhood and I wanted to please him."

There was such a gentle smile on Ethan's lips that she could feel her heart breaking. "You do not need to justify yourself to me, Lottie," he said softly. "You chose to inform your brother of my plans to protect what you believe in. The fact that you chose to trust an unworthy man is not your fault."

Lottie bit her lip hard. Oh, she truly had chosen the wrong man in whom to invest her love and her trust. In the beginning she had wanted Theo to be her white knight, to save her from the trouble she had brought on herself. It had made her vulnerable to her brother's manipulation. Ethan was right that in the end it was her principles that had prompted her to act; those wholly unlooked for, wholly unexpected and indeed completely unwelcome moral values that had forced her to betray him for the greater good of her countrymen. She could not regret her actions. But she deeply regretted that she had trusted Theo when he now proved himself a traitor.

And yet in some ways she and Theo were two of a kind, she thought bitterly. Both of them had seen their world crumble when they were no more than children. Both of them had grown up knowing they had to fight for everything they wanted. They had both sold themselves for money and security. They were more alike than she wished to admit.

"Most affecting," Le Prevost mocked. "Give the plans to me, *madame*."

"No," Lottie said. "If you want them you will have to take them from me."

Le Prevost shrugged. "If you wish to make it difficult. It makes no odds, *madame*. I shall have the information I seek and then…" A slight gesture with the pistol underlined his meaning.

"You cannot kill me," Lottie said. "I am Theo's sister! He would never countenance it!"

Le Prevost's lips curled into a smile. "Alas," he said, "you know too much, *madame*. Your brother will understand why I have to act as I do. Leave no witnesses, no hostages to fortune. You will both die—" He bowed ironically to Ethan. "I will have the plans and will sell them to the British at a very high price. *Enfin*—" his eyes gleamed "—so simple and so profitable."

"I challenge you for the papers," Ethan said. His voice cut through the thick tension that blanketed the room. He straightened up, strolled forward for all the world, Lottie thought, as though he was the one holding the pistol, not Le Prevost. Then she saw that he was armed. He must have picked up the sword they had taken from Gregory's house that night in London, which had subsequently been left in the umbrella stand in the hall.

"Show some honor for once," Ethan said to Le Prevost. "Take the challenge."

Le Prevost threw his head back and laughed. "A good try, St. Severin," he said, "but I have chosen my weapon and I am holding it. I would be a fool to accept the challenge of a man who bested me only last week on the practice field."

And then Lottie heard a very faint sound outside beyond the orchard, the creak of wood as someone crossed the stream from the fields and stepped on a loose board on the bridge. She tensed, straining to hear. Was someone coming? And if they were, would it not simply be Theo, come to finish what Le Prevost had started? Le Prevost was taking aim now, his gaze holding Ethan's, that terrible, triumphant gleam still in his eyes.

"A poor end for a man who was such a hero," Le Prevost murmured. "How amusing that I should do the British such a favor as to kill you, St. Severin, and for this they are not even paying me." He jerked his head toward Lottie. "Any last words for your inamorata? A moving farewell?"

There was the sound of the chink of metal from outside. It could have been no more than the chain on the well stirring in the wind, or it could have been someone brushing past it as they approached the house. This time the men heard it, too, for they froze. For a split second Le Prevost's attention was distracted. He turned his head and in that moment, with a strength borne of terror, Lottie picked up the chair she had been clutching and spun around. It caught Le Prevost under the chin and he fell backward. The pistol exploded and Lottie felt a sharp pain through her shoulder and grabbed the edge of the table to steady herself. Her legs suddenly felt as weak as water, slipping away from her. The light in the room wavered and dulled as her head spun. She fought desperately to hold on to consciousness.

There was the hiss of steel as Ethan drew his sword and Le Prevost scrambled to his feet. The blades rang against each other in a swift thrust and parry. There was desperation in Le Prevost's strokes, controlled fury in Ethan's. He forced Le Prevost back and back against the wall. Le Prevost grabbed the candlestick from the mantel and threw it at Ethan's head. Ethan ducked. Le Prevost followed up with a punch that just missed Ethan's jaw.

Ethan stepped back, recovering his breath. "You fight by no rules I recognize, Jacques," he said silkily, "but then we knew that, did we not?"

Le Prevost's response was a renewed attack but he was losing focus and skill now, and Ethan repeatedly beat back his blade. Lottie saw his guard falter, saw Ethan press the advantage, and suddenly the swords locked together, the men chest to chest, and she cried out as the blades wavered, then Le Prevost lunged forward with a mad shout and as Lottie watched he seemed to impale himself on his own blade and for a moment he hung there before he fell. She gave a cry as his body hit the ground and rolled over to lie against the grate.

Ethan discarded his sword and ran over to her.

"Lottie!" He caught her in his arms and she could feel him shaking as all the fear and tension and relief fused into one and he pulled her close. His mouth was pressed against her hair and he was murmuring endearments and she wanted to hold him tightly and hold him forever, but it hurt, it hurt so damnably badly that she could not repress a slight moan and he loosed his grip at once. In the firelight she could see his fingertips smeared with her blood.

"Lottie." His tone had changed. "You were hit—"

"Just a scratch," Lottie whispered. The room was wavering again. She felt light-headed and faint. Ethan was tearing up strips of some material—hopefully not her pink spotted muslin gown—to make a rough bandage. She could hear him swearing under his breath as he worked, as though if Le Prevost were not already lying dead on her carpet he would have sent the man to his maker a second time over. He ripped the dress from her shoulder before she could protest and wrapped the pad around and under her arm, pressing it down and tying it tight, which seemed to hurt all the more. Lottie felt horribly sick.

"I have to get you to a doctor," Ethan said.

"No." Lottie struggled to sit up. Her head might be spinning but there was one thing that she knew with absolute clarity, and it was that Ethan had to get away. For his sake, and even more importantly for Arland's he had to go now, before it was too late.

"Theo is coming," she whispered. "You will be trapped, Ethan—if we tried to turn him in to the British no one would believe our word against his that he is a traitor. And I cannot let you kill him." Her head felt so heavy; she rested it against Ethan's shoulder and wished she had not for it felt so natural to be there in his arms, to curve into the protective shelter of his body. It felt so right, when she knew she had to give him up now once and for all.

"The British will hang you now," she said. "You know they will. Either for conspiracy—" she gestured toward the plans, blood-spattered and crumpled on the floor "—or for murder. You have to get out whilst you can. Go now."

Ethan had heard her out in silence, his eyes burning dark in his face. He bent to scoop her up. "If I go then you come with me," he said, and his tone was uncompromising.

Lottie held him off. It was the hardest thing she had ever done when she wanted to cling to him. "No," she said. "You know I cannot."

He made a move toward her. "You can and you will."

"I would slow you down," Lottie said. She gestured toward her bandaged shoulder. "Be sensible, Ethan! We would not get beyond a few miles! Besides, they would be looking for us. A man and a woman and a boy traveling together—we would be spotted at once."

Ethan's jaw was set in the obstinate way she recognized. "I am not leaving without you."

"You must," Lottie said. She struggled to her feet. The room spun about her like a top. Her legs felt weak, trembling. "I cannot travel," she said softly, "and I have no reason to run. But you…" She placed a hand on his chest and felt his heart beat against her palm. "Not only do you have to go for your own sake, Ethan. You know you have to do it for Arland's sake."

There was a silence. Ethan was looking at her and there was stubbornness and tenderness in his eyes, and she thought of all the men who had left her from her father to her husband to each and every one of her lovers, and she looked at this man who would not leave her and she felt her heart turn over out of love for him.

"You told me…" Her voice was husky with tears. "You told me that you had failed him," she said. She clenched her hand against his shirt front. "This is your chance, Ethan. He is a boy. He needs you. You cannot fail him now."

Ethan's arms came about her and this time she did not wince. "Lottie," he said. His touch was full of love and anguish and gentleness, and she knew his decision was made.

"I will come back for you," he said fiercely. "I swear it."

"I'll come back for you," her father had said on that golden summer morning so long ago, and she had believed him. Now Lottie looked at Ethan and wanted to believe with all her heart. She felt the hope within her, the hope she had thought had been quite extinguished by the cynicism of experience, flicker and not quite die out.

"I know," she said. "I know you will." She forced her lips into a smile. "Now go."

The words had barely left her when there was a rapping at the door.

"Lottie!" It was Theo's voice. "Open up!"

Lottie gestured toward the window. "He's alone. You go that way. I will keep him here to give you a good chance of escape." She put a hand on his arm and felt the unendurable tension in him.

"Ethan," she said.

He covered her hand with his, swift and sure. She could sense his eagerness, knew that he hoped she had changed her mind about going with him, even as they both knew it was hopeless.

Oh love, how shall I live without you...?

"Pass the letter to me," she said steadily. "And also my pistol from the desk drawer. I will feel more confident when I speak to Theo if I have that in my hand."

The hammering at the door was increasing and Theo's shouts growing louder in volume. "I will break down the door!"

Ethan hesitated. "What will you do with the plans?"

"You know I cannot allow it to happen," Lottie said. She met his gaze very directly. "I am sorry, Ethan."

There was a small spark of warmth and laughter in his eyes and she felt it, too. So odd, when her heart was breaking.

"I understand," he said. He crossed to the desk and took out the pistol, laying it on the table. She watched as he bent to pick up the papers. He did not hand them to her. He thrust them into the fire and watched the flames take them, watched them curl and burn and shrivel to ash.

"I am sorry, too," he said, "but I could not betray my comrades. It will not happen now anyway. Not if I am not here to give the word."

There was the sound of breaking glass. Lottie stood on tiptoe and kissed Ethan. For one long, endless moment they stood in each other's arms and then there was the sound of rapid steps in the hall and Lottie stepped back.

"I love you," she said.

"I love you, too."

It was cold, so cold, without him beside her. Lottie picked up the pistol. It slid comfortingly into her hand. The door shuddered back on its hinges as Theo ran into the room. The window slammed behind Ethan. Theo's gaze went to the lifeless body of Le Prevost and lifted slowly to meet Lottie's. He made an involuntary movement toward the window and Lottie raised the pistol and he kept still.

"Good evening, Theo," Lottie said. "I believe that you and I have matters to discuss."

CHAPTER TWENTY

November 1813

"EXCUSE ME, MA'AM," Margery said. "There is a carriage drawing up outside. I do believe you may have visitors, ma'am. Are you At Home, ma'am? Shall I prepare to make tea?"

Lottie put aside the magazine that she had not been reading and smiled at the maid.

"How vastly exciting," she said. "Who will it be today, I wonder? Yes, Margery, by all means put the kettle on."

These days, Lottie thought, Margery had lost a great deal of her apprehension in dealing with the nobility, becoming almost as smooth as the best-trained butler. In part this was because the Marquess of Northesk had called several times in the past couple of months and was so gracious and courteous to Margery that she glowed with pleasure at each visit.

"I do believe that Margery is a little in love with you," Lottie had teased Garrick Northesk on his most recent visit. "She does not make her rock buns for anyone else."

Northesk had laughed. "I do tend to have that effect on maidservants," he said.

It was Northesk who, in the dark days after Ethan

had escaped, had persuaded the authorities to allow Lottie to stay at Priory Cottage. Theo had disappeared; no one knew where he was, but Lottie had the oddest feeling that he would reappear one day, for better or worse. In the meantime she had her friends—rather more friends than she might have expected under the circumstances—and the surprisingly stout support of the people of Wantage helped a very little to ease the pain of losing Ethan. It made it easier, she thought, that she was totally respectable these days. She had absolutely no desire to run off with the curate because not only was he prodigiously unattractive but there was a space in her heart that only Ethan could fill, and without him she wanted no one else.

The ladies of Wantage still asked her advice on fashion and sometimes, shyly, on matters of the heart. Mrs. Ormond visited, bringing Mary Belle with her, "for where the Marquess of Northesk sets the tone," she announced grandly, "I am sure that I am not too high in the instep to follow." Miss Cromarty, the retired schoolmistress, made Lottie gooseberry jelly laced with brandy to ward off the chills of approaching winter. Mrs. Fenstone, the doctor's wife, knitted ugly shawls for her.

"I imagine," Lottie said to Margery, "that she thinks that if she forces me into hideous clothing so that I look like a frump, she believes that there will be less likelihood of me running off with anyone's husband."

Northesk had called the previous day with news; he had had word at last of Ethan and had heard that he had got Arland on his way to safety in America.

"Don't ask me how I know," he had said, with a faint smile, "but you may take it that it is true."

"Thank goodness," Lottie had said, but it felt as though Ethan was a long, long way away. She had fidgeted with her teaspoon and had avoided Northesk's gaze as she asked, "Was there any word of what Ethan plans to do next?"

She had spoken lightly, pretending not to care, afraid of showing the depth of her loss and longing. Ethan's last letter, scrawled in haste, had been intimate, private, full of love and it had lain next to her in bed these two months past until it was now so crumpled it was illegible.

Northesk had tilted his head to one side—a gesture so like his half brother's that Lottie's heart had missed a beat.

"There are rumors that Ethan has been sighted in places as far afield as Paris and Edinburgh, Cornwall and Spain," he had said gently, "but I believe them all to be false. It is not even known if he is still in England. With Ethan there are always rumors, stories and legends."

"I know," Lottie had said, sighing. "He is like a will-o'-the-wisp. Sometimes I wonder if he is real at all."

"I think he is real enough," Northesk had said, giving her a dry look, and Lottie had blushed.

Northesk had risen to leave then, but as he took her hand to bid her goodbye he said softly, "I believe that Ethan is coming for you. Now that Arland is safely away, he will not forget the promise he made. You must be ready."

He had smiled, that heartbreaking smile so like his

brother's and was gone with a word of thanks to Margery on the deliciousness of the rock buns. Lottie had stood by the window, watching him walk away, and had wondered on the quirk of nature that had made Ethan and Garrick Northesk so similar in some ways, and yet she felt dizzy at the mere thought of seeing Ethan again, whilst Northesk, a fine man, a handsome man, left her entirely unmoved.

It would not have been so in the past, she knew. Once she might have invited Northesk to her bed, seeking from him the same comfort to ward off loneliness, the same elusive happiness that she had wanted from all her lovers. But now, having known Ethan, she could accept no counterfeit.

She shivered. Would she ever see Ethan again? Would he still want her? She knew what Northesk had said, but there were so many doubts and fears in her mind. They stalked her at night when it was dark and she was alone and the bed was cold and empty.

Bearing in mind that she now had other visitors, Lottie hurried to tidy up the little parlor, smoothing the covers on the chairs and pushing her latest piece of poor embroidery under a cushion.

"Lord and Lady Grant!" Margery announced from the doorway, and Lottie dropped the embroidery frame in shock and gave a cry.

"Lottie! Oh, Lottie!" Joanna Grant practically ran into the room and enfolded her friend in a vast hug. The first thing that Lottie noticed was that Joanna was hugely pregnant. Hugging her was like trying to get her arms around a barrel, but she tried her best, holding Joanna as tightly as she dared, which was not very tight in case the baby popped out. She felt the tears sting her eyes and block her throat, and she tried very hard to swallow them but they kept rising up again. In the end she gave in to them and then she realized that Joanna was crying, too.

"Jo, darling…" She tried an approximation of her previous, languid style, but it was impossible. "Oh, I am so happy to see you again!" she burst out. "I've missed you so much!"

"I didn't know!" Joanna grabbed the handkerchief that her husband, Alex, was proffering and dabbed at her streaming eyes. "Oh, Lottie, we were in Mongolia and I didn't get your letters, and I had not heard what had happened to you and when we got back I was so upset and worried for you that I made Alex come out here immediately—" She ran out of breath.

"You look marvelous!" Lottie said, smiling radiantly at her, holding her at arm's length. She smiled at Alex. "I can see that your marriage is a vast success."

Joanna laughed, grabbing Alex's hand. Her eyes met Lottie's, full of mischief.

"Who would have thought it?" she said.

"I am very happy for you," Lottie said sincerely. Joanna, she thought, looked much as she always had, elegant and stylish in a striped blue silk gown with the most adorable little spencer over the top, but there was a softer glow to her now than Lottie remembered. It was as though Joanna had lost her brittleness, she thought. Happiness had banished her sharp edges. She had grown into the person she was always meant to be.

Alex had discreetly withdrawn to let them talk and

had strolled over to the window, pretending an interest in the handkerchief-sized front garden. He was looking as handsome as ever, Lottie thought. It was embarrassing to recall that she had once tried to seduce him. Perhaps that was one memory that she would immediately expunge no matter how honest she was being these days about her past failings.

"How are you, Lottie?" Joanna said, an anxious little frown creasing her forehead.

"I survive," Lottie said lightly. She looked from Joanna to Alex. "I suppose you both knew that I would one day come to this?" she said wryly.

Alex smiled at her. "I would never be so ungallant," he said.

Joanna grabbed her hands again. "What can we do to help you, Lottie? Do you have enough food?" She looked Lottie up and down. "Or clothes?" she said dubiously.

"I know I look a frump," Lottie said. "These days I do not regard it."

"Lottie!" Joanna sounded horrified. "Now I know you really must have suffered!"

"How did you find Mongolia?" Lottie enquired as she rang the bell for refreshment. "I hear it is very… empty."

"Oh it was dire," Joanna said, waving her hands about expressively. "But I am used to these places now." She flashed Alex a smile to soften her words. "And they did have the most delightful textiles. We brought back some beautiful carpets and rugs, and a jacket made of silk and brocade that I am sure will be all the rage next Season—" She broke off.

"Pray do not worry about my sensibilities," Lottie said. "I am sure I shall never be an arbiter of London fashion again. Although I do believe that I have made a great difference in Wantage," she added. "They are now only two years behind the trend rather than ten. And the ladies are flatteringly quick to consult me on their wardrobes."

She was amused to see that the arrival of Margery with tea and cakes clearly reassured Joanna, who could see now that although her clothes might no longer be from Bedford House, at least she was not starving.

"So will you continue to live here?" Alex asked. "It is a charming little cottage, and the town seems very pleasant."

"Oh, it is delightful," Lottie said. "The Pallisers are content to ignore me and they have been prevailed upon to give me sufficient of a pension to enable me to live quietly." She smiled at them both. "And I really am quite reformed. I have lost my taste for scandal."

"Well, I suppose it is something that your father's family finally agreed to help you," Joanna said, wrinkling up her nose in disgust. "But they could have acted long ago. What a bunch of mean-spirited hypocrites! Oh, if only I had been here for you!"

"You are here now," Lottie said. "That means a very great deal to me."

"But can we do anything to help?" Joanna pressed.

"You can come and visit me often," Lottie said. "It may not be as exciting as traveling to Mongolia, but Wantage has its charms."

"Of course we shall!" Joanna said. A small frown

touched her forehead. "We had planned to stay a few days, at any rate. I understand, though, that the Marquess of Northesk calls…." She broke off.

"I am sorry," Lottie said quickly. She was remembering the old scandals, and the link between Joanna's family and the Dukes of Farne. "Northesk is a good man," she said. "He is Ethan's half brother and is the one who persuaded the Pallisers to pay me my pittance."

"I know," Joanna said. "I heard he had been very good to you." She waved a dismissive hand. "I do not blame Northesk for my brother's death, though I know Merryn still does. No…" She shook her head. "It is old history and I am only glad and grateful that he was here to help you when we were not."

"How is Merryn?" Lottie asked. She glanced across at Alex. "And your cousin, Francesca? Did she enjoy Mongolia, too?"

"Oh, Chessie enjoyed the trip enormously," Joanna said, laughing. "I think some of the Devlin spirit of adventure is in her blood! And Merryn is well. She has been staying with a bluestocking friend of hers whilst we have been away. They have been writing a history of the Welsh Marches from 1250 to 1350, so I hear."

"Lud, how dull," Lottie said, "though each to their own, I suppose."

"You look blue-deviled, Lottie," Joanna said, leaning forward to place a consoling hand on her knee. "Alex and I thought that we might go to the country fair at Uffington this afternoon. I hear it is marvelous fun. There is cheese rolling and even a balloon ascent! Why do you not come with us?"

"Why not?" Lottie said. It might be amusing to get out of the house for a little, she thought. It was a fine autumn day and perfect for a brisk walk up on the Downs. The days when she had considered a country fair beneath her interest were long gone. Really, she thought, she had once been the most unconscionable snob.

In the end the fair did prove to be rather fun. They all took a pony and trap from the livery stables and clattered up the track onto the Downs. The fair sprawled over several acres of Lord Craven's land at Uffington and the air was thick with the scent of gingerbread and pipe smoke. There were acrobats, jugglers and a fiddler playing jigs and reels—and a contingent of soldiers from the Berkshire Volunteers to keep the peace as the drink flowed and the crowds became more raucous. There was a shooting gallery and a contest to climb a greasy pole.

"A pity that Gregory is not here," Lottie observed to Joanna. "He would have won that one with ease."

In the fortune-teller's spangled tent she had her palm read by a gypsy woman who predicted that she would have many lovers, travel to distant lands and find a tall, dark foreigner whom she could not resist.

"I've already done all of those things," Lottie sighed. "Are you sure you are not reading my past rather than my future?"

The balloon was tethered on the flat area at the top of the hill. Scarlet and gold, it rippled in the air, tugging on the ropes that bound it to earth. The men who had been attending it earlier were taking a short break at the pie seller's tent before the balloonist, a famous aviator called Thomas Howard, was due to give an ascent as the highlight of the fair.

"You would not ever get me in that thing," Lottie said, transfixed by a combination of fascination and terror. "I am afraid of heights."

Alex started trying to explain to her how the balloon flew but she could make no sense of the science and after a moment she stopped trying and allowed his words to flow over her head. It was odd, she thought, how she could miss Ethan at such random moments. Sometimes hours went by when she did not think of him and then some small circumstance would remind her, perhaps finding something he had given her, a scribbled sketch or a piece of music. The most painful reminder was catching sight of someone who bore a passing resemblance to Ethan. For a heartbeat she would catch her breath and feel her heart surge, but already she would have seen it was not Ethan and the disappointment would flood back.

Now, for example, she had seen a man in the milling crowd about the balloon, a man dressed casually in jacket, breeches and boots, who had the height, bearing and coloring of Ethan, who looked so like him that she waited for the customary flare of hope and excitement and the fall straight after. It did not come. She stared, whilst her heart started to race and her fingers clenched Alex's arm so tightly that he fell silent.

Ethan was coming toward them, cutting through the crowds, intent, purposeful, utterly single-minded, his gaze fixed on her. The roar of the crowd died to a whisper. Everyone was staring. Far away, as though in a trance, Lottie could hear the shouts of children and the high thin music of the violin.

Lottie grabbed Joanna's hand to steady herself. "Jo…" Her voice was a thread. "Am I dreaming?" Then she realized that Joanna had never met Ethan and would not recognize him. But now he was close and she knew there could be no mistake.

"Of all the arrogant, dangerous, brazen exploits—" she began, but she was shaking so much that her voice faded away.

"So that is Ethan," Joanna said. She laughed. "You have to go with him, Lottie. In the balloon."

"I can't!" Lottie gasped. She could not tear her gaze from Ethan as he covered the final few yards to her side.

"Don't be ridiculous!" Joanna was holding her tight and pushing her forward at the same time. "Do you remember when Alex came for me on the *Sea Witch?* You have to be brave."

"I always wanted to be swept off my feet," Lottie said. "I envied you so much."

Joanna released her. There were tears in her eyes. "This is your chance, Lottie. Go!"

"Why did it have to be like this?" Lottie wailed.

"Because," Joanna said, "this is Ethan Ryder and I hear he never does anything by halves."

Ethan reached their side. "Take care of her," Joanna said fiercely. "I don't care who you are, but if you hurt her I'll find you."

She pushed Lottie into Ethan's arms, and he swept

her up and swung her around and deposited her in the basket of the balloon before she could so much as squeak. Her heart was thundering against her ribs and she was shaking as she struggled to her feet.

"I have no luggage!" she shouted.

"I didn't need any!" Joanna called back. "And neither will you!"

"Please look after Margery for me!" Lottie shouted. "And my canary!" She saw her friend nod.

Ethan was releasing one of the ropes, and after a moment Alex Grant sighed and went to help.

"Might as well be court-martialed *again*, I suppose," Lottie heard him say, "for helping an enemy of the state escape this time."

"Hurry!" Lottie cried. She could see the captain of the Berkshire Militia running toward them now, pistol in hand, shouting at them to stop. The two men who had been guarding the balloon emerged from the pie tent, rubbed the crumbs from their faces and also started to run in their direction. The crowd followed, as crowds do.

The ropes slackened suddenly and the balloon lurched. The basket rocked as Ethan put one hand on the side and leaped in. He put his arms around Lottie, and she clung to him, turning her face against his jacket, digging her fingers into his lapels as though that would steady her in this mad world.

"This could all go horribly wrong," she said, her words muffled against his chest.

"It won't," Ethan said. He sounded so confident that against all sense, Lottie actually believed him.

"You came for me," she said. She gripped his jacket and gave him a little shake. She could barely believe he was there. "Ethan," she said again, "you came back for me."

Ethan smiled, a smile of blazing triumph and tenderness that made Lottie's heart swell with pure joy.

"I said I would come," he said. "Don't say that you doubted me."

"No," Lottie said shakily. "Never."

She heard Ethan laugh. The balloon was rising, but terrifyingly slowly. Lottie could see Joanna's face, a look of horror on it that would have been comical had it not frightened her so much. The captain of the militia was almost upon them, taking aim, until Alex tripped him at the last moment, and then the updraft of the wind caught them and the balloon shot up into the sky, clearing the top of the hill.

Ethan kissed her, a heart-shaking kiss that swept her away. The scent of his skin was so familiar, the touch and the feel of him, that Lottie's head spun with recognition. Her heart expanded with love, opening up like a flower, turning to the light. There was so much to say, and yet now that the moment had come, so little real need to say it….

Ethan let her go at last. "Is this not frightfully dangerous?" Lottie whispered, looking up at the billowing silk of the balloon with a great deal of trepidation.

"Frightfully," Ethan concurred.

Lottie glanced at him. "You are enjoying yourself," she accused.

"Hugely," Ethan said.

"Do you know how to fly this thing?"

"I am not at all sure that one can fly a balloon," Ethan said. "You go where it takes you."

"Well, I hope the wind is in the direction of the coast," Lottie said, holding tight as another upward draft caught the balloon and it picked up even more speed.

"It is," Ethan said. "With a fair wind we may even make it as far as France."

Lottie looked down at the tiny figures running around the field below them and at the carved figure of the White Horse, which looked so much more impressive from the air than it had done on the ground. She felt the wind ripple through her hair and the sun warm on her face as a loving touch.

It felt like living.

It felt like happiness.

Ethan put his hand over hers and she smiled up at him and nestled closer into his arms. They stood wrapped together as the balloon rose higher until it was no more than a speck on the horizon, drifting away.

SOME SIX HOURS LATER, two of the villagers of Burley in Hampshire reported an astonishing sight. They swore they had seen a falling star, dropping into the heart of the ancient woods in a flurry of red and gold. But they had been on their way home from the village inn at the time, so no one gave their story much credence.

Later still, a small boat slipped from its moorings at Milford on Sea under the cover of darkness and headed out into the English Channel.

The British Army searched for Ethan Ryder and his

scandalous bride from Land's End to John O'Groats but although many sightings of them were reported, they were never found.

They were the *on dit* for years.

* * * * *

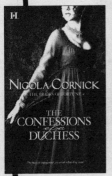

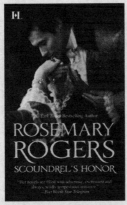

REQUEST YOUR FREE BOOKS!

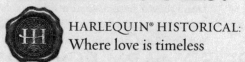

HARLEQUIN® HISTORICAL:
Where love is timeless

2 FREE NOVELS PLUS 2 FREE GIFTS!

YES! Please send me 2 FREE Harlequin® Historical novels and my 2 FREE gifts (gifts are worth about $10). After receiving them, if I don't wish to receive any more books, I can return the shipping statement marked "cancel." If I don't cancel, I will receive 6 brand-new novels every month and be billed just $4.94 per book in the U.S. or $5.49 per book in Canada. That's a saving of 20% off the cover price! It's quite a bargain! Shipping and handling is just 50¢ per book.* I understand that accepting the 2 free books and gifts places me under no obligation to buy anything. I can always return a shipment and cancel at any time. Even if I never buy another book from Harlequin, the two free books and gifts are mine to keep forever.

246/349 HDN E5L4

Name _____ (PLEASE PRINT) _____

Address _____ Apt. #

City _____ State/Prov. _____ Zip/Postal Code

Signature (if under 18, a parent or guardian must sign)

Mail to the Harlequin Reader Service:
IN U.S.A.: P.O. Box 1867, Buffalo, NY 14240-1867
IN CANADA: P.O. Box 609, Fort Erie, Ontario L2A 5X3

Not valid for current subscribers to Harlequin Historical books.

Want to try two free books from another line?
Call 1-800-873-8635 or visit www.morefreebooks.com.

* Terms and prices subject to change without notice. Prices do not include applicable taxes. N.Y. residents add applicable sales tax. Canadian residents will be charged applicable provincial taxes and GST. Offer not valid in Quebec. This offer is limited to one order per household. All orders subject to approval. Credit or debit balances in a customer's account(s) may be offset by any other outstanding balance owed by or to the customer. Please allow 4 to 6 weeks for delivery. Offer available while quantities last.

Your Privacy: Harlequin Books is committed to protecting your privacy. Our Privacy Policy is available online at www.eHarlequin.com or upon request from the Reader Service. From time to time we make our lists of customers available to reputable third parties who may have a product or service of interest to you. If you would prefer we not share your name and address, please check here. ☐

Help us get it right—We strive for accurate, respectful and relevant communications. To clarify or modify your communication preferences, visit us at www.ReaderService.com/consumerschoice.

HHI0R

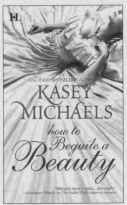

NICOLA CORNICK